SEVILLE

ALSO BY PAUL A. MENDELSON

FICTION

In the Matter of Isabel

The Art of Listening (stories)

Must Have GSOH

Their Exits and Their Entrances

The Forever Moment

Any Lengths to Please (novellas)

The Makings of Emily Jensen (novellas)

FOR CHILDREN

Losing Arthur

The Funnies

Henry the Half-Time Hero

Henry Jaffa and the League of Not Really Very Super Heroes

'I absolutely loved this book! Touching and very funny! William is a classic character! And Luisa is a wonder! It's a beautiful and scary thought meeting your younger selves, with seemingly limitless passion and endless possibilities ahead of them, after years of marriage and spent possibilities. Still smiling after reading Paul A. Mendelson's book. So damn great.'

Steve Armogida, Emmy-nominated screenwriter,
School of Rock, My Family.

'Loved *Seville*. It's fabulous!'

Niall Perrett, film producer (USA)

'A superb novel. From the aptly numbered room 381 and the magic of Seville, Paul A. Mendelson's novel takes you on a journey of discovery, using the past to inform the future, and weaves a mystical tale of relearning the meaning of love.'

Paul Harrison, BAFTA-winning director,
Ballykissangel, Touch of Frost

'Mendelson manages the near impossible, combining a premise that continually reels you in, with writing that jumps from the page. The dialogue and scenarios feel so close to life, while the narrative stretches the imagination. *Seville* should be available on the NHS – a 'booster book' to remind us how much pleasure and wellbeing can be gained from the simple act of reading.'

Chris McGuire, author of *Crooks and Nannies*

READERS' REVIEWS

'An enchanting novel. Paul A. Mendelson captures beautifully a couple in crisis who find themselves again.'

Harriet Curtis

'A real delight. I found myself wondering what it would indeed be like to meet my honeymooning self and husband.'

Daryl Jacob

'The plot is unique – very strong characters - it's a beautiful work.'

Anisa

'Totally mindblowing. Exquisitely written with a gentle humorous style. A five star gem.'

JR Cowton

'Touching and thought-provoking. Not just a great read – it's also made me want to visit Seville.'

P Barnes

'A real page-turner. With twists I wasn't expecting. Written by an author who clearly knows the ups and downs of love.'

J Ro

'*Sliding Doors* meets *Groundhog Day*!'

Anon

Seville

Paul A. Mendelson

The Book Guild

First published in Great Britain in 2025 by
The Book Guild Ltd
Unit E2 Airfield Business Park,
Harrison Road, Market Harborough,
Leicestershire. LE16 7UL
Tel: 0116 2792299
www.bookguild.co.uk
Email: info@bookguild.co.uk

Typeset in 11pt Minion Pro

Printed and bound by CPI Group (UK) Ltd, Croydon, CR0 4YY

ISBN 978 1835743 058

British Library Cataloguing in Publication Data.
A catalogue record for this book is available from the British Library.

FSC www.fsc.org MIX Paper | Supporting responsible forestry FSC® C013604

To the extraordinary young woman with whom
I honeymooned so many years ago in Seville.

And have been honeymooning ever since.

"Sometimes," said Julia, "I feel the past and the future pressing so hard on either side that there's no room for the present at all."

Evelyn Waugh, *Brideshead Revisited*

"There are more things in heaven and earth, Horatio,
Than are dreamt of in your philosophy."

William Shakespeare, *Hamlet* (1.5.167–8)

"Och, away ye go!"

William Sutherland, 1995 and 2025

Seville, Spain

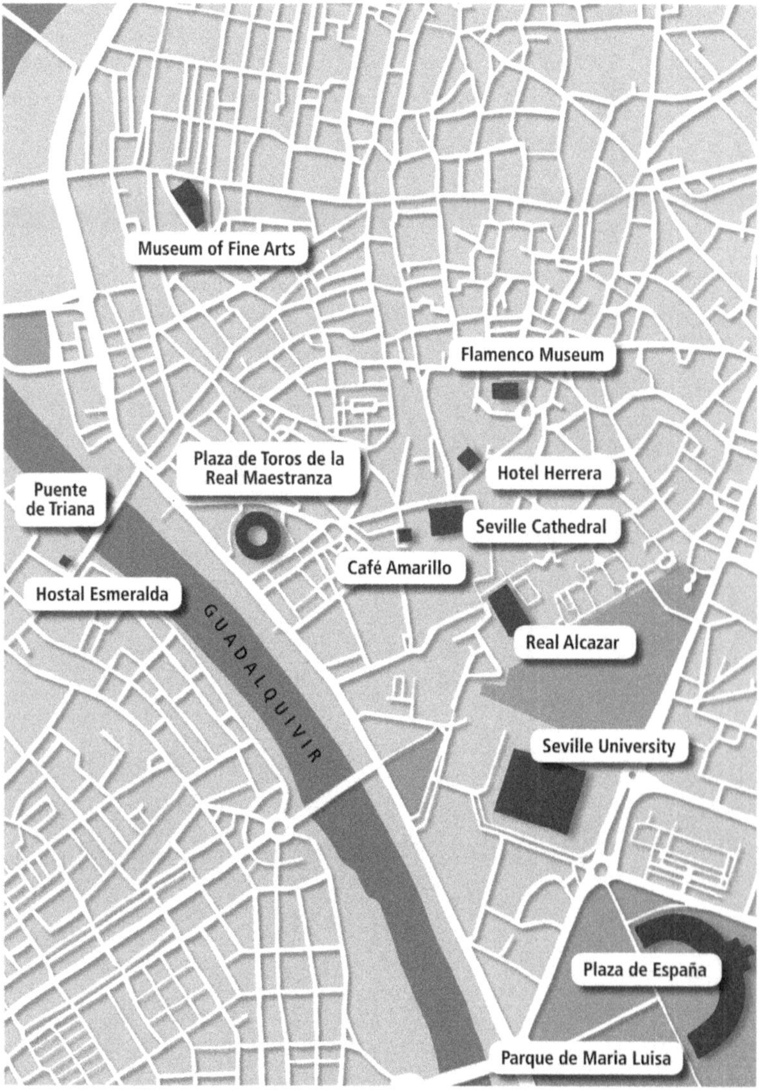

PROLOGUE

The ball of candle wax is still small; he began it only last year.

Gnarled and knobbly, it sits in his quivering palm. Suddenly he grabs it between tiny thumb and forefinger and thrusts it out in front of him, expectantly. Hopefully.

The young boy senses the intensity of darkness, despite the tailored lighting all around. Perhaps it is the lateness of the hour or the daunting solemnity of the occasion that adds to the sensation. Even though the people surrounding him appear far from solemn and he's not yet quite sure what this particular night is all about.

He has heard there is magic in the very air.

Yet he desires one thing only. More, he is certain, than he has ever desired anything in his life. Not that he ever looks back. Or even forward. There is only now.

And here it comes.

The biggest candle he has ever seen, slowly dripping its own scalding essence as it moves down through the dark, sultry air towards his outstretched hand. The flame almost frying his fingers. He can see only the eyes of his benefactor; all else is hidden.

More wax glides towards him, adding to his store, to last year's solidified bounty. If some of it drops onto his sweaty hand, sizzling the skin, so what? Provided the aggregation justifies the pain.

Maybe this year he will beat the rivals in his classroom.

Maybe this time will be his triumph.

It is going to be a very special week.

NOW
(2025)

CHAPTER ONE

"I DO KNOW HOW to pack a suitcase, Luisa."

William Sutherland is not in a holiday mood. He rarely is when he's about to go on holiday and seldom even when he's actually there. Apparently it's something to do with his never having had holidays as a child. Or being Glaswegian. Or both. William is not prone to self-analysis. He only gleans this particularly unhelpful observation from his wife, Luisa, the one who's trying to help him pack his suitcase and getting little thanks for it. The one who had bags of holidays as a child.

"I know you do, William. I know also you are angry if your shirts have the creases."

"I should have packed last night," he mutters. "If I hadn't had that bloody report to write for Sandy. We don't want to keep the kids waiting."

Luisa shakes her head. She knows they will be packed and sorted in plenty of time and the kids – who aren't really kids at all, not any more – wouldn't mind waiting. Not after a lifetime (at least for one of them) of being hurried.

She is feeling slightly lightheaded, which she thinks

may be because she is teetering on the cusp of diabetes and hasn't yet eaten, even though it is still very early.

But somewhere she knows that this particular feeling isn't her pancreas playing up. It is because she is sick with fear.

"Can I make you some eggs?" she offers.

He doesn't answer. She is sure that he has heard but she can't yet be certain, even after thirty years, whether he is mulling or simply ignoring.

Finally. "Er, no. No, thank you. I'll just have my cereal."

Luisa knows that, to William Sutherland's Catherine -wheel mind, eggs take time but cereal you just pour straight out. So she isn't going to argue that they'd be ready for him by the time he's through. That in fact it would be swifter for him than preparing his own morning muesli and fruit concoction. She simply nods and closes the bedroom window, muffling the familiar sound of Surrey rain they'll soon be leaving well behind.

He can hear her walk into the kitchen and the humming begin.

It's a humming of childhood Spanish melodies, of which she's not even aware but which either enchants or irritates him. More often, these days, the latter.

William sits on the newly-made bed, removes his glasses and releases the breath he has been holding in. He realises that this will waste valuable packing seconds, but he also feels that he deserves a brief breather, given the circumstances.

He looks blearily around the bedroom.

He can't deny that it is a comfortable room, sunny even, despite the weather. And most probably decorated and furnished in the best of taste, albeit a tad continental. Luisa is the one with the flair – this has never been his province. The bed works, at least for sleeping, although his sleep is never great. (This reminds him – he must ensure that he has packed all his pills. Some in the suitcase and the same again in the front compartment of his battered laptop bag, just in case their baggage goes to La Paz.)

The only feature in this expensively cosy room he could definitely live without is the painting, if you could call it that, mounted above the bed. It's there because William refuses to hang it in the living room, a decision that Luisa has tactfully passed off to its creator, their son-in-law, as wanting to have it where they can wake up to it every morning. Which they bloody do, although William tries very hard to keep it just outside his peripheral vision. At least this is one opinion he shares with his wife – it really isn't a very good painting. And unfortunately, in this case, knowing the artist doesn't afford it the least extra cachet.

Luisa has left her wardrobe door ajar. Moths will get in while we're away, he thinks crossly, although he's not totally sure if moths still do this. He suddenly recalls the smell of mothballs in the old tenement flat, one of several lingering smells from childhood, still there on his mother when they'd carried her out. A potent smell yet one of the comparatively harmless ones. Except, of course, to moths.

This week, he is being told, is a time for remembering. As if he didn't have enough to do.

He catches himself in the mirror and puts his glasses back on. William has never been taken with the way he looks, although Luisa has often told him how attractive she finds him. Not for some time now, that's for sure, but he does believe that on those historic occasions she genuinely meant it. Even if he sensed there was always the implication that others might see things differently.

For the life of him he can't see it now, even with his vision restored. All he can see is that proud terrain where his once-untamed, almost maple-red hair ran luxuriantly free, now a somewhat desolate archipelago of wispy, balding grey. And below the still half-closed, pastel-blue eyes lie clearly permanent gullies that time and life have dug into milky, Scottish, sun-shy skin. Bit jowly too, Father William, he thinks, and a future candidate for Red Nose Day – probably the result of too many business lunches, mostly at his expense and for too long not converted into business.

Perhaps he should go easy on the paella this week, although he suspects that eating for Britain might be the one thing he will enjoy.

The doorbell interrupts his assessment.

"William," calls Luisa, "they're here!"

" Damnation!" he mutters, before telling himself that he should be quite relieved they're early when he had been expecting them to be artistically late.

He stuffs a final shirt into the case. One that Luisa recently bought for him, on her way back from quietly delivering six others to the Help the Aged shop.

Sod the creases.

*

"You're going to have such a wonderful time, you two. I'm so jealous."

"*Sí*. I cannot wait, Marcus. It has been so long," says Luisa to her son-in-law from the back seat of the small car, with appropriate excitement. Then she remembers to add, once again, "Thank you so much for – everything."

The eager young man swivels round awkwardly in his seat, to nod acknowledgement. A gangly nod, trendy NHS-style glasses bobbing on his beaky nose, dirty-blond hair in need of a good cut swirling with the motion of car. It's a kind face, she thinks again. A face that will keep her beautiful daughter happy, she decides, if never in luxury, although can we ever truly know about these things?

"Oh, Mummy, you don't have to keep thanking us," laughs Claire. "It's our pleasure. Really."

William can see his daughter smiling in the driving mirror. That adorable, gap-toothed smile. The darkly beautiful, wonderfully mischievous face. Their eyes meet and for a moment he softens. His face lights up, as it always does when he sees her. For a moment the familiar numbness recedes.

"It's a huge thank you from me too, darling," he says, which sounds almost sincere. "Think you're ever going to learn to drive, Marcus?" he asks. He can hear his wife sigh softly beside him. William doesn't care.

"Doubt it, William," laughs Marcus, trying bravely if unconvincingly to rise above the familiar disdain. "Artists make rubbish drivers – ask the insurance companies."

"Make rubbish pictures too," mutters William, but mercifully almost to himself.

"You'll probably be amazed how all the memories come flooding back to you," says Claire, who hasn't been alive long enough to have the sort of memories she's talking about but has an unshakeable faith in romance. "And remember how you guys told me that you promised yourselves you'd go back there one day?"

"Did we?" says William, who remembers no such thing. "Well, that must have been a long time ago, darling."

Nobody comments, so the words hang uneasily in the still-dark, pre-rush hour air. Not unexpectedly, their English-teacher daughter moves things along with a vaguely appropriate quote.

"'The past is another country. They do things differently there.'"

William immediately responds, as if challenged. "Oh easy-peasy! LP Hartley, *The Go-Between*."

"Loved that old movie!" cries Marcus. "Julie Christie and—"

"We're talking about the book," grumbles William, his favourite game with his only daughter crassly interrupted. His wife throws him a look. "Film was good too," he offers. "But, at the risk of being a wee pedant, sweetie, it's 'foreign country.'"

"Correct! Just testing. So what's your holiday book this time, Daddy?"

"What do you think?" interrupts Luisa. "Company Report numero 6432!"

The entire car must feel Marcus tense. It certainly hears his intake of breath.

"*Away ye go!*" William mutters, crossly. "I do read other things. Mebbe I've got a lot of work on, eh? A few wee bills to pay?"

Luisa can see her daughter wince at the familiar question marks in her father's voice. The younger woman leans over to stare concernedly at her parents in the mirror. Not easy, as their older heads aren't exactly together. She stares for a few seconds too long, considering she's also switching lanes on a tricky, four-lane motorway. Words unspoken, shrugs exchanged.

William thinks, not for the first time, that life is so full of looks and shrugs and winces and nods that perhaps we need never really speak at all. Which would suit him just fine and cut out all that unnecessary small-talking he's never fully mastered.

It would certainly save him having to tell Luisa about the meeting he intends to set up while he's out there.

"Will you peeps be needin' to book a pick-up for the way back, guvnor?" chirps Marcus, in an accent of his own devising, to break the silence. Yet somehow it appears to do quite the opposite.

The AVE train pulls out of Madrid's brand-new Atocha station. Overflowing, the young man muses, with businessmen, holidaymakers and, most probably, considering the destination, pilgrims, although this is a word he associates with Chaucer and Bunyan, not a world approaching the dawn of a new millennium.

He cannot wait to leave this city, even though he knows that it is most probably splendid and he has only been here three days. Not enough time to "do" the museums and galleries (which, for him, is no great misfortune). But sufficient to make him seriously question that famed Spanish hospitality and love of family about which he has been told so much.

His only consolation is that, for probably the first time in his life, somebody else understands how he feels. Or, if this is not quite possible – he wonders indeed if this could ever truly be so – at least allows him the right to feel it.

And that same somebody's hand has hardly been unentwined from his since the entire journey began.

CHAPTER TWO

"OH, FOR FUCK'S SAKE!"

William knows that he should probably replace his old mobile. But what can he do – he loves it and it seems to like him reasonably well. So he would defy anyone to respond less vociferously should a rowdy group of guys with "Kevin's ~~Stag~~ SHAG Do!!!" crudely printed on identical white T-shirts come roaring through the concourse of Gatwick North Terminal and knock their beloved phone out of their hands, mid-business call, with a loaded trolley. (But not as loaded as they will be when they pour off the plane in Prague or Kraków or one of those other premarital, cultural high spots.)

He only just manages to catch the cascading object before it can be crushed terminally under foot. Looking up, after another expletive, he spots two small children staring unblinkingly at him, huddled into the folds of their unimpressed mum.

"Oops!" he mutters, in genuine contrition, because these days he is usually quite able to hold himself together and harness his famous temper. "So sorry, guys! Pardon my French." He smiles warmly at the kids and slaps the back of his own hand in mock chastisement.

"Oh fuh fffffs ake!" says the smallest child.

The family twirls back to face the line, unaware that this exchange is being watched from a distance by a smartly dressed and wearily attractive, Mediterranean-looking woman, a short, middle-aged traveller with medium-length, expressively cut dark hair and a figure that hovers precariously between voluptuous and BMI red flag. She moves with vague curiosity towards them.

"Making friends?" she says to William. Despite the earliness of the hour and the strain of the occasion, her chestnut eyes still sparkle, should anyone care to notice.

"Connections. Never too soon. Should I give them my card?"

Before he can look up, because he knows who she is, Luisa hangs a small plastic-bag on his hand. Puzzled, he opens it apprehensively, as if it might suddenly ignite, and removes a brand-new copy of *The Night Manager*, by John le Carré.

"Didn't I read this…?"

"Back in 1995? Only the half of it. You left it at that café the last time. *Our* café."

"*Our—*?" William glances at Luisa with irritated yet genuine admiration. "How do you remember it all – like it was yesterday?"

She looks down at the rescued phone, now clutched tightly in his hand like an errant child. "Perhaps because I am not always thinking about tomorrow."

*

Coming across William and Luisa Sutherland, of Richmond, Surrey, as they stroll silently through the final passport control and along the wrinkled corridor that leads, like a birth canal, towards their waiting plane, one would be forgiven for thinking they were strangers simply walking in the same direction. The balding, slightly stooped, middle-aged man, grabbing more complimentary newspapers than he or his politics could possibly absorb. The fetchingly mature woman in her tailored navy raincoat, shuffling patiently behind.

Or perhaps the onlooker might just assume they were so long-married that they had no further need to make those wearisome shows of togetherness that younger couples feel obliged to affect.

"I have to make a wee phone call," mutters William. "When we—"

"Of course you do."

He senses the urge to respond, but it would be nothing that he hasn't said or snapped out before. And – to be honest – he doesn't have the energy. Nor has he the least desire right now to prolong conversation, which even he reckons does not exactly augur well for the sort of holiday that traps two people together, like some kind of experiment with mice, without access to friends, family, proper television or, of course, work colleagues. Not that mice watch a lot of TV or have a particularly cordial working environment, but he still sees a parallel and wonders if the object in both cases isn't to observe as they tear each other apart.

Which is why William clings to his phone and prays that his laptop hasn't mysteriously uncharged itself between home and Boeing.

The silence continues on the plane.

William reads the reports that his dutiful PA Suzy has prepared and prioritised for him, whilst Luisa absorbs herself in her brand-new guidebook. A glossy tourist bible to a city she knows only too well and which William is pretty certain won't have changed that much in three decades. Or indeed in several centuries. Isn't this why people visit in the first place?

Isn't this why he and Luisa are trundling back?

Yet, even within this familiar silence and almost defining it, Luisa is doing that thing William feels she does so well. He wonders whether she has always done it. Whether she was doing it when they first met, in Glasgow of all places, so many years ago. Wonders if she is, in truth, one long, drawn-out, Iberian sigh.

Right now her audible sighs are over the number of Scotch whisky miniatures William is ordering from the British Airways steward. An order accomplished with the traditional "waving of the empty" so familiar to catering staff of all nations. She sighs as a small child in the seat in front of them leans over and duly emits an inevitable sticky dribble onto William's not particularly smart, yet not especially casual, M&S trousers – and which he won't let his life-partner wipe away, although she has the tissue primed and waiting in her hand. She sighs again as he taps out yet another polite email to someone even he is convinced won't respond.

She sighs loudest when the professionally chirpy announcement finally drifts through the plane. Before they know it they will be arriving at their destination and thank you for travelling with us. But William, by now a connoisseur of sighs, knows that this time the expressive exhalation of stale and unwanted air has a certain continental tinge and the definite hint of an excitement that wasn't there before.

As the massive wheels impact with God knows what force onto the near-to-melting tarmac, the whole plane joins in with the sighing. William even finds himself doing it. But with the distinctive timbre that only a dour Caledonian, on a particularly grumpy day, in a city he would rather bite off his legs than revisit, can summon up.

He is glad that he has packed his book at the top of his rucksack.

In fact, he has treated it with far more respect than his shirts or his trousers, despite her kind and repeated offers to do that perfect folding. The sort, with its wee pats and tucks, that only women appear able to achieve. Including his ma, which always surprised him, as the rest of the old tenement flat was a bomb-site.

He loves to read, of course he does, but he has had little opportunity so far. Or – more importantly – to write. They have either been talking or eating or making love (and, on one notable occasion, all three). But, now that she is jabbering so fast to the older Madrilenas sitting opposite, with their bulging handbags and equally overflowing sandwiches, he can probably devour a few chapters before the train pulls in. He loves this author, so he hopes he won't be disappointed.

And, who knows, he may even scribble the odd word. Actually, no "may" about it. He has set himself a certain number of words per day, as he has it on the best authority that this is what you do. But he is already behind and it is making him cross.

The trouble is that Spaniards talk so bloody loud.

He is sure that this isn't just him and his prejudices, etched even deeper by what has happened over the preceding few days in the capital. Her city. Days that mean they are on the train to their real destination earlier than intended.

He cannot understand or even make out a single word. He wonders if this is because they also speak faster than any other nation. Or perhaps you always think this when you can't make out a single word.

Then two words suddenly sing out, because they are already familiar to him and the jabbering women keep repeating them over and over again. Semana and Santa. Semana Santa. Semana Santa! It is almost as if they are warning them. Why the hell should we beware of Holy Week. Be 'feart' of Easter?

Semana Santa!

Finally she turns to him. "They are saying us we will not find the place to stay this week. They are saying us everywhere will be completo – filled."

"Full. Bugger! We should have booked. I told you we should have booked. I even marked out some nice cheap places in that new guidebook we got given. We should have phoned ahead. We should've—"

"Is okay, cariño. It will be fine."

"It might not be," he insists. Because he knows that things often aren't.

She just grabs his hand and continues to talk to the concerned older women, fast and loud. He muses that, curiously, where this impenetrable, unshared language should form a barrier between them, it actually adds to the enchantment and draws them even closer. He feels immensely proud of her, having this wondrous facility that he lacks.

"Gracias," he says, and opens his brand new book.

CHAPTER THREE

BY THE TIME WILLIAM has settled his bulky laptop back in its bag, alongside his unopened paperback, and locked his phone onto the local network, Luisa is already at the top of the staircase, her upturned face equally locked onto the already scorching Andalusian sun.

Ignoring the smiley platitudes of the crew and blocking egress for a planeload of over-agitated passengers, acting as ever like they're on the Titanic and the lifeboats are filling, Luisa's warm eyes slowly close in what anyone observing would recognise as almost cartoon-like bliss.

"Hell's teeth," says William, squeezing through to join her. "Feel that bloody heat."

As this is exactly what she is doing, Luisa sees no need to respond. Instead she glides down the steps, beaming at the huge sign ahead that says *SEViLLA*. She almost wishes she could claw up the burning runway with her elegant hands, like an ancient warrior returning triumphantly home after years in battle.

This time it is she who strolls ahead towards the glistening terminal, raincoat neatly folded into her bag.

The sleeves of her maize-yellow blouse, newly bought to kick-start an optimistic joyfulness barely apparent at the time of purchase, are now briskly rolled up, revealing firm wrists and sturdy forearms in desperate need of warmth.

William has issues with foreign sun. It isn't that he is totally against it; he has had enough continental holidays over the years to have gradually mellowed and built up some pale-skinned, factor 50 resistance. Yet he still finds the relentlessness with which it assails its addled victims from a cloudless sky both enervating and tiresome. And he has forgotten to bring a bloody hat.

At least the terminal itself is beautifully air-conditioned. He recalls, as he usually does on such occasions, that he once had a client who designed precision air-conditioning systems. So, naturally, he has a professional appreciation. In fact, rarely does William Sutherland go anywhere or do anything without it summoning up a business he advises, did so in the past or would dearly love to be doing so in the future.

Right now, however, he is more focussed on the speed with which Luisa is making her way through passport control. He can't quite see why she is in such a rush. Baggage takes its own sweet time and he'll be the one ripping the cases away from the carousel, probably ripping his tricky back in the process. Luisa has long ago stopped suggesting that they grab a porter, as he would rather endure sciatica than penury. And, of course, such functionaries are never anywhere to be seen.

When they finally emerge into the packed arrivals hall, William immediately scours the attendees. But a croaky voice right beside him still takes him by surprise.

"Señor Sutherland."

It is clearly an old voice, yet firm and unwavering. But what most unsettles William is how its owner has managed in seconds to single him out so definitively from all the other pale and nondescript British travellers streaming into the concourse. It isn't like one of his tedious conferences, where dangling lanyards give the name away.

"Aye?" he says suspiciously, turning, along with Luisa, to face the prescient greeter. "Mebbe." Although, of course, there's no mebbe about it.

The man – who offers them a warm and crinkly smile, as though they're already quite well-acquainted – is indeed old, although not perhaps quite as aged as his deeply lined skin, like the grain of an old church pew, might lead observers from a fresher, more temperate clime to presume. He wears a crisp, white, short-sleeved shirt, a comfortable pair of blue denims above sandalled feet and holds in his strong, calloused hands a card that reads "Hotel Herrera", the hotel that the kids – at God knows what expense – have generously and unnecessarily booked for them.

Before William can enquire as to how he was picked out so effortlessly from the cohort of equally pallid Englishmen, the elderly man has grabbed both their cases and is wandering jauntily off.

Luisa looks at William and smiles, made proud perhaps by an elderly compatriot's Herculean energy. William is too busy attempting to snatch back the cases to notice. An unseemly tug-of-war ensues, observed by one and all, which – despite his years – the more practised hotel employee finally wins.

"Aye, okay then," concedes William, with disgruntled magnanimity. "Gracias, Señor."

He watches as the nameless retainer strolls away, accompanied this time by Luisa. She is already chatting to him in their unnecessarily loud and rapid native tongue.

"I'm William," mutters the empty-handed Scot, wearing his laptop bag and his abandonment. "My – señora, Luisa. Special occasion. Let the celebrations begin!"

*

The comfortable rear seat of Hotel Herrera's magenta Fiat minivan suits William just fine.

Luisa, who doesn't want to make the aged Spaniard feel like a driver, although this is of course exactly what he is or he wouldn't be driving, has plumped for the passenger seat up front. William notices that the two new pals haven't paused for breath since they met, but has no idea what they're jabbering about.

Actually, he doesn't really care, as he is on the phone to his PA before they are even out of the crowded car park. He is also smoking, which he suspects breaks all sorts of Andalusian ordinances. If he doesn't exactly crave a cigarette now, he is enjoying one in anticipation of all those he will most definitely crave, but may not be permitted, as this holiest of weeks progresses. And, as an optional extra, it really pisses off Luisa.

What he doesn't do is pay the least attention to all the distinctly un-British stuff carrying on right outside his dusty window. The stuff that most newly arrived visitors embrace with a glee totally disproportionate to the actual content – a single palm tree, some excitable arm-waving locals, left-hand drives. This would be to concede that he is on holiday and not just working from van.

"Uh huh. Did Sandy get back to… Yes, the sun *is* shining. Very hot. The frying-pan of Europe, apparently. Do you have that number, Suzy? I *really* need that number." To anyone else he might already sound like the heat is getting to him. To Luisa, were she even bothering to listen, it would just be normal William-temperature. "Zero three five… Aye, really pretty, gorgeous… Seven two… *And* historical. If we ever get out of this bloody traffic…"

He opens the window, then swiftly closes it, as the heat roars in. "…Four eight – No, no oranges yet… I *know* that Seville is famous for… *and* barbers, but I won't be needing one of them either… three six two… *If I could just get to see this guy while we're here, Suzy – it'd make the whole bloody trip worthwhile.*"

The jabbering in the front seat stops.

Luisa, who has been doing the lion's share of it, looks round at William and glares. From her handbag, she slides out a compact but clearly expensive camera, the camera of someone who most probably knows what she's doing. William knows what she's doing. His spouse of thirty years is telling him she's going to have a bloody good second honeymoon, regardless of who she is having it with.

She begins to take photos of everything around her, even though Seville – or at least the Seville for which they apparently came – hasn't really begun. All he can see are relatively old but as yet undistinguished buildings, huddled together in the heat; people doing what people do everywhere, only more noisily; small family cars carrying anything but small families.

"Can't you go down a side road, Señor – please – *por favor*?" says William, who has already had quite enough of sluggish, Southern European traffic. "*Diversione*!" he hazards, his Spanish still consisting mainly of English words pronounced wrongly and loud.

"*Sí, sí*," says the driver, taking no notice.

Luisa continues her homeland conversation. "My husband is forever in a hurry. He always wishes he is somewhere else."

"And you," asks the driver, whose name she now knows is Pablo, "what do you wish?"

She turns to look at the old man. Caught out by the pointed question from this timeless-looking stranger with the half-closed, yet somehow bottomless, grey eyes.

"What are you saying? *Luisa?*" demands her husband, who, whilst never over-keen on being involved in conversation, can still feel quite marginalised when left out of one.

"I say you should not smoke." He can hear the smile that in good times is so much a part of her voice and knows she is saying no such thing. But, before he can challenge her, if he can even be bothered, the smile grows louder and considerably less wry. "You know, William, when I come back to this place, it feels like the time has stood still."

William glares at the long line of cars in the rippling heat.

"Feels like every bloody thing's stood still," he says. "Except the exchange rate."

The tall, unshaven man hands out postcards as they come off the train. Most of the arrivals – the ones with excess baggage and bewilderment, who are the only ones he targets – shake their heads or avoid the glossy object like it is a recklessly lunged knife.

Then somebody plucks a card from his outstretched hand.

"Hostal?" says the postcard man urgently, shouting above the noise of the heaving station. "Very good. Very cheap."

"I like the last bit," says the young man, shifting the bulging rucksack on his shoulders and examining the card. He adds a swift "Sí, sí," which is almost all he knows. He shows her the picture on the card, which is indeed appealing but could, of course, have been doctored.

"I know this wee street!" she cries, happily. "Is in Triana. Is ok."

"You go fast. Taxi. Andale!" urges the older man. "Say to hostal, it is Miguel."

The girl nods gratefully and moves off. The young man follows. He still needs to check out the place in their new guidebook– Hostal Esmeralda, he likes the name – to see if it's one of the promising few he's already marked out in felt-tip.

No way are they taking a taxi.

CHAPTER FOUR

NOW THAT THEY ARE a few miles further in on the hearse-like drive to Hotel Herrera, William Sutherland might well be thinking to himself that this is indeed more like it.

Were he not totally disinterested in even glancing out of the window.

Narrow streets of ancient and often quite grand buildings, almost caramel in the sunlight, would otherwise warm his eyes. People thronging these impassable thoroughfares in huge, sweaty, city-clogging numbers.

He could hardly miss the more intimate landmarks; colourfully tiled (so many tiles!) and plant-filled forecourts, ornately wrought balconies strung with riotous flowers and slightly less riotous underclothing. And glimpses, through the crowds, of pretty, tree-framed plazas. All there for the funereally passing eye to see and the assailed ear to catch, as local shoppers and vendors mingle noisily with tourists and with those other locals who, for this wondrous holiday week only, are almost the same as tourists. Minus the guidebooks and the bottled water. And the cameras. And some, but not all, of the awe.

Should he bother to look.

When he does finally glance up from his phone, as if to bestow upon Seville the honour of a Sutherland's attention, he sees something that – had he been a first-time visitor – might have sucked the heat right out of his body.

As indeed, he now recalls, it once did.

It is a person – judging by its size, a substantial male person – shrouded from dusty sandalled toe to solid neck in a gleaming white robe, whilst the head and face are themselves enclosed and totally concealed in an almost excessively tall, conical white hood. One that falls right down like a loose, shapeless snood onto the shoulders, the only barely identifiable features being dark eyes peering out through narrow slits in the fabric.

William would dare anyone to witness this harmless, indeed penitent, vision and not instantly think of those chilling newsreels of the Ku Klux Klan. The same way he is sure no informed person of his generation can listen to the stirring Ride of the Valkyries without picturing helicopters spreading napalm.

"Beginning to look a lot like Easter," he mutters to no one in particular, then notes that the hooded figure is swinging a laden shopping bag from El Corte Inglés, the celebrated chain store. Which, William thinks, is letting the old penitent side down just a bit.

And now the drums begin.

You can almost detect the ears of each person in that same crowded street suddenly twitch and turn, like those of a more alert and wary animal, as adults and children stop whatever they are doing and cock their heads in the direction of the percussive and increasingly thunderous sound.

Even William senses something, like a change in the very texture of the air. Luisa and her new amigo abruptly end their conversation.

"*STOP THE CAR!*" shouts Luisa. Once in English and then in Spanish.

William, alongside his surprise, is intrigued that the English version comes first. Perhaps because, for the purpose of barking orders, this is by now her language of choice.

Responding to the second bark, Pablo halts the minibus with a jolt. Despite the slowness of their journey, William and his dodgy spine bounce painfully against the minivan's reinforced rear.

"Shit! What are you – *Luisa?*" She is already opening her door. "Where the hell are you going?"

"Please, do not swear. You come – please come, William."

"Come? Where come?" *And why am I sounding like it's not my language?*

"Here. Now. *This*. Or I see you at the hotel. Is up to you."

With the groan of a devout long-sufferer, William throws open his door, just missing a passing elderly lady of around one hundred and ten on her moped.

"*Away ye go!*" he tells Luisa, using his trusty, catch-all phrase, as he shuffles round the paused minibus and gently grabs her arm. "You can't just wander off willy bloody nilly. This isn't Richmond! Are you sure we can trust…?"

He nods towards Pablo, who clearly isn't Richmond either yet seems to sense instinctively that he is being singled out. The old man turns to him and gestures – *GO!*

William hesitates for a few seconds, then lets go of Luisa, grabs his trusty laptop bag from the back seat and slams the door.

Before he trundles off towards the accumulating sounds, he slowly clicks his neck, arches his back and bobs his head forward then to the rear a couple of times. Luisa waits, as she has always waited, unwilling to disturb this unbreakable, possibly therapeutic ritual.

Now he is ready and able, if not necessarily willing.

"Just be careful," he says, concernedly. "You're not twenty-two any more."

CHAPTER FIVE

IN HIS TIME WILLIAM Sutherland has seen enough reportage of rivers bursting their banks, flooding helpless streets with an intemperate fury. This is how the historic city's winding passageways seem to him now, as a torrent of excited people flows unstoppably through alleys and *calles*, past bustling shops and rainbow stalls, jostling Catholics and non-believers alike.

All surging towards the sound of the drums.

Yet, being predominantly Spaniards, they are chatting and shouting and munching as they scamper, all at maximum volume. Some are dressed very smartly, in Sunday suits and church dresses, out of respect for the occasion, with many of the women in fashionably high heels, despite the cobbles and the chaos. Dragging children, dogs, shopping trolleys and darkly widowed grannies in their colourful wake.

The shopkeepers and restaurateurs, who have seen it all before, attempt to divert them with goods and menus. They point to exquisite Andalusian crafts at 'practically give-away' prices and empty tables that won't be empty for long. Inevitably, a few tiny tributaries trickle off. But they're matched by equally determined shoppers and diners pouring out of tiny doorways, bags in hand and tummies full, anxious to swim with the devoted tide.

William finds himself fearful that Luisa will be toppled and crushed in the good-natured but no less unstoppable stampede. His spouse is quite solid and strong, perhaps a bit too solid, he thinks uncharitably, but her regular workouts haven't made her any taller. Yet she weaves and winds her way through her compatriot throng with such relentlessly single-minded vigour, becoming more Spanish by the minute, that it is he who is in greater danger of being overwhelmed.

"*Scusi. Perdón.* MOVE! *Luisa...?*"

He finally catches up with her at a small but tightly packed crossroads, in perfect time to catch what is clearly a massive and meticulously drilled procession. Medieval, unchanging yet curiously contemporary.

Even William recalls that this entire gang, numbering in their hundreds and perhaps even thousands – *Nazarenos* in their pointed hoods, humble penitents stolidly bearing their crosses, altar boys, bandsmen, churchgoers and clergy – will have set off some time ago from their own local parish church and are treading their slow, solemn way to the magnificent cathedral in the spiritual heart of this great city. Or maybe they're on their way back – he would have to look at the map. Not that he actually cares.

But here they are, the guys in the conical hats, and not just in white this time. This cohort of intensely serious and devout men, scores of them, many barefoot, sport hoods of the deepest purple and carry not shopping bags but massive brown candles or silver sceptres. Despite knowing that these are just ordinary, self-effacing believers, simple, peace-loving members of the community, processing in proud anonymity, they still give William the shivers. Calmly they ignore the ranks of justifiably rapt humanity lining the streets or waving from narrow balconies, their eyes fixed firmly on the road ahead or the heavens above.

This is no victory parade, unless the victory is that of a religion whose ceremonies have endured, undiminished by outside forces, for hundreds of years. He has no idea of the pecking order or whether these anonymous guys are more or less important than the men behind them, men who are struggling – or pretending to struggle – with huge wooden (or pretend wooden) crucifixes.

But the ones to whom his heart goes out, and for whom he feels a genuine respect, are the ranks of men directly under the gigantic object now heaving precariously into view. Teams of dedicated and sturdy volunteers, the *costaleros*, who move the dais-like structure forward to the slow but exacting rhythm of the drums.

They're all burly, medium-sized men, of necessity around the same height, so that the ancient float or *paso*, a gleaming riot of burnished gold and silver, heavy as anvils, bedecked with velvet and candles and freshly cut flowers, maintains its precarious balance as it proceeds on its meticulously preordained journey.

He recalls with incredulity that these thirty staunch believers are supporting, with their impossibly strong arms, the entire weight of the beams and the sacred panoply that towers above them on the revered and immaculately sculptured floats. All they wear, to reduce any cranial impact as they bounce and sway under at least a ton of wood, are rough cloth turbans around their heads. Yet, all that the onlookers can see of these noble bearers, until they stop for breath and water or, he suspects, something stronger, are their firm, richly tanned feet in sandals or trainers, peeping under the thick white cloth that falls, like a room service tablecloth, almost to the ground.

Like so many of the *pasos* that William is certain will process past him this week – and God knows there will be a host of these floats that pass in the night – this towering structure bears, within its classical depiction of a pivotal Mystery scene, the tortured yet still somehow benign figure of Christ on his cross.

Surrounded by floral tributes and yet more candles, this Sevillano Christ gazes down lovingly on all. It would be either him or his poor mum up there today, sculpted yet almost too real, thinks William. They're the headliners.

William sniffs the air, scented with incense, freshly baked snacks and human sweat, and looks around for Luisa. She is nowhere to be seen.

He is certain that she will turn up and is not entirely unhappy to be witnessing this undeniably impressive spectacle for a few precious moments on his own. Or indeed spending the entire day on his own, just him and the world and his laptop. Which he knows, if he truly thinks about it, is not how things should be.

So William is truly not going to think about it.

He rarely does, because thinking alters little and dwelling in regret doesn't pay for dwelling in Surrey. On his office pinboard is the quote "nothing is certain but death and taxes", sent to him on a postcard by a jovial client, but he's pretty certain that this is optimistic bollocks. He knows in his heart that some things are set in stone and precious little will change between the two of them, William and Luisa, thirty years on, even on this week of supposed 'connection', like a LinkedIn of the spirit. Except, of course, their financial security, that will be sure to change, Sod's Law, if he doesn't stay forever on the ball.

So he mustn't forget – he *has* to make that phone call. Who knows – perhaps the gentleman he will be calling is actually sardined within this or a similarly overstimulated crowd right this very minute.

Suddenly his attention is diverted.

William finds himself standing next to a small boy, hardly more than six or seven years old and unusually fair for a local. He is clearly with his parents, a Spanish couple, warm and loving, with whom he seems very much at ease.

Something about the child stops William cold.

He knows that he must not stare, that it would make the child and his parents uneasy, yet he finds that he can't take his eyes off the boy. Short, newly-trimmed Easter hair, with that barber's trademark point at the nape, pale blue eyes, crushingly innocent face. And a smile of such wonder.

William's heart begins to pound, at the same time as his mind rebukes him for his foolishness.

Not now, William. Not here. Creepy is not a good look.

The boy is clearly unaware of William. Or of anyone. He is consumed by the procession and especially the float, as he stares upwards, open-mouthed, at the timeless magic passing slowly by.

"Señor – *Señor!*"

The screech of the old *gitano* woman tears William away. A new scent has entered his awareness – hardly surprising as she is thrusting a sprig of rosemary almost up his nose.

He shakes his head and backs away from the tiny and almost toothless Romani vendor. Not that there is much room for evasion in the solidifying crowd. She moves in deftly for the sell, staring into his glasses and his brain, muttering impenetrable incantations, which he assumes are about her crippling poverty and his desperate need for a herb best known for flavouring lamb. He waves her off with a vehemence that almost sends her entire stock flying. The shrieked imprecations hang in the air as she shuffles off to another victim.

And then he sees it. Ploughing towards him.

A bus, of a kind he doesn't recognise, but then how the hell does he know the buses of Andalusia? What he does know is that it has come out of nowhere. Hurtling down the narrow street directly opposite, which he had assumed was fully blocked off to traffic and pedestrians.

It is approaching at such speed that he doesn't have time to wonder why no one has noticed it or why they aren't instantly scurrying away in terror. Or indeed how come the Nazarenos around the massive float aren't either scattering in religious panic, coned hats wobbling, or rooting themselves to the spot in frozen fear.

Why is no one screaming to God, when surely today of all days he can't be far away?

William calls out for Luisa but he can't see her in the crowd. The sound of the drums and the golden, high-pitched trumpets is deafening.

All he knows is that the bus is coming.

All he knows is that he has to save the child.

Reaching out, he grabs the small boy by his tiny, warm arm and wrenches him tightly into his body, at the same time pulling both of them away as best he can in the throng, out of the path of the relentlessly oncoming vehicle.

Only it doesn't come.

The bus, of whatever vintage, simply fades and disappears. Like a vapour or a ghost. Touching nothing, disturbing no one.

Well, no one except William, who manages to gaze inside the spectral vehicle for just a fraction of a second before it totally vanishes. He glimpses, standing next to the phantom driver, a young couple huddled so closely together. She has a bright red bag over her shoulder, he sports longish hair of a not dissimilar hue and a tattered duffle-bag on his arm.

And then they're gone.

The passengers, the driver, the bus.

And all sense of reality.

"*Señor!*"

The appalled father is staring at William, as he yanks his confused child back into the safe harbour of his sane, Sevillano family. William notices, amidst the angry scowls and muttering, and a fist raised in righteous and quite justifiable fury, that the man has a small but vivid purple birthmark on his cheek, in the rough yet distinct shape of a star. This strikes some distant chord in William, even as he is quite busy noticing that the man is no more keen on being stared at than on having his child snatched.

"*William?*"

"*Luisa!* There you are. Did you see it?"

The advent of his wife has probably saved William Sutherland, potential child-abductor, from being beaten to a deserved pulp, but such an outcome is not even on the fringes of William's tormented mind right now.

"See what? See you grabbing somebody else's child?"

"Luisa—"

"What were you thinking?"

He notices that the afflicted family are moving well away from him and further into the crowd, as if at this moment they would prefer to be mown down by a horde of crucifix-bearing penitents or a gigantic, multipedal Son of God.

"The bus, Luisa. *Coming straight at us! Full speed! And then it...*" He shakes his head. "Please don't stare at me like that."

"Whisky on a plane. Is like three whiskies on land. And you had three, so—"

"Oh, please!"

"And now you are smoking again."

"Brace yourself for the crack cocaine. *Luisa...?*" But he stops and sighs, realising that this conversation is pointless and his delirium tremens a given. He shakes his head once more, as if to reboot his troubled mind. Could it be the whisky? Surely not – although God knows he needs one now. "Okay, fine. Well, maybe we should just check that Pedro's not made off with our luggage. And I *have* to make that call."

"Or else you die. And his name is Pablo. Not every Spanish man is Pedro. So go."

"Luisa—"

"Go. GO! I stay here."

He stares at her, as the all-too-familiar anger surges up and momentarily shunts aside whatever shock and humiliation has recently flooded his system.

"This wasn't *my* bloody idea, you know! This 'trip' – at my busiest time. What with – everything else."

Her hands move towards his neck. He doesn't flinch as she releases the fraying strap of his laptop bag, which has become tangled, not for the first time, under his collar.

"It is this place," she murmurs, as she briskly straightens him out. "*Thirty years, William!*" She gazes all around her. "I cannot believe where we are."

"Neither can I, Luisa," says William, as he moves off into the thickening crowds. "Neither can I."

Luisa watches him shoulder his clumsy way through the masses, towards a hopefully quieter street. Well before he is out of sight, she turns back to catch the tail-end of her first procession in so very many years.

Before it passes her by.

The bed is soft and so is she. So soft that he sinks into her like a weary traveller, finding a berth at last.

And then the giggles begin.

Laughter infused with the joy of finally being here. Alone together, after having been encircled by people. Whilst outside there are so many thousands more people, but folk they don't know and who would pass by him without judgement or disapproval.

He is so hot for her but he knows the heat isn't all of his making. Even with the small window and those flaking, blue shutters wide open to the tiny courtyard below, the unfamiliar, subtropical air is so still and dry. There isn't the whisper of a breeze to cool their coiled and sweating bodies.

Perhaps they should close everything tight, he thinks, but wouldn't this simply seal in the stifling air, with no hope of escape? She should know about these things; this is her country after all. And, for some quite recent years, her city. But she doesn't seem aware of anything beyond the two of them and this moment.

He wonders how she does this.

He has never been outside of Britain, barely ventured beyond Scotland, and a part of him feels even now that he should be out there, in the heat, exploring the city. Broadening his mind, gathering "material" for his writing. And, hopefully, what might pass for a tan on his pallid, northern skin. But it isn't this part of him that is making the decisions right now. And, anyway, his personal tour guide is clearly on her break.

At least it will give him an appetite for those wee plate things she has told him the locals like for their lunch.

CHAPTER SIX

"**AQUI ESTAMOS, PASE POR** *favor!*"

Pablo lets the triumphant thump of baggage on a nimbly nudged-open door tell William just how proud he is to be ushering his new British guest into habitacion 381, Hotel Herrera, Casco Antiguo, Sevilla.

Indeed, were William observing the old man's face right now and not simply flinging his laptop bag onto the inviting king-sized bed in weary relief, he would notice a degree of proprietorial satisfaction more normally reserved for people who have single-handedly reinvigorated a crumbling building marked for demolition. Or at least who possess such an edifice in its entirety.

But all that William sees is a large chamber in semi-darkness, with its shutters sensibly closed. It could, at first glance, be any hotel room in the world (save for the UK, where a kettle and tea bags are provided as a matter of course and to avoid riots).

Dumping the suitcases on the racks provided, the stocky driver/porter/Jacobo-of-all-trades scoots with impressive agility across the refreshingly cool bedroom, neatly avoiding a low, oak-like table in its centre. He flings open the shutters, bombarding himself and everything around him with radiant if somewhat merciless afternoon light.

Adding tour guide to his resume, Pablo beckons his new guest over, in the certain knowledge that this William Sutherland hombre will go *loco* over the tastefully tiled and curling, wrought-iron balcony, with all that lies sunnily beyond.

But William, still understandably shaken by recent events (or *non*-events), is already at the minibar. He is relieved to discover sufficient miniatures of a Scotch to which he is not entirely indifferent and which is hopefully non-hallucinatory.

He reckons he needs to return as soon as possible to that – he struggles for the word – *stasis*, yes, in which he recognises that he lives and in which he is thankfully just about able to manage his work and his existence. Whilst he would be the first to concede that the balance of his daily life is most probably far from perfect (and, come on, whose is?), it suddenly feels a whole lot more grounded than the heart-thumping, body-shuddering anxiety he's experiencing right now in this indifferently pleasant room.

There is a large and rather beautiful bouquet of flowers on a nearby table. Yet his troubled mind barely takes this in as he finally obliges a perfectly back-lit Pablo with the requisite attention.

"*Catedral!*" enthuses the old man, pointing excitedly, as if William might otherwise fail to spot one of the grandest and most breathtaking places of worship in the civilised world, just a few hundred metres from this railing. "*Muy bien*." Even the man's heathen guest can detect that the fervour bubbling over in room 381 is as much spiritual as architectural, and William has the good grace to endorse it.

"*Aye. Muy bien. Multo muy bien.*" Which seems to do the trick. And he has to concede that the massive and overwhelmingly ornate, Gothic cathedral, so golden in the unremitting sunlight, is indeed deserving of a proudly pointing finger.

"'*Hagamos una iglesia tan hermosa y tan grandiosa que los que la vieren labrada los tengen por locos,*'" quotes the old man, although William recognises only a word relating to madness at the end and wonders if it is referring to him.

The moving and slightly oil-stained finger moves on and upwards to the soaring bell tower, once Moorish minaret and now landmark of every local guide book and postcard and T-shirt in Seville, standing proud against the unrelenting sun.

"La Giralda! Muy famoso."

A vague memory stirs in William. *Yes*! They walked all the way up that tower, surely they did. He and Lu, as he used to call her in those days. It's the sort of thing they would have done, when they had all the energy in the world and that same world didn't sit like a rock on their shoulders. And curiously, to his surprise, there hadn't been any steps, at least not until pretty near the top.

"There were ramps!" he cries out. "Huge ramps. Aye. For the horses." Pablo's face is a tableau of incomprehension. "Ha! And she tells me I never remember anything!"

"Ah, *felicitationes!*"

"Excuse me?"

This is a word William knows, but he is not exactly certain on what the old man is congratulating him. His prodigious memory? Then he sees the bottle of champagne chilling in a bucket of ice on a side-table, with a small hotel-card around its golden neck. William reads it and nods, not totally overjoyed.

"From my business partner. Sandy." As if Pablo cares. "*Gracias*, pal. I'd better not be seeing the bill for this when I get back!"

William decides to open the bottle there and then.

Taking it onto the balcony, he sets it down on a small, tiled table. Yet, as ever, the call of his silent mobile proves too strong. He proceeds to dial a number, hardly aware that Pablo has parked the old retainer schtick and is watching his every move. Yet William knows, as he makes the call, that the old guy is still around. They never leave without their tip.

"Ah. Spanish answer-phone," he explains, over his shoulder, as he watches visitors down below stream into the cathedral. He wonders if there's an entry fee – they could be making a fortune. Mind you, the upkeep... "*Hello... hola...* No, still rabbiting... dear Lord, sounds like he's reciting Donkey-bloody-Oaty! ... Ah... finally! *Hola, Señor Barbadillo? It's William Sutherland here. From London. 'Matheson Sutherland'? Er... Ron Parfitt suggested that I – we – I'll call again, shall I? Try to catch you... Aye. Er – adios.*"

William remains on the balcony as he tries to open the bottle. He decides he has to make another call.

"This was all my darling daughter's doing, Ped... Pablo. This 'second honeymoon'. Well, her and the 'artiste' she went and married. Don't ask me how they afforded it. I'm just calling to say, y'know, we've arrived in one piece. And of course thank you. But she doesn't seem to…" William tries to keep the disappointment out of his voice. No need to display your emotions to the staff. "You got kids, Pablo? Er – *niños*?"

Pablo makes a five with his hand. Then another five.

"*Jesus*! And you can still lift a case!" He clicks off. "Clearly too busy for her old dad. Ah well. Care to join me in a—?"

He turns to find that Pablo has gone. Saved me a euro or two, thinks William, as he finally pops open the champagne.

The cork flies onto the empty balcony directly adjoining his. William finds himself wondering, as he always does, if a potential client might be staying there. Stranger things have happened. In fact, they've already bloody started.

"Let the party begin," he announces to nobody at all.

CHAPTER SEVEN

LUISA IS ALSO ON the phone, although she can barely hear anything above the clamour of the swirling crowds.

She remembers this historic, metal-arched bridge, The Puente de Isabel II, or Puente de Triana as she used to call it and assumes the locals still do. She can just about glimpse the muddy River Guadalquivir down below, as she moves westward with the joyous masses, a different gang of Nazarenos and apparently most of Seville. Making for the ever-vibrant and proudly distinctive Triana district, on its almost-island. Every week seemed to be a *fiesta* here, she recalls. The bars, the flamenco, the street music. But perhaps this is because she was young.

And just perhaps she can feel young again, she thinks, on such a special week. As young as she is trying to sound, in this curiously difficult courtesy-call to her daughter.

"Well, for *me*, memories," she responds lightly to the effusive, yet clearly anxious, interrogation from London. "Of course. Wonderful memories. But, Claire darling, you know your daddy. He never remember anything… Eh?… No, *no bullfight!*"

She finds herself smacking her hand against her bulky leather bag and shouting at her mobile, as if to show the totally disinterested world processing around her that Luisa Sutherland has no intention of *ever* watching an animal killed for sport. "We do not go to bullfight on the honeymoon, my darling, so not this time. You will not see me dead at *corrida*!"

Luisa only half hears her amused daughter talking about methinking and protestething too much – which she knows is just her funny way of speaking. The older woman's nostrils are suddenly assailed by an aroma that, despite the anatomic impossibility, goes straight to her heart.

"*Churros!*" she says out loud.

Now her daughter laughs, that uninhibitedly rich and infectiously dirty roar. Encouraging her – *go on, Mum, you're on holiday* – as if the pancreas gives breaks to its customers the way credit card companies are wont to do.

Luisa is at the tiny, kerbside stall now, surrounded by jostling patrons of all ages. Each one a part of that blissful, time-honoured ritual – the ecstatic dipping of a steaming, deep-fried choux pastry coil into rich hot chocolate, followed by a hungry stuffing somewhere near the region of the mouth.

Around them, Christ and his wooden disciples wobble and sway to the relentless beat of the drums. And she wonders once again why God, in whom she no longer believes but still chastises on a regular basis, would make something that tastes so good contain within it such potential for harm. Not unlike sex in many ways, she ponders, wistfully.

"No," she tells her daughter, "no churros," thereby informing herself.

Luisa moves reluctantly away and swiftly changes the subject. "Perhaps your daddy, he will go see the bulls fighting this time." And now, naturally, the question comes. And the mother answers with a harmless lie. "Er, yes, he is here. *Sí*. Of course... But he walks very fast up ahead, you know, as he is always doing."

Luisa finishes the call with a kiss and puts on speed, as if trying to catch up with her mythical husband.

Scuttling through the crowds and into Triana, she surprises herself with her dogged determination. Why did the middle-aged Spanish lady cross the bridge? What exactly, she wonders, is on this other, so perceptibly different side of the city, this earthily picturesque *arrabal* with its craft markets and potteries and tile factories, that is making her so anxious to find it? And what yearning has impelled her to follow and now overtake this particular procession? One of so many in this extraordinary city, flowing, like the river, in all different directions.

She thinks she knows, but she isn't as yet certain. Even her recall, universally acknowledged as far superior to that of her spouse, is not faultless. Nor is she sure why she is tapping her mobile again, finding a number that isn't in its stored memory but firmly lodged in her own.

Yet, before it even connects, to a distant office some thirteen hundred miles away, Luisa Sutherland, late of Madrid, now settled in suburban Richmond, finds herself frozen to the spot. Eyes shaded and unblinking, barely disturbing the turbulent surge, like a pebble in a stream, quite unable to move.

Making her own tiny almost-island, she stares at something right in front of her.

Something that sends an almost electrical tremor juddering through her system.

Something she thought she might never see again.

Luisa isn't yet as certain in her mind as she is in her heart. So she burrows deep into her capacious but sensibly inexpensive leather bag. Her Mary Poppins bag, as William once called it, not entirely with affection (since, on a recent occasion when he had to hold it for her, the bloody thing nearly wrenched his back). From its infinite depths she fishes out a small, fake-leather photo album, brand new despite its incongruity in this digital age.

She can sense that her movements are unnecessarily frantic, as she flicks it open, scrabbling for a page. Luisa knows that she can't actually calm down and also that she doesn't altogether wish to.

Finally she sees it.

A photo of a small, prettily tiled courtyard, a stone fountain at its centre, with a spouting, snub-nosed cherub doing the honours and stone benches all around. Embraced by abundant orange trees bestowing some welcome shade. It's an image from thirty years ago, most probably to the day. And there, smiling into the expertly adjusted lens, is a gangling young man with a straggly beard almost the same hue as his strikingly red and less strikingly managed hair. Despite the unrelenting sunshine, he holds a small, black folding umbrella.

Luisa looks back into the courtyard, outside whose closed gates she stands transfixed. It is empty now, but the fountain, the stone benches, the faded, old tiles are much as they were three decades ago. Even the trees seem unaltered. She finds herself staring upwards at a small, first-floor bedroom window, its freshly painted shutters swung open to welcome the Easter light. Luisa wonders who is behind those shutters right now and if they might be anything like…

"Hello… Luisa…cariño…?

The crackly voice on the phone spirals her back to earth. Just as the surging, chattering, churros-fuelled crowd picks her up like flotsam and drags her helplessly onwards towards the next busy square. The next procession.

So she doesn't see the heavy front door of Hostal Esmeralda opening.

NOW
(1995)

CHAPTER EIGHT

WILL SUTHERLAND, OF GOVAN, south-west Glasgow, knows that, in order to be a proper writer, you have to balance your reading time carefully with those moments when you should actually be putting pen to paper. No point citing your influences if they have influenced nothing more than a vague ambition or a nagging dream. And, in those circumstances, who in God's name is going to ask you anyway?

So back into the fading, plastic sports bag that he always carries, bouncing over the cheap but essential suntan oil and equally essential duty-free Marlboro, drops the newly purchased le Carré. And out come the worn yellow notepad and requisite chewed-up Biro.

The gentle trickle from the fountain soothes him, as he squats on its comfortingly cool surround. Legs that haven't seen shorts since childhood (and won't be seeing them any time soon) stretch out onto the tiled terrace. Despite wifely entreaties, his toes are still firmly encased in sensible, un-summery shoes. He makes sure his pale, northern face is gently shaded by trees from the ferocity of the Andalusian sun.

Will is just about to start scribbling, in the rare but welcome silence, when he senses that there is someone else close by.

He can almost feel the foreign eyes staring at him. (Well, foreign to him.)

Will Sutherland looks around to see a handyman/gardener whom he hadn't even noticed. The man is quietly tending some flowering plants, in beautifully ornate ceramic pots, that sit in a corner of the courtyard. He is small but solidly built, with the sort of tan, Will reckons, that comes not from basking in the sun but labouring under it. He is convinced that there is a difference, as indeed there has to be between lines etched by toil and those simply doled out by nature.

The man's stare begins to take on a quality of permanence, which disconcerts its object.

"You'll know me the next time, pal," says Will, with the confidence of a guy whose accent is impenetrable.

The man turns back to one of the orange trees surrounding the courtyard and deftly picks a luscious low-hanging fruit that sits glistening in the sun. He bites into it with almost theatrical relish and smiles invitingly at Will through strong, juice-stained teeth. The young man nods and the older guy tosses another orange his way. Will catches it one-handed and immediately sinks his teeth right through the skin, giving it an even bigger bite.

The shock is immediate and his face contorts into a mask of pure repugnance Unfortunately, just as a lovely young woman emerges from the hallway.

"*Will?* I am not nice for you?"

He stares grimacingly at his wife of a few days, who is looking so fresh and soft and utterly disconcerted. Instinctively she gazes down at her crisp, brightly flowered dress and slim, bare legs, then back at her sour-faced new husband.

"Eh?" says the young man, before he understands. "No – no, Lu. *Jeez!* You're – you're lovely. You look gorgeous. Beautiful. Wow! *It's the bloody orange!*"

It was almost worth the anguish for the radiant, open-hearted smile he receives, a smile that elides into a giggle so throaty and uninhibited that it sets the large camera around her neck and the silver cross beneath it swinging wildly.

"They are not for eating! *Mermelada.* Marmalade, *sí?* Silly… Willy."

He acknowledges her "English" naughtiness, laboured as it is, with a raised eyebrow, as he rises from his perch. Will knows that he could listen for hours to that gentle, laughing voice, like the tinkling of the fountain but with the earthiest undercurrent, and believes that he always will.

Before he moves on, he swiftly clicks his neck, arches his back and bobs his head north and south. The young woman waits patiently, as she has already learned to do, then nods towards his bag. A small, black umbrella has slipped out and almost into the fountain. He retrieves it and notices the amused handyman shaking his head.

"Reckon we should see just a tiny wee bit of Seville, now we're finally up?" he asks her. "BETWEEN WILD AND FRENZIED BOUTS OF CALEDONIAN COPULATION!"

This is clearly for the benefit of the older man, who can no more understand it than Lu. But her attention has moved on – she has caught hold of a scraggy, white cat, who either belongs to the hostel or thinks it does. She is nuzzling it to her breast with almost maternal affection. Will can't understand why, despite the cosy charm of the picture, he suddenly feels such discomfort and an even less explicable impatience. It isn't as if they have a schedule – there is absolutely nowhere they need to be.

He tries to park his irritation, even as he acknowledges its familiarity. He's being childish. Perhaps it is simply the drums that he can hear in the distance, moving closer beat by beat, sending their insistent rhythm to his heart.

The young man checks his watch, as he always does, but it appears to have died on his wrist. He shakes it, listens to it, winds it and even thumps it against a readily available tile. Nothing. So he discards it crossly into the fountain. "Time to go."

"*Will!*"

"One day," he vows, with a sudden seriousness that takes her by surprise, "one day, Lu, I am buying myself a solid gold Rolex. And a – whatever posh women wear for you."

"Oh, gracias, Señor. But the time she is not so very important to me."

She holds up the camera and frames her photo. Flame-haired, pale-faced husband and trusty black collapsible brolly.

"Say *mañana*!"

Will knows how much in love she is with her camera – he has teased her that it's almost as much as she's in love with him. So he plays up to it and adopts a sequence of poses, his personal favourite being to take a mouthful of water and mirror the naked cherub in the fountain. Spitting out the liquid in a perfect stream, he pulls down his pants to reveal more than a hint of pale, Glaswegian buttock.

So intent is he on making his new bride laugh that he doesn't notice an elderly Spanish couple emerge from the hostel.

"We are lucky it is not Michelangelo's *David*," says the man, with a twinkle, as he leads his equally amused wife out of the courtyard.

Will is struck by a sadness that is almost like an old friend as he watches them go. "Why couldn't *they* be your parents?" he mutters.

He sees Lu wince at this and he can't help but feel some small satisfaction. She gently frees the collar of his fraying shirt, where it is curling beneath itself.

"What's that smell?" he says, sniffing the air and changing the subject.

At first she thinks he means her, but then the familiar aroma hits her. "*Churros!*" she cries, with childlike glee.

"Okay," says Will, who has no idea what she is talking about but knows an excuse to move on when he hears one. He taps his bare wrist, where the apology for a watch once sat. "Come on then, Señora Sutherland. Let's take a wee shufti."

Lu waves adios to the handyman, who still watches them unashamedly.

They move through the wrought-iron gates to join those happy many who have suddenly congregated outside in anticipation of an approaching procession. But not before Will manages a courteous, "Thanks for the orange, *Señor*!"

A few seconds later, a young receptionist comes out into the courtyard and starts to look around. "Telefono – Señor Sutherland?" she announces, without great enthusiasm, to no one in particular. The handyman shrugs at her and goes back to his tending.

The scraggy white cat finds some shade under a tree laden with oranges.

NOW (2025)

AND

NOW (1995)

CHAPTER NINE

WILLIAM SUTHERLAND DOES NOT have the slightest interest in ceramics.

But he knows of a man who does. Which is why he is on his mobile in one of Seville's smartest stores, right opposite the cathedral, giving the informed assistants heart failure as he swings his laptop bag millimetres from their well-stacked but vulnerable shelves.

He had done his homework sufficiently to learn that Seville is especially celebrated for her exquisitely decorated tiles. He now reckons that you would have to be registered blind not to know, as you can't move for the bloody things. They're brightening up every wall, floor and balcony in town, including half of the ceilings, and enhancing indoor and outdoor furniture in neighbourhoods rich and poor. You'll find them in the best (and worst) homes and restaurants, public toilets and private palaces, cemented into pavements and even hanging on ladies' pendants.

Azulejos is apparently the buzzword. William reminds himself to use it whenever the opportunity presents itself.

He is on his phone now to ensure that opportunity comes knocking with pipes and drums within the next seventy-two hours. His world apparently depends upon it.

"So – maybe I could take you for a meal," he invites the recorder of Spain's longest answer-phone greeting. "You and your Señora. A 'night on the tiles', as we – *Oh*, are you sure? Well, gracias… No, no, you choose… Of course I know your product. It's of the highest quality. And, as for your *azulejos*, Señor Barbadillo… mm? … Oh, okay… Cristobal. Well then, you must call me—" He stops talking mid-sentence. Words dangle in the humid air.

The little blond boy, the one from that first procession, the one who he… *that* boy.

He's staring in through the window. Now. At William.

The sun and the reflections it creates are quite blinding at first. To William's confused eye it looks as though the boy is throwing delicate crockery up in the air. But no, it's his small hand that is moving up and down. The crockery is still, of course, on the shelves behind William.

Yet the boy is hurling something skywards. It's like a ball of some sort but not smooth, nothing that a child could bat or bounce. Irregular and knobbly, it seems to contain different colours swirling haphazardly within. And quite suddenly he remembers.

Wax!

Yes, from the candles. Children – young kids and even teenagers – would hold out their tremulous hands in the darkness towards a candle's flames. Dear Lord, that was such an age ago. And now the child is smiling. Or at least he is until his father comes along, sees William frozen in the window and snatches the boy away. Again. The purple birthmark on the man's cheek, in the shape of a ragged star, looks almost as angry as he does.

Without even thinking, or wondering if he is about to appear on some sort of watchlist, William wanders out of the shop. He doesn't hear the sighs of relief from the petrified assistants. And barely even registers the words he himself employs to close this hitherto most critical of phone conversations.

"We'll – er – speak tomorrow then. Aye. Good to talk, Pab… *Cristobal*."

The heat hits him like a fist as he leaves the impressive air-conditioning behind him. Hot and blinded, he changes his glasses to the ones he keeps for abroad, the old prescription with the expensive tinted lenses. An extra for which he couldn't quite justify forking out again this time round. It's a parsimony Luisa tuts about each time he slips them on, even though she knows that with his skin he tries to keep out of the sun as much as possible anyway. Beetroot isn't as yet the new shade of black.

William has absolutely no idea why he is walking in the direction of the cathedral. Luisa must be back at the hotel by now; the parade can't have taken that long to pass by. And, as the Gothic Catedral de Santa Maria de la Sede, along with its accompanying bell tower, is the city's most celebrated landmark on this or any other week, as indeed it was on that earlier Semana Santa, it would undoubtedly be somewhere she would wish for them to revisit together.

Perhaps this is why he is going alone.

CHAPTER TEN

EVEN FOR A CATHEDRAL this one appears unusually dark.

William wonders if perhaps they had installed the stained glass to face in the wrong direction or they're using ecologically friendly, low-wattage candles. It is only when he trips over the bulbous foot of an ancient wooden pew and falls to the floor that he remembers how lazily his old sunglasses actually adjust to the shade.

The flagstones are certainly cool but they're far from giving. He manages by sheer luck, as he topples, to shield most of his head with his outstretched hand. But his efforts are finally thwarted by his own laptop bag, as it swings sharply around his neck and smacks its weightiest corner right into his ear. He finds himself deciding to stay just where he is for a while, prone on the ground like some overzealous pilgrim, until his universe rights itself once more.

"*Señor?*"

When he finally raises his throbbing head a few painful inches, all he can see through the dimness, aside from the offending stonework, are the delicate, sandalled feet of a young woman. A bit higher and slender but firm legs fill his gaze: exquisitely smooth legs, he still manages to remark despite the pain, leading gracefully up to the fluttering hem of a fresh, summery dress.

"*Señor...*" comes the sweet voice again, like a fragrant echo.

The wondrous legs begin to bend, deep brown knees move towards him and finally a small, elfin face looms into view, closing in on his. It's a dark face with long, dark hair encasing it, but of course everything is still bloody dark. He removes his accursed glasses and exchanges them for the current model.

Now he sees her.

"*JESUS CHRIST!*" he says, quite loud.

He can hear the people around him gasp, for reasons he would be an idiot not to understand. But William Sutherland feels like an idiot right now. Or perhaps a madman. Because standing directly in front of him, or rather crouching purposefully to help him up, is his wife, Luisa Sutherland.

Yet not as she is today.

He is staring – well, of course he can't be, but it certainly feels like it – into the perfectly entrancing face and chestnut eyes of Luisa Sutherland, circa 1995.

Actually, no circa about it.

This would be Lu (very newly) Sutherland, April 1995. If indeed it were her, which obviously it isn't, patently can't be, despite that long forgotten yet all too recognisable glow. Easter 1995, to be exact. Or Semana Santa, as she would say. If the apparition could speak, which he very much doubts, as of course she isn't actually there, despite earlier evidence to the contrary.

"Señor? *Estas herido?* English? ARE – YOU – BUMPING – YOUR – HEAD?"

"Huh?" mutters William, who is rather impressed that he can mutter anything at all.

He tries to process exactly what this "person" is saying, in a voice of pure velvet that is beginning to stir vague and not wholly comfortable memories. He finds that he can't venture much beyond the fact that she is actually making far more recognisable sounds than he is. So he lets the gentle creature, this unexpected doppelgänger, assist him slowly upwards from his awkward, leg-worshipping position, while he forms an appropriate response. Wondering vaguely, as he rises, how come you can feel a hallucination's touch.

"English?" he answers her, finally. "Aye. Well, no. Glasgow. So not really. Or at all actually. But I speak the English. Of sorts. I'm sorry. To be staring, I mean. It's just that you look so like—"

"Like?" she repeats, with a slight smile.

"Just – someone I know. Used to know. Well, I still do, but – a long time ago. I'm so sorry. Again. Had a bit of champagne. Quite a… They say everyone has a double somewhere. And I had a few doubles, on the plane, I'm afraid. I'm talking gibberish."

The young woman seems bemused. "I am sorry – my English it is not so good." She stares back at William now and is looking quite disturbed, although probably not nearly as disturbed as he is. "You *shiver!* You are shocking, I think. No – you are shocked. *Sí.*" She offers her arm. "Perhaps we walk—"

William can only nod. She really does look so like Luisa. As was. She even *sounds* like young Luisa, with that alluring vocal combination of the dulcet and the earthy. Although, of course, young Spanish women all sound very much alike to him now.

He takes her arm.

"Are you on your own, sir?"

Sir?

"Yes. No. Well, sort of. My wife and I are—"

"Lost?"

"Aye," he nods in agreement. "Lost."

"*My husband and I too!*" she yelps in delight. "He always walk everywhere so fast. Even on the holiday. But I tell him, if it happen, if we are losing each other in all the people, then we meet here. In catedral. Even Will, he cannot miss a catedral!"

If William was shivering before, he is going way off the Richter scale now. They can probably feel his heart tremors in Catalonia.

"W-Will? YOUR HUSBAND'S NAME IS *WILL?*"

William is shouting. He knows this but he can't seem to stop.

He watches the solid, decorum-abiding, cathedral-respecting people around him and even way off in the distance turn as one to stare. Yet, disturbingly, the stares have the quality of those you would direct at someone who is totally insane, rather than simply disruptive or over-exuberant. Even the guys wandering around in the conical hats seem dumbstruck and he can only see their eyes.

"*Sí,*" says the young woman, who appears just a tad disconcerted herself. "Will. Is little for William. He is a

Glasgow-wegian also. We meet when I am au pair in Newton—"

"No. NO!" he begs. "Please. God! This isn't happening."

William staggers away, trying desperately not to pass out or collapse onto the hard stone again. He cleaves a ragged path down the longest, most awe-inspiring nave in Spain and into the beating heart of the massive cathedral, heading towards the great, boxlike choir-loft.

Not that he is heading anywhere. Or appreciating anything. Just reeling. The memory of that non-existent bus suddenly charges back at full speed into his brain.

Crowds are beginning to sweep in. The next float is clearly expected to arrive, after its slow journey from some honoured neighbourhood chapel, and they're after ringside seats. William feels like he is about to career into each and every one of the innocent bystanders, like a helpless driver whose brakes have just been severed. Or an errant float powered by too much sangria.

And everywhere he looks there are scenes from the life, or more usually death, of the Christ. Carved, painted, sculpted, etched and scribbled. By old masters and the youngest disciples. Hardly unexpected but nonetheless taunting. He knows that this is probably the deepest of sacrileges but he feels that somebody out there is bent on crucifying him too.

"I'm not even Catholic," he mutters, before noticing that the concerned young woman, this impossible visitor from another lifetime, is once again directly beside him.

He decides to make a stirring effort to appear vaguely normal, even though the current situation is about as far from normal as an alien invasion of Richmond. "Lost, is he? Young… Will. Och, well, there's an old saying. Coleridge? Tennyson? Someone dead, anyway. 'Tis better to have loved and lost—'"

"'*Than two in the bush!*' Will, he tell me this!"

"*Away ye go!*" William wonders briefly why he is finding himself so utterly charmed by a situation that might have come straight out of Satan's playbook. It's like meeting Godzilla and wondering if he'd like a biscuit. "So – er – so, how are you finding Seville?"

"By the train."

She sees him chuckle at this and he can tell from the glow in her eyes that she considers it a friendly, uncritical laugh. So she giggles too, as she slowly gets the joke. "Oh. *Perdón*. We have just arrived. From Madrid. We see my parents there. But I have been the student in this place. Here – in Sevilla."

"Aye. At the art school."

The young woman is quiet. The whole vast, Gothic edifice appears to go mute with her. *How the hell am I supposed to have known that?* he wonders.

"*You have artist's hands!*" he explains swiftly.

Oh brilliant, William. And now she's inspecting her wee hands, the dear thing. Hands that he fondly recalls. Smooth, unadorned hands, that once seemed hardly ever to leave his own.

So, we might as well go the extra mile. "I used to be a detective."

What?

"*Like your Sherlock Holmess!*" she cries with glee, her marvellously long, shiny hair swinging around her face and picking up every colour from the glorious, sunlit windows.

William is about to reply, with God knows what further nonsense, when without warning the great organ of the Catedral de Santa Maria de la Setes suddenly launches into something excessively loud and suitably sombre. He reacts with an involuntary but massive jolt, as if the sonorous notes have been injected directly into his system.

He notices, however, with some puzzlement, that the young woman – okay, Lu; he has to accept that somehow this *is* Lu – doesn't appear to register any surprise or awareness at all. But, of course, she is Catholic and he knows that the delicate, silver cross she wears at all times around her alluring neck has borne witness to some serious cathedral-going and organ-listening. Even if her recent choice of husband is testament to an unfortunate and, as many around Madrid and its environs pray, merely temporary lapsing. (William reckons they would have willingly loosened up their views on divorce, or even honour killing, just to see the back of him.)

They find themselves strolling together towards one of the smaller chapels, away from the crowds and the clamour.

He can't, in all honesty, flatter himself that this is because, despite her lyrical, four-day-old marriage, she has suddenly found a considerably older, balding stranger with eye-bags and a business paunch utterly irresistible. Yet the knowledge that she may simply be needing to reassure herself he isn't about to slip into a coma doesn't appear to diminish his excitement. Even though this is the weirdest, creepiest, scariest thing that has ever happened to him in his life and may hopefully just turn out to be a result of that unfortunate bang on the head. Didn't something of this ilk happen in *Dallas*?

"Will, my husband, yes – he say he is trying to make the big surprise for me this week." William knows exactly what the big surprise is, but he is damned if he is going to let himself slip again. "I am sure it is bullfight." There you go. "I cannot tell him I hate the *corrida*, can I?"

"Er, no," says William safely, if anything is safe in this madhouse. "But you're fine. I tried to get bullfight tickets here years ago. *Hopeless!* The bulls' relatives buy up all the best seats."

He can see her struggling with this one, so he taps a nearby information console, with superb digital close-ups of the cathedral's hottest features, as a way to change the subject. Yet, to his surprise, her expression has turned from vague puzzlement to shocked incomprehension.

"Why do you do this?" she says.

"What? Make a joke? Check the info?"

"No. Touch this nun. They do not like this."

"Touch the—?"

It takes only a couple of seconds to go from wondering what the hell she is talking about to knowing what the hell she is talking about. And he realises that the latter is so much worse.

"I'm so sorry," he explains/lies. "It's this arm. I injured it once, on a detecting job, and sometimes, you know, it has a life of its own." He waves it around to furnish credence to this rubbish. "The nun – did she notice?"

"I do not think this. You are very gentle."

"That's the one consolation. Aren't these paintings interesting?" He waves an all-encompassing arm around at whatever art is in the vicinity. "You *can* see the paintings?"

"*Sí*. Of course. I do not wear bad sunglasses. Ah, you like the art, yes?"

"I've learned to," William confesses. "I used to hate it. Totally. Couldn't see the point. It was my wife who taught me to really appreciate…" This makes him pause, just for a moment. "Aye, right enough. Dragging me to galleries until I finally succumbed. Until I really 'got' it." Again, he seems lost in thought. "Well, she used to. Not these days. We don't do so much these days."

The young woman nods, as if sensing a meander onto rockier terrain. Or maybe she just sees the sadness on his face.

"So. If you are okay, Señor…"

"*DON'T GO, LUISA!*"

A gasp. "How you know my name?"

"Aah," he mumbles, the "shit!" unspoken, hearing the drums in the distance and hoping they're coming to drag him away. "*Your bracelet!*" *Thank you, God.* She looks at her bracelet, on which her name is indeed engraved into the silver, but he would have needed eyes like a bat. "Eyes like a bat," he explains. "Could I maybe just take a wee look at your guidebook? Please. I-I need to find my wife again."

The young woman burrows into her bright-red shoulder bag and he suddenly recalls, as if memory is like a sharp knee to the groin or the stirrings of a migraine, how she so used to love the colour red. *Do we go through phases,* he wonders, *and did I somehow get stuck in sepia?*

She removes a glossy new guide to Seville. A wedding gift, that's it, from an old schoolfriend of his, presented to them and gleefully unwrapped there and then, in the hope it might be something fruitier.

As Lu passes the book to him, it immediately ages and crinkles in his hands.

Oh – Fuck!

William thinks he is going to pass out again, but he manages to look into her face, expecting to see a mask of pure horror swiftly overlay those beautiful, untested features. But, mercifully, she is looking not at the instantly worn and yellowed pages but in the other direction.

"Ah, I think I see my husband."

"Oh no," says William quietly. "Oh, dear Lord, no."

Without saying another word, fearing he might crumple or simply expire in the chapel, he stumbles out through a convenient but unnecessarily heavy side door.

When young Luisa finally looks round again to say goodbye, the man is gone.

Will she ever understand the Scottish?

*

William Sutherland reels into the screaming sunlight without any sense of where he is going.

It is some minutes later, and on the other side of the river, before he realises that he is still gripping the young apparition's guidebook. Warily, he begins to flick through its pages, now suddenly well-thumbed and weary with age.

A gift card, showing its years and emblazoned with fading printed confetti, slips into his trembling hand.

CHAPTER ELEVEN

LUISA IS ALSO STARING at confetti. This time on a photo of similar vintage.

She sits in a pretty, shaded square that she still remembers from her student days, barely a stone's throw from the river. With a café cortado and her favourite golden fino on the table beside her, she flicks through the small faux-leather photo album she has put together, somewhat tentatively, for this unpredictable week.

The first picture is of her far-younger self – could she ever *really* have looked so young and slender – as she leaves the Central Registry Office in Glasgow's George Square with her brand-new husband. She's ducking playfully under a shower of coloured paper and a less colourful shower of Scottish drizzle. Not the wedding she had been hoping for. But then, of course, he was not the husband her family had been hoping for. They would sooner have travelled to Hell than to Glasgow (in fact, they had suspected the two were twinned) and William's ailing mother could never have managed the journey to Spain, had this even been an option.

Luisa finds her hand instinctively moving towards her neck, as it so often does, searching for the tiny silver cross she hasn't worn or even owned for years.

Before she flicks onwards, she calls William again. He hasn't been picking up his phone, which can only mean he has fallen asleep after all those whiskies, although even this doesn't usually stop him. He would most probably answer the phone from his coffin, she reckons, or at least check the Wi-Fi. She leaves another message.

She should be making her way back to the Hotel Herrera, to begin their gifted time together, but there's just one more stop she wants to make en route.

Another, sunnier photo. This time of a café, but not the one she sits at now. This picture is of *their* café, the pretty one so near the cathedral, the one with the bright-yellow and black awning. The café to which they kept returning, wherever they had visited and whatever they had been up to that day. Doubtless it has gone now or at least changed colour, yet she still recalls exactly where it was. And there in the thirty-year old photo is Will. Her Will. Sitting outside, at a small table, waving. She can hardly remember him when he looked so happy and finds herself shivering, because this makes her feel so sad.

Another wedding picture now. Of a later wedding. This occasion far less fraught.

She can see that this time her husband, once so cruelly disapproved of, is manfully affording his own son-in-law at least a modicum of respect, even if it can't really be mistaken for affection. Yet there's no mistaking the love in the older man's eyes for the bride, that intensely joyful young woman, blended to perfection from a mixture of races, letting loose her expansive, gap-toothed smile. Those satin-sheathed, fist-pumping arms are upraised in pure triumph. *Got him!* The spark never seems to diminish, thinks Luisa with a grateful smile, and she prays that it never will.

One more photo, from a much earlier time, one she knows that she cannot and must not overlook, despite the pain. Not this week, of all weeks. And then she should move on.

"You are very pretty lady."

She looks up with a start. The handsome African man is selling jewellery. It's curling over his outstretched arms like a family of lazy snakes and is quite beautiful, but she's not in a buying mood.

"And you are full of shit," she says.

"*Sí*," the smiling man agrees. "But you are still pretty lady."

She nods a brief, amused thank you. At my age, she thinks ruefully, you take what you can get.

CHAPTER TWELVE

HE WOULD LIKE TO say that the old hostel has hardly changed over all the years.

But William can't honestly swear, hand on heart, that he recalls how it used to look in the first place. Yet, after his mind-bending experience just a half-hour earlier, William Sutherland is delighted he has even the wherewithal to push open the heavy gate.

He wouldn't have paused here at all, especially now that he has finally picked up all Luisa's missed calls and texts. Yet the name *Hostal Esmeralda* had been highlighted in felt-tip in the newly purloined guidebook. And he had spotted, with some satisfaction, the (inevitably) tiled nameplate as he came off the bridge. He just hopes he doesn't meet anyone he used to know.

Such as himself.

The courtyard, which even he has to admit is rather appealing, with its trickling stone fountain and abundant orange trees, is empty, save for a stocky, deeply tanned man in his forties, fixing a downstairs shutter. William gazes around and finally up at a first-floor bedroom, whose own perfectly functional blue shutters are open to the day. He senses the handyman staring fixedly at him and looks away.

"*William?*"

"AHH!!" The old guidebook slips out of his hand, as he turns slowly around. "Oh, dear God, it's you! Luisa."

"Who else knows you in Seville?" she asks, reasonably. "The Virgin Mary?" She looks at him – something is wrong. "William, you're trembling. Are you okay?"

"No, not really," he admits, retrieving the mercurial book. "Luisa, the most surreal thing has just happened. Possibly."

"You have been drinking," she interrupts. He has no idea whether this is a response or a new question.

"NO! Well, just some champagne." He stares at her. "It was from Sandy." He notices that for a brief moment she looks vaguely uneasy, just before she smiles.

"Oh. Well, this is kind," she says, almost dismissively. "Why are you here, William?"

"Here?" He is momentarily confused, as if the question is unexpectedly existential. "Oh, this place. Well, I was just passing and – you see! I *do* remember stuff, Luisa! Hostal Esmeralda! As in, you know, Quasimodo and Esmeralda. The Lunchpack of Notre Dame." He laughs but she doesn't join him. She is looking up at that same little first-floor bedroom.

William grabs the opportunity to stare directly at her, examining her upturned face with the most intense of scrutinies. Something he is certain he hasn't done in years. Why would he? Luisa flinches disconcertedly when she becomes aware of this, as if finding herself suddenly married to an overzealous dermatologist. So he judiciously dims down the glare.

"Luisa," he implores, "forget the drink. Please! It *wasn't* the drink. At least I – you will not fucking believe who – what – I just – huh?"

She has noticed the old guidebook in his still-trembling hand. Gently taking it from him, she flicks through its well-thumbed pages. He can only watch as she begins to read aloud.

"'*There are 115 processions during Semana Santa. They each proceed from their parish church right through the cathedral. But if it rains really badly, a procession can be cancelled.*' Now this you underline!"

"Yes, okay! But, Luisa, the guidebook. You notice how old it is? About thirty years old. Well—"

"'*BECAUSE some of the floats date from the thirteenth century. So the people have to wait until the next year, when the sun is shining.*' Only you would write under this – 'pack umbrella'. You and your bloody rain!" Yet she says this with at least half a smile and indeed appears strangely touched. "William – you keep the book all this time?"

William nods, sentimental old fool and shameless liar that he is. But the triumph is short-lived.

"No – you did not just 'remember' this hostal! It has the big circle here in red. Where you write 'cheap 'n' cheerful' with two ticks! *Sí* – I have the memory now. There was a guy here, at the station. With a postcard!"

"Our hotel's nice," says William. "It's got Wi-Fi." He can sense that this is neither a cultural nor emotional highlight. "Oh, and the kids sent lovely flowers. Well, Claire did. I tried to thank her but she was busy." He grabs her arm, startling her. "Luisa, just now, after I'd been to the ceramics shop—"

"The *ceramics* shop? William, we have to talk."

"What am I bloody *trying* to do?"

The handyman suddenly coughs. They turn to see him point suggestively towards the upstairs rooms. William and Luisa both vehemently shake their heads.

In harmony for once.

CHAPTER THIRTEEN

"SEMANA SANTA – IS very romantic this time of the evening, no?"

Will is too busy for Andalusian dusk or romance. He is checking the menu outside a classy restaurant, in a narrow, lopsided building on the winding old Calle Sierpes. A second later he collapses onto the cobbled pavement, clutching his chest. Lu looks down at the writhing figure and gasps.

"Will – *querido*!"

People hover around, faces showing a mixture of horror and fascination, but mostly fascination. Music plays obliviously from lively pavement cafés up and down the busy, tree-lined street. As Lu kneels down beside her stricken lover, the onlookers graciously stand just a few millimetres back.

"Brandy, quick," he mumbles, grimly. "But not that Fundador stuff. Cognac – as it's a special occasion."

He's not sure whether his new wife is going to laugh or cry. Happily, she decides on the lighter option and smacks him.

"Bet your pal Pope John Paul 2 gets his cut this week," continues an encouraged Will, standing up, unscathed. "'*Luigi, I weel take ze tapas bars, you do ze marzipan nuns.*'"

"You are idiot," she says, smacking him. "And el Papa, he is Polaco, not Italian."

People wander away, looking for tapas, chopitos, processions – anything but young love making a fool of itself in their wondrous city.

"*Details*. Have you seen these bloody prices, Lu?" He laughs but when he looks at her his smile has gone. "Mind you, one fine day—"

"We do not have to eat in the expensive restaurants, *cariño*," she protests, because she already knows this tune by heart. "We have only to eat together."

He brushes the long, shiny hair from her face and kisses her with a gentleness that surprises even him. What is it about this person that makes his anger, an emotion he truly feels he must have imbibed with his mother's milk, fuelled with his father's hobnailed kicks and nurtured since with unwavering passion, seem to diffuse like incense into the balmy, orange-blossomed air?

They don't notice the man who now approaches, speaking in a fluent Spanish that makes Lu spin round in wonder.

"*Dios mío!*" she cries, in the city where He is most probably listening.

"*Bloody hell!*" cries her husband, ignoring the occasion.

His new Mrs Sutherland already has her arms around the beaming interloper and is chattering excitedly in Spanish. The young man grins at Will who shakes his head and smiles affectionately back.

"*Away ye go!*" continues the temporarily deserted husband. "And remind me again of the Spanish for 'what in buggery are you doing here, you posh Scottish tosser?'"

The young man, who's clearly too tall and fair to be a local, favours Will with a reply that is so posh and Scottish that it barely sounds Scottish at all.

"Didn't actually learn that on my year here."

"Bet you heard it often enough."

"I tried to call you at your digs. Must have just missed you."

Will looks puzzled. "We only just *found* our 'digs'!" He separates his wife from the newcomer and puts his own arm around him, pulling him away. "I know it was your first time, Sandy, old chum," he says quietly, "but the best man's job usually ends with his speech."

"Damn," says the taller guy, smacking his own forehead.

"*Paloma!*" yelps Lu, in delight. "Is Paloma! I speak to her from telephone in hostal but she never say this thing!"

Now Will gets it too. "Jesus! The sodding bridesmaid!"

"But never the blushing bride." Sandy smiles, winking at Lu. Will clocks this, but his bride is already scouring the crowds at the pavement cafés.

"Paloma is *here*, Sandy?" says Lu, looking around.

"Well, not *here* here but we're meeting up again later on. She's got a job down the road. At the casino." He can see his friends staring at him. "She *invited* me, guys, at the wedding! For *Semana Santa*, with her folks on the other side of town. Would've been churlish to refuse. Could've caused a diplomatic incident." If Will rolls his eyes any more, they will spin out onto the cobbles. "Now don't you fret, oor Wullie, I won't cramp your hard man of the Gorbals style."

"Govan, actually," mutters Will. "Different class of squalor," but Sandy is already kissing Lu goodbye and starting to dance his way down the heaving street.

"Later," he cries. "Flamenco, disco, *casino*! Och, no, you dinna dance, do you, Guillermo?"

"Don't you worry, pal," calls Will, "I've got all the moves."

He looks at Lu, who is laughing. He laughs too. "Can you believe that guy? My ma used to practically curtsey when I brought him home from uni." He shrugs. "Bet even *your* mama would approve of him."

Lu doesn't say anything, because there's nothing she can say that would help. She wishes she could have changed the last few days, that her parents could have seen what she sees, tried even for a moment, just for her, to locate what it is that she loves. But, more than anything, she wishes that their opinions didn't matter. She is sure that they don't matter to her – well, she's pretty sure, or at least they don't matter to her as much as they clearly do to the man she has chosen. Perhaps because, for Will, they are simply another part of a sad pattern that is now almost a part of him.

She watches him as he looks back longingly into the smart restaurant, with its huge hams hanging from the dark wooden beams and the fashionably cracking *azulejo* tiles on the walls.

"Well, mebbe not today," he concedes. "But here's a promise, darling. On our last night here we'll – we'll go to this real snazzy place, with a rooftop terrace open to the sky and a rare view over the whole of Sevilla. There's one I ticked in yon book of ours. And we'll share a huge bloody cocktail."

"With the cherry on the top, *sí*?" says Lu, realising with a start that she no longer has the guidebook. No matter – she knows the city by heart. She must tell Will about that poor sweet fallen man she met. The one who made off with their brand-new gift.

"Aye. And one of those wee, wooden brollies!" he enthuses. "But, for now, I saw this nice, cheap caff in a square just down the road."

He takes one final look into the cool, darkened restaurant. He can make out a middle-aged couple near the window, sitting in total silence, with their most probably exorbitant bottle of fine red Spanish wine. "We'll come back here when we're unspeakably rich – and famous. Won't be long, my darling! Won't be long."

Lu just sighs and points her camera at Will.

CHAPTER FOURTEEN

"DAMN PAPARAZZI!" SAYS THE balding man, as the flash goes off.

The restaurant is already quite full, mostly with tourists who aren't inclined to wait until the absurdly late hours at which the indigenous population chooses to eat. Yet curiously only one couple, this quiet middle-aged couple, appears to register the flash of a camera on the street outside.

"They'll track me down, wherever I am," he persists, but notices that his partner still doesn't give a smile. He can't have missed one: he is staring quite hard into her face.

"Why do you look at me? All the time since we come here, you stare like you are seeking for something. It is not nice."

"Can't a guy stare at his wife in Spain? No wonder we Brexited."

William knows that he can't keep scrutinising Luisa, like a map that could tell him where exactly he lost his way. So he checks his watch, as he so often does. It's an elegant object and far from new. The leather strap has been changed several times, as has the glass, but the face, with its slim Roman numerals, seems – timeless. He notices that Luisa is also looking at it, yet clearly not to check the hour. Their eyes meet, as if a distant memory is suddenly being shared, not in itself unpleasant yet one of which neither chooses to speak.

"William, are you all right?" she enquires, with some concern. "That thing this morning – with the boy. And you are looking so pale. Even for you. This working, it makes you ill, I think. We are not so young now. And, please, no more wine this evening."

He lifts the bottle, a tad tauntingly, then pours what little remains into his wife's glass. His hand remains holding the stem, as if in some way he is holding on to her.

"Luisa, seriously, you *have* to listen. Please. It's not the booze. Or the work – *not that you ever actually ask me about the work...* This morning, at the cathedral, when I tripped—." He looks around at his voluble fellow diners. "Is it me or are Spaniards the loudest folk on earth?"

"Is not you. We are loud. You went to Catedrale, without me?"

"Aye. Er – sorry. We'll go again. Together. That's why we're here, isn't it? Well, that and the tapas!"

He must make sure he has the right words. It has never seemed more important. Yet he has the abiding fear that once he hears these words, however apt and well-chosen, as they stream from his own quivering mouth, it will downgrade the momentous events of this afternoon to just the symptomatic display of a nervous, alcohol-induced crisis. Which he may well have believed it to be, were it not for that worn guidebook now nuzzling against the ever-faithful laptop in his bag.

"You see, after I went off on my own—"

"Do you remember this place?"

Frustrated by the interruption, he nonetheless hears himself following her tack. "I'd have remembered these prices! We never came here, I'm certain of it." A random thought strikes him and he isn't sure why. "Oh, by the way, thanks for the le Carré. Sorry. I should've said." He shakes his head. "I used to read so many novels, didn't I?" Now he's almost talking to himself, as he looks around the bustling room, but seeing only a time long gone. "Even thought that maybe one day I'd—"

"William," she interrupts again, "I think we should use these days. This occasion. To – you know. If you are not 'too busy.'"

"No, I'm not 'too busy', Luisa," he says, crossly. "And here's my bloody starter for ten. I saw *YOU* today. The young you. Right there – in the cathedral!"

There! Now it's out. He has said it. Make of this what you will. That your husband of thirty years is finally losing the plot, most probably.

"Aah," she smiles, "and did I look like this?"

Out comes the photo album, as if he has simply plucked a tender memory from the ether and given her a welcome prompt. He is instantly confronted with a photo of their younger selves, in the courtyard of the Hostal Esmeralda. Taken no doubt by an accommodating member of staff or fellow guest.

"I make this book – for the occasion. '*William y Luisa. 1995 to—*'"

Luisa halts mid-pitch. She senses, through the uneasy stillness, a stiffening reluctance across the table. Yet she decides to flick doggedly on, as though William, once teased by glimpses of what's in store, like the trailer for a film he has been desperate to see, will find it impossible to resist.

She pauses at their wedding pictures. Harmless stuff. Heartening, in their innocent way. And then on to that photo of the Yellow Café, with William sitting under an umbrella – for heatstroke prevention this time, not showers – offering her his wave and that funny, vaguely uncomfortable, half-smile.

Luisa feels certain that William will warm to this, touched by happier recollections, but his anguished face soon tells her otherwise. Perhaps he misses his red hair, she thinks, the way she misses her impossibly slim figure and the innocent sparkle in her eyes. And everything else that speaks of being young and unburdened and having the rest of your life ahead of you.

Or perhaps, as Claire almost said, the past is a foreign country. And somehow they've mislaid their passports.

Yet she knows that it runs far deeper than this. And that they both miss what's missing – what got lost along the way. Something that a few snapshots pulled from a handbag, like a conjuror's dazed rabbit, can't so easily retrieve. Long-established fault lines, which a few days in a familiar city, however resonant the memories, may serve only to turn into chasms.

And still she turns the page.

Now a young Sandy sits there, at that same outdoor café, beaming into the camera. He has his arms around them both and his chair close to Lu's.

Even more swiftly onwards. Through the years. Photos of children.

"I'll go settle the bill." William is on his feet and

moving away. From her and especially from her fake-leather memory-bank.

Luisa drains her glass and shrugs at the elderly couple at a nearby table, who appear to have been watching them with barely disguised interest. She wants to tell them 'I *do* ask him about his work' then wonders if she does or if she simply complains about it. She doesn't notice her own husband looking back at her.

Rattled. And scared.

*

As he slips the restaurant bill into his wallet, which he does religiously, even when there isn't the slightest chance that he might claim it back, William pauses. He always takes this breath, perhaps just for a second and regardless of how pressed he is. The photo inside the worn and tattered leather, of Claire as a small child, never fails to capture those tiniest bits of heart and mind that aren't ground away or otherwise engaged.

He has barely registered the musicians playing in the busy street beside him. A talented guitarist and a hyperactive trumpeter, they perform what he has to assume is authentic local music, tailored for maximum reach and generosity. It is sufficiently on-message to cause little Spanish girls to leap up and practise their flamenco for clapping onlookers. Some are even in their tiny traditional costumes, which they must have insisted that they wear tonight and perhaps all of this special week.

As he looks up, William notices another not-so-little Spanish girl, moving with accomplished grace in her comfortable footwear to the local beat. Playfully clapping her hands and stamping for her smaller companions.

Luisa hasn't caught her husband watching her, which only adds to the moment. William is quietly able to observe his delighted wife strutting her stuff with flair and vivacity, almost blurring under the string of festive lights, utterly lost in the music. As if he has simply happened across an accomplished native lady of a certain age and decided that she merits a brief interruption to his journey.

He spots others watching in the crowded night-time street and wonders if they find this person attractive. He wonders also, despite those piercing memories unwittingly summoned back, whether he himself still finds her so. Or whether he merely feels, given all the evidence available, that he surely should.

Yet he recalls now, as the events of today sink in, how very attracted he once was. They talk of falling out of love, he thinks, as if it's an accident that happens in a moment, whilst in truth it's love that slowly falls out of you.

Finally she spots her familiar watcher and beckons him, somewhat unkindly, to join her in the dance, knowing that he would far rather jump off a bell tower. As he stands his ground, she shrugs and proudly flamencos towards him, smart holiday skirt swirling, sensible shoes stamping, pointing her camera even as she moves.

"It's like they've taken everything anyone's ever known about Spain," observes William, "and delivered it here in a truck."

Luisa is about to take his photograph – even though she knows it is something he has never fully enjoyed and dislikes even more these days – when a young Spanish woman approaches them. She takes the camera gently from Luisa's hand and helpfully pushes her towards her unenthusiastic husband, for the perfect, romantic shot. The couple try to pose politely for this kindness, so that they can all swiftly get on with their lives. But life, as so often happens, gets in the way.

Another woman, misreading the scene, assumes the photographer is a friend or daughter of the couple, who would surely prefer to be a part of the picture rather than simply its facilitator. So she virtually shoves this innocent third party right between William and Luisa, snatching away the precious camera with a single swipe.

The bemused Sutherlands have no idea whether to protest or endure, nor how many more innocents will be recruited to this farce, whilst the good-natured stranger in their midst tries not to giggle. Happily, the photograph is swiftly taken and the helpful locals soon depart, each delighted in her own kind way with a job well done.

Luisa looks at William. He seems torn, as if waiting for some sort of permission to react. But he can't help it. He has to laugh. And Luisa finds that she has to join him, wants to join him, the mirth erupting like a flamenco troupe bursting in full flamboyant glory onto a stage. For a brief moment they roar and chortle together.

But inevitably the laughter ebbs. And dies. Leaving them somehow even more bereft than before.

"Maybe we should be getting back to the room," says William.

"What for, William?" says his bride of thirty years, on this their second honeymoon, and walks slowly away into the crowd.

CHAPTER FIFTEEN

THE PLAZA DEL CABILDO, just around the corner from the cathedral, is brilliantly lit. So, when William finally catches up with Luisa, having navigated his way with less agility but more brute force through the festive night-time throng – all of whom appear to be seeing the entire medieval world and every passing nun through the lenses of their smartphones – he has no trouble recognising what she has been aiming for. And vaguely regrets what he called out to her on the way.

"See, is *not* an 'el McDonald's' by now," she taunts him back, as she probably still doesn't know the expression 'oh ye of little faith'.

Across the small square is the establishment to which Luisa has been referring, since long before they arrived, as '*our* café'. The one in all the photographs.

William seems to recall them patronising a load of differing establishments last time round and the sangria being equally disgusting in each. But he keeps this opinion to himself and simply expresses surprise that Café Amarillo still has a yellow awning. Luisa doesn't bother to explain to him that *Amarillo* is Spanish for yellow. He should know some bloody Spanish by now.

"*See! Just as it was!*" she exults.

There you go.

And there's even a young couple cuddling there, glimpsed through the roiling night-time crowd, sitting quite possibly at 'our table'. The crowd momentarily thins, drawn in different culinary rather than spiritual directions, and William realises with a sudden chill that he knows this particular loving couple rather too well.

Oh God!

The wild sensations William felt earlier this afternoon, which have been racking his body in the subsequent hours like major aftershocks, even as he tried not to think about them, rush back in with a new ferocity that almost fells him. It's not just *her* now, invading his present; it's *him* too.

A matched pair!

William Sutherland knows his own system, the inner workings that busily churn away and keep him just about upright and functioning. He is pretty damn certain that this is becoming too much for them. He knows too, without the slightest doubt, that he has to get Luisa out of here, get them both out of here, if they have any chance of maintaining their sanity. And, however precarious, their 'status quo'. Even if this sighting – as he still more than half suspects, despite mounting evidence – is merely his own personal and highly perturbing delusion.

And yet he simply cannot move.

He wonders why it is demanding such a colossal effort on his part to draw himself and his still oblivious wife away. Like an addiction he can't quite sate or an attraction too fatal to resist. But, of course, he tells himself, how could it not be so? How could anyone with any curiosity – no, simply with a heart that beats – turn away from such a scenario?

Yet, somehow, for both their sakes – for *all* their sakes – he knows that he must.

"Okay. Seen it. Still yellow after all these years." He turns to go, the demon vanquished. For now. "So let's—"

"This girl – why does she wave to us?"

What?

He turns back and sure enough the young woman is happily trying to attract their attention. He knows that Luisa won't have been able to make out the faces yet; her eyes aren't what they were. Nor in truth can he – it's Lu's brightly patterned dress that he recognises from earlier. But it's only a matter of time.

"YOU SEE THEM TOO?" he cries, anticipating the inevitable.

"Excuse me?"

"I thought it might just be me."

"You thought *what* might—?"

Luisa doesn't complete the question, because she doesn't need to. The young woman is striding briskly towards them, with a huge smile on her face and words of utter nonsense emerging from between her full, smiling lips.

"*Sherlock Holm-ess!*"

"*Ay, Dios mío!*" gasps the more mature version, suddenly not so mature, clawing for her husband's arm with the affection of a rabid pit bull, in painful parody of former companionship.

Lu beams at them both in sheer delight. William could put this down to her undiluted elation at seeing him once more, after their last magical encounter, but recalls with a twinge that this is much more how Lu sees – or saw – the entire world.

"Hello – again!" she enthuses.

"Oh, hello there – Luisa," responds William, grateful at least that his lips still move. He has grave doubts as to the stability of the almost calcified figure he is now supporting on his arm.

"You have my book of Sevilla?" asks the young woman, not unreasonably. "I think perhaps I am losing it."

William, who also thinks perhaps he is losing it, tries to smile. "'Tis better to have loved and lost – than to gather no moss."

Lu laughs sweetly, whilst patently not comprehending, and displays her perfectly white teeth. This playful, almost flirting banter does absolutely nothing to restore Luisa's equilibrium. Or indeed her sanity. What comes next serves simply to seal the deal.

With a shrugged apology, William digs into his bag and somewhat warily returns the crinkled old guidebook to its rightful owner. At which point, as feared, it instantly becomes brand new again in her welcoming young hands.

If Lu notices this, it mercifully doesn't register. But she surely can't fail, thinks William, to hear the long, high-pitched yelp emanating from the older woman beside him, as if she has just been publicly impaled on a skewer. Thankfully, Lu is far too courteous to remark on it, sounding as it does like Luisa is in torment over surrendering a volume that wasn't hers in the first place.

"*Gracias*," she tells William, running her long fingers delicately over the glossy cover. "Thank you. You will join us at our table, yes?" She explains to Luisa. "My husband – he is Glasgow also!"

Luisa can only respond with a demented nod.

William's protests – that the young couple would surely prefer to be on their own – go unheeded. (He almost adds "on your honeymoon" but recalls just in time that Lu hasn't as yet let slip this important nugget.)

As Lu moves back to her table, expecting her invitees to follow, Luisa finally spots young Will. She can't as yet make him out too clearly – just enough to confirm that the world is ending and she is going totally insane.

"AYYY!! I cannot breathe. I am going to be sick." She turns to William. "You *knew*? How can you not tell me? Most husbands, they tell their wives a thing like this."

"I did *try*, Luisa," protests William, limply. "You'd only reckon it was the drink talking." He realises how unsteady he is and how chilled the evening-warm square has suddenly become. "I have to say – you were a very lovely young woman." This observation doesn't appear to calm her. Nor does his adding, "*Are!* Still. Are."

"No. This is nightmare. I dream it, yes? This is not real, William."

"Well," sighs William, shaking inside quite as much as Luisa is doing in plain sight. "Only one way to know for sure. But at least they don't recognise us!"

They turn to each other, then park that thought. For later.

CHAPTER SIXTEEN

THE TABLE FOR FOUR sits well out into the teeming square. Away from the main entrance and yellow and black awning of the enduring Café Amarillo.

As he and Luisa have been invited over, William has to assume that the young couple are kindly offering up two spare seats. Fortunately, from William's point of view, he can't see any of his own contemporaries sitting there. To any other onlooker on this Easter week of 2025, the table is currently quite empty. And, in this city, on this week, quite desirable.

He wonders how it would play if another couple from today were actually parked at those very same places where the young couple sit so innocently. He can only guess that it would endow Will and Lu with some sort of weird double image – and that you wouldn't see William for dust.

But how do you work out the rules for a situation that so totally transcends them?

The older couple walk slowly towards their young hosts, whilst their legs quietly inform them that they shouldn't honestly be relied upon for much support in the imminent future.

"This man, he is *my* husband," announces Lu proudly, as the older couple slump into their plastic chairs. Around them everything else seems totally normal, people drinking, laughing, constantly playing with their smartphones and tablets, which only serves to make the situation even creepier.

Wait until they see William and Luisa chatting to thin air.

"Hi, I'm Will?" says the young husband, a distinct question mark in his voice. He appears quite bemused by two extremely nervy-looking old farts plonking themselves down in front of him.

"Hi, I'm W—"

William stops himself just in time.

He is already hugely relieved – whilst also just a tiny bit irked – that the younger couple show absolutely no signs of recognition, or even the vaguest niggling unease, as they confront their older counterparts. But for Will and Lu to hear their own names thrown back at them, by total strangers with similar accents, would be – at the very least – unsettling. Yet he finds himself at a total loss.

Until he spots a passing waiter deftly transporting a tray of drinks, on his way to a larger table. On the tray is a familiar brand of gin.

"*Gordon!*" he announces. "Yeah. Gordon. And this is my wife… er… er…"

Luisa is beyond stumped.

Helplessly, she follows her husband's eyeline to the same moving tray. "*Fanta!*" she cries, with unwarranted exuberance. She can feel the younger couple's eyes on her. William's too. "I was orange when I was born," she explains feebly. "Jaundice. You cannot call a child jaundice."

The newlyweds just nod. Lu, being Spanish, doesn't quite understand. Will, being British, doesn't understand either.

William notices that the young couple sit very close together. Hands constantly brushing, shoulder nudging shoulder, needing always to touch. Every word spoken by the one absorbed with the eyes as well as the ears of the other. He is also conscious that he and Luisa have set themselves down quite far apart, with bags of shoulder-room, eyes facing resolutely forward. It would seem perverse to shuffle up now into snuggle mode, should he even wish to do so.

"You are on holiday here, yes?" asks Lu, now that the curious introductions are over.

"No," responds William, then feels Luisa's eyes on him. "Well, yes. Of sorts. Thirtieth anniversary. 'Pearl', isn't it? That's an oyster with a bit of grit. We were here on our honeymoon."

The younger couple are beside themselves. "*We are on OUR honeymoon!*"

"*NO!*" cry William and Luisa, in a mock astonishment that, by rights, should fool no one.

"Hang on. More importantly," says Will, "Rangers or Celtic?"

To Will's delight, the older man begins to sing "*Follow, Follow, we will follow Rangers*" to the tune of a well-known hymn, even though William is well aware that they both, for their sins, support Partick Thistle. But he knows that this is a standard Glaswegian test of religious affiliation rather than specific allegiance. Within seconds, Will is joining in. He only stops when the shirt William is wearing begins to buzz and vibrate.

"What the hell is *that*?" asks the younger Presbyterian, pointing directly at William's throbbing breast-pocket.

"It's just his—"

"PACEMAKER!" announces William swiftly, cutting Luisa off and frantically thumping his bulging chest, until the unfortunate buzzing terminates of its own accord. "Anyone for a drink?" he croaks, through the pain. "Before I die."

William rises to find a waiter. So does Will.

"I'll get them," insists the younger version.

"*Away ye go!*" says the older. "You're on a budget… I imagine."

"*Away ye go!*" responds Will. As they look at each other, he seems a bit perturbed, as if the older guy might think he is taking the piss. "I mean, it's okay. Really."

They both find themselves standing up to summon one of the busy waiters, each man waving competitively in a totally different direction.

"That's our waiter," exults Will. "*Señor!*"

Luisa, who isn't as yet one hundred per cent in the loop or the loopiness but is catching on fast, momentarily wonders, amidst her barely controllable trembling, why Will is summoning a passing monk. Her current husband's muttering under his breath "A pint of Benedictine" doesn't really help. Nor does it ease her growing nausea when the men suddenly click and stretch their necks, backs and heads in an almost identically choreographed routine, like two robots of differing generations who both love Michael Jackson.

Meantime the waiter goes off, clearly in search of richer pickings.

Luisa takes a deep breath, stretches a smile across her face that looks as natural as a child bride's at a forced wedding and wades into the madness. "So – Will – you look like married life, it is suiting you. Yes?"

"Ask me again in thirty years, Fanta! But, hey, way too spooky. Two Glasgow lads and we each marry a Spaniard!"

William and Luisa are in there like bullets, intent on dispelling any more hints of creepy coincidence. Unfortunately, not with the same faked history. Luisa proudly claims herself an Argentinian, just as William is rooting his exotic wife in sunny Puerto Rico.

"*And* Argentinian!" continues her biographer bravely. "Moved to Buenos Aires as a wee baby. Her mum did Evita's hair." He dare not even look at Luisa now. But he can hear the familiar sighs kicking in.

Lu, bless her, is totally fascinated by this. "Aaah! I think your children they must have the interesting blood."

The young woman can't fail to notice that the hitherto twitchy older couple seem suddenly very still. Their faces appear in an instant to have softened and jointly sagged, the rabbit-in-the-headlights look replaced by something more profound, its roots far deeper.

"Oh. *Perdón*," she apologises, on the cusp of mortification. "Perhaps you are not – do not have – *lo siento*!"

"*Is fine!*"

Luisa is swift to ease the poor young woman's discomfort, the pangs of which she feels, not unnaturally, as if they are her own.

"We have a beautiful daughter. Her name is Claire. *Sí*. We adopt her, from a children's home – when she is three years old. And now she is married lady."

Luisa Sutherland can't believe that she is sitting there in her old café telling herself her own future, yet at the same time it feels strangely natural. She looks at William, as if to convey "*how weird is this?*" But his full attention is fixed on Lu.

"And now our nest is empty," says William, with a sad smile. "She used to *tweet* such a lot."

The young couple stare at him as he realises just how baffling this wordplay must sound.

"I miss her so much," adds Luisa, moving them all swiftly on.

"We *both* miss her, Fanta!"

"*They give us this whole holiday!*"

Luisa is suddenly lightening up, as if she has resolved to park the gargantuan madness of this entire grotesque situation. Just until she can be somewhere safe, in which to collapse, scream, vomit or simply lie down and die. "I tell Claire that many years ago, on our honeymoon, we make this promise. To come back again to Sevilla after thirty years! But young couples they make these promises—"

Luisa can tell that the younger woman is clearly moved by this. It would appear to resonate quite neatly with her own romantic thinking. As indeed it would, she concludes, since it was her that thought it. Yet when Lu responds, idly playing with the cross on a silver chain around her neck,

Luisa realises that the past still has its ability to catch her unawares.

"Ah! Will and me, we want *many niños*. Then they will give us many holidays!"

Luisa finds herself unable to speak. She simply gazes into the younger woman's luminescent face, absorbing the hope and wonder in those tender chestnut eyes. Until she is interrupted by a dismissive laugh from the brash young man with the shock of red hair.

"And many bloody bills!"

It's almost a snort, the distinctive timbre of which Luisa recognises, to the extent that it makes her want to smack him. Or at the very least take the young fool publicly to task.

Fortunately the voice of what can only be a New Yorker breaks in.

"*Thank God – two vacant seats!*"

William and Luisa stare up at the newcomers in horror.

The two middle-aged ladies, each adorned with ornate, baroque sunglasses on glittery strings and festooned with guidebooks, point professionally decorated fingers at the one remaining table in Seville with two seats still unoccupied.

The first lady, the larger of the two but only just, elects herself spokesperson. "We spotted you guys at our hotel. The Herrera? The city's like a can of sardines tonight. And those processions!"

Her partner (and William, at least, has formed the view that they probably *are* partners, berating himself at the same time for the assumption) picks up the conversation, whilst looking dangerously as if she is about to sit on Lu.

"But once you realise the guys are just plain folks and not the Klan – okay if we join you?"

"NO!"

There is no mistaking the decisiveness in the seated couple's voices nor its frantic intensity. The two New York ladies are clearly taken aback. But hardly more so than the younger pair, whom William and Luisa can of course see but immediately realise that the American visitors, thankfully, cannot. Meantime, Will and Lu are quite politely trying and failing to seem unfazed by their new acquaintances, who have just screamed with loud and synchronised negativity into the empty air.

The slightly larger newcomer sings to her friend, as if by putting the words to music she somehow cocoons them. "*We've interrupted somethinggggg, Shelby!*"

"*Vamos*, Marilyn. *Adiós todo el mundo*," says the other.

The women smile uneasily and sidle off, hand in hand. William and Luisa, who never go out of their way to offend unless absolutely necessary, nod a pleasant yet still utterly disconcerting goodbye.

"So!" says Will, striving for a normality that is rapidly dissolving in the sultry evening air. "Er – how *was* Sevilla in 1965?"

"*NINETEEN SIXTY-FIVE*?" yelp the older couple in bewildered unison, immediately screwing things up again on the 'normal' front.

It is William who catches on first. Gamely, he attempts to steer the storm-tossed and by-now seriously leaky craft back into the shallows. "Oh. Yeah! Er – thirty years ago – Fanta? Backwards from today? *From 1995*?" He is sounding increasingly desperate. "*On our honeymoon?*"

Out of the corner of his eye he can see his wife of thirty years struggling, as if someone has just told her that the world is flat after all and unfortunately the table she has chosen is perched right on its crumbling edge.

"Yes. *Married April 1965!*" William laughs, manically. "Well, as the poet Philip Larkin famously said – 'sexual intercourse began in 1963'. So we were in at the start, Lu."

"*Gordon!*" Luisa's admonishment at least reassures him that she is back in the game.

"I *love* Larkin!" exclaims Will, clearly delighted to be returning to more stable ground. "I'm an English graduate. Glasgow Uni. But where on earth did you two meet – a Scot and an Argentinian?" The solid nudge that Lu gives him doesn't chasten him in the least. "Hey, you went and married a writer, Mrs S! *Everything's* a story."

They barely notice the flicker of sadness that sweeps across William's face. And why should they? He is moving on with some urgency, his apparent quest now to elicit information from them. Information that, of course, he already knows, yet somehow needs desperately to hear again.

"Writer, eh? Aye… well. You must have a fine imagination, Will."

"Will is so good with the imagining, Gordon," boasts his new wife. "I say to him, Will, one day you will write the books for children and I am doing the pictures." She smiles a bit sheepishly. "Is good to dream – yes?"

Luisa looks wistfully yet not unkindly at William, needing with a curious urgency to check on his reaction. To her surprise, he shifts his chair even further away from her, edging himself closer to Lu.

"British Embassy - Buenos Aires - 1963. I was out there to help our Israeli friends find Nazi war criminals—" He is aware that Luisa is staring at him open-mouthed, but he doesn't care. 'Gordon' is on a roll. "—When into my office trots this lovely, young, Argentinian woman. Wanting to tell me of - of an elegant brothel that a notorious ex-SS commandant is known to frequent. Aye. She'd seen through his disguise, Lu - as a… porcelain salesman. *Azulejos*." He is watching their faces - the young couple are riveted. And why wouldn't they be? "That was enough for us to find our man - in the bedroom of one of the 'working girls'. Who just happened to be - you guessed it—"

As the couple gawp, Luisa nearly chokes.

Will - thankfully - has the grace to move things on. "O-kay. So - what do you recommend, Gordon? Y'know, that we do here in Seville?"

"Well—" begins William, but Luisa is in there, before he does any more damage. Perhaps only William can pick up the genuine fear in her voice.

"You must do - exactly what it is you were going to do, Will. *Exactly*!" She rises abruptly from her chair, realising, as she stands, just how rigid her entire body has become. "Now I think we let you get on with your honeymoon. Gordon? *GORDON!*"

"Eh? Oh. Yeah. We'd best be—"

"*Wait! Por favor.*"

Lu is standing too. And holding out her bulky camera to Luisa, who almost instinctively takes it. Whilst it can't help but suddenly look its age, it is clearly in the most capable of hands. She swiftly adjusts it, with a familiarity that might confuse a more suspicious mind. Now she signals the couple to sit down close together and smile, instructions they are only too willing to obey.

On the move himself and scooping up his precious laptop-bag from beneath his feet, William notices that a shiny paperback book has slipped out of the dark holdall on the ground next to the younger man and fallen behind a chair. He casually picks it up, noting with a smile that it is indeed Le Carré's *The Night Manager*. Luisa's recall was, as ever, total. He slips it back into Will's bag, amongst the notepads and pens and duty-free fags, where it belongs. Enjoy!

Luisa takes the photo. Fortunately, the newly old camera appears still to be functioning. She hopes, for the youngsters' sake, the roll of film inside it is too.

With waves, nods and some relief they leave the blissfully ignorant, albeit faintly bemused, honeymooners to enjoy their evening. As the older couple have every confidence they will.

Neither William nor Luisa notices Pablo, sitting at a small table beside the café entrance. He enjoys a quiet coffee and a Ducano as he watches his new guests stagger helplessly away.

CHAPTER SEVENTEEN

"IN MIRACLES, LUISA, WATER *turns to claret!* In miracles, the Virgin Mary pops in for tea! In miracles, I clinch a deal without everyone wanting something for bloody nothing!"

William barrels unsteadily through the good-natured crowds that mill idly around a small shopping street quite close to his hotel. The throng, happily oblivious to the time-clash phenomenon taking place in their midst, are on their leisurely post-tapas, pre-dinner way to do some late-night, classy designer or tourist-tat shopping. And catch the evening's next procession, which is visibly and noisily imminent.

William just wants to lie down.

Preferably with his mouth wide open, under an optic of upturned Scotch.

Nothing makes sense any more and he's bloody sure no one round here is going to help him, not even the local archbishop. "Moving in mysterious ways" is no succour to him right now and the drumming he can discern coming closer is as nothing compared to the drumming in what he used comfortably to call his brain.

Pilgrims with rosaries and agnostics with cameras receive equally short shrift, as he bangs elbows, bags and the occasional well-placed knee against anyone daring to stand in his way. Children and old people included. An equal-opportunity bruiser, he's not even being British and saying "sorry" all the time. They don't apologise in Bedlam.

He proclaims his bewilderment over his shoulder to his similarly shell-shocked wife, who this time is struggling to keep up through the swirl.

"In miracles, I make a profit during this sodding downturn," William continues relentlessly, "and we don't have to wonder where our next bloody euro is coming from! So don't talk to me about miracles!"

She wasn't, actually.

Luisa was thinking that at least the evening's lunacy had kept him away from the constant checking of his email. Which – when she considers it – is a miracle in itself. But as soon as she catches up with him, he turns round and shouts into her face. This is, of course, in order to be fully heard above the chatter but also because he wants to shout into her face.

"*I'm a bloody marketing consultant from Govan, Luisa. We don't DO miracles!*"

Even as he yells this out, some inner commentator tells him that these particular words have most probably never before been bellowed within the ancient walls of one of the great cathedral cities in Europe, on the most important week in the Catholic calendar.

And now, of course, the procession arrives.

Right on schedule, he imagines; no *mañana* for this lot. There's no way he or anyone else can move around and beyond it. More Nazarene hordes, more parishioners with a cross to bear, another vast band of brothers from the *hermandades*. And, rising up above her ravishingly floral and candlelit nest, precious metals glinting, Mary herself. The newly bereaved and exquisitely carved mother, gazing down with such heartbreaking love and grace on all her children.

From a tiny balcony just above them, an elderly man, surrounded by his family, suddenly begins to sing.

Even William, who thinks he can never be surprised again, is stopped by this. It isn't that the voice is so very beautiful, at least not to him, but somehow the depth of untarnished emotion sends it close to heaven.

A small woman, dressed entirely in black, whom he discovers standing peacefully beside him, tells him "*saeta*". He has no idea what this means but he guesses she is putting a name to what he is hearing. It feels spontaneous, this "*saeta*", as if the impenetrable words the man chants so fervently come directly from his heart not a hymn sheet.

It is Luisa, long-lapsed Catholic, who breaks the spell. "So – *what?* We ignore this? How, William? How we are to ignore this 'not-miracle'?"

"I don't *know*, Luisa! Don't ask me – I just don't—" Disconcerted, he looks up at the singing man, but his own words speak of more earthly matters. "Did you see how she looked?"

Luisa knows that he is talking about Lu. Formerly Luisa Montero. Lu Sutherland for the past four blissful days. As Luisa was. As Luisa never will be again. "Full of life," she ponders. "Full of dreams."

"I'll give them a wake-up call in the morning."

Luisa grabs him with an urgency that takes him unawares. "No. You do nothing with them! You hear me, William? *Nothing!* ... SUDDENLY I AM SCREWING NAZIS IN BUENOS AIRES?"

William adds this to his list of things rarely said at Easter. As, evidently, do those around him who understand English. Unfortunately, this would appear to be almost everyone. A young Australian couple, who have their cameras at the ready for the procession, swiftly snap off a couple of Sutherlands, just in case anyone should ask them if they met a still-attractive, middle-aged, Argentinian Nazi-screwer on their travels.

The bystanders appear to be awaiting William's response with some interest. To their everlasting disappointment, his phone rings. They don't pick up Luisa's long-suffering sigh and of course William has heard that particular sound so often that it ceases to register. It probably wouldn't resonate even if she shinnied up onto that balcony and turned it into a song.

"Sutherland," he answers, although he can barely hear anything over the drums and the irreverent, yet paradoxically deeply respectful, Spanish crowd, most of whom appear to William to have brought their entire families along: 'from crib to crone', as he might have phrased it, were he still writing ad copy (which, somewhat to his own regret, he hasn't done for quite some time).

Mary is now staring indulgently down at him, so he turns away.

"Oh, *hello*, Señor Barb—Cristobal. Good of you to... yes, I can talk. Just. ...Oh? Well, thank you. Yes. Er – *sí*. I'm sure that would be grand." He looks to Luisa warily, as if to check out whether it would indeed be grand. "…No, no, she'd be delighted. Really."

William watches his wife as she stares up at the majestic float, which appears to sail past them into the blue-black, sultry night on a bed of flame. And he wonders, for a moment, why she is gently stroking her no longer unlined yet quite unadorned throat.

CHAPTER EIGHTEEN

"HELLO - THIS IS *William Sutherland...*"

It isn't. Yet, of course, it is.

Will Sutherland, cocky yet pensive, is trying to adopt the weathered tones of a considerably older man, a gentleman of curiously similar origins to himself (and, unbeknownst to him, of very similar name), whilst he holds a cheap plastic sunglasses case to his ear. Will intends this to represent a phone. Not a mobile phone, as he still knows relatively little of these. Nor is he aware that in just a few, swiftly passing years these quiet, scented gardens in which he promenades, on this short-sleeved, starry night, will be infested with them, like luminous bats.

"...Aye, the famous novelist and millionaire playboy. That one!" His amused and adoring wife of a matter of days gives him a look of mock disapproval. "...*Monogamous* millionaire playboy. And this time round we'd like something just that bit snazzier, *por favor*... Certainly with a minibar! And a jacuzzi... Aye – no, *two* helipads, my wife and I never heli together."

He hears that glorious chuckle and turns, as ever, to drink her in.

She seems to glow in the moonlight, as if the night has switched her on like a singular son et lumière, giving her flawless skin and that flowing, midnight-dark hair a lustre that, at least to a young man hot with love, matches the dazzling floats in their glory. She holds an orange in her hand, plucked from one of the trees lining their way, and is stroking it tenderly.

"Lu...?" His voice has become more serious, which causes her to stop and look at him. "D'you reckon we will come back here? But, you know, rich – like that old couple."

"*Together*, *cariño*, like that couple," she responds, equally serious. "Rich or not rich. We make this promise also, yes? Our thirty *aniversario*. Two thousand and – and twenty-five, *sí*? That we are here again, in this place."

Will looks at her, his eyebrows raised and that wry, worldly-wise smile, one she already knows so well, on his barely shaven face. That he should react to this notion with such scepticism both surprises and unsettles her.

"We are surviving Madrid. And my parents," she protests. "What can be worse than this?"

"Their sodding dog," he replies, which at least lightens the mood, if not the sentiment.

A little boy is skipping towards them, with his parents. He holds a knobbly sphere of wax, which he tosses up into the air and catches clumsily in both small hands. They notice a distinctive, star-shaped birthmark on his cheek.

"Is very old tradition," explains Lu. "Their balls grow bigger every year."

"Yeah, well, they would," says Will, seriously. So seriously that she completely fails to register the joke. He smiles anyway, happy to amuse himself, then points to the orange in her hands, which she is caressing so sensually that he can hardly believe it isn't deliberate. "Do you mind not doing that?" he says.

She glances down, as if to examine what she is doing. If it wasn't intentional at the outset, it most certainly is now. She raises the ripe orange to her lips and sniffs it, then slowly rolls her tiny tongue around its bumpy outer edge, finally taking it in both hands and rubbing it sensuously over her full lips, her chin and down onto her soft, warm throat. By the time it reaches the undone top buttons of her light, summery dress, Will has decided you can only have so much promenading of an evening.

"Come on, Señora Sutherland. And bring your Jaffas with you."

*

If there is a particularly Andalusian way of making love, it may well involve rolling around naked in a tiny, moonlit room, on a narrow and rather lumpy double-bed made even more lumpy by a generous helping of Sevillian marmalade oranges. Whilst all the time these natural aids to romance explore and massage the body's most sensitive zones.

Giggling is most probably optional but in this case the option builds to such a crescendo that the persons responsible actually roll off their bed of warm citrus and onto the hard, wooden floor. Fortunately, this does not unduly interrupt the task at hand, as Will and Lu Sutherland are nothing if not tenacious.

CHAPTER NINETEEN

IN A SMARTER, BETTER-APPOINTED bedroom just a few hundred metres and three decades away, that "old couple" – yet still not what William and Luisa Sutherland, on their better days, would consider over the hill – lie far apart.

William has donned his eye mask, to deter the fusillade of early morning sunlight from disturbing his already rocky sleep. Luisa wears a tooth guard, which helps to prevent the stressful grinding she gathers she does in the night from giving her headaches in the morning and an arthritic jaw for life. She has performed her creaming and her plucking and is ready to switch off the light.

They both know, however, that they are not going to grab much sleep tonight.

"What do you think they're doing right now?" asks William, raising his mask. Yet he doesn't turn to Luisa. He stares straight up at the ceiling. "Three guesses," he answers himself ruefully, his imagination filling in where his memory fails.

She doesn't say anything. So he proceeds to worry out

an explanation. For something that he knows can support no earthly rationale whatsoever.

"It's like, I dunno," because he doesn't, "it's like two parallel lines have just gone whoomph!" He smacks his hands together at this point with such unanticipated vehemence that Luisa's teeth almost bite through the plastic. "We've got our own Bermuda sodding Triangle!" Despite his best efforts, William finds himself reduced almost to tears. "I don't understand, Luisa. I just don't – *those two young kids!* I hardly recognised them. They certainly didn't bloody recognise us."

"It is this week. Semana Santa. Some people say there is magic here. I cannot explain this thing, William."

He turns to her now, removing his eye mask altogether. She registers his look of utter bewilderment and returns it with a look of her own, one not totally drained of affection. Even though the turmoil in her heart and mind, she believes, is quite the equal of his own.

Yet neither expresses any desire simply to pack up and go back home to Richmond. Leave all the madness here, where it belongs. Forget it ever happened; keep calm and carry on. The thought simply does not occur to them.

Very slowly, as if he thinks this might, in some ingenious way, disguise the fact of his moving at all, William shuffles across the massive, king-sized bed, until he can sense the warmth of his wife's thigh through her summer nightie. Luisa feels the unexpected yet still-familiar contact of his legs on her skin.

She is surprised, it has been a while, but she doesn't edge away – and not simply because, were she to do so, she would most probably fall off the bed. But she does lean over and nudge the bedside light, so that it angles against the wall, its harshness dimmed, without banishing visibility altogether. Deftly, she seizes the opportunity to slip off the dental guard and toss it in a drawer.

They kiss, gently at first, letting their bodies softly entwine before their mouths confirm that this is more than a friendly goodnight squeeze. Not that even these have been over-abundant in modern times. She feels his excitement as she senses her own gradually building, not dynamic as yet but still here and present in a way she might not have anticipated even hours before. Although she had wondered, as they were planning this trip – and possibly even hoped (admittedly without that level of yearning that borders on distraction) – whether this might indeed be an integral feature of the week's 're-tracings'.

His hands, as they gently caress, making delicate patterns on the soft material covering what she considers her still reasonably firm breasts, don't leave her totally cold. Even if she does feel curiously and almost stupidly self-conscious. The newly redawning familiarity, the quiet comfort of two people grown apart but still so very far from strangers, slowly begins to bring its own welcome and much needed rewards. Lovingly yet urgently, he slips her nightie over her shoulders.

And then she sees his eyes.

They're closed, which is fine and as she might have wished, as indeed her own had been for some seconds. But, in that moment, she suddenly *knows*. It is as if she can journey behind the lids and directly into his mind, intruding on the dreamscape he is trying so desperately to keep to himself.

She can see *her*. The other woman.

Her younger self.

She cannot be certain of it. Yet she is certain of it.

And now, with a clarity that scares as much as it fascinates, she can see the two of them, young Will and just-as-young Lu, making a love so passionate that it resonates through the years, rocking her life and her world. She can picture – in fact she can't stop picturing – their naked, thrumming bodies, clenched and rolling, flesh unblemished and strong, glowing with sweat and youth and hope. As if their sexual acrobatics are being projected in an open-air theatre, to an audience dumbstruck with admiration.

But now the cast is changing.

It is the older man, the weary fifty-three-year-old currently nuzzling and stroking her with passionate and rediscovered intensity, whom she 'sees' with this beautiful young woman. The woman she once was but clearly is no more. The woman reintroduced sharply and miraculously into her middle-aged husband's mind; the girl who has so innocently attracted his interest and so sweetly commandeered his attention. In a manner this older woman knows that she has not done for so very long.

It hurts more than she can possibly explain.

She wishes with every cell in her overwhelmed body that it could just be over and is at least reassured that it will be very soon.

CHAPTER TWENTY

THE MORNING SUN MAKES its warm, languorous way over a proudly unchanging city. A city now miraculously cleaned-up from last night's processions and anticipating, with the unwavering confidence of centuries, many more to come. It slowly gilds and brings new life to ancient buildings, as it crosses the easy-flowing and not so easily cleaned-up Guadalquivir, Spain's only great navigable river, and enters the picturesque district of Triana to the west. A district waking up to yet another day of celebration and service.

Sol takes time out from his full spring schedule to sneak through the gaps in the shutters of a pretty little hostel, alighting first on an apparently thrilling book in English by a writer with an assumed French name. This is in the possession of a young Scot who didn't enjoy any apparent literary thrills the night before. He is dozily blinking-in dawn's early rays, as he eases himself free from what he was happy to look upon as an alternative source of adrenaline.

And he begins to snort.

The young woman beside him lies with the rumpled sheet half-covering her slowly stirring body, like that proud lady with one exquisite breast exposed on those French coins she herself has seen on trips with parents and friends. Which, of course, rings no bells with him. Otherwise he would doubtless be referencing it, instead of just snorting.

Finally she turns, vaguely disturbed by the weirdness beside her.

Result!

"I couldn't get the bullfight tickets," Will explains, rearing his head, with its thick red and totally un-bull-like mane, "so I had the bull come to us."

"It is only your head that is big," retorts Lu, reaching a lazy hand down under the sheets.

"Give it thirty seconds, darling. What's the Spanish for Durex?"

She stares at him. "What is the English for Durex?"

"Er… jonnies? Condoms?" Pointing downwards. "Contra—"

"Ah – *el preservativo*."

"Aye. *El preser*… Okay. Well, maybe sometime you could get, you know, more *el – por favor*. From the—"

"*Farmacia*."

"Exactly. *Farmacia*." He strokes the unbelievably soft, olive skin below her collarbone. "We don't want any little *accidentes*."

Lu's still sleepy face doesn't intimate that this might not be quite the catastrophe her new husband clearly envisages. But she catches him picking up on her slight *que sera* shrug, so she swiftly lightens up. "Little Willies!"

she laughs. “There is only three nights now here. How many do you have?”

He holds up ten fingers. Which makes her give that ethereal yet so very bawdy laugh he loves. And allows the Govan bull to rear once more.

CHAPTER TWENTY-ONE

WILLIAM SUTHERLAND IS DRESSING carefully in front of the full-length mirror.

He knows that this is something he rarely does these days, unless he has an important client meeting. So virtually never on holiday. (Although, hopefully, this week will be different.)

The husband is having to make do with whatever natural light is teasing through the blinds, as he doesn't wish to disturb his sleeping wife. He realises that he could simply wait and she would be more than willing to tell him exactly what fashion crimes he is committing. But curiously, on this first full day of his hardly longed-for trip, he fancies a brisk start and a tad more personal grooming.

William looks over at his huddled bedmate, recognising the tiny shifts and movements that signify her slow, reluctant transition towards day. Luisa could sleep for Britain – or siesta for Spain – yet this time William senses in himself none of the usual resentment. In fact, there's something approaching affection here. Or, if not quite those dizzy heights, at least a hiatus in the conventional irritation.

William Sutherland is actually feeling not too bad about himself.

He ponders if yesterday – despite its almost heart-clogging madness – hadn't concluded far better than he might have expected. The fact that this outcome also makes him feel strangely uneasy is one he will park for the time being. It seems clear to him now that any attempt to resist phenomena currently doing the Andalusian rounds will prove less than futile. So he might as well simply surrender.

Yet isn't he that guy who always needs to be in control?

William convinces himself, in the language of lunacy, that normal service will naturally be resumed when they return home to Richmond. As indeed he has been convincing himself, for some years, that his life, or at least what passes for it, is as normal as he can expect – indeed, as anyone could expect. Even if normal isn't the same as good. Or satisfactory. Even if it is in fact dry, slow and nagging, like a tiny, repetitive throb that doesn't ever convulse or cripple yet never actually abates.

He is not usually in favour of holidays or trips, as he feels that they only stir things up. Which is why, William suspects, his more passionate wife is so keen on them.

But perhaps yesterday – last night – was a watershed. One that he may never fully acknowledge and certainly could not easily explain – yet equally clearly will not ever forget. He will have to see how the rest of this craziest of (holy) weeks plays out.

He wonders if there might be a further mystical encounter any time soon, in this spiritual Disneyland. He wonders also, with some alarm, whether in fact this might be exactly what he is wishing for. *Dear Lord!* He reminds himself not to forget to take his morning blood pressure pill.

Behind him the gentle rumbling builds.

"*Buenos días*," he says, with a warm smile. "Sleep well?"

Luisa doesn't answer. She simply nods, as she struggles out of bed, unrumpling her nightwear in the direction of decency, and pads towards the bathroom.

William is fully aware that his wife isn't a morning person, so he won't take offence at the lack of conversation. But he can't help but find it curious that she should be so intent on covering herself even further, with the flimsy robe she has left draped over a chair, when she's going to be removing the lot in a matter of seconds.

He knows that this hardly reflects well on him, but he can't help but compare his wife's ample figure, one that William did genuinely appreciate last night, with that of the slender young woman who keeps lingering to the last detail, like a seductive melody, in his mind.

Yet he immediately feels better about such thoughts when he realises that they may, in some legitimate way, be flattering. In fact, he might just compliment Luisa on how grandly she has managed over the decades and indeed, so far from letting herself go, as others in their circle have done, how well preserved and attractive she still is.

Then he realises that this is just as monumentally crass and incorrect as his original thinking and wonders whether there shouldn't be some sort of marital Geneva Convention to afford immediate guidance on the spousal battleground.

And perhaps a historian in this field of human conflict might explain how you can quite happily have comfortably enjoyable sex with a person with whom you are still quietly and attritionally at war.

"So. What do you want to do today?" he asks, but she has already closed the bathroom door. He tries to be as casual as he can, albeit louder, with the next question. "Hey, remind me, just out of interest, where did we go – this time today, last time round? Y'know, the first full morning of our trip."

For some reason, possibly because he hasn't entirely woken up himself, William reckons that this is sufficiently subtle for her to consider it as no more than a sentimental, perhaps endearingly nostalgic enquiry, rather than what even he senses it might really be – an attempt to take whatever cataclysmic oddness happened yesterday to its far-from-logical conclusion. Or at least onwards into a further and probably even more terrifying new stage.

William hasn't ever regarded himself as a man with an addictive personality, despite the smoking and the whisky. All right, there's the work too, which Luisa mentions at every opportune moment, but of course this is so far from being an addiction as to be laughable. Unless the addiction is to pure, unadulterated survival. And the whole human race has that monkey on its back. He reassures himself that he has seen first-hand a true addiction at play and this simply isn't him.

Yet he feels those strange and not totally unfamiliar stirrings inside of him. A fluttering as if a dynamo is slowly charging up within his gut and a hollowing even further down. Sensations that say to him something is happening in my life, something devouring and all-consuming, quite possibly even dangerous, which despite every sane impulse I'm not totally certain I wish to curtail. Should this even be one of my available options.

"*Luisa—?*"

She clearly hasn't heard him. Or is choosing not to respond.

He switches on the bedroom light and checks himself out again. He realises, with genuine regret, that he really doesn't look that great – especially compared to the younger, hairier guy, that one just across the bridge, who is most probably still rutting for Scotland. But perhaps "distinguished" might hold the fort for attractive or striking. And at least his colours don't clash today. He is almost sure of this.

"*Me*, Lu?" he answers an unasked question from the mirror. "Well, I'm a novelist. And a scriptwriter. Oh, you know, London, Cannes, LA. You've probably seen some of my work. I subtitle well."

If it freaks William Sutherland out that he is having an imaginary conversation in a hotel bedroom – located somewhere that he hadn't particularly wanted to be – in which he lies to his innocent young wife of another bygone era (who has no idea who he really is and thinks he's a man in his fifties, living contemporaneously with her in 1995) then he manages to hide it well.

Perhaps it might just begin to strike him as total bloody insanity, with God knows what permanent consequences to his psyche, if Luisa's mobile, sitting on her bedside table, doesn't decide to ping at this particular moment.

He is suddenly and overwhelmingly angry.

An anger that bubbles up with boiling fury, like an unstoppable geyser, from the pit of his stomach. Although, in fact, it *is* quite stoppable – he has developed some basic mastery over the years and is rather proud of the fact. He hardly even raises his voice these days. He rarely has the time or the energy.

William isn't the least bit disgruntled that an incoming text has been flagged – Luisa is entitled to these. But it tells him that not for the first time she had clearly forgotten to switch off her phone, so that it wouldn't ping loudly during the night and wake him from his ever-precarious sleep. A slumber that, once disturbed, might never regain full traction.

Of course, it hadn't actually done this. William had slept unusually well, due in good part to a simple bodily reaction no prescription drug has at yet managed to replicate. But it is still worth reminding his thoughtless wife of her oversight, as it might even the score just a fraction and elicit a rare apology. Some momentary contrition to temper the endless series of sniping altercations and exchanges, alternating with brooding silence, that have become the bedrock of their lives.

He moves slowly round the bed and picks up the phone. Perhaps he will return it to her bag, with the ringer pointedly off.

But first he will just steal a wee peek.

It takes him mere seconds to read the few, tiresomely abbreviated words. Yet he knows, once read, that their resonance will last him a lifetime.

He also realises, with some surprise, that despite the mounting fury, he is not overly surprised at all.

William carefully sets the mobile back down then just as softly picks it up again. He is not so familiar with this particular model, but it doesn't take him long to check through his wife's text history. Or at least that history she hasn't judiciously deleted.

He finds nothing more of interest, no more fuel to the rising flame, although he does feel slightly envious of the girly "chats" Luisa has with their daughter. Nor do the old photos, some of which she has preserved in digital form, with skills he can still admire, astonish him. The smiling young girl at school. Their family dogs over the years. The cheeky, fair-haired little boy. The usual suspects.

Silence. The sounds of showering have subsided.

William feels that logically he should storm straight into the bathroom, full of righteous husbandly wrath, textual evidence in hand. He would most certainly be entitled to do so and can't really explain what is stopping him. Or perhaps he can. Perhaps he senses, if only vaguely, those accusations she may throw back, misguided though they would undoubtedly be. Accusations he doesn't particularly want to hear at this moment. But now is hardly the time for self-analysis.

Although he does wonder, just briefly, if he has been waiting for this. And even, somewhere, wanting it. Like that second shoe dropping onto the floor above. But this was, of course, before yesterday. Before last night. Before William lost all grounding and his time went out of joint.

What was it Lu had said in the cathedral? Something about being lost.

He looks around, taking in the joyous flowers, the old-fashioned photo album, the celebratory bottle of champagne, which is probably by now as flat as he suddenly feels and so far has only been enjoyed by one.

Snatching up his laptop bag, William loads it instinctively with the contents of his bedside shelf, as if he is somehow grabbing hold of his own life or what's left of it.

He leaves without slamming the door.

*

On his quiet departure from the bedroom that his daughter had kindly booked for him, William Sutherland is pleased to discover one of the hotel's lifts, directly across the corridor, with its steel doors open.

As if it has been waiting just for him.

He thinks to himself once again that, had he been the one making the booking, he would have ensured that their room was situated a good few yards from such an obvious sleep-disturber, and finds himself surprised that Claire has never picked up the clues in all these years.

The lift isn't empty.

Pablo is there, nodding to him, although William can find no obvious need for a lift attendant. Perhaps he is simply on his way down and for some reason has opened the doors to this floor. William is almost pleased to see him.

He begins to talk to the older man before the doors are even closed. Even though he knows that his words are pure gibberish to his smiling companion.

"Ever know something about someone, Pablo? I mean, deep down? But you really didn't want to know you knew it?"

"Manchester United," says the wise Sevillano.

*

William doesn't see the look of surprise on Luisa's face as she emerges from the bathroom, encased in her gown once again. His absence is, of course, the cause of it. Alongside the discovery of her mobile phone, which she is almost certain she hadn't simply flung onto the recently vacated bed.

CHAPTER TWENTY-TWO

LU SUTHERLAND CAN'T GET the older couple out of her head. And she wonders why.

She wishes she could share her thoughts with her new husband, but it doesn't feel like particularly rewarding territory. Not after they already discussed it in the park last night and he had that strange look on his face. Not when Will wants to immerse himself totally in Seville and discover, with his writer's eye, everything that had made her fall so in love with the place. Before she did the same with him.

That was the time when she was plain Luisa Montero, daughter of the haughty Monteros of Madrid, chastely studying her art and photography. The season she met Sandy Matheson, on his university year abroad, a happy meeting that persuaded her to come to Glasgow, of all places, as an au pair to friends of his family, in order to improve her English. Her "command" of which she now knows Will loves, because – although she can't herself detect it – her speech still has more than a nip of "Glesga" in the mix.

And, anyway, it's quite hard to share anything when your *hombre* walks so fast. She has to expend all her energy just to keep up with him. (You learn to move fast in Glasgow, he tells her, because you're forever "skedaddling" away from someone.)

This already simmering day they are in the famed Plaza de Espana, for which she deliberately hasn't prepared Will, as she knows that it will blow him away.

"*It's so frigging old!*" he cries, his head turning like one of those slowly revolving cameras they used and abused in his annual school photos, trying to take everything in.

He embraces the vast half-circle of historic brick buildings in all their magnificence, with their landmark tall towers north and south, inevitably tiled alcoves, a multi-bridged, canal-like moat big enough to take small boats and the even more predictably tiled fountain at the centre. "It's sort of Arabic, isn't it, with a bit of your medieval stuff thrown in. I'd say Renaissance – do you know that word?"

Of course she does. And now she has her fun. "It is built in 1929," she exults.

He looks at her, but he isn't smiling. "You're taking the piss," he says.

"*No*, Will!" She looks suddenly unsettled. "Is not the piss. It is built for the very big *Exposicion*, yes? You say World Fair, I think. Like many of the buildings in this city. Is funny, *sí*?" She tries to placate him. "But is in very old style. Of course."

"Like mock-Tudor," he says, to total bafflement. "Although some of us peasants don't awfully care to be mocked."

Lu may not have known Will Sutherland long, but she's already familiar with the flashes of anger that can flare up out of nowhere. They had a few days of it in Madrid, understandable and expected, which she did her very best to tamp down. She has been hoping it will be calmer here. Without parents. Without disapproval. And without that casual belittling she more than suspects preceded her by many years and on too many bad occasions. Yet she knows already that the plates beneath are unstable and the shifts are never far from the surface.

Perhaps, she muses, their meeting with the older couple has unsettled Will too. Compounded by their subsequent talk in the park, conversation that seemed so harmless and even romantic at the time. Her dreams of their returning here in thirty years, his of being rich enough to come back in style. His fears perhaps that they might not.

She thinks that maybe marriage is like a collaborative piece of art, such as one of those huge murals in the Alcazar Palace that she loves and wants to show Will, or even a modern performance piece, begun with strangers whom you may have chosen for their gifts but who you can only hope have the same vision as yourself. And you can't ever fully know how it will turn out or exactly how the other person sees it, until it is nearing completion and the creators can step back and reassess. Perhaps this is what that long-wed couple, in whom she detected a certain undefined sadness, are doing this minute. Stepping back thoughtfully. On their *segunda luna de miel.*

Yet, as she looks at his tightened face, she is already wise enough to know how to save today's suddenly fraught situation.

"*What is the movie you have seen with this plaza?*" she challenges, then smiles at his blank look. "Is one of your favourites."

She can tell from the way his wary eyes immediately brighten and sparkle, the set of his face softening even as his brow furrows, that he is on a new and thankfully more placid trajectory. As he silently reels through his personal "ten greatest" in the Odeon, Renfield Street, of his mind. He revels in challenge and is not going to be defeated.

"Too easy. *The Graduate*."

Lu just stares at him until finally he laughs. Relieved, she joins in the laughter. "Don't tell me," he warns. "Dinna you dare tell me!"

"I do not dare this," she promises. "I dinna."

He walks around, talking to himself, determined not to be beaten. "None of my fave movies are set in Spain. Except for maybe *El Cid* and truly it wasn't that brilliant. So yon bloody building is probably standing in for somewhere else." Will looks at Lu and she is nodding. Unlike her, he can't of course compute that the emotional temperature of the day is entirely dependent on his solving this devilish riddle.

"Don't nod. Don't even think to nod. Okay, you can nod a wee bit – just 'cos you're so bloody cute when you nod."

She nods again, even though no further clues have been offered.

"Right," he mulls. "It's Moorish, isn't it? Like Hula Hoops. They're very moorish." She looks totally blank. "Dear Lord, have I consigned myself to a lifetime without wordplay? Me – Glasgow's future greatest novelist."

"You have ten seconds, mister the big head. *Diez – nueve – ocho—*"

"You're a hard wee woman, Señora Sutherland… Moorish… Moorish… Arabs. Arabic. Oh shit!" He smacks his head, in ecstatic parody of the eureka moment. "It's Lawrence, isn't it? *DH Lawrence of Arabia!*"

She nods her head in glee, although she is still a tiny bit bemused.

"That's the one thing you still didn't know about me, Missus S. I *love* TV quizzes. Contests. Competitions. *And game shows!* Gimme a game show and I'm happy as a pig in – Hey, I just missed being on *University Challenge*, you know, 'cos I went to the uni try-outs let's say a wee bit the worse for wear."

Will greets the classic, Twenties building, a civic hymn to Baroque, Renaissance and Moorish revivals, with new admiration, his eruption of mere minutes ago almost forgotten.

Lu Sutherland wonders, for a moment, if this is how it is going to be. That she will have removed herself from a comfortable, privileged world she has always known, in this vibrant and steamy country, to act as a coolant for the pale yet fiery love of her life.

And she knows that, whatever the challenges, she couldn't be happier than she is right now.

Just to prove it, she takes another photo. Her new husband standing resolutely, if precariously, on the tiled rim of the faux-historic fountain, with a large and not over-clean white handkerchief swept over his mouth, to "protect" himself from the cruel Arabian sand.

She is relieved to notice, too, that whilst he says nothing

out loud, Will does gently hold out one of his hands and slap it jokily yet contritely with the other. At the same time as he looks into her glowing eyes and gently but distinctly mouths the word 'sorry'. His entire youthful countenance suffused with a love that couldn't be more requited.

CHAPTER TWENTY-THREE

THE GUITARIST ISN'T DOING William any favours.

It may be a genuinely old *bodega*, with its gnarled beams and hanging hams, an authentic five-star haunt for TripAdvised, pre-processional tourists ("*best tapas in town – be prepared to stand*"), but he deems it far too early for music.

Not too early, however, for the overpriced and rather large Scotch he is downing morosely in the semi-darkness. He glares at the offending musician, back-lit by a morning sun that lingers, like an underage customer, at the doorway. If the guy rashly asks him for a request, he already knows what it is likely to be.

William rummages in his laptop bag. Even he is sufficiently self-aware to know that he is totally obsessed with – and permanently lopsided by – the contents of this particular hand luggage. His bulky laptop, the old-fashioned jotting pads, diary, power bank, back-up power bank, EEC travel adaptor plugs, a selection of coloured pens. And, of course, the stacks of business cards and company brochures. Luisa jokes with him, although the digs are not so jokey these days, that he carries enough cards to give one to every person he passes in the street. And that most people already have one.

He slips out one of the glossy brochures. *Matheson Sutherland, Marketing Consultants.* He had wanted a pithy slogan stripped across the bottom of the front cover ('We mind your own business' or the like) but Sandy had thrown that idea right out of the park. Told him it was the old advertising copywriter coming out. Prospective clients, he had opined (as he tends to do, in that smarmy, seductive brogue) want testimonials from their fellows or, even more potently, their betters, not off-the-shelf platitudes.

He flicks open the brochure.

Staring out at him in full colour is that familiar and to him rather bland face, smiling with appropriate yet not overweening confidence. Neighbouring him, in a similar square of his own, is Sandy Matheson. His dearest friend from uni days, perceptive matchmaker and longtime partner, looking unnecessarily handsome and un-balding. The wavy, dirty-blond hair has hardly changed, thinks William, either in style or generosity, from that honeymoon picture in Luisa's accursed album. Nor has that smile beneath the fine Roman nose; a smile reeking of a well-born assurance, one that the guy hasn't just slapped on for some smarmy photographer.

William closes the brochure and throws it back with some force into his bag.

"Okay, Señora Sutherland," he announces into the darkness, half-rising from his hard wooden seat, "*the second so-called honeymoon is over!*"

The offending document lands next to the paperback he has just bunged in there from his bedside, more out of habit than design. He knows bloody well that he is not going to waste good festering time on a novel, however tense and well-written.

Yet something about it catches his eye.

It is probably the deliberate dimness of the bodega, in contrast with the already glaring sun, but the vaguest disconnect just registers in his 40%-proof breakfasted brain.

He removes the paperback until it picks up the light.

The first barely downed slug of whisky moves swiftly back up into his throat.

In his hand he holds a brand-new paperback copy of *The Da Vinci Code.*

What the hell—?

He turns it over and around, as if – like some basic yet still impressive conjuring trick – it will revert to John Le Carré's *The Night Manager* before his very eyes.

It doesn't.

So he drops it and burrows somewhat frantically back inside his bag, just in case the 'manager' is still lingering somewhere in one of the many convenient nooks. Perhaps the rogue Dan Brown has simply been slipped in while he wasn't looking, by some kindly, book-sharing stranger.

And then he remembers.

Last night. The Yellow Café.

Just before they were quitting that hostelry of madness, William had spotted a paperback novel that had slithered out of his younger self's open and somewhat tatty sports bag. So, of course, he had graciously tucked Mr le Carré safely back in. Who wouldn't? Allowing the young man to continue with its reading, hopefully to the dramatic end this time round. A pastime he clearly enjoyed and that William still does, given the time. Which, of course, he rarely is.

He picks up the celebrated yet unfamiliar novel again, but this time his hand trembles so violently that he is scared the chunky new book is going to slip right out and topple his not quite empty glass. So he gently sets the bestselling thriller back down on the table and drains his Scotch. For safety's sake.

The sweat that runs down his face has nothing to do with the temperature of a city on the boil. No fan is going to ease it.

He has to speak to her.

Now.

CHAPTER TWENTY-FOUR

THE TWO FRIENDS FROM New York, seated at a nearby table on the pretty sunbathed terrace of Hotel Herrera, watch the attractive, if somewhat worn, European lady with barely disguised interest. Why is she on her own, they wonder silently and not so silently, with her continental breakfast untouched, staring at her phone as if it is about to bite her?

With an urgency the couple can only assume has something to do with this same phone, the perturbed woman suddenly rises from the table. She nods politely, clearly recalling them from last night's bizarre snub, but without overt embarrassment. At which they have taken no offence, because life is too short and they have suffered worse slights in their day.

By the time Luisa returns to their bedroom, William has already let himself in. He always insists on at least two keys, even at a B&B, for this very reason. He is standing on the narrow balcony, holding a thick paperback in a grip that leaves his pale fingers even whiter.

Before she can speak, not that she has any idea what she would like to say nor what he might even wish to hear,

William reels round and barks at her. Yet with none of the words she is expecting.

"*When did I get this?*"

Luisa has absolutely no idea what he is talking about.

All right, he is waving a glossy novel in her direction, like a Bible-basher on a busy street corner; but it can hardly be this that is straining every muscle in his face to breaking-point, nor causing the disquieting look of pure terror in his eyes. Not after what he has clearly just discovered on her phone.

Her silence appears simply to fuel his panic.

"The book, Luisa! The *BOOK!*"

She can hardly believe what she is hearing.

"Oh, we talk about books now! The Semana Santa reading group. Then perhaps we move on to the weather. Will it rain very hard this Easter Sunday and stop the processions? Hmm…"

"This novel, Luisa. The paperback. Just *answer* me!"

She looks around, as if God or someone closely connected might afford her guidance as to why her husband, having only just discovered his cuckolding, should be retreating into the safety of literature. Or at least literary phenomena.

"Do you not remember even this?" she asks, a touch tentatively, as if her next question to him could well be about the name of the current prime minister or the date of his next birthday. "You are saying to me you are the only person on the planet who has never read this book. Yes? So I buy it for you at the airport. As a present. *Jesucristo!*"

Now he is simply gawping at her. Dumbstruck. *The airport?*

Luisa Sutherland does not know, at this critical point in her life and marriage, whether to be scared, sad or angry. Although she really feels she ought to be at least one of these. Yet she finds herself opting for the purely practical. She will simply do her best to ignore the perversity that is being aimed in her direction and accept that it has been a most peculiar couple of days.

"William," she begins calmly, although she is patently feeling far from calm. "Now is the time we must talk, yes? And perhaps not about airport books?" Her question doesn't deflect the manic stare one bit, so she simply continues. "I know we do not do this so much these days, the talking. But if any time is the right time, with what has happened just yesterday, with what is happening today..."

She leaves it hanging. She really doesn't need to spell it out in all its tawdry detail, does she? The text that she is now certain he picked up – and, who knows, perhaps somewhere way deep down this was her intent – will have articulated it all too clearly.

He moves towards her at some speed. She manages not to flinch. But he walks straight past her, making for the table in the centre of the room. So she simply carries on, afraid of the sudden silence.

"When did we stop the talking, William? We used to talk so much – WHAT THE HELL ARE YOU DOING?"

He has picked up her handbag.

At this point it would not have totally surprised Luisa Sutherland if her husband of thirty years had temporarily forgotten his gender. She notices with surprise bordering on relief that it is the small photo album that has now attracted his goldfish-like attention.

She can only watch in bemusement as he flicks through the carefully chosen mementos. Until he hits a happy snap of the two of them so long ago, sitting with Sandy at the Yellow Café. His old pal's right arm is draped casually around Lu's bare shoulders. This is apparently all the proof William needs.

"*He was already coming on to you that night!*"

"What night? Who?"

Luisa checks out the photo William is brandishing. And sighs.

"Here? *1995!* You crazy? He was with Paloma!" The sigh becomes a groan. "It was Paloma taking the photograph! He has had two wives since this day."

"Still found time for mine though, didn't he?" He continues flicking. "Still found time for my fucking wife! Or for fucking my—"

Luisa speaks very softly. She knows that it's a forlorn hope but she also knows that if she cannot be forgiven she must at least be understood. "Yes, William, this is *exactly* what he found for me." She doesn't wait for him to process this. "Please, will you sit?"

William has no intention of sitting. He is staring at the album. He doesn't believe he will ever sit again. Perpetual motion is the effect he is going for, as if this will recharge some particular mechanism inside his body and make his suddenly broken-down life function and move on once more.

Luisa sits on the unmade bed. She wonders briefly if she should have hung the *no molestar* sign on the door. And she recalls how a younger version of the man currently circling around her had hung a similar sign quite effectively from a place for which it wasn't strictly intended.

"I do not do this to hurt, William." She ignores the scoff from above. "You must believe me. No, why should you? It happened. You know this now. Four years ago – you were on another 'new business' trip. *Two days before your own daughter's wedding! Two bloody days! Leaving me to—*" She is finding it difficult to breathe, so she slows down, in the hope he will too. "Sandy he is coming with his gift for her. For them. He could see how sad I was. How sad and angry. And so – alone."

"And since the Samaritans don't make house calls…"

"*Oh por favor!* I am not proud of this. It is not – who I am. Not who I want to be. Sandy, he is still – a good friend. Not more than this."

"A friend with benefits. A friend who texts – *sexts* – on 'second honeymoons'…"

"A friend who *listens*! Who *cares*. But where were *you*, William? Where have you been, for so much of the time?"

William doesn't even have to think about this. "*Working*? Supporting us all through a pandemic? Doing a job I hate? I sure wasn't out screwing your best pal." He shakes his head in disbelief. "He *introduced* us, Luisa!"

She gently pats the bed beside her, as she looks at him, but she might as well be doing some housekeeping.

"I had the hopes, William," she says sadly. "That this place – this week – could make things better. For us. For you and me." She shakes her head at the sheer futility. "Could perhaps maybe, you know, *change* something."

Luisa has no idea if it is these few so very halting words that galvanise William, delivering him in an instant from his angry stupor, or if he is simply on another bizarre trajectory of his own. Like that weirdness with the book.

She hears the drums down below, as they intrude on their painful awkwardness. And she can only watch while he revolves at some speed, like the little man in shorts on an elaborate Swiss clock, before propelling himself towards the door.

Yet suddenly he stops and takes another glance at the photo album, lying open on the bed. Hadn't he noticed something, as he swiftly flicked through it just now. What was it? Something that surely wasn't there when she first put the album together, nor even when she tried to show it to him in the restaurant just last night.

Something that is suddenly everything.

"I – won't be long," he mumbles.

Because, even now, with his head swirling and a madness in his eyes, he thinks it inappropriate to leave a room without at least saying something.

*

William isn't surprised to find the lift opening for him. Seeing Pablo inside, spruce and waiting patiently, simply confirms that this really isn't an ordinary morning.

The descending guest stares straight ahead at the closing door, as he quotes from something he once read on a very educated wall. "'*It is easier to forgive an enemy than to forgive a friend.*'"

The older man reels off some words in Spanish. It sounds like something about the weather. And nothing that indicates the older man is responding to anything that has gone before.

"Aye. That's as may be, Pablo. But hey, what if it's not

too late? What then? The Señora wants change – I'll bloody give her change! What do you think?"

But when he looks hopefully at the retainer, all the latter says is, "Manchester United."

CHAPTER TWENTY-FIVE

"*YES... YES... NO... BOLLOCKS!*"

There is a skill to pouring cheap Spanish wine down your forehead, from a glass pitcher or *porron*, and allowing it to glide past your eyes and along your nose and trickle into your waiting mouth. Despite his steady hand and patrician nose, Sandy Matheson has yet fully to perfect this skill.

As the young women at the table laugh, along with some of the more indulgent onlookers at the Café Amarillo this pleasant spring evening, the misdirected red wine spills gently across the table and onto Will's open notepad.

The pad sits right next to him, alongside his trusty ballpoint, so that, should inspiration decide to strike, its target will have the tools neatly to hand. Unfortunately, the previous strike now looks like being alcoholically blurred or at least partially sodden. Its creator can only moan in anguish, as the more practical Sandy quickly grabs the dripping page and begins to lick it dry.

"Mm!" he enthuses. "Sutherland. His fruitful Rioja period." Will finally manages to retrieve the precious pad.

"I tell you, Wullie," says the erstwhile best man, wiping his damp face with a napkin, "I'd bite my arms off to be a writer—"

"—But you 'never had my disadvantages'. Yeah – yeah. Your bloody wedding speech. I was there, pal, remember?"

"Only just! I had to dance with the bride for you! Crap job but—"

"Tough Guys Don't Dance. Ask Norman Mailer."

Lu and Paloma laugh, accepting that this is their role, just as it is the guys' job description to prance around like overgrown schoolboys and chatter in an English neither young woman could possibly understand. Paloma, almost as dark as Luisa and a good six inches taller, drapes a long, slender arm lovingly around her old art school friend, delighting in the occasion that has brought them together, first just a few days earlier in a wet and chilly Glasgow and now proudly back here in this bridesmaid's own home town.

Sandy begins to talk in his unaccented Spanish and Lu immediately responds. Closely followed by raucous laughter from all but the slightly irritated groom.

"Queen's English, *por favor!*" Will insists, taking another swig of wine from his glass.

Sandy turns to him and whispers softly, "She says she loves a canny linguist. Least I think that's—"

Will roars and spits his half-gulped wine back over his notepad. It is the girls' turn to look baffled. He simply smiles at them and pours more cheap Rioja.

Lu, realising that no translation will be forthcoming (and that this is possibly for the best), hands Paloma her camera with detailed instructions. She manages at the same time to pick up most of the ensuing conversation between the *hombres*, which is now quieter and appears to have taken a more serious turn.

"Listen, amigo, I wasn't kidding," she overhears Sandy inform her new husband. "What I 'telt' you back home. If the old novellas don't pay off. I mean, I hope they do, sure I do, but awful tricky. The two of us could always team up and make a pile. Maybe not day one, but bloody soon thereafter. My business skills and *impeccable* family connections, your – godgiven talents. Hey, matey, you can still write! Ad copy… press releases… *invoices!*"

Before Will can respond, Lu is there. Friendly but firm. "No, Sandy! Will and me – Will and I, yes? – we make the big deal. I do my working – I am a good teacher, I think; I have assisting job in a very nice Glasgow school – Spanish and art. And I have little bit of money from my abuelita. While my husband is writing his book."

Will shrugs to Sandy. What can he do – the boss has spoken.

They hear Paloma whistle and the three of them turn as one, smiling broadly, arms around each other, to be captured forever in a memory that will survive the years.

But Sandy isn't letting go so easily. "I'm just saying, Lu – classy *Madrileno* like you deserves all the happiness money can buy."

"Ayy!" shrieks Paloma, her statuesque body made even taller by both bronzed arms waving dramatically into the air. "Is bad time! I must go – to my work!"

Sandy, for reasons best known to himself, takes this as a cue. Leaping up – and narrowly avoiding another major spill – he segues into a rarely performed rock version of that heartfelt historical plea to Bonnie Prince Charlie to return from France. As taught more traditionally to disinterested Scottish schoolkids of a certain vintage.

"*Will ye no come back again?*

Will ye no come back again?"

Will is not going to be out-sung on his own honeymoon, having already been out-danced at his wedding. Luisa only just stops him from clambering onto his chair.

"*—Better loved ye canna be,—*

Will ye no come back again?"

Paloma laughs at the duo as she scuttles off with an elegant wave.

The young friends are totally unaware of a new voice now entering the mix. A voice from another age.

It is a gruffer, some might say more mature voice, with a Scottish accent only slightly tempered by years of Home Counties conversation. Yet this middle-aged voice can only be heard, whether they might wish it or not, by strollers chancing on a certain square in the Barrio Santa Cruz, on a sultry spring evening in Seville, during Holy Week 2025.

"*Will ye no come back again?*" sings William Sutherland, ageing marketing consultant and erstwhile tartan rocker, as he observes his younger self, who he knew would turn up here if he waited long enough, joining in vigorously with someone this older version can't see at all. Yet someone who, even allowing for the apparently rigid 'rules' of this existential chaos, he can picture in his mind only too well. A friend whose impromptu performance is being enjoyed, alongside that of her husband, by a beautiful young woman from whom William Sutherland is finding it extraordinarily hard to remove his gaze.

"*Will ye no come back again?*"

The trio conclude their curious, time-defying performance to audience responses that are much the same in both eras. Onlookers simply roll their eyes and shake their heads. Although a suspicion, by those encountering William singing totally on his own, of serious mental health problems adds a certain piquancy to the mix.

The older man watches as a thoroughly satisfied Will lifts his replenished glass and starts to move away from the table, towards the interior of the café. The man even manages a smile, almost as if he has enjoyed being transported for a few moments back to what was clearly a more liberating, less burdensome time.

Yet this nostalgic glow is short-lived, replaced almost immediately by a searing blast of anger that rages through William and scalds him at his core. This is sparked by nothing less than his being obliged to watch, in pure helplessness, as his young wife shuffles up close – too damn close – to nothing that William can actually see.

But then he doesn't actually need to.

CHAPTER TWENTY-SIX

WILLIAM SUTHERLAND HAS ABSOLUTELY no recollection of the toilet facilities at Café Amarillo on the week he first encountered the great cathedral city of Seville. Hardly surprising as he barely remembers the great cathedral. But he is gratified to find that, like that holy edifice, at least they haven't changed location.

He knows this because the first thing he sees as he enters the chamber is Will, standing thoughtfully at the urinal, glass of Rioja in his free hand, making room for further intake.

"Like me to hold it for you?" offers William.

William receives a look in return that would chill the blood on a dark Glasgow night, as the young man turns slowly to take in his pervy offeree. But then Will Sutherland instantly softens, surprised yet immediately contrite.

"Oh – er – Gordon, isn't it? Sorry about – I thought for a wee moment you were – say, how's it going?"

William is relieved to assume, from the level of Will's response, that the chamber is free of other pre-millennials invisibly urinating in the vicinity. So he gently takes the full glass from Will's hand. Of course, it immediately turns old and dusty, a few pathetic pink granules above a fragile stem. The younger man is, as William had hoped, too preoccupied to notice. (William is rather gratified, in fact, by how generally unobservant humanity can be.)

"Going as well as can be expected," says William.

"Glaswegian for fantastic. Were you sitting out there? You should have come over."

Will appears quite genuine in his hospitality, but William just shakes his head, struggling to keep the now vintage Rioja out of the light.

"Och, you don't want an old fart around. You're with your friend." He stares at Will as hard as he dares, without it seeming creepy. "At least I *think* he's your friend."

The young Scot may be an ardent student of English literature but William remains unimpressed by his appreciation of subtext. "Not just a friend, Gordon. You wouldn't believe it – the guy was my best man!"

"*Away ye go!* Well, you know what they say about best men, Will." This time he stares even harder. "They always win in the end." William can't help feeling he is employing the sort of dialogue that would have them both walking out of a cinema, but desperate times… "He's a seriously good-looking guy," he adds, without considering that maybe he shouldn't.

William is so involved in his dialogue of the deaf that he fails to become aware that a new patron has entered. A man from his own era who has observed this balding, middle-aged Brit hold an intense conversation with an empty urinal. But William does hear the sound of a lock firmly turning, as the visitor sensibly puts a solid door between them.

"Aye, okay," says Will, who also stares at William a bit oddly, now that his best pal's movie-star looks have come into play. "Well, I think mister gorgeous out there just offered me a job. Probably via his old man, who's loaded. Writing bollocks for fun and profit." He shrugs, thoughtfully, or as thoughtfully as he can, given the Rioja. "'The rich are different from you and me', Gordon—"

"'—they've got more money'. My Hemingway to your Fitzgerald. Highly appropriate, considering where we are. Spain, I mean, not the gents'. Well, here's another good one for you, pal. '*Never look a gift-horse in the mouth.*'" William moves pointedly closer. "Unless of course he's *snuffling* in the wrong place for his oats." Which even he thinks is quite pithy, as well as on the nose. Yet he's just beginning to wonder whether Will would still miss the bloody point if it was tattooed on his inside leg.

"Yeah. Well, I need money, Gordon, that's for sure. But listen, me and Lu have got it all worked out. At least in the short term. She works while I write." William just shakes his head. "And, in the even shorter term – I need *fags*!"

He retrieves his glass, liquefied once more, and moves off, leaving William bitterly frustrated.

Until Will suddenly stops at the door.

He turns round slowly, as if finally absorbing what was just said. And looks straight into William's eyes.

Without a word, he walks out of the bathroom.

"Well, that took its own sweet time," mutters William, as the man emerges gingerly from the cubicle.

CHAPTER TWENTY-SEVEN

THIS SPECIAL NIGHT'S CANDLELIT procession has no drums, no trumpets, no songs of worshipful joy. Save for the slap of Spanish sandals on the dark and ancient streets, it is for once solemn and silent.

Which doesn't mean that all its spectators are.

At least three are standing huddled together on a tiny and most probably historic wall, whispering away happily as they angle for a better view and the intrepid photographer amongst them for a better angle.

Below and around them a bobbing, bouncing, shushing crowd of the devout and the merely enthralled – kids, cameras and churros in hand – shuffle in quiet-ish respect, zealously elbowing away those who block their eyeline, in the hope they won't dare protest too loudly.

Despite the fruity Rioja working its own magic around his system, Will is still not too far gone to appreciate that what he is witnessing goes way beyond anything he might have imagined. He could hardly call himself religious and he's far from spiritual. Yet, to watch ordinary, decent people, imbued with an unquestioning faith, recreate a spectacle unchanged throughout the centuries – in a city whose history and grandeur overwhelm – well, it does something to his soul. Will isn't sure exactly what, as he has no idea what a soul actually is or whether he really has one. He finds it all quite confusing.

Made all the more confusing, this cloudless, indigo evening, by the encounter he has just had in a café toilet. With an amiable but clearly troubled man he has only recently met. Yet whose wisdom he is coming slowly and surprisingly to respect.

"Beats the auld kirk for razzmatazz, eh, oor Wullie?" says Sandy, the drink causing him to whisper just that bit too loudly. "*And* for silly hats."

To his own surprise, Will feels himself bristle.

He reckons that it has to be at the casual lack of respect his friend is showing towards a ritual for which his new wife, beyond the obvious photographic possibilities, has a genuine reverence. Lu's Catholicism has never been much of an issue for him, because she has sweetly made a point of it not ever being so. Even if this meant standing up to her parents, who clearly regard him as the red-headed *anticristo* from the North. He feels that the least he can do is to show some deference to the faith she still observes and to the iconic festival she has brought him lovingly almost two thousand miles to see.

But unfortunately this feeling only lasts a few seconds, because he is a bit drunk and can never resist a comeback.

"Do you think they use the pointy bits to jab open their cans of Irn-Bru?"

"Sshh," says Lu, while the guys giggle, but it comes out a tad spittily, as she has enjoyed quite a bit of that cheap wine herself.

Lu Sutherland knows that she probably shouldn't be standing on such a narrow wall, or leaning over quite so far, but how can she resist? This way you can capture not just the flickering candles, reflected in the centuries-old, zealously polished silver, but also the rapt faces of local children, up beyond their bedtimes. Some of the little girls amongst them, she notes with a melting joy, are actually wearing seriously starched communion dresses and tiny white mantillas.

"Course, we've seen it all before, haven't we, *cariño*?" says Sandy, smiling at her.

He accompanies this with a companionable, short-sleeved arm draping itself casually across her shoulder, easing her towards him and disturbing the heavy red shoulder-bag, along with her delicate balance. If he feels the glare coming from the other young man on the wall, he doesn't let on.

"Er, Sandy," mentions this young man. "My wife now? *Pal*."

"Point taken, *pal*," says Sandy, very slowly sliding his arm back across the downy nape of her neck. But he can't resist a parting shot. "If you'd stuck with me, Lulu, you'd be sitting down there, with the *alta burguesia*."

He points to a carpeted section, cordoned off with a golden rope, where older members of the community and the better-heeled tourists sit on red velvet chairs and enjoy a more expensive silence.

The wondrous *paso*, with its beloved and infinitely precious Virgen Maria on board, crucified son in her arms, seems suddenly so sublime, floating on high across a shimmering backdrop of night and stars. It is too much for a young art-lover, with any sense of beauty, to resist.

Camera practically welded to her face, Lu leans over just that bit too far, in search of the ultimate shot. Her weighty, leather bag, already sliding off her shoulder, now swings round in front of her and she begins to topple. Sandy's arms shoot out to support her, as do Will's, but the taller man gets there first. And stays perhaps just that bit too long, his hands remaining on top of her pounding chest for a few brief seconds after normal gravity has been resumed.

A guy might expect a jokey reprimand for this or even a semi-stern look of disapproval. What Sandy doesn't expect is to see his old university friend, his wiry carrot-top pal from Govan, lurch towards him at some speed, blue eyes ablaze. Nor does he anticipate Will concluding his swift trajectory with a solid push to the shoulder that causes the taller man not simply to desist but to lose his footing, stumble and then collide face-first with the wall.

Lu is too horrified to scream, although others around her, including the poor bleeding victim himself, manage to express their surprise. She just stares in alarm at her husband, who, to his credit, appears equally as shocked as she does.

Yet something inside him, some strutting bravado picked up on the mean school playgrounds and dark tenement closes of Govan, causes him to stare at her defiantly, as if the 'handy' guy got just what he deserved. He mouths '*what*?' to his stunned wife, although he knows what only too well.

The silence isn't going too smoothly.

Yet, some distance away, one interested spectator is as quiet as the grave. William Sutherland can't say that he isn't shocked by the sudden attack. But neither can he say that he isn't quietly satisfied.

He is far too absorbed in the drama even to notice that one of the large crosses passing noiselessly by is being borne by the stocky handyman from the Hostal Esmeralda.

CHAPTER TWENTY-EIGHT

LUISA SUTHERLAND CAN'T RECALL exactly when her fear of heights began to take hold.

She certainly doesn't recall having had it as a young woman. Perhaps it isn't a fear exactly, but an unease, a preference for not being in a place where she may be obliged to look a long way down. And a sense of – fragility. A certainty that everything in this world is breakable. She read once that vertigo at its core is an almost-overwhelming desire to jump. She may be feeling this now, as she clings so tightly to the balcony railing. Yet she cannot make herself loosen her grip and go back into the empty hotel room. A room in which she has already spent – and wasted – most of her long day.

The German couple next door have already returned, hot and sticky, from whatever attractions the afternoon had provided. They have showered and dressed for the evening's entertainment (after having, perhaps, become more pleasantly hot and sticky). Finally, they have taken the air on their own adjoining balcony, exchanging a few polite words with their neighbour, who clearly had even fewer words for them, despite speaking excellent English for a foreigner, and have then departed arm-in-arm to enjoy their still-sandalled evening.

And yet here she stands, staring out at the stern cathedral, its Gothic countenance lit starkly against the dark, velvet sky.

She doesn't even turn when she hears the door to the bedroom open.

"*Everything's going to be okay, Luisa!*"

She wants even less to turn round now. Her husband sounds wired, manic. As if his voice is running, even though his body is still.

"You won't understand," he continues, elatedly. "But don't worry."

She stands unmoving, her fists firmly around the wooden rail. Not understanding, yet still worrying.

She only alters her posture when she hears sounds of a rummage – and is slightly relieved to discover that this time it isn't her shoulder bag William is plundering but his own. The worn-out old laptop sack that is almost like an extra organ. She had only appreciated quite how exercised he must have been on his last flying visit to their room, when she'd noticed that he had left this precious holdall ungrabbed on the bed.

William appears beyond excited, sliding his hand almost sinuously into one of the soft, protective pockets. She watches, transfixed, as this elation switches instantly to alarm, as once again he brings his own slim consultancy brochure out into the light.

He glares at it, as if it is the most repellent item ever to have emerged from a person's work case, even though he himself had carefully packed it there, alongside several of its glossy fellows, just the day before.

Now he's opening it, although God knows he could quote the whole document by heart. She can see by the way the pages fall that it's *their* photos he is gawping at, like an idiot. His and Sandy's. Matheson and Sutherland. Partners and pals. Luisa recalls the morning of the photo session – William checking in with her for any catastrophic shirt 'n' tie clash.

Without wishing further to unbalance whatever is going on for him, but curious to know what exact manner of lunacy this is, Luisa treads lightly across the room.

What she sees makes the situation no clearer.

William is slowly running a shaky finger along the broken, off-centre nose of his partner, a 'blemish' the man had clearly contrived to make even more of a feature for the photographer by adopting a slightly cocky, off-centre stance. As indeed he usually does, thinks Luisa. Like a cheesy yet still appealing James Bond poster.

The only word that springs to mind to describe her husband's face is devastated.

But, as she watches, a lot more words spring almost unbidden from between her tight and angry lips.

"Why do you *stare* at this photo?" William isn't listening. "TALK TO ME, WILLIAM! I don't know – get angry this one time. *Sí*? *Throw* something! An ashtray – no, in here it is no-smoking – a vase! Make the passion. Instead of being a – a robot. Yes. A fucking, walking-in-and-out-of-fucking-hotel-rooms robot!"

He looks at her now, but it is a look of such helpless puzzlement that her heart almost goes out to him.

Concerned that he might suddenly flare up, but not necessarily in the borderline-acceptable, vase-throwing manner she has just mapped out for him, she lowers her voice and speaks from a well of shared memory, from which he might yet manage to sup.

"What happened to the boy who would break a man's nose just because he is looking at me?"

If William appeared astonished before, this seemingly innocent statement threatens to poleaxe him totally. And, yet again, his response to her is entirely off the wall.

"*You REMEMBER that?* It only just—"

She looks at him expectantly, even if his wording is a bit weird. At least he is raising his voice. Preps for a good, old-fashioned, perfectly normal fight?

The trouble with being pretty obviously in the wrong, she muses, despite whatever all-too-human motivation may have landed her there, is that it makes it a wee bit more difficult to lead the charge onto the moral high ground. But not, she assures herself, impossible. And they're finally engaging with each other. Aren't they?

But no – it's back to his bloody brochure. *Jesus!!!*

Luisa does a lot more sighing in Spanish, as she watches her clearly demented husband flicking through the brochure's familiar pages – pages he himself designed and supervised to the very last bullet point – in stupefying disbelief. Finally she scrambles across the newly-made bed (she did at least allow the maids to do that – she needed the company). Hitting the room phone with shaky fingers, she is astonished at how swiftly the summons is answered.

"Aah! *El conserje, por favor.*"

Perhaps it is fortunate that she doesn't hear William

address the photo of his now asymmetrical colleague. "What sort of an idiot would *still* be partners with a guy who smashes him into a wall? Still be *pals*?"

"*Hola? Necesito un boleto de avión a Londres... Londres... Sí. Emergencia. Inmediatamente!. Sí... sí... Okay. Muchas—*" She turns back to him, hoping for the slightest reaction. He clearly hasn't heard a loud Spanish word she has been saying. "How long do you keep looking at his bloody picture?"

"Until it bloody vanishes!"

Their eyes lock in a tableau of mutual bewilderment. And then her husband is across the room and out of the over-used door again.

This time with the laptop bag clutched firmly in his hand.

*

William doesn't even nod to Pablo when the lift doors open immediately upon his arrival.

To be fair, he can hardly see the man anyway, squashed as he is behind the two ladies from New York. They greet him silently and not without suspicion. The sort of greeting you might give a wife-beater, should you suspect that his spouse may be lying in a crumpled heap just beyond the bedroom door.

Yet, being both friendly and trapped, they decide to give him the benefit of the doubt. The slightly broader one, Marilyn, as he recalls, taps a guidebook. Between them they appear to own an entire shelf.

"Going to the processions?" she asks, although she

knows it would be pretty hard not to, as throughout this remarkable week they proceed to you.

William is not in a talkative mood. So he just nods.

"Y'know," adds Shelby, gamely, "we shouldn't really be here. Not this week of all weeks."

Despite his preoccupations, William sees no mileage in being rude. "Oh, I don't think the locals have burned gays for a while now."

"She meant because we're Jewish and it's Passover," says Marilyn.

The elevator opens and William scoots. Without even pausing for one of his Pablo chats.

There is somewhere he has to be.

CHAPTER TWENTY-NINE

"***I DO NOT BELIEVE*** *this!*"

Lu is starting to push open the heavy, wrought-iron gate, her trembling hand flat against the giant tile at its centre. Naturally, there is no reason why she should believe this, as it isn't true.

But William is quite convincing, as he points upwards to the small bedroom that looks out, as ever, over the pretty little courtyard.

"Fact. I'm pretty sure it was that room right there. With the shutters. I was just, you know, passing this evening. Out for a wee stroll," he explains, with a charmingly mystified smile. "And I recognised this place! Hostal Esmeralda. Aye. From – well, from when we stayed here, back in 1965! *What are the chances?*" He can't stop shaking his head in amazement. "But I never expected to see *you* staying here, Lu! Of all people."

Lu, who is genuinely mystified rather than just doing the face, also shakes her head in wonder. "Is big coincidence. This is the word?"

"'God's way of staying anonymous,'" says William. "Not me, sadly. Einstein."

"It is very late, Gordon."

William totally understands that now is possibly not the best hour to be trading obscure quotations from Swiss maths geniuses. "So why did I come across you walking back here all on your own, Lu?" he enquires, more pointedly. "*On your honeymoon!*"

The young woman, from three decades ago, looks at him with such a sadness that he finds his heart melting, in a way he can't recall having experienced for so many years. There was the wedding of course, not so long ago, his lovely Clairey and the painter, but this is different. Perhaps because he didn't cause the wedding, far from it, yet he knows damn well that the tears now pooling in this beautiful young woman's soulful and so familiar brown eyes are all his own work.

She pushes the heavy gate a bit more, this time with his help. William can't be certain but he senses that this younger Lu doesn't want their conversation to end just yet. He takes the chance and follows her into the courtyard. She can regard him as either a stalker or a friend – it's up to her.

When she sits on the rim of the fountain, cooler now that the natural oven known as Seville has dialled itself down, he joins her. It's a bit precarious but he manages. And she tells him exactly what her new husband just did to his slightly naughty, but basically innocent, best friend. She may struggle with the terminology, yet her mime of an angry push and its aftermath leaves little to the imagination.

"Welcome to Glasgow," remarks William, but almost to himself.

He notices that, as she talks, Lu picks nervily at her fingers. William knows the action so well – and recalls that Luisa, his current Luisa, was doing much the same less than an hour ago, in such differing yet still anxious circumstances. He wants so desperately to prise those lovely fingers apart, to stop the inevitable damage, but he doesn't dare. Yet he can't let it go.

"You'll spoil those artist's hands," he says, with a gentle smile.

As she nods, Lu leans over, opening her arms. A white cat suddenly appears in her lap, as if from nowhere. William jolts for a second, until he reminds himself that he is apparently 'permitted' to see artefacts (and domestic animals) of Lu's era, provided they are actually being held by her or by Will.

There are clearly rules to this madcap game, but William wishes to heaven he knew who was making them. For now he can simply enjoy the sight of a delightful young woman offering a slightly scrawny animal the unconditional affection William recognises as so much a part of who she is. Or at least of who she used to be.

And this is why, as he fondly remembers, he was so in love with her.

William is about to pursue the conversation when he realises that there is actually no need. The young bride wants to talk. Apparently his 'happening by' was simply one of fate's more kindly acts on this most cruel of evenings.

"He has so much of the anger inside of him, Gordon," she says, stroking the cat more firmly. "I know why this is. Of course I know why is this."

"From his brutal childhood and his sadistic dad," amplifies William helpfully, before her curious look signals to him exactly what he is doing. "Er – I'm guessing," he adds a bit feebly. "But you can usually tell these things."

"*Sí*," agrees Lu, innocently. "From his very bad papa. His father who is dead now. This man, he was so—" She stops, a bit embarrassed.

William senses that for her to go any further would be an unforgivable breach of trust. He isn't going to encourage or prompt her. Whilst she is hardly likely to tell him anything he doesn't know, it might be more than he would wish to hear.

He wants so much to ease her discomfort. He also wants rather a lot to pat her hand, but William knows that this is hardly appropriate and there is a good chance she might squash the cat.

"It's okay." He turns to look at her and this time a genuine sincerity burns in his eyes, surprising even him. "Trust me, Lu, he *will* learn to move on. To behave like a – well, like a grown-up. To tame that anger. Or at least re-channel it. And, you'll see, he'll be less like his nasty, thuggish drunk of a dad with every day that passes."

You're off on one again, William, he thinks, his lower back starting to twinge, as if on cue. Stuff coming up for you, stuff you didn't expect, revelatory stuff, but rein it in, pal.

"With your help and support, Lu. Naturally. With you on his side."

It is only as these words unwrap themselves that William realises they began somewhere deep in his heart, in his past, where he seldom goes these days. He becomes suddenly thoughtful.

"Although Will may not actually thank you for it," he says quietly. "Not ever thank you for helping him be the guy he never thought he could be."

Lu Sutherland smiles up at this kindly (if disconcertingly prescient) older man, who is now getting up to stretch and click in a manner that seems curiously familiar. Perhaps it's a Scottish thing. The gentleman seems so wise, but of course thirty years of a good marriage - or at least a marriage that has endured - must provide some insights.

"I hope, *sí*, that you are right," she says, with a familiar sigh. "I see all this good inside of Will. I do, Gordon. With of course the anger. But who can know?" Lu smiles, not entirely in happiness. "Poor Sandy. And he is just saying this night he want to give Will a job."

William says nothing. The expression clouding his face says everything.

"*Que?*" she says, then adds "*What?*" for his benefit.

William deepens his troubled look, knowing that he has a captive audience. "Can an old guy offer you a serious piece of advice, Lu? You *and* Will?" He takes her nod as a green light and moves forward at speed. "NEVER mix business with friendship! Never. Ever. Recipe for disaster. Trust me, ends in tears. Nip it firmly in the bud before—"

"*Am I interrupting anything?*"

They both spin round at the sound of the voice.

Will Sutherland looks extremely sober as he approaches them. And equally sheepish. With a huge measure of contrition thrown in.

William finds himself wondering, just for a moment, who this rangy, red-headed guy is. This patently anxious young man who has interrupted such an important tête-à-tête. Yet as he registers the genuine contrition, he finds his heart swiftly going out to him.

For his part Will, both hands held suspiciously behind his back, ignores William completely and stares, guilty and unblinking, at his wife. *Their* wife.

William is surprised to hear the coldness in Lu's greeting. He had always thought that came later. But, of course, he reminds himself, the smashed-face incident didn't happen first time round.

"How is Sandy?" she asks.

"Bloody sore, but still laughing." Will attempts a chuckle himself. "You have to admire his stamina."

"Do you?" mutters William ruefully, although it is patently none of his business. They turn to him, as if just remembering he is here. "I heard about the fracas," he explains.

"*Fracas*," says Will, in William's voice, which is obviously not hard to do. "Great word. Fracas." He stares hard at the unexpected third party. "What're you doing here this time of night, Gordon? Hunting more Nazis?"

Before William can bang on about the random nocturnal stroll, his practically photographic memory and the roots of coincidence, Lu begins to sniff quite loudly. So of course all eyes go back to her.

"What is this smell?"

She can't stop sniffing. William has a go but isn't sure whether a smell can travel thirty years. And, if it can, whether he'd really want to be there when it arrives.

Will is a picture of innocence. "Well, I don't know, Lu. Hospital, mebbe?"

She hands William the scrawny white cat and moves towards her grinning husband.

Happily for the older man, the young couple don't notice that the transferred cat has instantly become its own skeleton. William drops it in horror, praying that it reverts back to cat and he doesn't have to explain a pile of bones on the ground. It certainly disappears from his view. (William is not a particular fan of cats and dead ones hold even less appeal.)

Meanwhile, Lu is trying to move around Will, but he keeps deliberately turning away, so that she can't ever discover what's behind his back. This game goes on for some seconds. Whilst, to anyone else, it would most probably be sick-making, like a lovers' mouth-to-mouth chewing-gum exchange, William is totally fascinated. He finds himself taken by his own former playfulness and his young wife's gleeful willingness to play.

Finally she manages to double-guess Will and land up behind him, where she finds a greasy paper-bag and a tiny cardboard pot.

"*Churros!*" she yelps, triumphantly.

"Not exactly The Ritz, Seville," he says, apologetically.

"No, is better! I LOVE the churros."

"You can only eat them if you promise to get chocolate all over your wee Iberian face."

"There is not another way!"

William watches with genuine enchantment as Lu grabs one of the doughy coils and dips it into the still-warm and nicely sticky chocolate. Her young husband can't stop smiling at her. Yet William can detect the apprehension there, the burning need to make reparations and the justifiable fear that an oily snack may not quite be enough.

He has no idea of time, as he gazes at the loving young couple with unexpected warmth and an almost infinite sadness. William knows that he is smiling but is clueless as to how to desist and return to his more pressing agenda. Nor if, to be honest, he even truly wants to. He can almost feel the anger in his eyes dissolve into an embarrassing moisture, as this attractive pair play silly buggers just inches from where he sits.

Finally, Lu remembers that he is still there. "Oh, Gordon, I am sorry for this. Churro?"

William shakes his head. He would dearly love one but it would be way past its sell-by date. Like him, probably.

"So, Señora Sutherland," says Will. "I did a very bad thing, didn't I? A wee bit of an angry young Glasgow man thing. Very bad. Totally unforgivable." He looks so serious. "Am I forgiven?"

To William's surprise, Lu turns back to him, a tiny smile on her face, above the chocolate. "What do you think, Gordon? About forgivingness? In the marriage."

I'm sorry?

William looks like he doesn't think anything.

He appears totally speechless. And gormless. As if someone has casually asked him for his take on the latest advances in string theory, rather than sharing an instantly accessible concept that has been around since humans became human. His raddled mind churns wildly, as he processes the extraordinary yet stupidly obvious enquiry that his wife's younger incarnation has just hurled at him like a grenade. He knows that he has to say something or he will just appear rude.

"'Forgivingness'? Hmm. Well…" *Come on, William, Gordon, whoever I bloody am.* "Well, I suppose, if simple 'forgivingness' is the way a couple can get back – you know – to how things were. To how things ought to be…"

His speech fades, his turbulent mind absorbing the words he has just heard leaving his own mouth. As if they're front-page news to him too.

"*This is what I think!*" cries the young wife, in elation. And William believes for a moment that he is very wise.

Lu stuffs a churro into Will's mouth and follows it up with a long, chocolatey kiss, both of them totally unfazed by their audience. The older man feels almost like one of the family, relieved that they are totally oblivious to the turmoil churning deep inside him.

Will the younger clearly isn't finished. "I've fallen on my sword bigtime wi' Sandy," he says, "but I need to make it up to you, Lu."

"You give me churros!" she laughs.

But Will just shakes his head. This clearly isn't sufficient.

"Hey, Lu," he says, "we *were* planning to go to the casino tonight! See Paloma in action. But well, I dunno, maybe now—"

William has absolutely no idea how the notion currently galloping into his brain like a Spanish stallion has arrived there, nor what the hell it thinks it is doing. He just knows he has to run with it.

"Mind if I make a wee suggestion?" he says, then steams straight on. "You *must* still go! Exactly as planned. But this time – with a psychic Scotsman on your team!"

Predictably they just stare at him.

CHAPTER THIRTY

THE BUILDING WASN'T ALWAYS a casino.

William thinks that it was probably built as a palace. He assumes, rightly or wrongly, that in this once-royal city most grand buildings of a certain era were originally palaces or some ducal equivalent. Proudly flaunting those ornate carved crests at their top and the grand, balconied windows below, they were clearly ideal spots for looking down on warriors marching past in triumph or for being envied by peasants looking resentfully up. But he really doesn't have that much of an idea and, to be honest, he hasn't the time to mull on history right now.

He is simply relieved that the place remains here thirty years on, still lit up like Christmas and still with a constant flow, through its revolving doors, of not particularly smartly dressed or attractive people, some looking more cheerful than others.

He is also hugely impressed that he recalls where it was, although a surreptitious visit to Google Maps didn't exactly hurt.

He does wonder briefly, as the curious threesome

stroll together down a thankfully quiet side street, how he would have been able to explain Google to his young friends, had they caught him at it. He could, of course, have informed them that he had only just invented it (the name a cool abbreviation of, say, his own fine Scottish handle – 'Gordon… Ogilvy' – and the whole thing simply a prototype) but he had a feeling that the tiny, pocket-sized phone would have freaked them out well before he could have segued into enhanced lying mode.

It suddenly reminds William of a book he had loved as a boy, one that his favourite teacher had loaned him, because the man must have recognised that here was an imagination at work. It was Mark Twain's *A Connecticut Yankee at the Court of King Arthur*. Dear Lord, he hasn't thought about this in years. Or of the kindness of Mr Paterson at Govan High, the first guy who persuaded him that, despite his provenance, he could *be* something, that he could write himself into a career, although the English master most probably hadn't been thinking of slogans for portable air-compressors.

"So this is your brilliant reconciliation plan?"

The young man's dour scepticism shocks William out of his reverie. "We came here on *our* honeymoon, Will," he explains, enjoying a rare excursion into truth. This very same night, the night of the silent procession, as he has thankfully recalled. "Nearly lost my shirt. Fanta was not happy."

"Well that's encouraging," says Will.

"I do not like *juego* – the gamble – Gordon."

"I know, Lu," says William, who recalls only too well. Then, realising that he shouldn't know this at all, he recovers swiftly. "I know how you might feel. See, I didn't like the *juego* either. *Until* I discovered I had a sixth sense." And are my bollocks ever going to stop coming out of my mouth? he muses quietly.

"Yeah, right, Gordon," says Will, who doesn't believe the bollocks either. "And I'm the third witch in *Macbeth*. C'mon, Lu."

"How's your team Partick Thistle doing these days?" says William.

"*What*?" says Will, eyes widening, suddenly a lot more impressed. "Can you see us wi' a win coming?"

"I said I was psychic – not a bloody miracle worker."

William turns to an equally awed Lu, with a knowing smile. "How do you think I was such a good Sherlock Holm-ess?"

William Sutherland – detective, psychic, master of coincidence, eponymous inventor of Google – has no intention of accompanying them through the revolving doors, however convinced they now are of his "powers". It was bad enough just walking here.

He has deliberately remained a few feet behind the youngsters, watching as they glide unwittingly through the bodies of people who look to William as corporeal and contemporary as himself but might as well have been ghosts to his 1995 counterparts. He certainly didn't wish the same thing to happen in reverse and for Will or Lu to witness him ploughing through their fellow travellers and their bulky cameras, without a second glance.

He tells them what he believes they need to know, in as much detail as he can muster from the first time round, then slips tactfully and quietly away.

To his surprise, he knows now what he has to do.

*

Will thinks he has died and gone to Monte Carlo.

The small casino is as heart-achingly glamorous as he imagined it would be, the movies being his only real frame of reference.

Okay, the seated men gambling aren't in immaculately tailored tuxedos or look like oily oligarchs just off their luxury yachts. And the women haven't all poured themselves into gorgeous gowns that shimmer under massive chandeliers, along with the tiny beads of excitement that lie like translucent pearls on their stupendous cleavage. But the tables are there, brimming with decks and chips and card shoes and roulette wheels. And the staff are suitably smartly dressed, possibly more so than the clientele, each one dealing and shovelling and croupiering with consummate skill and élan.

Will Sutherland is as happy as a dog with two dicks and informs Lu of the same.

And now he spies a couple who complete the picture, making it truly *beyond* worthwhile.

The man is about Gordon's age, but so much classier, with a full head of rich, silver hair and a tan that Will is convinced won't fade with the season. From his wrist a chunky gold Rolex the size of Big Ben appears to be sending beams of wealth out into the room. The Rolexed arm is made even more impressive by being confidently rested on the naked back of its owner's considerably younger and more beautiful companion.

Lu takes this in then observes that her husband isn't just taking it in but laminating it, framing it and sticking it on the biggest wall in his dream house. So she gives him a nudge that manages to be simultaneously playful and corrective.

He shrugs an unconvincing apology and tries to recall what Gordon has just told them. Struggling at the same time not to wonder why the hell they should believe this curiously omnipresent old guy for a single second.

Okay, I'm getting something. Now try to remember exactly what I'm going to tell you. At 2AM the staff will change...

There are no clocks in the place and, of course, Will's watch is at the bottom of a Triana fountain. So he takes Lu's hand and holds it until the tiny watch face informs him that the time is ripe. And, sure enough, Gordon's next prophesy is equally accurate, as they knew it would be, although God knows how he got there.

The croupier on the busiest table is a local girl, someone you both know...

Lu and Will see Paloma. Despite their smiles, she stays absolutely professional.

...But you'll need to pretend you don't. If you want to stay on her table.

Paloma's workstation is the roulette table and she manages it with the utmost seriousness. Will can see that his wife's best friend from art school, a practising artist, is proudly earning the money she needs to survive. Her long, slender arms poised for action, she is interested only in making profits for the house, without hopefully upsetting too many punters or errant pilgrims.

The three friends exchange very small and surreptitious smiles.

Will is tempted to put all he can afford on the date of their recent wedding. Number six. *Nombre sei.* Good as any. He's been bloody lucky with it so far.

You might be thinking – I'll put all I can afford on our wedding date. Number 6.

Him again! That voice in his head. Somehow it sounds so familiar to Will, and not just because of the Glasgow accent. But he only met the guy last night. Okay, Gordon was back again this evening at the café, hovering next to him at the urinals and, ah, yes, again just now at the hostel, when Will made the walk of shame. But the man is still a stranger, if not quite a perfect one.

Well, don't. Put it on – hold fire, it's coming – yes – no – yes – Will, your dad's birthday!

This surprised both of them. But not as much as the explanation.

About time the belt-wielding old shagger did something for you, isn't it? Oh. Er – sorry, went into a bit of a fugue just there.

Will glances briefly at Lu and smiles. She doesn't return it, as she is too busy preparing her fulsome lower lip to be firmly bitten by small, strong, perfect teeth. Which she does to maximum effect as soon as he starts to put all of his chips on 17 and then pauses, as he remembers that prescient voice.

Ah but DON'T do it this first time round. Don't be hasty like I – don't be hasty. Wait for the next spin.

Paloma spins the wheel. Lu swiftly grabs back the chips parked beside Will as the teasing, taunting little sod of a white ball whirls swiftly round and smoothly round and slowly round, with that jarring, clickety-clackety racket that sounds like nothing else in the world but can be more poisonous than a rattle snake.

It ends its tantalising journey on the totally untalismanic number four.

Will and Lu breathe a sigh of pecuniary relief.

*

The city is gently winding down as William strolls back to his hotel.

The processions are long gone and the huge, yellow street-cleaning trucks are making their own less devout but just as driven pathways through the candlewax - and petal - and pastry-strewn streets.

He carries a fresh bag of churros and some warm chocolate, but he isn't dipping.

Deep in thought, he is more confused but also more determined than he has ever been. Yet a part of him is still able to notice how frequently he can walk through a place with his weary head bowed and his eyes looking relentlessly downwards. He realises this now, because he finds himself counting discarded McDonald's cartons and feeling almost upset that this should be one of the markers distinguishing this extraordinary city from the one in which he honeymooned.

As he resolves henceforth to spend more time looking up, a painful thought jolts him.

"Aye, *that's* where I made my big mistake first time round! But hopefully tonight, guys—"

He segues into a far more important thought. As he mumbles over and over to himself, in some considerable confusion, one single potent word.

A word that doesn't actually exist.

"*…Forgivingness…*"

*

Will is just as confused yet perhaps even more determined. Which is why he is asking Lu with such urgency for the chips she still holds in her hand. When she shakes her head, he slips into pleading mode, with a bit of imploring thrown in.

Finally, as Paloma makes her last call for bets to be placed, there is a loud gasp from the croupier in question and a firm tap on his shoulder.

The rookie gambler finds himself looking first at Lu, whose eyes have grown impossibly wide. He turns slowly to see a large black toreador hat, under which is some unruly blond hair, a noble, smiling-through-adversity countenance and a heavily bandaged nose.

Sandy manages to explain the situation to Paloma in dumb-show. Putting the entire roulette game on hold, he points accusingly at his old friend, like some righteous, Old Testament prophet, then mimes a sharp push and equally dramatic stumble. With a face-smash for dessert. Will joins the charade, for all their benefits, by faux-disembowelling himself in contrition. The other players round the table are intrigued at the same time as they are pissed off, because they are here to lose money, not get involved in childish games.

Paloma, regaining her professional composure, makes one more *final* final call, aiming it directly at her damaged boyfriend's so-called best amigo. Time is so nearly up.

A preoccupied Lu makes her fatal mistake. She rests the chips she holds on the rim of the table, so that she can minister to Sandy, who makes no bones about his yearning for a good minister. Seizing the opportunity and ignoring the others, Will grabs the chips and sets them firmly down on the temptingly resonant number 17.

Every single one of them.

His distracted young wife suddenly realises where most of their honeymoon money has gone. Lu can only watch in helpless horror as the ball revolves, its demented rattle piercing her brain like a particularly sadistic torture devised by Torquemada himself.

Sandy watches too, the throbbing pain in his face tempered by the smell of excitement just inches away. And the scent of a probable blow-up thereafter.

The innocent, unknowing ball comes to a stop. On number 17.

"YA FUCKING DANCER!" yells a delighted punter, which is probably not an expression he picked up at a casino movie, even in Glasgow. And hardly the insouciant cool of his dreams.

Will turns to Lu, who looks more relieved than elated, and hugs her in that feet-off-the-ground, solar plexus crushing way that only love and a totally undeserved windfall can elicit.

But Lu can spot the fire in her new husband's eyes, a glow that to her mind almost matches his hair. She is seriously concerned that he doesn't blow all their newly-won chips, the colourful motherlode Paloma is delightedly pushing towards him. That he doesn't immediately squander it on the date of his ma's last hospital visit or his first wet dream or some equally arbitrary number that will set them back where they started. Or worse.

She catches Sandy's gaze. He shrugs, knowingly. The intimate exchange of two people who have never had to worry much about money, as they jointly fear for someone dear to them who patently has.

Shaking her long, shiny hair in a resolute twirl, she grabs Will and practically drags him away from the table towards the cash desk, suspecting that, whatever she does, this wad of pesetas is not going to be in his wallet for long.

CHAPTER THIRTY-ONE

"LUISA?"

There is no way William Sutherland can know that at the exact moment he is powering up the stairs to habitacion 381 of Hotel Herrera – because he is impatient and the bloody lift stubbornly refuses to arrive (*where are you, Pablo, when I need you?*) – his disquieted wife is kicking her heavy suitcase through the same lift doors three flights up in preparation for her final descent. Had he appreciated the almost farcical nature of the situation, at three o'clock in the morning on this singular Semana Santa, he might not be so stunned when he opens the bedroom door and walks into an empty room.

"*Luisa?*" he calls again, just in case she is hiding playfully in the spacious wardrobe or stifling giggles behind the half-open curtains.

He hears the bell, as the lift arrives back on his floor. Returning to the corridor he notices that Pablo – *who else?* – is waving at him. Not a come-quickly wave, more the wave of an old friend happy to be reacquainted.

Sod him, thinks William, charitably, but he moves towards the lift anyway. He still carries the greasy bag of cooling churros and the essential chocolate dip in his hand.

"Story so far, Pablo. Now that you're asking. Looks like my magical mystery meddling only went and got our loving threesome *even bloody closer!* And maybe just a wee bit richer."

Pablo nods. Of course he does. William reckons that if he told the older man he was going to chuck him head first off the Giralda Tower, the man would smile, nod and reference that most iconic of English football teams. Yet somehow this doesn't stem William's flow. Perhaps lift-confessions are the Holy Week variants of the elevator pitch.

"But perhaps, Pablo, I have been barking up totally the wrong tree!" he exclaims, slapping his head in a *eureka* moment, as he recalls this evening's surreal conversation, (not that they aren't all surreal) at the Hostal Esmeralda. "Or even the wrong bloody forest!"

The lift doors start to open but William sees no sign of Luisa.

"What's '*forgivingness*' in Espagnol?"

"Churros," responds Pablo.

"No it isn't." He shoots out of the lift, unshared local snacks and all.

He glances around the deserted lobby, although he knows that the odds on finding his missing wife here are pretty unenticing. A restraint he recognises as peculiarly British prevents him from asking the young man dozing off at the reception desk, beneath a large TV screen, whether he has seen a woman in the vicinity vaguely resembling the woman he came in with.

If he had to capture his wife, for identification purposes, in words or actions, the descriptors short, dark and well-rounded would probably cut it, with a patently sharp mind and a genial attraction. Easily outlined to a weary receptionist, even with indigenous pastry in hand.

Yet if asked to go beyond the superficial, flesh out the identikit version, he couldn't readily think of a suitable sequence to describe the lack of connection, that perpetually postponed meeting of minds, the familiarity that brings occasional comfort, more often the reverse, but in truth simply is. Or indeed the growing distance between them, the sense of being wholly apart from each other when each should be a part of the whole. And current circumstances – vacated room, deserted lobby – imply that this sorrowful gap is most probably wider than it ever has been before.

But now he has a sense of how to fix it. Or at least how to begin. Thanks to – well, who knows? But he has always been a problem-solver, hasn't he? For pity's sake, isn't this what has kept them afloat all these years?

The lights of an approaching car draw him towards the entrance. A cab is pulling up and from the shadows of the hotel's forecourt he watches Luisa emerge, dragging her suitcase.

"*LUISA*!" he yells, rushing towards the revolving door, Britishness suddenly abandoned.

If she hears, as she surely must, she doesn't acknowledge him. He pushes the doors so fast with his forearms that he almost sends himself round for a second time. But instead he topples out, one foot clipping the other, and manages to halt just inches from her furious face.

"*Where the hell have you been?*" she almost screams at him.

For a moment he is silent. She has clearly been waiting for him for hours and no explanation, true or false, could possibly ratchet down the white heat of her anger.

"Doesn't matter," he says, weakly. "Walking. Thinking. Where the hell are you *going* – at this time of the night?"

"Well, it isn't the casino."

He just looks at her in astonishment. Why would she recall this now? Unless…

"Oh, of course, you still remember this," she continues angrily. "Because you make the money. Always the bloody money."

William is staggered yet again by how swiftly old memories can be erased in another's mind and replaced at a stroke with fresh new ones. Memories he has himself created only this same evening, by interacting with a young couple just down the road and half a lifetime away. He has no idea what to say to this.

"I've got churros," is what he comes up with, although this is rather stating the obvious, as the bag he holds is now sodden with grease and the accompanying pot can be filled with only one thing tonight.

"Well, aren't you the lucky one?"

"No," says William.

"It is three in the morning," responds Luisa, "I am five kilos overweight, I have the raised cholesterol and a sugars problem – and I am probably leaving you. You still think churros are the answer?"

"Not on their own."

"There is a hotel at the airport," explains Luisa. "And then tomorrow the first thing…"

"Will *he* be there to meet you?"

Before she can answer, if indeed she intends to, William sets down the churros on a wall and grabs her suitcase.

"Be careful of your back," she cries instinctively.

"*Señor!*" protests the driver, at the same time as the impulsive case-grabber is assailed by a pain that predictably shoots up his spine and attacks all available muscles.

"*Jesus Christ!*" he yelps. "You can tell who most of the bloody clothes belong to!"

Luisa takes advantage of the spasm that is by now almost like a family friend and snatches back the case, telling him that she told him. The couple continue to tussle as the great cathedral gazes silently down.

"Don't leave me, Luisa. *Please.*"

She turns to look at him in disbelief. That this plaintive, softly spoken entreaty could find such yearning expression in a man she believes she knows so well rattles her for a moment and sends her off-stride. But he hasn't finished.

"I've learned stuff today, Luisa. *Important* stuff. About moving on. About you and me. Well, mostly me." He moves tentatively towards her, as if scared that she might recoil. "One more day. Just the two of us, together. Brand-new start, eh, in this bonkers bloody place. Feels right – doesn't it? Luisa?"

The cabbie, who is also gazing silently down, has had enough. He mutters a curse, leaps back into his purring cab and roars off.

"*Tu puta madre!*" suggests Luisa, as she watches him go. Angrily, she starts to look around, still gripping her case in readiness. As if another cab is just waiting to take up the slack.

"One more day. All I ask."

He thinks about adding the "forgivingness" bit, his golden legacy from those younger, wiser souls, but senses that whilst the concept might be lodging itself quite seamlessly into his own psyche, and can hardly be the worse way to move into the future, Luisa may not be in the frame of mind to be publicly absolved just yet. However magnanimous the gesture.

And so he just parks the notion and waits for an opening. It will come.

She sets her case down. Without quite looking at him, she shrugs. "What is one day – after thirty years?"

William exhales deeply, the way his overpriced osteopath has advised him, and lifts the case. She eyes the churros still on the wall and grabs one, as her husband gazes at her with a genuine fondness, which she notices but hardly recognises – it has been so long.

Luisa indicates with a gentle motion of her head that he should set the case down again, and he finds himself suddenly filled with a new sensation that feels strangely like hope.

"So, tell me, William," she asks him, with some interest, alert despite the hour. "Tell me this important thing that you learn from wherever you have been. Please. This great big something about you and me, well mostly you, that will make tomorrow so different."

If William has gleaned anything over the years, it is that, when an unanticipated opportunity arises, you seize it.

"Okay. I'll tell you exactly what I've—" He suddenly stops as a not unfamiliar panic takes hold. "*Tomorrow?* Oh shit! Luisa—?"

He stares at her, as a look not unlike horror takes over his face and one not a million miles from total puzzlement envelops her own. Her eyes ask "what?" as her mind wonders briefly if he is having a stroke. With his next words, she reckons that a stroke is too good for him.

"I'm meeting this big client tomorrow. Y'know, the one I came here for? The ceramic king himself. *Azulejos*. He exports all over the world! Señor Barbad—"

Luisa doesn't need to hear any more. Certainly not what the idiot's name is. She grabs her case and stomps slowly but angrily back into the hotel, leaving her irredeemable spouse hapless and helpless.

"You're invited too," he mumbles weakly.

Although, as he recalls the finer details of the man's generous invitation, he suspects that this isn't exactly going to make his second-honeymooning wife reckon all her birthdays (or anniversaries) have come at once.

CHAPTER THIRTY-TWO

"BASTARDO!"

After the great cathedral and the famed Alcazar Palace, the magnificent Baroque-style Plaza de Toros de la Real Maestranza de Caballeria de Sevilla is the most visited monument in the whole of Seville and generally acknowledged, especially by Sevillanos, as the Mecca of bullfighting. (Not an inappropriate comparison, when one considers the reverence in which this pursuit is held in certain Spanish circles, even as her other great religion is being celebrated just down the road.)

The matadors who practise their hazardous art in this beautiful but challenging ring are amongst the most celebrated 'killers' in Spain. And their fans, all twelve thousand of them on capacity days, the most unforgiving. The statue outside the gates, that of the bewitching but tragic gypsy Carmen, cigar-girl and dusky Sevillian temptress, welcomes the world to the glamour and spectacle that is the essence of *corrida*.

So there is no reason in the world why kindly Señor and Señora Barbadillo should presume that their female guest this afternoon, at the commencement of the season, would rather find herself in the seventh circle of hell.

"*Bastardo*!" is the word she keeps muttering under her breath. But not so far under that William – who needs no translation this time – isn't hugely relieved that she's not seated right next to his ebullient prospective client.

Señor Barbadillo, a florid Sevillano in his mid-sixties, with a belly that stubbornly refuses to stay contained within his expensively loud, short-sleeved silk shirt and chest hair that feels the same about his collar, is extremely proud of the seats he has obtained for his new friends from chilly London. And the influence it took to secure them.

"You are very lucky, my friends. These seats in the *Sombra*, they are like the gold."

When William looks quizzical, the man patiently explains that the seats here are divided between those in the "Sol" – the unrelenting sun – and the ones in which they find themselves: "Sombra" – the shade. With more than an inference that only peasants, or tourists who know no better, occupy the former.

There are representatives of all species here today. The *Maestranza* is buzzing. And, if Spaniards can be noisy in trains and restaurants, even in cathedrals, they excel themselves in bullrings. It is as if their reputation as the highest decibel form of humanity is in constant danger of challenge and they have to keep reasserting its dominance.

William can spot a few obvious tourists here and there, amongst the over-animated spectators. They're the ones whose heads appear to swivel all around, like that kid from *The Exorcist*. But he is fairly certain that the bulk of the crowd is composed of locals and their compatriots, many of them *corrida aficionados.* All primed for a pleasant afternoon of chopitos and carnage.

Señora Barbadillo, a striking, raven-haired woman, considerably taller and probably slightly younger than her husband, leans over to add more colour to the introduction. Like several of the ladies around her, she holds a small bunch of flowers. Perhaps, ponders William, these are to be thrown into the ring. Or maybe they are just to mask the smell of death.

"Is finest *corrida* in Spain," she says proudly. "So – in whole world, *sí,* Luisa?"

"My cup is running over," says Luisa, who does some more muttering for William's benefit. "I cannot believe you do this. To bring me here *again*!"

It takes a moment for William to absorb what she has just said, amidst the music that has just been turned up to max. And of course he's pretty tired – neither of them had the best of silent nights. He can't even look at what is going on down below – he can only stare at Luisa.

"Luisa, this is very important. We need the money. My business is – *AGAIN*?" He's shaking his head. "Luisa, we never came here. We couldn't aff—" Suddenly a brand-new memory from a new long-ago rushes in, like a diverted river discovering its freshly altered course. "Oh bugger," he mutters.

He starts to look frantically around the arena, especially the hot seats, whilst at the same time placating his wife and offering his hosts his full attention. He has never multitasked so hard in his life.

Señor Barbadillo feels that his own importance needs

reinforcing one more time. Or perhaps he has simply run out of conversation. "No *sol*, no sweatings."

"Aye. Perfect," says William, still thrown by Luisa's last remark. "Very – generous of you, Cristobal. Eh, Luisa?"

"Perhaps this time I ask a matador to put me out of my misery. With a big sharp—" William feels that a nudge at this moment would not be inappropriate. But it only seems to make things worse. "Ooh, sshhhh… *Clients!* Ssshhhhh!!! I see her husband gives her flowers."

"I gave you churros." Her scoff reverberates around the ring and down the ages.

Señor Barbadillo, who William thinks would have to be deaf and blind not to pick up the tension in the costly seats to his right, carries on gamely with his hosting. "Somebody say Jesucristo is not the only death we think about in Sevilla this week. But the bulls, William, they do not get up again on Sunday!"

He gives a huge, irreligious roar at this, then looks around to see if anyone else, equally rich and well-connected, has caught the multilingual wit emanating from Barbadillo, the tile-king. His wife clearly has and scolds him quite unconvincingly. "*Cristobal!*" She too is not averse to looking around, presumably to check if anyone is acknowledging their suitably *Sombra* presence.

William joins in dutifully with the laughter. He has discovered over the years that a subtle mimicking of the reactions or emotions of prospective clients is more likely to encourage a warming disposition, leading on to even more warming contracts. He has laughed at some shit in his time. He draws a line at overt racism or sexism but, hand on heart, he can't honestly admit to having sacked or rejected any client because of it. He salves his conscience just a tad by overcharging them.

And now the trumpets sound.

The crowd goes quiet, or as near to quiet as they are able, which isn't actually that close. The participants – toreros in their suits of lights, embroidered with silver or golden thread, picadors on horseback, *banderilleros* or flag-men and their crew, including the mozos or sword handlers – all enter the arena. The band plays life-affirming paso dobles as the cheers erupt and the players take up the formalised positions that ritual dictates.

Finally, the bull arrives, adorned with the rosette of his proud estate, unwitting star of the show.

This one, obligingly shaking his massive head and snorting wetly, is a jet-black and achingly noble beast. As William assumes they all are, at least at the outset. His enormous neck bulges on cue, mighty shoulder muscles glistening dangerously in the sun – no *Sombra* for him – as he kicks up dust and wonders what the hell he's got himself into. He is about to be tested for ferocity by the banderilleros, flaunting their magenta and gold dress capes. As the discerning crowd makes its own informed assessment.

He is not about to disappoint.

All this is explained in great detail to William, who finds himself genuinely fascinated – he has been wanting to witness this spectacle for over thirty years. Yet it is also beginning to feel disconcertingly familiar and he is starting to realise why.

"*Tercio de varas*," announces Cristobal, "with the – the lances, *sí*? The matador he watch the bull very very carefully, he study him with his whole head, while the *banderilleros* they do the workings with the capes." The portly host turns to William, genuinely hoping he is as impressed as he should be. "And then he is doing the *veronica*."

He is puzzled to see that his esteemed British guest is now staring fixedly to his right, well away from the action and deep into the sun-drenched rabble, with his mouth wide open and an expression of pure shock in his eyes. How can anyone not be held spellbound by the prospect of *veronica*?

"Señor – William? It is okay?"

It is very much not okay. Yet there is no way William can tell the man what or who he has just seen. And it isn't Veronica. He only knows that he is feeling some empathy with the bull.

*

Across the *Maestranza*, in the now scorching *Sol*, almost all eyes – and a lot of chunky cameras – are on the *picadores*. Working in pairs, they prance the ring on their blindfolded and seriously well-padded horses, goading the bull with their lances. One pair of eyes, however, is firmly closed and pressed painfully tight into the shoulder of a young and totally absorbed red-headed man.

Will tries gently to turn his young wife's head back, so that she can see what she is desperately trying to miss. He can't understand for a moment how she wouldn't be enjoying this, her national sport. Especially when he has had to pay so much for the seats. They're in the glorious

Andalusian sunshine, for pity's sake, watching angry bulls being mercilessly goaded and tormented. Even allowing for massive sunburn and definite heatstroke, how much better can life get?

"Hey, Señora Sutherland, meet me halfway," he says affectionately. "At least open your eyes."

*

"So – what do *you* do, Señora?" asks William, with more assurance than he's feeling.

He realises he is fast slipping down the client sociability league and needs to clamber back up before it's too late. Gamely, he tries to ignore what right now he – and, thankfully only he – can see just a few metres and several sunny degrees away from him.

"I am *flamenco*," announces Señora Barbadillo, her large hands fluttering in unconscious confirmation.

"Of course you are," says William, like he knows.

Señor Barbadillo, proud husband, exclaims loudly, "The best in Sevilla!" His Señora tries and fails to look modest. "She is *sixty* years age this Sunday – the Easter Sunday!" She doesn't even try not to look disgruntled. To his credit, her Señor senses this. "I tell him because you look *forty* years, *cariño*. Younger! You feel the legs, Señor. *Feel!*"

William really isn't in the mood right now for feeling any sort of limbs, even those belonging to the spouse of a prospective client, although he has probably done worse in his time. Nevertheless, he leans across the expansively soft belly of his host and extends an arm. His fingers touch and then grasp the solid, sixty-year-old calf muscle that is being exposed for his benefit. He whistles, which feels both stupid and appropriate.

"Very – substantial. You hear that, Luisa? You want to feel Señora's—?"

"I give you lessons, William," offers the owner of the leg. "Good prices."

William pictures his wife dancing so joyfully in the crowded street with that sweet little girl, flamenco impromptu, the night they arrived. And the numbing paralysis that appears to set in, freezing every cell in his resistant body, whenever such activity is offered or even mentioned to him. He remembers now, with a helplessness bordering on despair, that he couldn't even dance at his own wedding. In that tiny room above the pub, the one crowded with friends, bereft of family, reeking of Tennent's lager and lust. Not even when roaring drunk can he lose this almost primal hostility to simply moving with the music.

"Sorry, Señora, two left feet. Ask my wife."

"My husband does not dance," responds Luisa, although no one has actually asked her. "It is when he is at his most stiff."

William stares at her, but Luisa is looking away from him and around. He knows that it won't be long before she spots what he has already seen, with God knows what consequences. He knows also that it would be wildly imprudent of him to stare again in that direction. But he simply can't help himself.

He already suspects that the day – along with his life – is turning into the aptly named bullshit and there is absolutely nothing he can do about it. Yet he can't help feeling, amidst his paralysis, that he is not entirely free from blame.

Over there, in the *Sol*, he observes poor Lu, who is looking everywhere save into the ring itself, in which he assumes the picadores of her own day are happily breaking down ligaments and making proud animals bleed.

"Strictly Come Lancing," he says, to keep the conversation going, before he realises that of course his hosts have no idea what he is talking about.

Lu finally – and inevitably – spots him.

Now she's nudging Will excitedly. He's clearly too engrossed to take any notice, but she still waves across to the cooler *Sombra*, in innocent delight.

The distinctively raw smells of blood and sweat suddenly assail William's nostrils and strike a chord of familiarity in his tumbleweed head that scares him half to death. He realises with mounting dread that his own mind and memory are inexorably changing, along with those he has been trying – with admittedly mixed results – to affect.

"Our lives fall apart and *still* you work. Now here is bloody miracle," mutters Luisa, without looking at him. William watches as she picks at her fingers. He tries gently to draw her hands away from each other but she pulls them sharply back.

"Not leaving me with much else, are you?" he responds, attempting to catch her eye. But she is staring pointedly down into the ring, as if she would witness even this atrocity rather than engage with the person who dragged her here. "Luisa, I *had* to make this meeting. Things are pretty tough right now. You know this. The guy's business could make all the—"

She isn't listening. Not any more.

"*I can SEE them!*" she yelps. "Oh, *Dios mío*! There – in the *Sol*!" William closes his eyes, as if this will erase what they are both now acknowledging. "*Sí*! Of course! *This is where we were sitting!*"

There is no point in William explaining that he couldn't get bullfight tickets for love nor money back then. That isn't even history now. What do they call it – false memory? But how on earth did he—?

Before he can stop himself, he blurts out what his feverish mind has just churned up. "Dear Lord! I bought the seats from a bloody scalper outside the ground, didn't I? *With my winnings!*"

Luisa isn't listening. Not to his ramblings. She is too busy taking the barrette from her hair and shaking her head slowly, languorously, like one of those glossy shampoo commercials for emerging, less sophisticated nations that her husband used to write when they first moved down to London. The hair, still rich and lustrous, isn't as long as it was back then, nor as flowing, its natural colours given a modicum of tasteful help. Yet at once she seems more sultry and, just as swiftly, several degrees more Spanish. William can admire the brazen femininity, at the same time as he wonders why the hell she is doing this. And, more disconcertingly, for whom.

Their host is clearly impressed, which can't be all bad. Beaming at his attractive guest, he nods down towards the ring. "*Buena*, Luisa?"

"Makes me proud to be Spanish."

Señor Barbadillo nods happily. Him too. Yet the tiniest doubts still linger. "The bull, William – he has very good life. All the grass and ladies that he want!"

"Ha ha! Big surprise for him now," mutters Luisa, which really doesn't help. "I cannot sit here and ignore them," she whispers crossly to William. "It is like I insult myself." She stands up, drawing noisy sighs from those behind her. "Perhaps I go cheat on you with my husband, eh, William? Like the Argentinian *puta* that I am."

William rises too, but is drawn back down again by his host, before the grumbling aficionados behind him can become amateur picadores.

"*Luisa*?" he whispers urgently. "NO! It isn't safe. You don't know what you're getting into."

"Where does your wife go?" asks the podgy Señor, not unreasonably.

"*Sol*. She wants to work on her tan." Which sounds stupid even to William, but not as stupid as explaining that his mercurial spouse is rather set on visiting 1995.

CHAPTER THIRTY-THREE

WILL AND LU ARE both waving now, but this time it isn't Luisa who has caught their eye.

"Might have known *he'd* have the bloody posh seats," says Will, with begrudging respect. Lu has explained to him the way the pricing works here, which is clearly quite different from Firhill Stadium, at which Partick Thistle play and where sunburn is rarely an issue.

They're looking across into the *Sombra*, trying to catch the eye of their broken-nosed and bandaged friend, as he enjoys the action in relative comfort, his left arm planted firmly around Paloma. He's nodding contentedly as his new love, a native of Seville and clearly no stranger to the *corrida*, proudly points out the finer details to him.

"Next time," vows Will, his eyes not leaving Sandy's damaged but enraptured face, "we'll be the shady ones."

Lu strokes his face and dabs some more suncream on it. The novelty has clearly worn off and skin is already competing with hair in the ruddiness stakes.

A sudden movement beside them causes both to look up.

Luisa is standing in the neighbouring aisle, untrammelled head held high, one elegant hand perched perkily on a cocked and available hip. The other hand lightly taps the young man's shoulder. Will immediately gives her a delighted smile, which she just as instantly returns. But this time Lu is holding back. Perhaps it is the way the older woman's gaze is aimed directly and rather too narrowly at her husband. And most certainly not down there at the ring.

"Oh, hi, Fanta!" says Will. "Bloody great to see you."

Lu tries to catch the eye of the older woman, this still-attractive stranger who is gazing down at her husband almost coquettishly. And what's with the hair and the pose? she wonders. It seems curious, such wilful abandon on a woman that age. She certainly wouldn't carry on like this.

"It is good to see you also, Will." Now the older woman acknowledges Lu, but as a casual afterthought. "*And* you."

Luisa has a vague sense that the spectators of her own era, those contemporaries who sit in the same two seats that she is currently addressing, are staring at her and wondering who the hell she is talking to.

They appear to her as no more than indistinct ghosts, eclipsed by the impossible reality of the infinitely more vivid young couple from her past. And, of course, Luisa has absolutely no awareness of the young couple's immediate neighbours, those innocent denizens of a previous millennium, who are reacting in a similar manner towards Will and Lu as they watch the young couple converse with a patently empty aisle.

"I had to pay some wee scalper a small fortune," explains Will, "but we struck it lucky last night, didn't we, Lu?" Lu shrugs – she has had luckier days. "Thanks to good old Gordon." He catches Luisa's confusion but it doesn't seem to bother him. "Mind you, I should have bought Señora Sutherland here a seat facing the other way round!"

Luisa laughs, as if her own attitude to the *corrida* is just so different.

She lifts her head to bask in the sun's merciless rays, content to shrug off the blight of a long Richmond winter and an unpromising early spring. "I like it better here in the sunshine, Will," she tells him. "I become Spanish again." It takes her a moment to understand why the attractively bearded young man looks so surprised. "*Argentinian!*" she swiftly amends. "So, Will, you have the *cojones* for the bullfight?"

"I've supported Partick Thistle since I was seven, Fanta. I'm used to slaughter."

"*Sí* – but when your team lose, I do not think they are this night's main course in a Glasgow restaurant."

The two of them fall about at this, and Luisa takes the opportunity to rest a hand on the young man's pleasantly firm forearm. She can feel his rusty hairs rise, as if in attraction to her welcoming palm.

Neither notices that Lu is looking pure daggers at her future, more worldly self.

*

In the not-so-comforting shade, William tries to summon back his errant wife with fruitless flicks of his wrist, as if he is watching her wander obliviously into quicksand, too far out to be thrown a rope. His bemused neighbour can hardly fail to notice this, but is still unfailingly polite.

"Your wife, she know these people?"

"Er – quite a coincidence actually, Cristobal," says William, as casually as he can feign. "They're her cousins."

"*Sí*? ...But they are Japanese, Señor."

"Talk about bulls and bloody china shops," says William, to himself. Because he has nothing else to say.

*

The *banderilleros* strut their stuff with practised arrogance, deftly swishing their gold and magenta capotes. Their brief – to pass and position the now weakened but still ferocious and understandably enraged bull.

"So, Fanta, these guys are—?" asks Will, with genuine interest. But Luisa, now sitting close to him in the aisle, isn't exactly certain what manner of spectacle he is looking at. For all she knows, rain could have stopped play back then and a local girls' band are ruining gems from the musicals. She hopes against hope that more information will be forthcoming. "The guys with the fancy kebab sticks?"

Luisa laughs in relief. "Ah, *banderilleros*! Is funny because we use this word also, Will, for the tapas on the little sticks."

She catches Lu rolling her eyes at this, as her head turns away from the skewering. Luisa really doesn't recall herself being so possessive, but the evidence is staring her in the face. She decides to ignore it.

"Well, now that the *picadores* have wounded the poor bull," she explains, "these guys they come in to make it so much worse for him. You really like this, Will?"

"Reminds me of Govan on a Saturday night. Or my old man on any night. No bull."

Luisa smiles at this, as she undoes another button on her blouse. And smiles even more as Lu's bright eyes almost disappear into the top of her head. Finally, the younger woman speaks.

"Poor fat old thing. To be so close to death. On the last of its legs, I think you say." With this she looks directly at Luisa, the sharp little *banderilleros* making their mark.

"*LUISA!*"

Both women swivel instantly at the impassioned cry of a balding Scotsman, now making his urgent way down the aisle. Unfortunately, both women also respond with a "*sí*", which causes the young couple to stare at the older woman in confusion. Luisa just shrugs – easy mistake to make.

"Er… fancy seeing you two," says William. He smiles pleasantly in greeting, although his heart is racing, along with his mind and every sweat gland in his body, as he envisages all the ways this could go so horribly wrong.

"Again," adds Will, shaking his head.

There you go.

"*Again*?" queries Luisa, looking at William, who decides to keep his own counsel.

"Aye. *And* again," Will ploughs on happily. "Hey – thanks for 'numero 17', Gordon. It paid for these wee seats and more. He's got the gift, hasn't he, Fanta?"

William tries to compute how much Luisa might be remembering. She clearly recalls them winning at the casino, which of course only happened this time round, but obviously struggles with how the kids came up with that winning number. It is as if his "interventions" still only belong to him. For now.

If the gods are playing with us, thinks William

Sutherland, then they're clearly making up the bloody rules as they go along.

"Oh! Do you like to meet our friend Sandy?" says Lu, out of left field, or perhaps to divert the brassy older woman's attention from her new husband. The younger version is pointing up towards the classier seats. "We tell him all about you – the second honeymooning people."

Sandy?

William and Luisa just look at each other. But before she can put a clamp on her tongue, Luisa nods excitedly as she gazes around. "Ah, *sí*. Of course. He was here also – *is* here! In the *Sombra*."

"How the crap do you know that?" asks Will, not unreasonably.

Luisa has no answer to this. At least none that won't set the world reeling.

"*She's psychic too!*" exclaims William, in desperation, realising that another 'new' memory has settled in his wife. "We belong to a club. Can I borrow my wife for a second?" He grabs her, his mind reeling. "Jaffa! No – Fanta!"

Luisa stands, using Will's shoulder to support her. "It was so good to meet you again, Will." She smiles with a sadness that goes right over the young man's head. "After so long," she murmurs, letting out one of her especially deep, soulful, Iberian sighs.

As a grim-looking Luisa follows her husband towards the exit, Lu watches the older couple with undisguised fascination. She senses quite an argument brewing. Looking back thoughtfully at her own husband, she sees that he too is preparing himself for the kill.

CHAPTER THIRTY-FOUR

"I OWE YOU AN *explanation? You were screwing my bloody business partner!"*

William and Luisa Sutherland are conducting the ding-dong of their lives in full, if indifferent, earshot of random spectators, as they hastily leave the *Maestranza*. Indifferent save perhaps for one young woman down below in the *Sol*, who would look at anything rather than the artful slaughter that holds everyone else rapt and breathless.

William has no idea where they are going, geographically or emotionally. Yet, like the spectacle they are forsaking, he senses an impending climax he is powerless to control.

"*And* your best friend," responds Luisa, her anger equalling his own. "See – even here you are putting the business first!"

"Because he was giving you the business first!" William points back to the *Sombra*, although by this time they are outside the Plaza de Toros and the lively spectators can be heard but not seen. "And now you're looking up at the posh seats to check if you can see him again."

And to think I was going to absolve you, he muses. Well, sod "forgivingness". Yet, even amidst the *madre* of all rows, he still can't help fretting that he has left a great potential client back there, rapidly losing his potential.

They could, of course, remain stationary and continue their argument, perhaps in a quiet corner or a deserted street. But William and Luisa are not well-versed in the etiquette of all-out, stand-up rows, as they don't form a major part of their disputational repertoire. It would seem that William has quite successfully trained himself out of them, scary as they were, since his more volatile youth. With Luisa's quietly calming assistance. Something she now appears to regret, as she would far prefer the sparky firebrand she just left at the *corrida*, the one with whom she was shamelessly flirting, to the distant automaton Will Sutherland has become.

Whatever the reasons, the sheer momentum of their flare-up propels them away from the historic building and towards the banks of the swiftly flowing Guadalquivir. They find themselves crossing the familiar bridge into Triana, although a trip down memory lane is probably the last thing they need right now.

Luisa tries to stare into her husband's face, ensuring that her words bear their intended weight, but shorter legs mean that she has to walk that bit faster just to keep up with him. William has no intention of slowing down, despite having no obvious destination in mind. So her words come out in a breathless rush, bouncing off his stiffening back, which isn't quite as she would wish them delivered.

"Tell me this," she pants. "Just this. What sort of a husband is it who is so married to his work, he prefers to screw his laptop?"

"At least it responds to my touch," he fires back, walking even faster, as if in a rush to return to his past.

"Oh no, William. Oh no. It is not me who is dead inside."

Now he stops. Now he turns.

"Just keeper of the dead," he says quietly, but not quietly enough. He watches his wife's face crumble, as if the underpinning, always so precarious, has finally fallen away.

"*Bastardo!*" she spits. Then does the same in translation. She shakes her head and mutters to herself, in the way one does when pretending a comment is not for other ears. "Sometimes I think you do not remember even his name."

Before he can answer this, not that an answer springs readily to mind in the face of so monstrous an allegation, she scrabbles into her heavy bag. Out comes the little photo album. As he watches, wanting to protest but still not finding the words, she flicks desperately through it.

He briefly sees again the happy photo of Will and Lu at the Yellow Café, taken just the other evening by the "older" Luisa – the snapshot that certainly wasn't there less than an hour earlier that same evening, when she thrust the newly-compiled album at him in the restaurant.

Another small amendment to their history.

Finally, she comes across the treasured photo of that beaming little boy, with what she always called his *lapis lazuli* eyes and the blond hair just tinged with red.

She thrusts the photo directly in front of William's face, a gesture that makes passers-by wonder unsurely if the man is losing his sight or the woman is losing her mind.

"*Jamie Eduardo Sutherland!* Ring a bell, *sí*? JAMES! Like your papa. So that 'good can come from bad'. This is what you say, yes?" Her voice begins to crack and not just because of the unaccustomed shouting. "But where is the good now, William? Where is it now?"

She walks to the end of the bridge and then stops, unsure of where to take her anger and her misery. This time William hesitates, but only for a moment. He knows that he must follow her, because there seems nowhere else to go. With the discussion and perhaps with the world.

Memories begin to flood in, flowing with the speed of the river just below their feet. But he senses that there are certain places where he cannot go. Not here. Not now. If there was ever a time for silence…

"Just do not say it!" She has turned back to him and is staring him out.

"Easter Sunday." He had not meant to say it. But he said it.

"*He said it!*" she tells a bemused passer-by, in disbelief. The elderly woman, dressed entirely in black, just shakes her head, which Luisa takes as a sign that this thoughtful stranger is just as appalled as she is.

"What've I got to lose, *cariño*?" retorts William, in self-defence. "How's this for total recall? Stroke of midnight. Easter Sunday. Year of our Lord, 1995. Very last night of our honeymoon. The bells were damn sure ringing then, for me and my girl. AND IF YOU HADN'T COME ON SO BLOODY STRONG—!"

"*ME*? You were like La Giralda in your pants!"

If she had hoped that no one nearby would understand English, Luisa is soon disabused. A couple of young lovers, laden down with plates and tiles from one of the Triana showrooms, suddenly burst into giggles and stagger away, so as not to offend the older, Spanish-looking woman, who is being pretty offensive herself. They almost daren't look at the poor old, balding guy, who is becoming quite red in the face.

"Perhaps I should have thrown an ice-cold sangria on it," hurls Luisa, unfazed. "Then I can go out and 'win the bread'. Our deal, yes? Our big bloody deal. While you be the famous writer and make wonderful stories about Nazis and whores." He tries to interrupt but she is on a roll. "Instead of having to find a job you say to me so much you hate. *Sí*. All my fault. I get 'up the duff' all on my own!"

"You had dreams too, Luisa! Your art – your photos. Our kids' books, together." He laughs wryly. "One *'el preservativo'!* See – that's a word I remembered. From the *farmacia*. Bit too bloody late. If only I'd trusted my Spanish, rather than my wife."

She glares at him, then walks angrily, tearfully away. Without even thinking, she finds herself moving towards the Hostal Esmeralda, the scene of the crime. How did they end up here?

How did they end up – here?

A more recent thought shoots back into William's feverish mind. The mind of a marketing consultant. Something that has been nagging him since his latest 'experiment'.

Maybe his earlier forays into altering lives and history were just trial runs!

Those relatively small-scale 'testing' exercises one is advised to conduct and ruthlessly evaluate, before going all out for that full, take-no-prisoners, global launch.

Phase 1 is done. Phase 2 will need to be something just a wee bit bigger.

A *whole lot* bigger.

To her surprise, Luisa feels William's warm hand circling gently around her wrist. She looks down at it and at his elegant watch that was once so special. As their eyes meet, welling with tears they would rather nobody witnessed, William suddenly knows what he must do.

"You wish it too, don't you, Luisa?"

He can hardly breathe, but he has to complete the thought, even though he is certain that she does not and will not understand.

"That things could have been, you know – different." She stares at him now and shakes her head, as if he is simply stating the obvious. Even when he says something that in truth is so totally overwhelming. "That we could *change* things."

Now she laughs. A sound bereft of mirth. Or joy. Or hope.

"Things? '*Things*'? Just look at us, William!"

Without being aware of it, they have reached the ornate, tiled gates of the hostel itself. But they don't look in. They don't see the stocky handyman turn from his pruning and watch them as they stare at each other, before they move off in separate directions.

Because there is nothing more to say.

Back in the hushed *Maestranza*, Lu hides her tearful face in Will's shoulder, as the lifeless carcass is dragged bloodily away.

CHAPTER THIRTY-FIVE

WILLIAM SUTHERLAND THINKS THAT there is probably nothing more poignant than a long-married couple lying next to each other in the darkness, neither partner sleeping, neither party acknowledging the other's state of wakefulness. Yet, somehow, rather than saddening him, this seems to etch resolve even deeper into his mind.

When finally, some hours into the night or perhaps early morning, he hears those familiar sounds that tell him his sleeping partner really has succumbed to the weariness overwhelming her, William slips gently out of bed.

He begins to dress in the dim light seeping through the curtains.

After he has completed this tricky endeavour, and is hopefully not resembling the unmade bed he just left, William stares down at Luisa. He whispers into the darkness, at a level he knows, from his own restless nights' experience, is unlikely to wake her.

"Goodbye, Luisa," he says, tenderly. "We'll get there, *cariño*. It's going to be okay."

Of course, William has no idea if this is true, nor indeed whether the "there" to which they're going to get is even attainable in this jumbled world that exploded for both of them just a couple of days before. He simply knows that anything has to be better than where, disastrously, they are in this moment. And where, as he realises now, they have been for far too long.

Now that he has, in some revelatory way, been reintroduced to the beguiling woman he married and with whom he has managed to live for three sometimes turbulent decades – this occasionally infuriating yet so often disarming woman, the unique and intrinsically decent person to whom he has been forced by some rare phenomenon to realise, over these past few unreal days, that he genuinely owes so much and for whom he believes, despite yesterday, despite a host of yesterdays, he has genuinely learned to feel "forgivingness" and perhaps a long-lost or at least much misplaced love – he is certain that he has to try to make things right again. To make things work again. For both of them.

Before he loses her forever.

William has never felt more resolute nor more determined in his life.

Nor more convinced that resolution and determination count for bugger all when you don't have even the vaguest notion what you're doing.

CHAPTER THIRTY-SIX

HE COULD DO THE walk to Hostal Esmeralda in his sleep. Which is probably just as well.

There is no one in the freshly scrubbed streets as William leaves the hotel (where, for once, he doesn't bump into the ever-wakeful Pablo). Nor is there much evidence, save for shop-window displays, that one of the largest and most spectacular religious festivals in the world is currently at its height.

The cathedral itself appears to be sleeping, as if storing energy in its ancient stonework for the upcoming Easter Sunday, *Domingo de Pascua*, the most important day in the calendar. Energy sapped, thinks William, from the hundreds of poor artisans and craftsmen who most probably expired during its construction. And then he thinks that such thoughts, whilst vaguely poetic and metaphysical, aren't really getting him anywhere much, so he stops thinking them.

He has no idea how long he spends on the old bridge, by now so familiar, gazing down at the gently mesmerising river, with no proper idea where it has begun nor indeed where it is going. For William this is just a halting point on his mission, until the time is sensible to proceed.

He really does wish that he had a proper, definitive plan. A honed-until-foolproof, long-term strategy for the future, with Sutherland and Co as the brand. But none has occurred and if he thinks that watching an endless stream of muddy water will clear his head and sharpen his focus, he is seriously disappointed.

The Hostal Esmeralda is just awakening as he pushes open the gate. There is no one in the courtyard but the shutters of his old bedroom, *their* bedroom, are open. He hasn't quite worked out how to explain his being outside their door so early in the morning and he knows that 'just passing' won't hack it this time. But in this brave new world, where different rules apply and lying through one's teeth feels perfectly normal, he is confident that something will occur.

The tiny reception desk is unguarded, which he takes as a positive omen, so William is able to slip through and up the stairs without being observed. He looks around but after thirty years he can't honestly say that the creaky staircase or the old tiles adorning the walls ring the slightest bells. Nor does the bedroom door when he finds himself outside it, wondering what to do next.

He has no need to wonder for long, as the door suddenly opens. Reeling back against an available wall, he feels suddenly sick with the prospect that this is happening today, now, and is the initial phase of his master plan, which isn't a plan at all but some species of desperate and clearly unrealisable dream.

The occupant of the small, first-floor room appears just as surprised as William. He is a man of a similar age, but better skintone, to the total stranger on his landing. Yet he bids him a hearty Australian (or Kiwi: William is never quite sure) good morning and slips past him down the stairs to enjoy his *desayuno*.

William doubts whether the man he just encountered is aware that he has been sharing a tiny room with a couple from the early nineties, but he knows that he shouldn't hang around to find out. He has not the slightest clue as to what to do next and doubts that he will have any firmer ideas after a good breakfast.

But he will at least have had a good breakfast.

*

It is well after nine when he finishes what was indeed an excellent breakfast. William supposes that if anyone can do a Spanish omelette, these guys can, and recalls with affection the myriad tasty omelettes he has enjoyed back home over the years, with Luisa and Claire and quite often with their closest friends. The latter of course did include Sandy, which makes him decide he won't think any more about omelettes right now.

He is not thinking about anything constructive when he finds himself on a bench in a small but delightful square, rich in statuary and bitter oranges, not far from the hostel. He is struck by the acres of emptiness inside his brain. William Sutherland, still apparently of Matheson Sutherland, whose mind is usually churning at such a rate, either with future plans or financial worries, long and short-term strategies, campaigns carefully targeted and dreams sadly unfulfilled.

He would do what the gurus advise and simply trust in the power of the universe, except he thinks that's a pile of shite.

As the city comes to life, the benches around the square fill with bright-eyed tourists. William watches them as they pore over maps on their phones and tablets, or more likely, he reckons, hit social media for their first fix of the day, indulging in the cyber-schadenfreude that only kicks in when flaunting to less fortunate connections back home a snapshot of Andalusian paradise these domestic observers possibly won't ever afford. (Or at the very least aren't enjoying right now.)

A large Nazareno all in white parks himself next to William.

They exchange a polite nod, which is all the more impressive when your head is masked and conical. Had he even wished to begin a conversation, which William doesn't, he doubts that they would readily find a suitable topic in common.

It is when William checks his watch – a habitual gesture, as there is nowhere in particular he needs to be and he has absolutely no idea where he is going – that he senses a pair of eyes examining it with interest. When he looks up at the eyes, which of course are all he can see of this encased man, he is surprised to find that they are staring at the elegant timepiece in what has to be pure admiration, as no one would linger this long merely to ascertain the time.

If William Sutherland didn't trust the universe before, he does now.

As he remembers.

CHAPTER THIRTY-SEVEN

IT TAKES WILLIAM A good half-hour to find the small jewellery shop, which turns out to be just around the corner from the Hostal Esmeralda.

He might have deduced this, with his Holmesian skills, had he really thought about it. But the frustration of tramping around the several streets abutting the square is far outweighed by his current elation, as he strolls down this final, exquisite little shopping parade. It appears unchanged over the centuries, save for the large, ground-floor windows and the merchandise behind the glass.

The shop is empty, so he decides to wait outside, until – well, until whatever he hopes will happen actually does. Or doesn't. In which case, he realises, he is totally stuffed once again.

"*Señor?*"

He spins round. A young man in a smart, grey suit has come out of the shop and is smiling at him.

"Mm?" responds William.

"Can I help you?"

"How did you know – that I was a Brit?"

"I have special powers. The government – they often call me in."

Ha bloody ha, thinks William. But he tells the man "I'm just waiting." He realises this sounds a bit odd, so he extends the wrist of his left hand from under the sleeve of his vaguely summery jacket. "I bought this watch here. Well, actually, my wife did. Your name was on the box – still got it, somewhere – and we were staying just round the corner." The young man is nodding, with professional interest. "She came here thirty years ago – this very morning. I think. Yeah. Pretty sure. Before you were born."

"I do not think so, Señor."

"You must be older than you look."

The assistant points across the road "I think it is there that she bought this."

William looks at where he is pointing. It is a small, specialist CD shop. He gawps at the young man in confusion.

"We moved. It is the gypsy inside of us."

William stares at him. Then rushes across the road.

*

The noise is deafening.

The CD shop, stocked mostly with secondhand or specialist items, along with some coveted vinyl, is quite small and narrow, yet stretches a surprisingly long way back. It is already quite full of customers, mostly Spanish, some of whom are happily singing along with the blaring music. This is William's idea of hell and the surge of hope he felt on that bench in the square swiftly evaporates into the music-drenched air.

Then he sees her.

The young woman is bent over what he assumes must have been a glass counter, with its most precious items displayed beneath. All sealed and secured, until a man with a special key can release them. It is obviously such a man, or indeed woman, with whom Lu is talking so volubly.

William's gaze lingers once more on her face. He stands transfixed, for a moment, by the aching beauty he still remembers. A beauty he recognises now as having deepened over the years, rather than being cruelly withered by them. Not just on the outside but – more importantly – the beauty that lies within. It isn't Luisa Sutherland that he is now wanting to change, he reassures himself, but simply the circumstances that have changed Luisa Sutherland. And of course himself along with it.

Which makes him even more determined.

William knows that he has to attract Lu's attention, across the decades, amidst all the noise and bustle. But he can't physically reach her. In his pulsating, musical world, there are stacks of CDs and a display of curious musical instruments, not to mention curious customers, barring his way. So he has to resort to an undignified yell.

"LU? HI!"

The young woman turns at this, as indeed do most people in the record shop, despite the racket they themselves are making.

"Oh. Gordon. How are you – today?"

She smiles at him with genuine delight, without raising her voice. Because, as he soon realises, there is no need. Her long-gone shop is most probably empty. It certainly isn't playing *Now That's What I Call Andalusian Music! 86.*

He finds himself wondering if she would offer so disarming a smile to any considerably older man she might be forever bumping into on her honeymoon or whether she considers him just the slightest bit attractive. Unfortunately he can't quite hear the words that might afford him some clue, as they are burying themselves beneath this same smile.

"COULD YOU SPEAK A LITTLE LOUDER?" he yells.

"Why?" she asks, not unreasonably, wondering why he doesn't just move a little closer. He really is a quite peculiar man, she thinks to herself.

"ER – MY EARS. YOU KNOW," he explains, pointing to his ears in case the concept is proving too tricky for her. "AGE!"

"Oh – OKAY." He can see her give a bemused shrug to the phantom jeweller. As well she might, for the elderly man, who is most probably six feet under by William's time, has no idea as to whom his pretty young customer is shouting. "THIS IS BETTER? YOU CAN HEAR ME?"

William turns to a fellow record shop browser, who is staring at him. "Bloody madness," he remarks. Which, whilst undoubtedly true, isn't totally satisfying as an explanation. "JUST! I HOPED I'D RUN INTO YOU AGAIN."

Lu just nods. Had she thought about it, she might have wondered how come this curious Scotsman keeps turning up in places she just happens to be. But she is a rather sweet and really quite innocent girl and the concept of stalking hadn't yet fully taken hold in mid-nineties Spain.

"I WANTED TO APOLOGISE TO YOU. FOR YESTERDAY," he continues.

"APOLOGISE? *PORQUE*?" she responds, getting rather used to this empty-shop shouting. She hardly notices the wary old jeweller swiftly returning and locking up the precious items he has only just taken out.

"You could apologise to us too, Señor," mutters a disgruntled music-lover.

William just ignores this. "CAN WE TALK SOMEWHERE LESS CROWDED?"

As the customers respond with a heartfelt "*por favor!*", Lu looks around the empty jeweller's shop and wonder, if Gordon, husband of the oddly named Fanta, is actually *insano*.

"I was making a gift. For Will," she explains, and, if he doesn't hear, so be it. "His watch, it is not working. And he must always know the time! I come back later. *Buenos días.*"

This farewell is to the jeweller, who finds himself both disappointed and rather relieved.

The CD shop customers are wholeheartedly the latter.

CHAPTER THIRTY-EIGHT

WHEREVER I WALK IN this city, thinks William, I find myself beside the sodding river.

He is trying to remain pleasantly casual, as he strolls with Lu, but in his head he is desperately seeking some place where there are relatively few people, at least from his perspective. And a location that most probably hasn't changed too much within the last thirty years. It takes only one mistake, he reckons, such as walking on a bridge that was only constructed in 1998, to freak out the poor young woman completely. Unless of course her Catholicism gets the better of her and she sees him in a new and rather more radiant light.

When he comes across what looks like a massive park, he beams at his young companion with genuine gratitude.

"Here is my favourite place in all of Sevilla!" she exclaims, throwing her slender arms wide, as if better to express her appealingly childlike delight. William feels he could almost pick her up and swirl her around, but he would most probably rupture something, even before she could begin fending him off with her small but powerful fists.

"Parque Maria Luisa. She is named as me. Luisa. It is so green," she enthuses. "You have been here before, yes? Much of it is done for the Exposicion. 1929."

"I think I remember it. The park I mean, not the Exposition! Isn't there a very grand building somewhere round here? Aye. They may have used it in some sort of film."

For a moment he notices a curious sadness wash over the young woman's face. But just as swiftly it has gone. "*Sí*," she smiles. "It is *DH Lawrence of Arabia*!" Suddenly William remembers and feels some of this sadness, yet he can't quite recall why. "Is also *Jardin Botanico*. Many beautiful trees and flowers. And *palomas*. The doves, yes. As my friend!"

As they walk along the tree-lined avenues and into the heart of the massive park, they occasionally side-step people who, to each other, aren't there at all. To William it looks like she's a wee bit tipsy and he can only assume that he must appear very much the same to her. So he tries to do his swaying just outside her eyeline. Then Lu says something that takes him completely by surprise.

"You and Fanta are having the big argument yesterday at *corrida*, yes?"

He hadn't realised that they had begun the row to end all rows even before they had fully quit the *Sol*. Or perhaps the young woman, an artist and photographer primed to observe, had simply picked up from their body language that a major storm was brewing. Yet, before William can explain or perhaps even defend himself, she surprises him once more.

"This is wonderful."

Wonderful?

"Is it? How so?" He is going to add "pray tell me" but she wouldn't understand and facetiousness is not the look he is going for.

"*Sí*. You are still together!" she explains in delight, as if it is just so obvious. "This is what marriage is, I think. The fighting and the making it up. The staying with each other. You are – how is it – an 'example.'"

She laughs at this, almost as if she is embarrassed. William just smiles thoughtfully. Perhaps this is the "example" he and Luisa have kept in their heads all these years. From their own honeymoon. He decides he won't go there – it's a maze out of which he'll never find his way and he's learning that, when magic intrudes, logic flies straight out of the window. And, of course, the "still together" bit sadly doesn't ring quite true.

They reach a waterlily pond. William is reminded of being dragged screaming by Luisa to Monet's home at Giverny and, to his surprise, rather loving it. He waits for this younger version of his cultural personal trainer to sit on a bench.

Her body language leads him to believe there is room beside her. As there is clearly still a bench there, albeit most probably not the same one, he parks himself next to her and prays that some predatory stranger from the past doesn't decide to sit down on top of him and strike up conversation with a beautiful young lady. One who is sitting quite on her own and appears to be talking to herself. (Hopefully, this latter activity would deter even the most determined lothario.)

"Fanta, she works, yes?"

He still can't quite get used to his wife being a fizzy drink, although it is not totally inapposite, so he just nods. Yet it appears that his inquisitor is after more.

"Ah. Yes, indeed she does. But you know, Lu," he says, thoughtfully, "I do think her main ambition was always to be a mum. Just that. *Mama*. And she was a bloody good one… Twice."

He shakes his head. Too much information.

"But eventually, Lu," William continues, happy to be telling the truth for once, "she did go back to college – when our wee Clairey was nine or ten. And Fanta's a full-time conservator now." He smiles at Lu's puzzled face, as she repeats the meaningless word to herself. "She preserves things. You know, old documents. Photos…" He smiles, wryly. "*Memories*." Now one of his own memories flutters back, one at which he is certain the young woman will be utterly amazed. "D'you know, she has actually held Shakespeare's will – right there in the palm of her hands."

Lu's face registers not so much amazement as shock bordering on total disgust. "NO?! *Dios mío!*" She cries out. "They still keep it? And they let the ladies to touch it?!"

It's William's turn to be puzzled. "Eh? A will is just a document, Lu, that— *Whoa*! You didn't honestly think—?"

She blushes sweetly. She did honestly think. At exactly the same moment, they each begin to roar.

"I cannot believe you thought—"

"Yes, okay, Gordon."

As if current complications aren't sufficient, an elderly nun chooses this moment to approach William with a collecting bowl. He hasn't the least intention of talking to her, nor of dropping coins into what will undoubtedly appear to Lu like thin air or worse, so he simply waves her off.

"I think you like the *niños*," says Lu, staring in the nun's direction, with a soft smile.

"*Huh?*" says William.

It takes him a while to work out that there must be small children in Lu's vicinity, or at least in her eyeline. Kids who most probably have their own children by now, but nonetheless it is at them she believes William is waving. He is certainly not going to disabuse her. Especially not when she has led him straight onto the avenue towards which he has been struggling so tortuously.

"Ah. You want a lot of *niños*, don't you?"

"Oh, *sí*," she laughs, although she is clearly deadly serious. "Many. But Will, he say that for the kids, you are needing much money."

"They aren't cheap to run, Lu."

"I know this. I do know this thing." She stares out at the lily pond, and perhaps also at the children. "But sometimes, Gordon, I think Will he will never have enough of the money. To be happy. Never enough to have the kids. Not even one kid. *Even if he wins at the bloody casino every single day!*"

Turning to William, Lu registers his shock. He knows he does good shock. Yet he also knows this doesn't mean that the shock isn't real.

"Excuse me, please, Gordon," says Lu. "Will, he say to me, Lu, bad things they are always around the corner. I say to him, we are not *around* this corner! We are here." William tries vainly to interrupt. "I tell him, Will, you are a good writer. I say this to him. But it takes the time. He wants to make the money from it now. He wants all the nice things he never had. I understand this. I do, Gordon. But not tomorrow. He wants it *yesterday!*"

William stays silent for a while, watching the water lilies gently bob. So much life beneath the stillness. He wonders if there are frogs here this time of the year.

Finally he responds, still gazing at the water. "It's hard to imagine what it's like to be poor, Lu. If you've never been there." She starts to pick at her hands. William watches. "What do your parents think of him?"

He has no idea why he asks this. It's not as if he isn't all too aware of the disapproval, the sneery rumblings that used to cause such pain and anger and feed his own lack of self-worth, like blood to a tumour. Perhaps it still smarts, he thinks with some sadness, even after so many things – and people – are dead and buried. Even after he had thought these feelings were buried with them.

"WHO CARES WHAT MY PARENTS ARE THINKING?! I am NOT my—"

He wonders if they can hear the shouting, back where she is. She's certainly looking around, a bit shamefaced. "Oh, excuse me. I am Spanish – always the shouting."

Shame the nun didn't hear it, he thinks. It might have finally sent her packing. (Where, sadly, a middle-aged Scot talking to his imaginary friend clearly hasn't.)

But now he's stumped.

He knows that there is something he has to tell her, some important wisdom that he needs to impart. A gentle but firm warning from a friend that will hopefully change her life going forward and equally hopefully his.

Yet this is something so out of left field, so intrusive and intimate, not to mention fundamental, that there is absolutely no way he can get there with this person. Someone who believes that he is nothing other than a kindly, if somewhat eccentric, stranger.

Then the drums begin.

They're still far off but he notices that Lu has unclasped her slim fingers and is tapping her guidebook. His old Seville guidebook with its Semana Santa section, the fragment so recently quoted by Luisa in her 'rain-warning'. The tiny sapphire in her ring sparkles as it catches the light. He bought that ring for their engagement, he recalls, from a stall in The Barrers, the huge Glasgow bric-a-brac market. Luisa had it reset in an elegantly thin, silver band, on – when was it – of course, their twenty-fifth.

Okay, so Lu can hear them too. Not the same drums surely – he has no idea how long drums survive – but most probably played to the same rhythm, accompanying the local procession at a similar time. There are not so many options and the great cathedral figures in them all. The idle tapping on the guidebook continues.

A long-buried memory now suddenly surges, sparked by the drums and the guidebook.

Yet a memory of something not in truth experienced. Neither then nor this time round.

Never too late.

He leaps up, looking back down at her hands as they grip the precious volume, encouraging her to join him. "You know, Lu, there's something I've been wanting to see for thirty years."

She knows that she should be getting back to Will. But he has told her that he wishes to write. Just for a couple of hours. Hours in which she could have found that watch.

But there is still time.

CHAPTER THIRTY-NINE

THE LIGHT INSIDE THE small chapel is dim, sepulchral.

Its heavy wooden doors are partially closed, with just enough room for the odd intrigued visitor to slip in. Most are content to wait outside.

A massive float rests on the ground in the semi-darkness, her ancient gold glistening. Candles are being carefully lit and freshly-cut flowers strewn, awaiting the final adornments. The Blessed Virgin looks down on her devoted band of brothers and sisters, as patient and indulgent as ever.

This *paso* reminds William of a prone camel, patiently resting in anticipation of an important passenger and a strenuous journey. The legs it requires to unfold, flex and ease itself jerkily upwards, however, are not its own but those of the devout huddle of white-vested men, the *costaleros*, currently swigging from water bottles and deftly winding thick cloth "turbans" around their heads, as they await the orders of their boss, *el capataz*.

Outside, in the narrow streets, the cohorts of Nazarenos and cross-bearers chat volubly and swap news, in order to get in as much soccer, gossip and bullshit before the long, slow silence of the procession.

William wonders if silence is more excruciating for Spaniards. He doesn't, however, express this notion to his guest, as it might appear inappropriate and she is in any case too involved in whatever she is looking at. Which he prays – to whoever is around – approximates in some decent measure to what he himself is observing.

As if on a signal, the sturdy men manoeuvre themselves beneath the enormous structure, ready to hoist it up.

"Lucky they're all much the same height," remarks William, "or Mary'd be in for a bumpy ride. Mind you, I've seen them stop at times for liquid refreshment and it hasn't hasn't always been water." He laughs to himself. "By the end of a long evening, Mary and her special son can be seen bopping around up there like they're having quite a party." He wonders for a moment if he is being disrespectful. After all, this Luisa still wears the tiny silver cross at her throat.

Yet he doubts Lu is listening. She watches spellbound – curiously, she has never thought to catch a procession at *salida*, its very commencement. Glancing at her, William begins his hastily conceived and most probably supremely inept master plan. He looks again at her guidebook, as if he has the power to reach beneath its glossy covers.

Here goes.

"Someone once told me, Lu, that there are 115 processions this week! Imagine, *115*! And each one starts off from its own wee parish church – just like this one – at exactly the same time every year." He turns nervously towards her. "You *can* see the float, Lu?" She looks at him as if he is mad, then simply nods. Perhaps in order not to derange him further.

"Anyway," he continues, briskly. "See, each one sets off on its own journey – same time, same place." He pauses, because he needs his next words to register, however mundane they may sound at first hearing. *"Unless, of course, it rains."*

She simply nods. Makes sense. As his daughter would probably say, no biggie. But he has more.

"Then obviously it's far too risky. I mean, some of these floats go back to the thirteenth century. That's even older than me!" He laughs, so she smiles politely, clearly more fascinated by the preparation than the conversation. "So – if rain stops play," he persists, "and things aren't *exactly* right, Lu – she just waits patiently for the next year." He waits not quite so patiently. Finally, after some seconds, she responds.

"And if it is raining the next year?"

Now she is on board – now he can dial up the intensity. "Well – there's a right time for everything, isn't there? Y'know, processions, honeymoons—" He turns to her and raises his voice above the clamour that is slowly building around him. "*—Niños.*"

She looks at him and is clearly surprised by the fervour that makes his blue eyes gleam in the darkness, like the tiny facets of her antique ring.

"Aye. Time it wrong, Lu, and things can get spoiled. As Rabbie Burns said, 'the best laid schemes o' mice 'n men gang aft a-gley.'" As she stares he ramps it up, to compensate for the dimness in the lighting and perhaps the obscurity of his reference. "Aye, plans can get ruined, Lu. Maybe forever. *Trust me, dear,* I know whereof I speak."

William fears he may be seriously overdoing it, metaphoring himself into obscurity. Yet he can tell that she is listening. He can almost see her mind processing this, accustomed as he is, after all these years, to the slightest shift in her expression. Time for a lightness of touch.

"Which is probably why we Brits always carry precautionary measures." As she turns to stare at him, he digs into his laptop bag and pulls out the least expected item from within its folds. "*Our trusty brollies! Da dah!*"

He waves his cheap, retractable umbrella jokily in the air and is relieved to see her smile. And indeed offer a slight nod, as if she might just possibly be starting to catch on. Big if, he thinks, but then notices, as the sleeve of his jacket glides up, that her attention has shifted to his watch. Without asking, she touches it, yet so delicately that he barely feels the pressure on his wrist.

She looks softly into his eyes.

It's a look he hasn't seen before, at least not this time round. Or at least not aimed at him. He intends simply to stare back at her and smile in a deeply meaningful way, as if somehow to nail down the points he has made so obliquely. To etch them into her mind. But as he moves towards her, his face just inches away from her own, he breathes in that familiar scent, takes in the almost painful loveliness, and finds himself dissolving, falling into her.

"Luisa—" he murmurs.

A blast of light suddenly hits them as the doors to the church are flung wide open and the huge, gleaming float is finally hoisted up with enormous love and strength to its full, processional height.

His lips gently brush her forehead.

The ancient float moves out of the darkness into the light, like a child leaving the womb.

CHAPTER FORTY

LUISA SUTHERLAND HAS NO idea where her husband has gone, but she has a pretty fair idea where she would like him to go.

After yesterday afternoon's post-*corrida* confrontation, with each partner attempting to insert the ultimate barb and pierce the decisive artery, they had continued the evening in a slow-bleeding silence, broken only by fractured mundanities that made the silence seem like bliss. As if each was watching the other slip farther and farther away, whilst still being mere inches apart.

Luisa has a vague memory of William whispering goodbye to her in the bedroom this morning. She was struggling to cling on to sleep, like a shaky bridge on the verge of collapse, yet has no real clue as to the literality of her husband's farewell. But he's certainly not out here with her now, enjoying a late breakfast on the hotel terrace. A breakfast she hardly eats. So perhaps it was exactly as he had spoken.

Even though she is quite in the shade, under a bright umbrella, Luisa still wears her sunglasses. She knows that beneath them she looks ravaged, although she can't actually remember crying. Perhaps it was in that rocky sleep.

"Excuse me? Er, *scusa mia*?"

She hadn't noticed the two ladies from New York, but they have clearly been noticing her. Their warm smiles don't quite mask the intense curiosity in their faces, as they stare at her and more especially at the vacant space beside her.

Luisa turns, instinctively removing her shades, so that she can engage with these total strangers more politely. Even though this is the last thing she wishes to do. She realises how British she has become, after all these years away from home.

The shock on the ladies' faces is instant and ever more transparent as they try feebly to disguise it. "Is okay. I – get the hay fever," explains Luisa.

The women nod and cock their heads to the same side sympathetically, although they clearly don't believe this for one moment.

"Oh, poor you!" says Marilyn. Then, all sympathy done, she thrusts her iPad at Luisa. "We were just wondering – could you take our photo?"

"We've seen you in town," endorses Shelby. "You know your way around a camera."

"*We're on our honeymoon!*" Marilyn almost yells this out. Luisa isn't sure whether this is simply background information or some sort of threat that if the photo isn't up to scratch it could blight the most important moment of their lives.

"They'll have to reconsecrate the whole of Seville after

this!" laughs Shelby, lightening the mood for at least one of her listeners.

Luisa, despite everything, is a professional. She takes the iPad and stands up. Moving around, she estimates where light and shadow best suit her subjects, whilst those subjects scrape their chairs around noisily, leaning as one in every direction to ensure they're both firmly in shot. The photographer dearly wishes she had lenses and dials to fiddle with, and some rope to tie the wrigglers down, but agrees to work around these limitations.

As she takes the first of what she imagines will be a considerable range of shots, in order to achieve the yearned-for result, a third party intrudes on the marriage. Pablo's concerned head has bobbed in from the side and is staring directly into the iPad.

"*Señora – aeropuerto?*"

Luisa watches the ecstatic if somewhat frozen smile on Marilyn's face dissolve. "The *airport!*"

The iPad nods.

"You're going to *miss* Easter Sunday?" says Shelby.

Luisa just sighs. "It cannot match the first one."

The New York ladies nod.

"Hard act to follow," says Marilyn.

CHAPTER FORTY-ONE

WILLIAM HAD NO IDEA that, in his absence, Seville has become such a modern, dynamic, avant-garde city. He feels that someone should have told him.

He realises that he is far more at home here, in the shadows of groundbreaking architecture such as he has just unwittingly encountered: the startling high-rise towers, the stunning new bridges, vibrant thoroughfares where history and ritual don't assail him at every turn. And he can maintain the comforting sense that commerce is still the major religion of the world.

He left Lu, somewhat reluctantly, a while ago. Hopefully now with more pressing thoughts in her head than simply buying him the watch he has been constantly wearing these past thirty years. Since then he has been wandering aimlessly around the throbbing new city, smoking his anxious way through his first ever packet of Ducados, which he reckons taste as bad as they smell.

He must have a Scotch.

Just one.

Or a couple.

While he waits for the world as he knows it to end. Or, more hopefully, to begin.

It's in the lap of – whoever, now.

*

Will isn't touching his beer.

It has been warming beside him, on his usual table at the Yellow Café, all the time he has been writing. He is perfectly aware that, when he is in creative mode, the drink – whether it be soft or hard, hot or cold – is simply his entry fee to sit for hours and piss off busy waiters. The guys who clearly prefer a table to be occupied by customers who drink like fish, eat like pigs and tip like they don't know the exchange rate. He once expressed curiosity as to whether Jean Paul Sartre did the same at Les Deux Magots in Paris, but Lu didn't know what he was talking about, so he pursued the conceit no further.

He hasn't yet noticed Lu, who watches him from a corner of the square. He is rarely aware of her observing him "at work", which she does quite often, or of the overwhelming love she feels at these moments. A love combined with an envious awe that someone can be so lost in the world of his own imagination that he is totally untouched by any of life's more readily accessed wonders.

As she finally approaches his table, she notices, on the vacant seat next to him, a small gift-bag from a local store. It could, of course, be something he has bought for himself. But, as he never buys anything for himself, because somewhere rooted deep inside him is the sense that he doesn't ever merit a treat or reward, it's a pretty safe bet that the gift is for her.

The first time he is aware of her approach is when she leans over to kiss him away from his narrative and simultaneously scoops up the gift-bag in a single whisk. Before he can stop her, she manages to pull out a little red beret, almost the same shade as the leather bag she is carrying. She has it halfway to her head before he shakes his own.

"Hey, you! That isn't for now."

"When it is for?"

"I'll tell you when it is for when we get to when it is for."

"You are the spoiling-sport," she chides, dropping the soft beret back, with exaggerated regret, into its temporary home. "Well, then, you cannot have what it is I have for you, until this time also."

He laughs, pulls her close to him for a hug and swiftly rummages in her bag as it hangs on her shoulder. Before she can stop him, he whips out a small, paper sack nestling on the top and withdraws it with an almost theatrical flourish. She grabs it back in some desperation, before he can open it, most probably because she doesn't want the world to see what she has just purchased from the local *farmacia*.

"This is not the thing!" she admonishes. "Now you must buy me *fino* and you read me what it is you have written."

He shrugs and lifts his pad with a flourish, preparing to impress her with flowery paragraphs she cannot yet fully understand. He is perfectly content to know that she will praise him unreservedly, regardless of comprehension, and give him the simple strength to carry on. He has never loved her more than at these moments and hopes that this will go on forever, although he strongly suspects that honeymoons never do.

A chill suddenly passes over him, as he thinks that he won't ever again be as happy as he is right now. And yet still he wonders, just for a moment, how he might enjoy right now even more.

CHAPTER FORTY-TWO

WILLIAM SUTHERLAND HAS NEVER been so scared in his life.

He had assumed that the whisky would calm his nerves. Or, if this didn't quite work, the second or third shot, along with those disgusting cigarettes, might just dull the edges. Yet, if he had to describe himself at this moment, the words "intensely sober" would spring to mind. A descriptor he has not hitherto found necessary nor the least bit useful.

There is something in the air and this time it isn't the Ducados.

The sky is as relentlessly blue and cloudless as ever, the Andalusian sun scorching believers and apostates alike, yet he can sense within the outward calm a definite trembling.

It is as if the world is gearing up for something, or a vigorous storm is due, but he knows that this is more of a British thing, where it seems you can't have three days of fierce and clammy heat without the heavens getting all overwhelmed and teary. Yet the universe does appear disturbingly askew right now, unsettled, an elemental mirroring of how he himself feels inside.

Or perhaps, in his arrogance, he is simply globalising his own, small-scale but intensely real panic.

William is almost relieved to see the familiar purple minivan parked outside the hotel as he begins his walk up the pebbled drive. His old pal Pablo is there too, gently ushering in the latest visitor, hefting her expensively smart leather case with the spryness of a man half his age. He notices William and waves in recognition. William feels inordinately pleased to see the old guy, although if he mentions Manchester United one more time he may just rip his lungs out.

This new guest looks rather elegant, he thinks, even from the back, as a set of well-manicured fingers dip crisply into a large and expensively soft, leather bag. She is not young: her clothes are too smart and timeless. Yet she is clearly fit and agile, the firm muscles in her tanned legs made more striking by the height of her heels, as she takes the steps to the door with a noticeable briskness.

Here is someone who obviously looks after herself, he reckons, because she clearly feels she is worth looking after. And who, judging by the instantly deferential look on the doorman, expects others to do the same.

As she disappears, this person who seems so at ease and at home, in a way he recognises he seldom is, William finds himself remaining in the courtyard, almost paralysed with anxiety.

Is the Luisa Sutherland he will very soon encounter going to be unchanged – when he turns up again, after so many hours, in their 'second honeymoon suite'? Or have her memories (and his too, presumably), alongside their histories and their lives, been irrevocably altered by today's not so subtle nudges. Transmuted by what he might just possibly have caused to come to pass thirty long years ago.

His head is reeling too much to ascertain what is really going on inside there. Or to consider any possible ramifications.

Perhaps, he thinks, he should simply prepare himself for one suitcase less, in a suddenly stark hotel room formerly occupied by a wife who, not unreasonably, grew tired of waiting.

She could be on her way to the airport right now, for all he knows, with that same angry cabbie. To be met just a few hours later by her duplicitous, crooked-nosed, smooth-talking lover. And, indeed, how could he blame her?

Or perhaps not. If all has gone according to what he could hyperbolically term a plan.

He suddenly feels an alarming, almost sexual rush of excitement, as it surges with terrifying speed, like an electric charge, through his veins. An oddly primal yet curiously illicit thrill rattles his frame, energising yet disturbing, like nothing he has ever experienced. His heart begins to thump, his breathing becomes more rapid. Sweat forms on his brow, as a fiery contest between overweening ego and genuine apprehension starts to play itself out in his head.

Then, just as swiftly, the 'symptoms' recede.

What the hell?

Not for the first time this week, William Sutherland wonders whether he is slowly going insane.

*

The room is pleasantly dark as William opens the door.

He is not surprised to find the shutters drawn on such a dazzling day. The sounds of the nearby shower in full flow are comfortingly reassuring.

Closing the door, he calls into the bathroom. "Only me!"

The shower finishes and a few seconds later the bathroom door opens.

Into the bedroom steps a shapely young woman, naked save for the large bath-towel she is draping casually around her head. Back-lit to perfection, she skips lightly on damp and immaculately pedicured bare feet to the shutters and sends them flying open.

"Hi, babe," she says, smiling over her shoulder at William. "Get those extra pillows?"

NOW?

CHAPTER FORTY-THREE

THE SHUTTERS BANG AND midday light blasts in on the stranger, in all her unidentifiable glory.

"*AAAHH!! Oh my God! I am SO sorry!*" yells William, immediately swirling away towards the door.

"That's okay," says the young woman cheerily, "no biggie – we can ask for them downstairs, when we go out. Hope you found your cigars."

Cigars?

She trots back into the centre of the room, casually flicking the towel over her glistening body. He can't help but notice that she is very attractive. To his amazement, however, when he fully takes in her smiling face and long, lustrous dark hair, she also looks disturbingly like young Lu.

Yet this is so obviously not Lu, young or old – and she is clearly not in the least embarrassed by his presence. She is either a vaguely demented exhibitionist or something is quite catastrophically awry. William so hopes it is the former.

"*Oh my God!*" is all he can say right now.

"You've seen it before, Willo!" And there goes theory number one.

"Have I?"

"Can you be an angel and pass me my lippy?"

He has no idea where her lippy might be and can only just work out what it might be, but anything that gives him a legitimate reason to turn away from the alluring yet terrifying vision jiggling around before him has its own therapeutic appeal.

Until what he sees in the mirror turns this briefly held assumption to ashes.

"*Oh – sweet – Jesus!*" he says, as the full horror strikes him.

It is still recognisably William Sutherland, but not as he knows it.

The vision before him now has a perma-tan that would make Donald Trump look like a Noh theatrical, a full head of what has to have been horrendously expensive hair, from whomsoever or whatever it came, and no obvious sign of – or need for – spectacles. He is clad in tight-fitting, designer clothing, in which he would never have been allowed to be seen dead, or wished to be seen at all. And yet, as he stares in appalled wonder, it is all just starting to become terrifyingly familiar.

Which is the most alarming sensation of all.

"Honestly?" says his new companion, smiling at him. He remains transfixed by his – or at least *someone's* – reflected image. "You guys are worse than we are. Hey, what time is it over here?"

He checks his watch and recoils yet again, like an over-the-hill boxer being punished for even trying. There, on his expensively bronzed wrist, occupying a slice of bodily real estate that, for exactly thirty years, has been the family home of a stylishly understated, high-end Spanish watch, is a solid gold Rolex about the size of a small meteor.

William knows that, before he slips into stress-induced catatonia, he has rather a lot of questions. Enquiries peculiar to this current stage of what might well be his life but is looking remarkably like somebody else's. Yet perhaps it is simply a life into which he has just stepped for some brief sojourn, like an Airbnb of the spirit.

"Who *are* you?"

She looks puzzled for a moment. He senses fairly swiftly that this may not have been the most prudent query with which to launch.

But then she laughs and puts on a truly appalling Scottish accent. "Well I'm braw, thank you, Wulliam – and hoo's yersel'?" He just nods, bemused. "Actually, I'd be better with my clothes, babe. Unless you were contemplating—?"

"Er no. NO!" he says, in panic, as he realises exactly what she is offering. "But thank you. For asking. You just – get yourself dressed. Now. Please."

She waves a patently gym-toned arm, her eyes still promising wondrous things to come, and trots back into the bathroom. William slumps onto the newly-made bed, wishing that it would gently fold up and clamp itself around his exhausted – albeit reconfigured – body, sucking him swiftly down into oblivion.

The uninhibited young stranger is back in seconds, beside herself with excitement, gesturing frantically towards the TV set.

"Oh – ooh! I forgot," she yelps. "Switch the telly on! Willo – quick!"

Willo?

"What on earth for?"

"You might just catch the end!"

"It's nigh, is it?" he says.

He struggles up from the bed and switches on the TV, to reveal what looks like a Spanish game show in all its blaring garishness. He doesn't understand the language but humiliation is somehow universal.

"*Well?*" demands the young woman, her eyes on the screen.

He steals a swift look at her, but he could be making her the sole subject of an intrusive, no-holds-barred documentary shot in IMAX 70mm and she most probably wouldn't notice. She is utterly transfixed, staring at the wall-mounted television as if it is a friendly, visiting alien and might just have a message pivotal for humanity.

"Well *what*?" dares William, although he has a dreadful feeling that he ought to know.

"I saw it in the lobby when we came in," she explains, sort of. "No offence, but I think you slipped up with the talent."

"Did I? The talent. Uh huh."

Suddenly it no longer seems quite so important that he should know who she is. What would be more infinitely more valuable, at this precise moment, would be to have the vaguest notion who *he* is. If she could just stop jabbering for a second.

"Mind you, perhaps she's perfecto for the Iberian market. 'Culturally appropriate'. What are the ratings? I'm assuming it's being recommissioned."

"Can I – get back to you on that?"

He senses movement beside him and realises that

the young woman is towelling vigorously as she watches, almost in time with the rhythm and mounting excitement of the show itself. If I don't move around, he thinks, I might explode. No man should have to go through this. He wants desperately to cry but it's not something he does and he feels it might not particularly enhance his situation. So pacing is the better option.

He finds, however, that he is not certain how to walk. There is most definitely a confidence in his stride that wasn't there before – perhaps it's the tight clothing – but he also feels that his legs are shaking so much that they're going to give way under such intense anxiety. The combination makes him seem like a drunk trying desperately to appear sober, as he reels around the room. Although, interestingly, the chronic back pain appears to have been sorted.

"Are you sleep-deprived or something?" she asks him in all seriousness. "You didn't even recognise your own programme!" If he could stare at her even more cluelessly, he manages. "*Sooner You Than Me*! – The one we've—" she makes finger-quotes "—'come to check out in Madrid.'"

William must have the appearance of someone whose brain has just ceased to function, because suddenly the young woman seems genuinely concerned.

"Is it your medication? Not going to peg out on me, are you?"

"I'm – hoping not to," he laughs. "Not with the National Television Awards coming up!"

How the hell did I know that? he wonders, having just managed to terrify himself. Or am I simply making it up as I go along?

He can't help staring at her and she's staring back, but not in such a good way as she was.

"Sorry," he says. "Must be jet lag. Ha! LOL." *What?* He'll be doing that finger-quote thing next or the 'I'll call you' gesture with his hand. "You know, you do look *so* like—"

"I mean, how would I explain *that* to your wife!" she continues, then watches him add an open mouth to the picture he is currently presenting. "Willo? You look like you've never seen me before. Oh God, you haven't got that Alz—?"

"*I'm 53!* I think. No, that's probably stayed the same. Only bloody thing that has."

William Sutherland gazes around the still familiar room, like it might provide some welcome answers, and tries to ignore the unfamiliar stranger's less-than-welcome bafflement.

She knows Luisa!

Probably from these damned TV awards, whatever they are. Somehow this makes it all so much worse. An adulterer! A betrayer! A love-cheat! Something of which, for all his sins, he could never have been accused hitherto. That was Luisa's territory and they were moving on from this, weren't they? '*Forgivingness*'.

But hang on, he thinks, as memories about his own past behaviour, brand new memories he most definitely doesn't want, begin to trickle mercilessly in.

"I have to find – an emergency tobacconist's. For – more cigars. Won't be a minute. Okay?"

He looks back at the young woman. She's totally locked-on to the TV. He nods, gives a feeble little wave and leaves the room.

CHAPTER FORTY-FOUR

AS IF TO REASSURE William that God is in Seville and all's right with the world, Pablo is there, waiting inside the open lift. He smiles at William, who manages to produce a small yet quite relieved smile in return, from his rapidly diminishing stock.

To the old man's surprise, this expensively dressed, professionally tanned and scientifically coiffeured guest suddenly grabs him by the wrist, his seizing-arm weighed down with the most massive gold watch the shocked employee has ever seen.

"*Señora Sutherland?*" yells William, into the man's face.

Pablo's eyes light up and he gives William a grin that is one part envy, one part admiration and a good slug of friendly disapproval. "*Ah! Señora Sutherland. Ooh. Bonito!*"

"Eh?" says William, confused. Until it registers. "No. No! Señora! … Señora *Luisa*! Older – maybe not quite as bon—" He tries to describe Luisa with his hands, in a vaguely geometrical way that Luisa, had she been here, might not find totally flattering. But then, of course, were Luisa still occupying room 381, he most probably wouldn't be outside it, clamping onto a poor hotel porter in total desperation, correcting him on the exact dimensions of his wife.

After the confused man has shaken his head a few too many times, William releases him.

"No, of course you haven't seen her. She's probably still back in Richmond, or wherever we live these days." He presses the lift-button himself. "This isn't the story I meant to write, Pablo. Cheating on the poor woman with some perky young – clone. *OMG – how many times have I done this?!* And when did I start saying OMG?!"

He catches himself in the mirror that takes up the entire rear of the lift and has to smile. "Mind you, I am bloody successful. Check out the TV in the lobby, pal. When you get the chance."

*

William knows that he can't stay away from that steamy hotel bedroom for too long.

It feels like the only place in town where he might be able to figure out what on earth is going on, although he already has a rough idea and it scares the hell out of him.

And there is still a sense, albeit sadly receding, that if he flops onto that comfy bed and falls into the sleep he so desperately needs, he may just wake up to find that this has all been a product of his not-yet-quite-moribund imagination. Or simply another out-of-body episode in the lunacy that consumes this particular week.

Yet something tells him that if he does actually make the tempting glide between those newly pressed, snowy-white sheets back in *habitacion* 381, he is not going to be enjoying much sleep.

As he walks past the old cathedral, stern and inscrutable as ever, he looks up once more at the towering La Giralda. William has no idea why his eyes are constantly drawing him towards this particular monument, with its seamless blend of the Moorish and the Christian. He simply supposes that this is what landmarks are designed to do or else they wouldn't take up valuable postcard space. He recalls that Luisa would often take him to an excellent but not inexpensive restaurant called La Giralda, in the leafy London suburb of Pinner, when she had an atavistic yearning for Spanish food but no desire to brave the West End to sate it. It seems like such a lifetime ago.

He burrows into his hip pocket for his trusty mobile, as he usually does every five minutes, albeit in less tight-fitting trousers, yet this time it is for different and markedly uncommercial reasons. He is surprised to discover, although by now he really shouldn't be, that the phone in his newly burnished hand is the fruit of a rather different vine. He finds himself rather liking the look and the heft of this unfamiliar machine, undoubtedly at the very summit of its range (*he's Willo Sutherland, for God's sake!*), at the same time as he is horrified by it.

Once he has fathomed out its functions, he checks his list of contacts, which is pretty extensive, although none of the names mean a thing at first glance. Which is not to say he hasn't actually heard of any of them but the fact they may also have heard of him smacks of new, yet not entirely unflattering, information. He wonders if this is what schizophrenia or dissociative personality feels like, although he suspects those poor folk don't dress quite so snappily.

Without thinking, he dials a number he has known for years, which has previously been accessible at the simple touch of a button. A woman answers but he doesn't recognise the voice.

"Hello?" he says, anxiously. "Who's that? ... Can I speak to Suzy, please? ... *My PA!* ... Oh – I must have the wrong... Sorry."

As he is clearly in a totally different line of work these days, there is no reason in the world why Suzy should still be his loyal PA. Still, he will miss her. He wonders what she is doing now. But he doesn't wonder for long, as he is already checking through the bank of stored photos in his new toy.

He employs his curious, yet increasingly confident game-show producer walk to weave through the distinctly less confused visitors to old Seville. Most of these are also using their phones for photographic purposes but they probably have at least some knowledge as to what photos they have already taken.

There aren't actually many pictures on his phone, so he obviously hasn't become any more interested in photography than he was before. Luisa is the photographer in the family, he thinks, not without some genuine warmth and pride. Especially considering he is cheating on her in a major way and the evidence of his deceit is currently riveted to a noisy TV programme, in a language she doesn't understand, not so many metres from here. (He feels thankful that his own daughter isn't involved with a dirty old man like him and wonders why on earth this clearly bright but demonstrably young person in room 381 would be. Although, let's be honest, he tells himself – you do have a certain mature, man-of-the-world appeal, Willo. And you're not *that* old.)

What does surprise William – along with all the other major shocks to his system – is that he doesn't actually feel quite as guilty towards Luisa as he reckons he should. As the William Sutherland he believes he still knows certainly should. Perhaps contrition is simply sidelined right now by that far more potent driver, revenge, considering her own past dalliance. Yet even this urge doesn't appear to be inflaming him with the same red-hot fury as so very recently. Maybe, he surmises, not unpleasurably, it didn't even happen this time round. Or it could simply be that deep down he's just shallow.

His attention is suddenly captured by a photo that knocks him sideways. Hey, look at this – me with the late, great Michael Jackson! Both of us giving a beaming thumbs-up into the camera.

"*Now we are talking!*" says William Sutherland, out loud.

When people begin to stare, he feels a curious urge to show them the photo. Who wouldn't? Yet he wisely resists and simply slips the classy new phone back into his classy new pocket.

Intrigued, yet still some good way from undisturbed, William seeks out what other treasures may be in there, as if it's some sort of amnesiac lucky dip. Ooh, car keys – to an Aston Martin! Some white pills in an unlabelled container – no idea what they are, but he should probably keep taking them, and finally, in another pocket of his shiny blouson (*who wears blousons? I do!*) a Cuban cigar in its slim, tin tube. So that's his errand completed.

He feels it's time to check out his new image once more before he heads back, just in case another change is in progress. A shop window provides him with much to reflect on.

William Sutherland Mark Two still takes him by surprise and still scares him more than a little, even as it slowly begins to impress. Something deep inside, a thought screaming to be heard within the demented soundscape of his mind, tells him that he really ought to fight off the getting too accustomed to this new and startling biography. And that, unlike the city where it is happening, this particular mystical blending of the ancient and modern is leading to madness rather than harmony.

The shop window is a riot of hand-painted fans, some clearly very old. Sensibly displayed wide open, in an array of colours, they proudly reveal their finely detailed craftsmanship. Not the least interested in decorative fans but drawn by reflective glass, he decides to check his reflection once again.

An attractive woman of around Luisa's age skips out of the shop with her husband. She is clasping a brand-new fan in evident delight. With a jubilant flourish she raises it above her head and makes a jokey, cod-sultry flamenco movement, which causes her husband to laugh and William to feel painfully wistful, although he can't compute exactly why.

He has to get back to that room. But there is one burning question he must ask on the way.

*

The young receptionist smiles at him as he approaches her desk.

"Room 381," says William. "The lady I am with—"

"There is a problem, Señor?"

"No, no. Not at all. Do you happen to know her name?"

*

Sooner You Than Me, a sentiment William endorses to the hilt, has finished by the time he returns to the room.

The excitable young woman is looking fresh and lovely, in a bright and very short summery dress, long slim legs tapering down to what seem to William the sort of shoes Luisa might own, only a bit glitzier, attached to heels of a height he knows she would never sport. Not if she wanted to do a decent walk in a city without aching for days afterwards.

"You took your time," she says.

"Sorry – *Tazmin*," he replies, emphatically. "Had to go to Cuba! Ha!"

"So – what are we going to do today?"

"Er… what would you like to do, *Tazmin*?"

"Everything!" she declares. "*William*."

CHAPTER FORTY-FIVE

EVERYTHING! IS EXACTLY WHAT William Sutherland and Tazmin Whatsername do on their first afternoon and evening here in Seville.

They walk the extraordinary city he feels he has been walking his entire life, yet apparently he just arrived here a few hours ago. He can't help noticing that his companion is more entranced by the designer shops than the historic buildings, but he manages to temper his disapproval by recalling that he didn't want to be here for any of it, until he tripped over a pew and met his wife's younger self in a cathedral and his whole world began to unravel.

He finds himself staring unblinkingly at the young woman, which she simply takes as her due. She has no idea that she reminds him so much, at least superficially, of someone he used to know. He wonders if he has had other affairs like this and if the young women have all shared a similarity, of sorts, to the one on whom he is cheating. Or at least her far younger version.

Fortunately, Tazmin is completely unaware of the puzzlement that clouds her lover's face, as they explore the tiny streets and even tinier boutiques. He is quite amazed at how much she can talk, without pausing for breath, and how little interest she has in anything he might have to say. Not that, to be honest, he is actually saying anything of overwhelming interest right now, if indeed he is even capable of doing so. He is almost relieved that his companion is stuck in transmit-only mode, as it gives him time to think.

He just wishes his thoughts could amount to something more practical than "get me the hell out of this" and "kill me now". If he could only find his way back home to Luisa (wherever home is; he'd need to check that out subtly with reception) then maybe things might sort themselves out.

Perhaps hope has not died after all.

This suddenly sparks off a fragment of another vague thought, something darker, unformed yet dreadful, that unleashes a chilling, almost visceral terror deep inside him, causing his heart to thud like a Sevillian drum and the sweat to pour once again. He can't quite get there. Not yet. Especially not with all the excited chatter just a few delicately scented inches away.

But he will.

He knows and he fears that he will.

Several shopping sprees and sangrias later, night begins to fall. They find themselves snacking on the tapas for which Seville is justly famous and through which Tazmin is making staggering inroads. He silently prays that these aren't mere appetisers for whatever else she may have in mind.

Then they hear the trumpets.

William swiftly grabs Tazmin and practically drags her out of the bar, pickled octopus in hand, for no better reason than this is something he feels the young woman must see and it may even stop her talking for a few blessed moments, although he has his doubts.

It soon becomes clear that, whilst Tazmin is sufficiently awestruck by the 'gobsmacking' candlelit procession to upload its highlights on her Facebook page, alongside pictures of every single tapas she has just tried, this is not the defining moment for her that it was for him when he first encountered it so many lifetimes ago. But then, he reasons, this young person hasn't been graced with the sort of spirited and spiritual guide he had first time round.

The insistent rhythm of the drums, solemn as it is, puts Tazmin in the mood for dancing. It isn't long before she drags William off in the direction of a new club she has tracked down on TripAdvisor ("*best disco in town – be prepared to stand*").

It is when she is leading him away that he feels a pair of eyes on him. Turning back to the procession, William sees that one of the Nazarenos, this time clad all in red, is not looking straight ahead like his myriad fellows, lost in his own spiritual world, but is staring directly at him. There is something about those penetrating yet soulful eyes that is curiously familiar.

He shakes his head vigorously, as if this might just ward off impending doom, but it is at this point that Tazmin happens to turn back and notice him. With a smile full of misguided understanding, she nods and runs a delicate hand across the upper part of his thigh. Yes indeed, perhaps they should just go back to their room.

Clubbing can wait until tomorrow. There are other ways to break into a sweat.

Oh God, thinks William, turning back to the Nazareno. But, whoever he was, he has gone.

An elderly man is sufficiently moved to render a croaky but impassioned *saeta* from his balcony, which makes Tazmin think it really is time to move on.

*

Pablo is manning the lift when they return but this doesn't appear to impede the flow.

"I didn't do politics at Warwick to produce tacky game shows all my life. No offence. The thing about television is you have to think outside the box. Are you ok, Willo?"

"*Buenos noches, Pablo,*" says William tiredly, ignoring the man's exaggerated winks and knowing smiles. He realises that there is no way in this incarnation that he could have known the name of the old fellow – the man wears no identifying badge – but Pablo doesn't appear in the least surprised.

As soon as they enter the room, Tazmin hurls her bulging bag of souvenirs onto the table. They hear the clack of all the "hand-carved", genuine flamenco castanets she has bought for her many nephews and nieces. In one smoothly choreographed movement, she swivels and switches on the TV. Clearly she has no intention of watching but it appears to be the natural background to whatever it is that she does intend and which cannot apparently be effected in silence.

"When you picked me out of all the candidates – even though I knew sod all about TV-prod, well, I thought – he must see *something* in me. And I don't mean 'you know'. You're not that sad. Are you?"

"Possibly," admits William. He watches her kick off her shoes and begin to massage her feet. He finds himself thinking that she really does have sensational legs. Perhaps he truly is this sad. "Time for a drink!"

"Haven't you—?"

"Drunk enough?" He knows that he had been hitting the Rioja pretty hard at that tapas bar. Who wouldn't? Yet he also knows that the blurriness in his aching head has nothing to do with alcohol. "Couldn't happen."

Tazmin suddenly shoots up and scurries across the room at some speed.

"*Lu!*" she cries.

William is immediately alert.

"WHAT did you say?" he shouts back.

For a moment the young woman looks alarmed. "I need the loo, William." She smiles through the discomfort. "This is a killing place. What on earth made you think of it?"

She closes the bathroom door, emphasising the question's rhetorical nature.But he answers her anyway.

"I have absolutely no idea," he replies, quite honestly.

CHAPTER FORTY-SIX

AS IT BECOMES INCREASINGLY clear that Tazmin Whoever is in the bathroom for the long haul, William Sutherland – Willo, to Lord knows who – mixes himself the strongest drink he can take without collapsing and walks out onto the balcony.

He gazes over the sparkling old city, its celebrated monuments cleverly illuminated to enhance their grandeur whilst still preserving their dignity. But they give him no pleasure. The ironwork of this elegant balcony might as well be bars of a cage, he thinks, or a prison cell designed by a master sadist. No, by Kafka. By a sadist who has read Kafka. He has no idea what the night has in store nor whether he will even survive it. Perhaps this is what those pills were for.

William really does feel quite sorry for himself, sorry for what he is fast becoming and for what he may well have wrought. Sorry too for Luisa, innocently thinking that he is 'in Madrid' (*finger-quotes*) on some spurious game show business. And also for young Tazmin, who apparently knows Luisa (and even creepily resembles her!)

yet inexplicably is here with him this holy, tawdry week. Does she have an agenda or is it he who is power-broker and the cards are unfairly stacked?

He does also wonder if such compassion on his part, or at least insight, will all too soon vanish, along with his long-established world view and whatever values he may once have had. Plus all those former, now clearly unsubstantiated memories.

Without pleasure, he takes a deep, audible breath, as if hoping the orange and jacaranda-infused bouquet of this unending spring evening might clear his befuddled head.

And then he hears it.

Another breath, equally deep yet infinitely more embracing. It seems to come from the balcony adjoining his own.

William turns slowly, to see the confidently elegant woman he believes he first glimpsed when she arrived here earlier today with Pablo. But he sees her now in angled profile. She sips white wine and is smoking a slim cigarette. As her head moves slowly round towards him, he decides his own serious drinking must have kicked in after all. Because he can't really be seeing this.

"*LUISA*?"

The woman spins round. And stares at him really hard. She shakes her head. Moves closer. Stares even harder.

"*Madre de Dios!* Is it? No! *William?*"

The glass falls from her hand and smashes into jagged crystals on the solid, tiled floor, the wine trickling swiftly down into the runnels. Her feet are bare, so she has to skitter instantly away from the danger, causing her to move even further towards him.

There's no question now, thinks William, in total shock. This woman, in a casually smart outfit he has never seen before, sporting a cool and clearly expensive hairstyle that is totally unfamiliar, is Luisa.

Yet a strangely different Luisa.

More stylish and sophisticated than he has ever known her. Trimmer, certainly; firmer, possibly; with a harder, more brittle edge that is evident in every movement she makes, every syllable she utters.

How can this be the woman he knows so well, whom he has known for over thirty years and left sleeping only this morning? In the same bed that is behind him now. Before he set off on his mischief.

The woman who, even in this seriously warped scenario, should be waiting for him back home, in some upmarket Greater London suburb.

So how comes she barely recognised him? Or he her?

And *smoking*?

"What are you doing here?" he demands, in fearful wonder. "Next door to me?"

"I ask you same thing! What do you do in Sevilla? Business?"

She looks genuinely surprised. As if he, William Sutherland, is the last person Luisa would have ever expected to see here in Seville, this week of all weeks. In the adjoining room. At the same hotel.

And the awful – yet now so painfully obvious – truth smacks William right in the heart.

He realises with a sad immediacy that if he is not to jump screaming off the balcony or collapse into a gibbering heap right here on the omni-bloody-present tiles, he has to work unquestioningly within these new parameters that he has just been given. To be a serious player in this topsy-turvy, down-the-rabbit-hole game.

At the same time, he has to sound like this is all perfectly, delightfully normal. That his mad fantastical storybook world hasn't just segued in moments from Gabriel García Márquez into Noël Coward.

"Oh. No. Not business," he says, ever so casually. "Just, y'know, passing through. Bit of much needed R 'n' R. But you look—"

"Older."

"No! Well, yes. Mebbe. No – you look – different. Aye. Different."

She smiles at this, as she tries delicately to avoid the wine-spill. He notices that she wears turquoise varnish on her toes. When did she start doing that, for pity's sake? But he soon has larger concerns than her pedicure.

"Different to who?" She smiles. "The young girl who went off in a London taxi twenty-eight years ago?"

Excuse me?

For quite some moments, William finds that he can't respond. The calculator in his brain is trying to convert a random figure into something that makes at least a scintilla of sense.

"*TWENTY-EIGHT YEARS?*"

It still comes out as a shriek that screams into the orange-blossomed air. Which he hopes no one else can hear.

"*Sí*. Time fly, eh? But you look – well, at least you have kept your hair." She moves closer to him. "Or somebody's."

He shrugs. He's certainly not going to justify a hairweave to this person, nor in fact anything else that has been done to him, at most probably enormous cost. Stuff that he can't as yet recall but is pretty certain he will in time. It just depends how long the fifty-three-year-old brain takes to reboot – when its wiring has been drastically abused and its memory given the most cataclysmic shock to its system.

Luisa can't help but register the look of total bewilderment on the face of her short-lived ex-husband, no matter how hard he strives for normality. Not unnaturally, she puts it down to his surprise at encountering her once more. Here, in the very city where they honeymooned, exactly three decades ago. She also notices that he keeps looking behind him into the bedroom.

"You are with someone. Your wife?"

"No. She's nothing like my wife – I'm assuming." The look of instant disapproval on her face makes William bristle. "*Oh come on, you can talk!*"

She seems quite taken aback by this. He realises that, of course, in this new reality, she most probably can talk and indeed just has. Without any trace of adulterous guilt. "So – what about you, Luisa?" he asks, adroitly changing the subject.

"Well – I did marry again, William. *Sí*. After our 'quickie'. But you know this." (*I don't as yet, Luisa, he thinks, but I'm bloody sure I will.*) "I am the optimist, yes? The glass half-full!" She looks down at her bare feet and smiles. "Well, until I see you."

"Yeah."

He realises that he has always loved Luisa's feet. He finds large feet rather intimidating but hers were and still are, even with their vivid embellishments, quite delightful.

He also realises he shouldn't spend many more seconds admiring them. He nods towards her bedroom. "Is he—?

"We are not together."

"Oh, that is *excellent*!" he says, almost punching the air, until he realises she isn't quite so exultant. "I am so sorry, Luisa. Kids all grown up?"

She shakes her head with a motion so brusque and firm that he immediately understands this is not an area ripe for further exploration. "And how about you?" she offers, swiftly enough for it to appear a change of subject, although it is very much the same.

"What?"

"Did you finally find that 'window'– for children?"

Now, quite unexpectedly, the terrible thought that has been lurking half-formed in his reeling head comes barrelling in, with a force that sucks the breath from his body and sends him grasping for the handrail.

"*CLAIRE!*"

He cries it out as his hand burrows into the unfamiliar, too-tight trousers for his wallet. He produces a Gucci billfold, which feels like someone else's that he has pocketed in error. There is no photo "frame" inside. No picture of his own wee smiling, gap-toothed, adopted daughter.

No Clairey.

There is little mistaking his desolation, yet Luisa does just this. Although even she is alarmed by the vehemence with which the man just yelled out his daughter's name.

"Well, I am glad for you. Fathers and daughters. Is special, no?"

He doesn't answer. He has turned his ravaged face skywards, as if the heavens might in some way provide a solution. Cursing himself that his beloved daughter hadn't been the first thing on his broken mind.

"So. Quite a coincidence," she continues. No response. "*William?*"

"Eh? Er – well, we did say we'd come back here in thirty years, Luisa. Ha! A promise is a promise."

"But I have a meeting here."

"A meeting? Oh. Right."

He is at a total loss as to where they go from here, but he knows for sure that they have to go somewhere, or he is indeed totally lost.

"Luisa, you don't fancy—?"

"Climbing over the balcony? No, William."

"No. No. A drink. You know, a – wee nightcap. Not in here. Obviously."

"It is very late, William," she protests.

"It isn't! Not for Seville. Sevilla. Please, Luisa? For – old time's sake."

"If I remember, they were not so good. The old times."

Weren't they?

"Here they were. On our honeymoon. I'll square it with – whatsername."

Luisa shakes her head, but she is smiling. It is not a smile he recognises. It is a smile that belongs to a different Luisa, a Luisa who has had a life of which he been no part for decades and that sadly he doesn't know at all.

But it will do. For now.

It will have to.

She checks her watch, which he can tell is more expensive than anything he might or could have bought her. Or that she – the other she, the one who clearly no longer exists – would have dared to buy for herself.

"In the lobby. Ten minutes," she says.

He nods gratefully to this stranger and walks back into his room.

CHAPTER FORTY-SEVEN

WILLIAM IS NOT ACCUSTOMED to stealth, nor built for it.

Even on tiptoes he can usually be heard through tightly closed doors. He is also not entirely certain that right now stealth is the most sensible solution. But he allows himself some slack. When you encounter your wife of thirty years, whom you only recently left in bed, and she tells you that she walked out on you in 1997, you can probably be forgiven for lacking a foolproof strategy.

"*Willo?*"

The proof that he's a fool is calling to him from the bathroom.

"Mm?"

"Sorry, babe. Bit of a dodgy tapas."

William feels like pointing out it could be any one of twelve. "Well, you just stay there, T-Thomasina, till you feel better."

"Sorry? – I think it was probably the—"

"Probably." He picks up the ice bucket sitting on top of the minibar. "Just going to get some ice."

Before the poor young woman can reply, he is out of the door and summoning the next lift. He leaves the ice bucket on the floor, reminding himself to fill it on his way back, from the machine he noticed way down at the other end of the corridor. Knowing that this is one of those menial tasks he will undoubtedly forget. As Luisa of the long-suffering sighs is never slow to point out.

Well, she was.

Inside the empty lift, which feels more like home than anything else on this batshit-crazy trip, he checks himself out in the mirror. Whilst still vaguely appalled, he is not entirely unimpressed. For the first time in his life he looks – aye, successful. Even if this isn't something he has ever hungered to be successful at.

Or maybe he has. Which is even more scary.

On its way down from tweaking his new hair, which William still does as tentatively as if he were stroking a barely tamed ferret, his unnaturally brown hand brushes over the inside-pocket of the gaudy blouson. It discovers a bulge. Curious, he fishes out a compact portable dictaphone, which he doesn't recall having ever owned. Yet, to his surprise, he knows exactly how it works and what he is going to recite excitedly into its eager memory.

"Idea for game show! Warring couples go back to where they honeymooned."

He immediately hurls the dictaphone into a bin in the corner of the lift. "Shut the FUCK up!" He can't help thinking of Jekyll and Hyde then recalls that as a kid he yearned to write like Stevenson. He wonders what his fellow Scot would make of this nightmare.

A notion briefly enters his head. He can kill himself

before the new, glossy, deeply superficial 'Willo' Sutherland can take him over completely. It's no more than he deserves and there's a bloody great tower right over there from which he could probably jump. Taking in both Christian and Moorish features on his descent.

Yet, as he waits in the lobby, he realises that he actually wants nothing more right now than to see her again, this new Luisa, if only for just a few minutes. Even if this is so very different a Luisa to the spouse he has clearly loved and lost forever. The new, alluring yet more than slightly intimidating Luisa Montero had, it appears, only briefly been his. And, on the available evidence, most surely never will be again.

William is pacing the reception area, too buzzed to keep still, when he hears the slow click of high heels on the surprisingly untiled flooring.

The Luisa from Room 383 appears like a vision, casually cool in a cream, silk blouse and minty-blue denims, shoulders draped in a striking red pashmina shawl. He recalls that she always did have a passion for the most vivid red and it always looked so good on her. He smiles admiringly.

"How is the Wi-Fi in your room?" she asks.

William is thrown by this, although it is invariably the first thing that he himself checks out on arrival. "Huh? Well, I can't say I… You look terrific, Luisa."

"I know this."

Well, *get* you, he thinks, although this unexpected degree of self-assuredness is both scary and exciting. But mostly scary.

Before he can continue, although he can't actually

think where to lead this conversation or indeed whether leading anything is remotely in his gift, he spies the New York ladies. They can hardly free themselves from the revolving doors, so laden are they with store bags and souvenirs. Instinctively he turns away, then realises there is absolutely no need, as they are not giving the slightest indication that they recognise him. And why would they – he arrived only this afternoon.

"You can't imagine them holding an Inquisition," says the slightly larger one. "They're so darling."

"Okay. Where do we go?" says Luisa, checking her watch. "On our – 'reunion'?"

"Wherever they don't have castanets," says William. "Or Taylor Swift."

On their way out, they pass Pablo at the door. He looks at the two of them, then up at William, and simply shakes his head.

*

It is William's idea to take a horse-drawn carriage ride through the city.

This feels suitably romantic, the sound of clopping hooves, buildings touched with the arrogance of history gliding slowly by in the intoxicating night air. He finds himself wanting more than anything to impress the hell out of this mesmerising creature he knows so well, yet hardly knows at all. She doesn't exactly leap at the notion with the enthusiasm he recalls the last Luisa having for soppy stuff, but neither does she sniff too overtly when he signals to the first driver in the rank.

As his persona right now seems to be about as fluid as a person can get, William sees no harm in answering whatever questions she may throw at him with answers that will most advance his cause. Although he is hardly any more solid on what this cause may be.

"Oh yes, a few novels," he tells her, "after you left. The critics have been very kind."

She smiles and points to the gold Rolex, sitting brightly on his wrist like a landing pad for a tiny helicopter. "I can see you have done well."

"Wanted their new platinum model but—" *Stop it, William!* "But what about you, Luisa? Tell me about yourself."

"Well, of course, you would not remember this—"

"Don't *you* start!" he chides, before recalling that it isn't this Luisa who has always accused him of never recalling anything. This one wasn't around long enough. He is finding this so tricky.

"O-kay. When I come to be au pair in Glasgow – when we first meet, *sí* – you tell me you will write books for the children."

"And you'd do the pictures. Of course I remember."

"Well, you remember also that you change this plan pretty quickly, yes? To the writing for the *publicitad*, the advertising? For much more money. You get nice job, we come to London – and I do not ever see you."

He recalls that they moved down to London not so long after their marriage, of course he does, because he suddenly had to boost his income. *Their* income. For obvious and rapidly growing reasons. Which I did, he notes proudly, and with some success. I supported us all and gave us stability. But how curious that this same migration occurred in both of his "lives", even though circumstances and – more specifically – dependants were clearly so very different. He finds this more than a little unsettling.

"But now I am the 'one-man-band'," she continues, oblivious to his turmoil. Or perhaps simply unstirred. "The words *and* the pictures. I am quite famous person here in Spain, William. If you are five years old."

Luisa is not looking at him as she tells him this, but she picks up his sudden, helpless intake of breath.

Her head turns swiftly back, so that she might understand why her harmless words should have shocked him so audibly. But, of course, she doesn't understand and he clearly wishes to move on.

"And you live here in Spain?" he asks, pointing in no particular direction.

"Madrid. *Sí*. I am coming back home all these years ago. After we divorce. Why not?"

"*Maestranza!*" shouts their driver suddenly, believing that his passengers are far too interested in each other and wanting to secure his tip.

William stares at the imposing bullring, now illuminated so expertly in a golden light, although he feels blood-red might be more appropriate. He shudders as he recalls what happened here only yesterday. Well, one yesterday. Another yesterday. When of course *this* William, the one with all the hair, was still apparently in an as-yet-unspecified London suburb, making final preparations for his naughty Spanish weekend.

"Bet your parents threw a fiesta when you came back home," he mutters. "Barbecued the dog – hopefully." She has the grace to laugh at this, which cheers him. "So, Luisa, we both achieved our dreams. Bloody well done us!"

She checks her watch again. William now recognises it as an exquisite Cartier. For a moment they sink back quietly into their own thoughts.

"Do you remember Sandy?" asks William, as if this is a sore he cannot stop picking, regardless of whose life he is living or whose ex-wife he is challenging.

"Of course," says Luisa, in some surprise. "I meet him when we are students here. You know this. He introduced me to you in Glasgow."

"Stay in touch, do you?"

She looks strangely confused.

"William, I married him."

CHAPTER FORTY-EIGHT

AS THEY STROLL PAST the tiny bars and cafés strung out along the riverbank, William watches the reflection of coloured lights ripple prettily in the water and thinks about throwing himself in. At the very least it might clear his head.

Of course Sandy went and married Luisa. Why wouldn't he, once William was out of the picture? Even if he had to move to Madrid to find her. William doesn't care to examine this too closely, but he just bets her excited parents bought a dispensation from the Pope especially for that rich, blond, Presbyterian bastard. Second time *fortunato*, Luisa! Yet patently that didn't last either. Which might suggest that Scotch and fino don't mix quite as readily as any of them had hoped.

"There is a café," she recalls, as they walk. "I pass it today in the hotel microbus. I am not certain, but I am thinking we have been there once, a long time ag—"

"Actually," interrupts William, warily, "we're better off with a cosy little bodega I know."

*

The Café Amarillo is as busy as ever.

The old, white-haired woman with the gold tooth and the stubby pencil behind her ear, who seems to manage the place and never sleeps, is there alongside her young and surly under-manager. William recognises them from his previous visits, but even if they might just have recognised him by this time, when in his last incarnation – big if, considering the flow of drinks and drinkers into the Yellow Café – he is obviously a first-timer to them now.

William tries not to make it too obvious to Luisa, but he finds himself looking determinedly around for two people whom he prays to high heaven won't be here.

Then he begins to wonder, inasmuch as his frenzied brain can, whether this sweet young pair would find him just as much of a stranger.

In this new reality, he and Luisa never did come back to Seville, did they? Or at least not to celebrate their pearl wedding anniversary. But whatever is going to set future events for the young honeymooners on this new and very different trajectory, one that William himself has clearly influenced and whose unforeseen consequences he is now sadly enduring, hasn't as yet happened to them in their own 1995 timeframe. So he and Luisa – the old Luisa – *must* have returned here this week and met them. And he must have, in his dubious wisdom, jiggled things around.

Or there would be no new bloody reality right now to be dealing with.

Like sitting here with a totally re-invented Luisa. The highly successful, single, childless one who left him in 1997. Because that last midnight of torrid Semana Santa love had proved, as intended, inconsequential.

He supposes it all depends on when new stuff kicks in and old memories finally die. Or, of course, what sort of a laugh the gods feel like having today. Because surely someone up there is playing with him, on this most extraordinary of weeks, in this bewitchingly other-worldly city. And logic, the rules we mortals play by – the rules that govern time itself – have most certainly been defenestrated.

Well, William Sutherland is sorry, but he doesn't quite get the joke. This alternative humour in his alternate reality. Or why he alone should be the butt of this celestial fun-fest, the helpless patsy being picked-on in the front row of life. Not when he's fighting for his sanity, whilst trying to remain Mr Rich 'n' Cool of Eurotrash.

"Who do you look around for?" she asks, as they reach a table.

"*No one!* No one at all. Just – looking. Nice place. Very – yellow. *Amarillo.*" How did he know that? He's floundering. Stay on message, William. "So – not surprised Sandy moved here to Spain. He always loved the place."

"*Sí.* He expand his father's business," Luisa explains, taking out a phone that he notices, with a faint sense of pique, is even smarter than his own. "I learn a lot from him, before we part. About the marketing. But you are also the successful man now, yes? I know you want this *very* much."

He shrugs modestly, without elaborating on the source of his riches, as Luisa beckons the young waiter with an imperious wave. "Johnny Walker, *por favor*. I think you like the Scotch, yes? *Y fino.*"

Once she has ordered, and even before the surly waiter has quit the table, she is checking her emails. He notices that her screen is a sea of the bold and unread and recalls how disinterested her predecessor was in all things electronic. Except texts, apparently.

Now she digs into her capacious bag, which he surprises himself by recognising as a genuine Hermès Birkin and of the softest leather. From it she pulls out a small pad and a silver pencil and diligently begins to scribble indecipherable notes. She proceeds to light a cigarette and make a phone call, talking in the fastest Spanish, ignoring William completely. Eventually she shrugs him a cursory apology, which he waves off. Of course he understands. People of the world.

William looks warily across at the uncleared table next to him, knowing exactly who he doesn't want to turn up out of nowhere and claim it. He notices a well-scooped ice cream dish and, beside it, resting against a tumbler, a small ball of candlewax. Very carefully William leans over to pick it up. He looks around for its owner, who has clearly left, most probably with his folks, to catch the next procession. Where he or she will discover, to their chagrin, that they must start all over again.

The lumpy ball feels warm in his hand, as he rolls it around, the knobbles of wax gently massaging his palm. William is so sad for the little boy, if indeed it is a little boy, who has been too full of his evening *helados* and excitement to "say goodbye" to his chair, as he and Luisa used to say, to make certain the kids left nothing of value behind.

Sensing a gap in the phone chat, he points to her mobile. "They're working late."

"I am working late. They are in Buenos Aires."

She continues to talk into her phone, her voice a tad louder and sterner than before. He finds that he can't stop staring at her. Even though she appears quite drawn and her familiar dark-brown eyes look tired, the "set" of her face seeming in some indefinable way different to that of her predecessor, he is taken once again by how beautiful she is. A profound beauty, he thinks, now that he has the time to examine it, of which this face is simply the outward expression.

He hears familiar laughter behind him, moving closer.

Will and Lu are on the side street beside the café, scouring the terrace for a vacant table. *Shit!* Before he can turn away, William catches the young woman gazing at him, but her gaze is blank. She looks away yet something suddenly causes her to turn back.

"Let's walk!" he tells Luisa, leaping up.

"*We only just sit down!*"

"We can sit down when we're seventy," he retorts, which right now doesn't actually feel that far off. He grabs Luisa's arm and lifts her right out of her chair. She's lighter than the last one, he estimates, and wonders if she's eating okay.

"I begin to remember you now," she says, but there is little affection in her tone.

It is only when they are well away from the Café Amarillo and its distractions that William notices he has absent-mindedly slipped the small ball of wax into the side pocket of his blouson.

CHAPTER FORTY-NINE

BY THE TIME THEY have crossed the good old Puente de Isabel II into Triana, Luisa has her high-heeled slingbacks in her hand and an expression of total disbelief on her face.

"Usually when I do marathons I wear the proper shoes," she moans.

"I never think of you doing marathons."

"I never think of you at all."

William realises that he is taking a massive risk in bringing this new Luisa here. But he is pretty certain that the young couple are by now happily settled into their own special café, lingering for hours over the single drink they can afford, until urges that are even less costly nudge them lyrically onwards.

He knows instinctively that here is the one place – the only place – he should be with this particular Luisa right now.

The ornate gates are closed but not locked. Through them he can see, with some relief, that the small courtyard is deserted. The only sounds are those of the ever-trickling fountain and the festivities far away. Smiling at the bemused and weary woman sighing beside him, he pushes open the familiar portals of Hostal Esmeralda yet again and beckons her to join him.

"What is this place?" she asks, following him through the gate without much enthusiasm. "Why do you bring me all the way across the bridge to here, William?"

He looks around the courtyard, although by now he reckons he knows every plant and tile, then turns back to confront an expression of utter bewilderment. "Oh. Well. It's just – pretty," he hazards. "Don't you think it's pretty, Luisa?"

She is not indifferent to beauty but she clearly doesn't feel she has to tramp across entire cities at unearthly hours to find it. He slumps down on the narrow rim of the fountain, sensing the tiny splashes of water on his hands and the chill of her disdainful shrug.

Luisa Montero of Madrid is clearly not going to work with him on this.

"I think I've made the biggest mistake of my life," he confesses.

"The hair?"

"Worse."

The woman has no idea what he is talking about. Nor, William suspects, has she the least interest in finding out. Yet she does at least walk gracefully towards the fountain, on those small, bare feet he still finds so attractive, even with their vivid turquoise toenails glistening under the twinkly, courtyard lights. She settles herself comfortably on the cool marble rim, albeit some distance away from him.

For a while they say nothing: Luisa because she is most probably waiting for him to elaborate, William because he finds he has nothing much else to say and sees even less point in saying it.

Suddenly – and it is as if he watches himself doing this, from some distant spiritual or perhaps not so spiritual plane – he moves closer to her. Very gently he lays his arm around her shoulders, his trembling fingers lightly brushing the skin where her soft red shawl has slipped down. The feel of her is so familiar, yet he can't actually remember when he last did this, when he last touched her with such affectionate intimacy. And indeed love.

How curious. This old sensation, with this new person.

Unfortunately the shock of an unbidden advance from a virtual stranger, however affectionate, almost sends Luisa into the fountain. Yet even as she hurriedly rebalances herself, William believes – perhaps just for one brief, glorious moment – that he can sense her hesitation. But, of course, he may be wrong, as she swiftly follows it up by drawing herself firmly away, pulling up her shawl and shoving him off with such force that he has to prevent himself from toppling over the edge.

"*What do you think you are doing? William!* How do you believe that you have this right? After twenty-eight years!"

"Seems like yesterday," he says weakly.

"*Oh, por favor!*"

William Sutherland reckons that he has never felt more hopeless and utterly lost than he does right now. Sitting beside this shocked, angry and totally perplexed person whom he knows so well, he realises with a sudden start that he clearly doesn't know her at all.

Is this what I've become, he wonders. And is this how I'm destined to remain – embracer of strangers, seducer of young women? A person abundant in hair and bling but utterly lacking in self-respect?

He looks at the woman. She is rubbing her weary feet and gazing anywhere but at him. If, for just one moment, Luisa, he tortures himself, you could remember what we once had, while I can still recall how much I have lost.

And then it strikes him.

The last and probably most futile gesture of a dying man. And a sudden memory he thought he had quite forgotten.

He leaps up from his perch by the fountain and rushes over to the nearest orange tree. Reaching up as high as he can, he selects the largest, juiciest orange he is able to liberate, noticing again that he no longer appears to have a back problem. Without a moment's hesitation, he aims his open mouth towards the glistening fruit and takes a giant bite. But this time he *relishes* it, bravely allowing its jolting sharpness to play tricks on his unsuspecting taste buds, as the guileful juice slithers between his teeth and out of his mouth.

"Mmmmm! Tart," he says, bravely relishing it. "Not you. I mean—"

She looks at the man as if he is totally insane.

For which he can't honestly blame her, as he suspects she may well be right. With a sadness that tastes more bitter than any dubious orange, he gulps down the remainder of his mouthful, concluding the fruitless gesture.

He is still gazing hopelessly at her uncomprehending face as it slowly changes.

Her glance rests first on him as he deals manfully with his impromptu snack. Gradually it ascends to the small, first-floor bedroom, now shuttered and unlit. After a few interminable seconds she turns to him, with a softness he knows he will never forget. A recognition that almost breaks his heart.

And he gives a nod.

For a moment neither speaks, lost in their own thoughts and memories. But William is not totally bereft of reason. He knows that it cannot last.

"I suppose we should be getting back to the hotel," he says.

She nods, still looking at him. "Yes. It is very late, isn't it?"

They stroll once again through the open gates and towards the ancient bridge. Uncomplicated sounds of people enjoying the tail ends of their evening echo from the banks. William and Luisa walk a few feet apart. But very gradually – almost despite themselves – they find that they are both moving just that bit closer. As the timeless and uncomprehending river flows beneath their feet.

*

The night receptionist is watching the TV on the wall behind his head, next to an array of clocks showing the current time in a random selection of countries. Another *Sooner You Than Me* beams out, compensating for its lack of volume with an unsubtle barrage of colours. William can't help but be quietly impressed.

"That programme!" says Luisa. "They are showing it all of the time." He smiles but remains sensibly quiet. "You and I should be on it."

"I'm sorry?"

Luisa walks towards the lift but doesn't say anything more until they are travelling up to their floor. "They find the couples who are doing the splitting up – yes?" He nods as new memories that don't totally thrill him come rolling in through the fog. "And they must each help with the choosing of the next partner, *sí. For the other one!*" He watches her, as she rolls her eyes. "What sort of a horrible mind—?"

He shakes his head in utter disgust as the lift releases them and they walk slowly to their adjoining doors. When she stops at number 383, he remains beside her, looking both desperate and quietly hopeful. The empty ice bucket is still there.

"Luisa—"

Before he can complete a thought that hasn't quite formulated in his fuzzy head, the door to number 381 opens. The extremely pale and seriously angry countenance of Tazmin Whatserface glares out, like a gargoyle from the cathedral. William immediately picks up the ice bucket.

"Where did you go for it – the North fucking Pole?!"

Luisa appears to recoil, taken aback by the anger or perhaps simply by Tazmin. The considerably younger woman stares disdainfully back.

"Ah," says William, loudly yet pathetically. "Er – Tamzin…"

"Close but no Cuban cigar! I've got the Spanish shits and yes, it looks like the biggest one is right here with me." She glares at Luisa, who can't hide the tiny smile on her face.

"*Who the hell are you?*"

"Me? I am nobody."

"Well, stop staring!"

"Taz-min, sorry – guess what? *This is my ex-wife!*" William announces it with a smile, as if Tazmin is bound to relish this happy coincidence as much as the next abandoned mistress. "She's staying right next door! What are the chances, eh?"

"YOUR EX-WIFE!! Did I die and wake up in a seventies sitcom?"

William has a feeling that nothing he could possibly say would improve the situation in any meaningful way. He looks helplessly to his newly discovered ex.

"It is like your programme, William," she says. "But would I choose you – Tazmin? *Sí*, perhaps I might."

He is still staring open-mouthed at Luisa, as she smiles and slips quietly into her room.

"*And you left me alone – for that!*"

He turns back angrily to the wronged yet patently wrong woman. "*That*, Tazmin, is someone I've loved and lost. Twice."

"Eeughh!" says Tazmin, unimpressed. "Well, not to worry." She segues into what he immediately recognises as gameshow mode and most probably one of his. "Congratulations, Mr Sutherland of Virginia Water. It's your turn to play *Second Chance*!"

She slams the door so violently that William can feel the aftershock through his hair weave. He remains staring at his own barred room and then at the equally impenetrable one beside it.

A squeak of wheels finally draws his attention away.

Pablo approaches, pushing a large, room service trolley. The old man just nods to William, as if he has seen it all before, although William doubts that in this case he has.

"Couldn't put a pillow on that, pal?" asks William.

"Manchester United," says Pablo, with sad yet now almost welcome inevitability.

CHAPTER FIFTY

EASTER SUNDAY

WILLIAM CAN HEAR THE church bells pealing all around the city.

He slides open the windows to his balcony and staggers out into the morning sunlight, narrowly avoiding the huge potted cycas plant, which he can't actually recall having been there before. But then Luisa has always had to point out anything she's planted at least four times before it becomes part of his world view. Or at least she used to.

The tiles on the balcony already feel warm to his bare feet, although it is still far too early in the morning. It was six o'clock before he was able to gain access to his room, now angrily vacated by its other guest. He thinks he feels more wretched than he ever has in his lives, yet he knows that this is, of course, not quite true.

Something bothers him about last night, something which the curious events of the evening have somehow parcelled up quite neatly and stored in the attic of his mind. Ready for him to unwrap when the time is right. Which clearly isn't yet.

A rustle of newspaper from the adjoining balcony tells him he is not alone. He doesn't even turn, but simply leans forward and rests his elbows on the wooden rail.

"Knew all the time, didn't you?" he says.

"'William Sutherland Productions'. Your name is all over it."

"I know! How *about* that! – Er, yeah."

Luisa sets down yesterday's copy of *El Mundo* on her table. "There were no novels, were there?"

William still can't look at her. He raises an unfamiliar, tanned hand to shield his eyes from the sun. "Didn't have the talent."

"You had the talent, William, but not the patience. This is why we part, I think. Where is your little girlfriend?"

"She lost her faith."

"And on Easter Sunday! … Did you think she looked a little like—?"

"NO!" he protests. "Not a bit! No way."

Luisa shrugs, unfazed by his vehemence. "Well, tonight it is all over. Semana Santa. Pouff – *terminado*! As if this has never been."

He swivels round to gaze at her. The expression of horror on his face shocks her out of her easy complacency.

"As if–? And the magic along with it, Luisa? *All the magic just – stops?*"

Luisa finds herself rising and moving towards him. He is shaking his head wildly, as he processes her words.

"But *you'll* still be here, won't you, Luisa? For a little while. You're not – *terminado*."

She smiles, a touch sadly. He notices that she is still in her dressing gown and also how good she looks, although she'd probably look even better, he reckons, if she gave up the cigarettes.

When she speaks, he has to strain to hear above the bells. "William, my meeting here tomorrow. Is not for business." He looks confused. "Sandy."

It takes him a moment to make sense of this single word, as if it's simply a random sound and not the most devastating thing she could say.

"He LIVES here?"

She shakes her head. "Barcelona. But we had the good times here. As students. Perhaps we try again."

He gazes into her eyes, which seem softer now in her clear morning face and so much more vulnerable. "And this would make you happy, Luisa?"

She shrugs, resignedly. "Are we not a bit long-in-the-face for happiness, my old friend?"

He has no firm evidence to counter this – God knows, his own life hasn't been one of unalloyed bliss – yet, curiously, he doesn't quite believe it. Which makes him even more desolate.

William shakes his head helplessly and goes back into his room.

*

By the time he registers the gentle but persistent knocking on his door, William Sutherland is almost dressed and trying to make some sort of sense of all the "stuff" from his pockets. He has no idea into what heady – or, more likely, appalling – worlds this set of keys will afford entry, nor the high-flying ailments so many pills are hopefully holding at bay.

He ignores the knocking. Until he knows for certain that it is not going to stop.

As he opens the door, Luisa – still in her dressing gown, but gripping her huge designer handbag as though her entire life rests inside it – looks up at him for a brief moment, then slips past and into the lonely room.

"I have made you sad, I think," she says, to silence. "Come – I buy you the big breakfast." He shakes his head but she is already moving on. "I remember you like it when I make the tortillas. See, William, I do remember some things."

She looks around the room and her quick, sharp eyes find ample evidence that someone has left in a hurry. She bends to pick up a single red castanet, stamped for some reason with the head of a bull, from beside the carved leg of the table. As she does so the little ball of candlewax dislodges itself from behind a crumpled handkerchief and rolls towards the table's edge.

"Souvenir?" she smiles, catching it before it falls.

William takes it from her hand and stares at it. "Some wee fella must have lost it last night. He'll be wondering where on earth it's got to. Probably been collecting it for years, poor lamb. With his dad. Every Semana Santa, just growing right there alongside—"

He begins to cry.

Without any warning or preamble.

Not just tell-tale moisture around the eyes, token indicators of a middle-aged man's basic humanity. Huge, loud, clumsy sobs, screamingly discordant primal wrenching, as if his body's reservoir has been breached and there is no way he can calm the surge.

The force is so great, the pummelling the body inflicts on itself so relentless, chest in spasm as it fights for breath, that he can't stand up any longer. It seems as if he is trying to gasp into himself all the air in the musty room, all the air in the world, and there just isn't enough. Can never be enough.

William shuffles backwards until his calves find the end of the bed, then seems to crumple down. Yet he doesn't flop. He just sits. The cries don't cease.

Luisa says nothing. She simply sinks down next to him, their bodies gently touching. And she waits.

After some minutes, his breath slows and he is able to speak. He offers her the explanation he feels that he owes.

"His name was Jamie. Jamie Eduardo Sutherland. You *see*, Luisa!" William doesn't pick up the confusion on her face. He isn't looking at her now. He is somewhere a long time ago, yet as vivid as yesterday. "Five years old. Just started 'big' school." He smiles, as his breathing becomes more even. "He was so proud, bless him. In his wee uniform. With his plastic Jurassic Park lunch-bag. He so loved his dinosaurs." He shakes his head, as he remembers. "It was meningitis. So quick. So bloody quick. There was no time. Perhaps today—"

"Oh, William." She takes his nearest hand, the one not gripping the mislaid, waxen treasure.

"I couldn't stop it, Luisa. I *couldn't*. If we'd had more money. If I'd—"

"What does money have to do with this?"

"*Everything*!" he cries. "Everything! I was determined it would never happen again. To any of us. I had to do *something*! Make money. Oh Jesus, I don't want to forget him! But I will, won't I? Like he never happened. Like he never left us."

William rises from the bed. He has to walk around. The need to talk to himself, to try to figure things out, overtakes the bafflement he must already be causing the elegant but bemused woman who watches him in silence.

"All this bloody – interfering with the past. *It's like I'm straddling two competing versions of my life!* But the old one's blurring – and the 'new' one's not at all where I want to be!" He turns back to her, as if suddenly remembering that he is not alone. "No offence."

She shakes her head, although she understands so little of what he is saying. But she beckons him back to sit with her, as if she understands it all.

"I never did, you know, Luisa. Forget. Not for a single moment. Despite what you – well, the last Luisa—" He sounds almost accusatory in his ramblings, as he swivels round on the unmade bed to glare at her. "*Somebody had to keep things going*! Somebody had to stay strong and 'win the bread.'" He sighs an almost Spanish sigh. "Love may be a team game, Luisa – but grief's a competitive sport."

Luisa can see that William, in his angry desolation, is confusing her with someone else. The mother of his lost son, most probably, whoever she was. Wherever the poor woman is.

"And – Claire?" she asks, nudging him on, away perhaps from the hopelessness.

"We couldn't have any more kids. Ironic, eh? *Niños.* We found Claire in that godawful children's home. But she was smiling. She was the only one smiling, Luisa. Wee gap-toothed smile. She's still got that." He begins to take deeper breaths, restoring equilibrium. "Clairey brought the fun back. And we did have fun – the three of us. Really. It wasn't always like— And then she left to get married. This was when things began to really fall apart. Forget the father-of-the bride stuff. I didn't feel I'd gained a son. I'd simply lost a—" He gasps as the bites of reality keep coming. "AND NOW MY CLAIREY'S GONE FOR GOOD!"

"They grow up, William. They move away."

He shakes his head. How can he explain? How can he possibly explain what he can't himself understand? He doesn't even try. He moves his hand away from hers and levers himself up.

On his way to the bathroom, he chugs some pills from the small jar on the table, whatever the hell they are.

Luisa remains on the bed but the bathroom door is open and she can see him suddenly shout at himself in the mirror.

"WHAT IF NO ONE EVER CAME TO ADOPT HER? OH GOD! WHAT IF NO ONE EVER CAME!"

He catches her unblinking eye and she takes this as an invitation of sorts to move towards him. "I do not understand all you say, William. I am sorry. But to lose a child. This I can only imagine." She shakes her head. "No – I cannot imagine this."

William notices that she is holding the wax ball and realises that he must have left it on the bed. She is stroking it so gently. This reminds him of something, but he can't quite – yes, he can. It's the same caring, loving, almost maternal way that Lu was stroking the scraggy hostel cat. And he feels something shift deep inside of him.

"I am *so* sorry, Luisa."

She raises her eyes to his face and sees something there that surprises her. Her ex-husband, from a brief, unhappy marriage so many years ago, a marriage she truly believed would last a lifetime but lasted no time at all, is gazing at her with an expression she can only describe as remorse. No, not simply remorse. Sympathy. Pity.

And she finds that this makes her really angry.

Luisa moves swiftly moves back into the bedroom, shaking her head rather too vehemently. He can only watch her as she practically disappears inside her vast red bag and grabs her phone. In practised yet still somehow frantic moves, she searches for something. What – a number? Surely not another email!

"William. *Por favor*. Do not be sorry, please," she mutters, head down, fingers swiping. "My life is full! It is *so* full. *Sí*. I have my books. My tours. My readings. I have two houses." She thrusts some photos in front of him. Look. *Look!* Now he understands. Sort of. More swiping. More thrusting. "Oh and see – my lovely nieces, my beautiful nephews. My family. *And all the niños who read my books. These are my children!* SEE! I am so—"

She ceases as dramatically as she began.

And suddenly this fine, intelligent, beautiful woman seems to William so much more gentle and so crushingly vulnerable. Yet still quite different from the Luisa he only just left and harder still to believe as a later version of the young Lu, with whom he's been so sweetly and devastatingly reacquainted.

She begins to pick mercilessly at her fingers. After a moment, he reaches over and gently parts her hands. This time she doesn't resist.

But now, like a badly cut film, the scene has abruptly changed. William is banging his head with his fists.

"*William?*"

"Aaaarrghhh!! The old stuff's going – from my head. It's disappearing, Luisa! I'm remembering new stuff. My first TV show. It was great! No, it was crap!"

"You surprise me."

Holding her shoulders in both his trembling arms, he talks directly and excessively loudly into her face. As if giving her the final briefing for a mission, one in which the slightest error could be fatal.

"Easter Sunday!" he cries. "We've only got a few hours. Until the music stops. Just a few short hours. Then everything goes back to – normal. New normal. *This* normal." She has never witnessed a man in such desperate panic. How did this happen?

"*The clock's ticking, Luisa!*"

"For you, it always was." He is already grabbing his things, throwing on his blouson and making for the door. "Where do you go?"

He stops.

"Er – not a bloody clue. But I have to do *something*, don't I?"

Turning back to her, he takes her hands. Tightly, as if some part of him wants never to let them go. When he talks, she is taken both by the intense sincerity in his voice and the fact that his words are total gibberish.

"I have to find them, Luisa! And – and make things right again. Like they were. Exactly like. Lord knows how. Not just for me. For *you*!"

For *her?*

He kisses her gently. And says again what he has already said not so very long before. "Goodbye, Luisa."

For some reason that he can't explain, William picks up the wax ball. And leaves Luisa Montero of Madrid alone in hotel room 381, awaiting her meeting, stroking the little silver cross that this time round has never left her throat.

CHAPTER FIFTY-ONE

WILLIAM SUTHERLAND HAS ABSOLUTELY no idea what he intends to do.

No change there, he thinks. But he does know that whatever needs doing has to be done before his old memory fades completely and Easter Sunday finally dies like the snuff of a candle. He hasn't a clue as to which may come first.

It is the old waitress who first approaches him at the Yellow Café. Do all elderly people in this city work 24/7? With a smilingly expansive gesture she offers him the choice of available tables. William shakes his head and takes the small waxen ball from his still-unfamiliar blouson.

"Someone left this here last night," he tells her. "The poor *niño* will be missing it."

The woman takes the ball with a knowing nod. He notices the surly young waiter in the doorway roll his eyes.

William wonders if this tiny yet somehow vital mission has really been the best use of his strictly limited time.

*

Where to start?

He traces his steps back to the cathedral. Naturally, the old place is even more a hub of fervent activity this resonant day – Easter Sunday – when its particular crowd-pleasing *pasos* process solemnly through the jam-packed streets and onwards through this grandest and most spiritual of passing places. Final performance this season, no encores, no eleven o'clock number. Resurrection same time next year, weather permitting.

But no Will or Lu.

He checks his Rolex, which tells him with merciless accuracy just how little time he has left before this holy week ends and his entire world along with it. They could be *anywhere* in this infuriating city, crammed as it is to riotous bursting point with myriad excitable strangers, none of whose histories he imagines have been quite as reversed and rewritten as his own.

Needles. Haystacks!

He decides to try the Real Alcazar, the celebrated royal palace that he still can recall as Moorish and breathtaking – and which he knows for certain he and his new bride visited at some late point in that perfect week.

Or at least he thinks he knows for certain.

Whilst the oldest working palace in Europe fails to summon up memories that are anything close to sharp and crystal-clear, he recognises with far greater clarity, as he walks around the shaded cloisters and courtyards at three times the speed of any fellow visitor, that his genuine appreciation of the Real Alcazar and its magnificent gardens, even now, owes so much to Luisa.

But, of course, Will and Lu aren't bloody here either.

At least not so far as he can tell.

Yet how can he possibly know that the moment he turns a corner, as in the worst kind of farce, they aren't just slipping away around another corner and into a sunken garden only a few feet ahead. Or perhaps they've discovered a secluded Moorish alcove, notorious for trysts amongst couples long dead, and are having a surreptitious knee-trembler (a delightful expression and indeed experience he still vaguely recalls sharing with his new bride).

Nor are the young couple, nooks and nookie excluded, at the Casa Pilatos. This grand Andalusian palace, with its precious *azulejos*, permanent residence of the Dukes of Medinacelli, is infuriatingly not even an extremely temporary home for Will and Lu Sutherland.

"Bloody waste of time!" he says aloud, as he rushes out of the stunning grounds. A middle-aged couple at the gate, overhearing this, immediately swivel on their brand-new FitFlops to find the next item on their unmissable ten list. (*TripAdvisor: There can be queues. Be prepared to stand.*)

*

William tells himself that he can't believe where the time is going, but of course the disbelief is minimal. There are clocks everywhere to remind him and he could never resist a clock. He has something the size of a clock on his wrist, taunting him with its sadistic, solid gold accuracy.

Inevitably, he finds himself back at the Yellow Café, hours later but none the wiser. His triple espresso grows cold as he pores over a tourist map and tries to remember what the hell he – *they* – might have been up to on their final day. A day that by now has precious little day left in it.

Looking up from his map, he sees the attractive woman of around his own age, whom he had noticed the day before as she coquettishly flaunted her newly bought fan. This time it is her turn to laugh, as her playful husband juggles with a couple of oranges he has clearly just plucked from a tree. William can't decide whether he finds them utterly delightful or a potent incentive to lose his breakfast.

Until an outlandish thought suddenly strikes him.

With the immediacy of a spike through his chair, he launches himself upright, spilling cold coffee all over his plastic-coated map and onto his stupidly expensive trousers.

There is something so madly delusional in the notion that has just occurred to him that, of course, it feels totally appropriate in the context of this week.

CHAPTER FIFTY-TWO

WHEN HE TURNS UP yet again at Hostal Esmeralda, William is just as exhausted from the street-pounding and procession-weaving, from rushing and pushing and scrambling, as he would have been in his old life. Which only confirms that Mr Hot Shot "TV" Sutherland pays someone to do his workouts for him.

The handyman is up his usual ladder, fixing yet another broken shutter.

William strides towards him and grabs the lower rungs. Before the stocky man can protest, William is shouting up at him, ignoring for the moment whether the object of his wrath can follow a single word he yells.

"Remember me, pal? I sure remember you! YOU'RE FROM THEIR TIME!" William can't believe he is saying this, and he's rather glad they're quite alone in the courtyard. Yet he knows that he is right. And that the long-buried memory for which he was scavenging this morning, after last night's orange-munching visit, has just kicked right back in.

"*Señor?*" says the apparently puzzled Sevillian, in

that wary manner universally recognised as a prelude to summoning the authorities.

William decides to shake the ladder quite violently, although he knows in his heart that killing the man right now, however satisfying, might not necessarily further his cause.

"Listen, amigo, I don't know what the hell is going on, or who you are – and I'm too bloody petrified to ask. But if I don't find those two innocent youngsters by midnight tonight and set them back on track – undo the damage I've done – I am totally screwed. Trapped for eternity in game show hell." He points to the small bedroom that he and Luisa once shared. "Please – this isn't about me! Forget about me. Do you want to split up that sweet young couple?" He pauses for a moment, his passion outrunning his logic. "One of whom, of course, *is* me."

The handyman moves down a couple of rungs and stamps hard on William's fingers with the heel of his old leather boot. William yelps in agony and leaps back out of range.

"*Bloody Hell!*" he cries. "Just because you're surreal doesn't mean you have to be nasty with it!"

"Plaza de Espana," mutters the handyman, under William's curses.

William believes that he has heard the man correctly – if indeed it is a man and not a spectre or a phantom or a product of his own, deluded brain. He certainly isn't going to hang around and re-pose the question. "Yeah? *Gracias*. Bit unnecessary, but *mucho... gracias!*"

He rushes off and out the gate, rubbing his injured hand. He doesn't see the handyman shake his head, nor does he hear him repeat "*Plaza de Espana!*" with a wicked laugh in his throat.

*

The Plaza de Espana is, of course, bloody miles away.

Or at least it feels like this, as William struggles and barges his way once more through the chattering, surging crowds. All doggedly tramping the streets in search of the week's final processions, even though they have probably witnessed incredibly similar processions all week.

He stops and ponders, just for a moment, for whom exactly he is doing this. Then he realises he doesn't have the luxury of stopping and pondering. And, anyway, he sort of knows.

The sun is sending meaningful hints about going down, after another steamy, full-on day, as William finally rolls up at Seville's confusingly grand contribution to the 1929 Exposition and begins his search. Alcoves and all. The haunting theme music from *Lawrence of Arabia* crawls unbidden, like an ear-worm, into his head.

William finds himself, forty-five fruitless minutes later, sitting on yet another trickling fountain, in front of the Plaza de Espana, alternately sobbing and cursing.

"*Marmalade-eating bastard!*"

He has totally run out of options. The unsuspecting pre-millennium honeymooners he is seeking so desperately, the couple who will now never enjoy a long marriage or thoughtful anniversary gift from a lovely daughter (or even that daughter at all), could be anywhere.

Yet *anywhere* is not on the maps in his pocket, his sexy new smartphone, his memory or his mind.

His expensive head has almost sunk into his chest when he glimpses them.

Strolling towards him, Easter Sunday smart, are his expansive hosts from the bullring. Señora Barbadillo looks particularly radiant, flashing those sturdy, flamenco legs in sheer black stockings, beneath a respectfully dark yet still summery dress. Her raven hair is jauntily topped off with a bull's-blood pillbox hat.

William can't believe how delighted he is to see them again.

"*Señor Barbadillo! Señora!*" He is immediately thrown off course by the utter bafflement on both their faces. "It's me. *William!* …We just went to the *corrida* together."

"No, Señor, we did not," responds the portly man, gently but firmly.

"No, of course we didn't," admits William, sadly. "Sorry to—"

Before he can finish, Señora Barbadillo suddenly grabs hold of his arm. To no one's surprise, she is extremely strong.

"How you know our name?" she challenges him.

Good question. "Er – flamenco! Everyone knows your name in Sevilla, Señora." He turns to go. "And your legs."

"Your name too, *William Sutherland*."

William swings back in amazement. The older couple are smiling and pointing excitedly to his blouson. He pulls it out like a flabby fold of skin and twists his neck round until he can make out "William Sutherland Productions", emblazoned on the reverse in gold script. He reckons he must come across like a dog chasing its tail, but it doesn't appear to bother his onlookers.

"*The more soon you are than I am!*" they cry exultantly.

"May we have the photograph, Señor?" implores his new, old acquaintance. "Today is birthday of my wife."

"Of course it is!" cries William. "*You're sixty!*" He can sense the Señora isn't thrilled with this. "So hard to believe," he adds hurriedly. "So hard. Doing anything special tonight?"

Señor Barbadillo's eyes take on the naughtiest gleam. "*Hotel*," he announces. "Is best and oldest in Sevilla. With *only* our family. Very quiet." He then steps forward and proceeds to give William a huge and bewilderingly conspiratorial wink, one that his wife cannot see.

William is attempting to process this nonsense when the flash of a camera, or perhaps a light suddenly going on behind, just nicks his peripheral vision. And moments later something flashes in William too.

A red glow?

He knows this means something. It has to do with the honeymoon, with Will and Lu, he is certain. But he can make no earthly or unearthly sense of it.

Until he catches the Señora smiling at him. And watches her red hat bobbing.

A hat. Something about a hat. A red hat?

And now he remembers. Or he thinks he does. It isn't much, in fact it's light years from much. But it's a start.

He begins to move off, but then turns back and shakes both their hands. "*Gracias*. Very *muchas*. Happy Birthday."

As he picks up speed, he calls back "*Felicitations*!" out of politeness and then, for some obscure reason, adds "*See you on the show!*" because it sounds the sort of thing TV folk like him say.

He can feel their puzzlement searing into the back of his limited-edition, corporate blouson.

CHAPTER FIFTY-THREE

"*MISSION BLOODY IMPOSSIBLE!*"

Night has fallen and William can hardly move in the tiny, clogged-up streets. In fact, he can hardly breathe. When he doesn't have someone's hair in his mouth or a meaty shoulder in his eye, his nose is stuffed with the heady scent of industrial-strength incense, garnished with sweat, rancid orange blossom and a thousand semi-digested tapas.

The frenzy of the masses to catch the last of the *pasos,* as they make their way towards and through the great cathedral, is palpable. The life-giving transfusions of wine and sangria provide the turbaned ones beneath the wobbly floats with new energy and a different sense of rhythm. William is certain that he can detect the hitherto stately drums and brass attempting to sprinkle a last-minute flavouring of New Orleans into the mix, but of course his sanity has been in question for some while.

And the Spanish are shouting.

To their partners, to their children, to Jesus Christ and to whoever is at the other end of their mobile phones shouting back. Lights beam up at the cathedral, with a far from medieval brilliance, and down also on those many passing solemnly or curiously or aimlessly through its massive and ornate Door of Assumption.

Rich, fulsome Spanish hair, some of it under starched white or black mantillas, shimmers and glints, reflecting the rainbow glow. As does the incendiary garb adorning this particular band of torch-bearing Nazarenos, making William think that perhaps these are the only flame-red items that he has been frenziedly dredging up in his scattergun and very far from total recall.

He is all too aware that his life-changing, sanity-restoring quest may very shortly come to a messy and fruitless end.

One of the fiery Nazarenos suddenly steps out of rank and stoops down.

William strains to follow the hooded man's descent, managing to peek through a gap in the crowd, which now appears to be pulsating like some multi-headed, short-sleeved organism. His eyes finally find a small boy with unexpectedly blond hair. William recognises him as the wee lad whom he rescued from an unstoppable and totally non-existent nineties bus and whom he later followed dumbly towards the cathedral.

Is the little chap an unwitting part of this torturous Passion play, William wonders, a boy with that painful resemblance to someone never out of his head? Although even this, the most searing memory of all, is slowly losing its sharpness.

Shouldn't this be a blessing and not the curse that it feels?

The kindly Nazareno is allowing red-hot wax to drip slowly from the massive candle he holds, gently easing it towards the boy's tiny, trembling hand. For a moment William wonders if this could be the same knobbly ball he returned earlier today, already amplified. Stranger things, of course, have happened.

The boy suddenly turns towards William and their eyes meet, through a tiny chink in the crowd. There is no look of surprise here, in the excruciatingly innocent, blue-eyed stare, and thankfully no fear. William thinks he might just have detected a rapid blink of – recognition? Gratitude? He feels his stomach quiver.

The crowd moves forward to the beat of the drums, as if in one throbbing, congealing lump, and the child is gone.

William strains urgently to catch just one more glimpse, to retain the image, as if this is suddenly the most important thing in his life. But he can no longer see the boy, or the kindly Nazareno, although of course the latter all look the same under there. Yet he does catch the blessedly non-judgemental eye of Christ, on this, his special day, looking indulgently down on one confirmed non-believer's helpless, hopeless despair. For a moment William thinks he sees him shrug.

A flash of a large – and, by now, classic – camera changes everything.

William looks up swiftly in the direction of the flash, although naturally it is far from the only one going off right now. Yet, somehow, perhaps because it is of a different vintage or simply the way it travels over decades right into his reeling head – like that flash he now recalls outside the pricey restaurant – it is indeed a one-off.

People are clambering onto ancient walls, railings and each other to snatch a better view, however obscured and fleeting. Some are being pulled away in a manner quite un-Christian.

William decides to weave through the crowd and, where weaving has its limits, to push and shove and gouge. Picking up speed, as he simultaneously summons up reserves of barely used muscle, cursing the ridiculous tightness of his trousers, he keeps his eyeline tilted skyward. At least he knows now what he is looking for, just as he knows the unlikeliness of his ever finding it.

Or them.

He catches the briefest glint of red.

It could be anything.

Yet this time it resonates inside his pulpy brain in a manner that has recently become so familiar, with its surreal sense of superimposition, like a dodgy palimpsest over the present. So that he knows it could not be anything else.

And finally he sees her.

Lu Sutherland, his wee, lithe, graceful Lu, perched precariously on an ornate railing, short skirt rising over impossibly slim, brown legs, as she strains and stretches. He spots her bright-red and finally permitted 'Easter-bonnet', firmly fixed on that dark, shimmering mane.

As she tries, as ever, for the one perfect shot.

Her equally bright-red bag must, he reckons, be rattling with rolls of used film. He recalls the albums that the *old* Luisa curated and preserved; expertly taken pictures, to be just as studiously ignored over the years by his unsentimental self.

William finds himself longing to pore over those glossy, bulging, repetitive, non-existent albums just one more time.

Now young Will is there, in his eyeline, standing directly below his intrepid wife. He holds onto an elegant, wiry ankle, supporting with infinite care this slender frame. As entranced as ever by her spirit and her form.

William moves towards them, along the packed street.

As he turns, he catches his reflection in a compact but well-stocked shop window. Through the serried ranks of tiny, take-home clay Nazarenos (the purpose of which is still lost on him, unless local kids battle with them in holy wars) he finds that slightly smarmy stranger staring back. Instinctively, he runs a Rolexed hand through his still alien hair and wonders what the hell to do now.

A powerful whiff of rosemary, nicotine and undigested beer, some six inches from his face, causes him to turn.

The wild little Romany lady seizes on his attention, as if her breath has been a genuinely persuasive calling card, and thrusts newly plucked sprigs of rosemary almost up his nose. Without a moment for doubt, William wrenches the Rolex from his wrist and hands it to her. He watches her stunned, rheumy eyes as they flash between him and the passing Christ, as though these miraculous men are simply two sides of the same, divinely provident coin.

"*Ayyyy! Muchas gracias, Señor!*"

She pushes her entire stock of rosemary down the front of his shirt, then snatches a few sprigs back. No mileage in being over-grateful.

William has forgotten her already. He is too busy attempting to yank out his hair weave. Anything to drag him back, in Lu and Will's eyes, to the already-strange person they seem to like and into whom they appear inevitably to bump. He has a feeling that the new Willo

Sutherland will only freak them out and that this would hardly further his cause. Whatever the hell that cause is.

But the hair-yanking only makes him yelp.

William reckons that whoever did it must have been amongst the best in their field. He wonders how much it cost him and whether he was able to put it down to the business. Then, terrified that the young couple will disappear forever from his gaze, he looks around for a less painful option.

He spots a man his own age a few ragged rows behind him, wearing a battered Panama hat. Struggling back to reach him, amidst shoves and curses, he offers up a big wad of euros, notes he discovers, without excess surprise, filling a silver money-clip in his trouser pocket. "Señor? Er… hat? Panama? Sombrero? Quanta—?"

The man immediately grabs the euros and joyously pops his hat onto his new friend's new hairdo. "On your head be it, boyo," he laughs, in an accent closer to Rhondda than Ronda.

Resembling a tad more the prototype William Sutherland, albeit more bronzed, he turns back towards Will and Lu's wobbly perch, in anticipation of a heroic plough through the decades.

They're no longer there.

Perhaps they are flowing with the crowds now, or at least their own contemporaneous, pre selfie-stick crowd, following the massive, candlelit procession in anything but silence towards the cathedral. Or maybe they are walking in an entirely different direction, seeking the proud band of brothers from another *hermandad*. Or even snatching a swift break, a drink, some low-budget tapas…

Shopping… strolling… lingering…

They could be bloody anywhere!

William knows all too well that they won't have returned to their little room just yet. Not on this pivotal Easter Sunday night. Not until…

He has no idea in which direction to jostle and shove. Towards the cathedral or away from it, in the direction of Triana, or along the riverbank? Families with wizened grandmothers in black and little girls in starched white communion dresses, are laughing and celebrating and falling asleep, because the night is balmy, the day is holy and they happen to be Spanish. Tourists watch the locals in delighted wonder and tourists from Britain wonder how people can be so full of joy and free from inhibitions whilst remaining relatively sober.

Come on, William! One last time – for pity's sake, remember!

He pushes through the crowds, choosing a direction at random – or perhaps just going where the obstacles to progress appear smaller and less likely to offer sharp-elbowed resistance.

Easter Sunday, 1995!

He finds himself slowly raising his hands to his temples, like a medium attempting to make contact with the other world. Where did the two of you go that last bloody night!

The two of us – where did *we* go?

Maybe I have got Alzheimer's, he thinks, although he'd challenge anyone to recall in every detail a holiday they took thirty years earlier, even if it was their honeymoon. *Especially* if it was their—

"*William?*"

William spins round to find a tall, good-looking man of a similar age, only slightly greying, immaculately turned out in a lightweight and miraculously uncreased linen suit. He seems quite similar to the charmingly confident and urbane man he had left in their mutual office, just a few days and another life ago. Similar of course, save for the broken nose he didn't have last week.

But of course, in this reality, the guy also didn't have time or opportunity to have a furtive liaison with his partner's wife, while the latter was on a new-business trip, so William swiftly realises that any hostility would be somewhat misplaced. Therefore he had better swiftly tamp down the righteous anger he is somewhat irrationally feeling.

All these thoughts are flashing through William's brain like lightning as he greets his old friend with surprise.

"*Sandy*!"

The other man reacts with an astonishment consistent with his not having seen his once best friend for possibly decades. William realises that they are not only on different pages, they're in totally different books.

"Dear Lord!" continues William, disingenuously. "What on earth are you doing here?"

"I could ask you the very same thing," laughs his old friend. "Luisa's here too, you know. Our mutual 'ex'. "

"*No?!*" says William in a cod surprise that has become second nature these past few days. "What are the chances? Er, I hate to be antisocial, Sandy, but—"

But what?

The infinitely more relaxed man shakes his head of real hair in nostalgic amusement.

"Same old Will. Always in a hurry. Hey, we must have a little *bebida* – the three of us. Like old times. Remember when I gatecrashed your *luna de miel* here?"

As William is about to simply nod and move on to Lord knows where, a vague but hopefully not unproductive thought emerges.

"How could I forget, old pal?" he says, with a casual yet searching smile. "The silent processions, that lovely casino win…"

"The broken nose…"

"Aye, sorry about that, Sandy. And, of course, *on Easter Sunday we…*" He stares hopefully into his old friend's far too unlined face. "We – er…"

Sandy smacks his tanned forehead and points gleefully upwards, to the nearby La Giralda tower. William swivels and follows his gaze.

"*We hit the heights!* Well remembered. Poor Paloma got dizzy from too much *vino de naranja* and all those steps, so we had to leave you two lovebirds—"

To Sandy Matheson's surprise, his old college mate suddenly beams, clasps the other man's well-manicured hands in what feels like an inexplicable show of gratitude then ploughs off through the crowds at almost dangerous speed.

"*Bless you, Sandy!*" the bolter calls back, as he goes. "Let's meet up again soon. In – in another life."

William doesn't even have time to consider that in this other, much hoped for life, this same man is someone he would very much like to smash into a wall all over again.

"'*Sooner you than me*', oor Wullie!" shouts the man in the slick linen suit.

CHAPTER FIFTY-FOUR

WILLIAM LOOKS UP AT the massive, ninety-one-metre, golden tower, with its famed weathervane on top, and thinks of The Lord.

More specifically, he thinks that The Lord only knows how he is going to climb up a monument this tall, in the already breathless, frantic state in which he finds himself.

If the Moors were as smart as all that, where's the bloody lift?

In this same roller-coasting loop of demented thought, he mulls over why, of all the places where he might possibly locate his and Luisa's younger selves, does that holy wee prankster, in whom he of course doesn't believe for a moment, park the pair of them at by far the highest spot on the old city map?

It is only when he barges his way inside the surprisingly spacious entrance that he remembers once more that La Giralda is actually composed mostly of ramps, not steps. He can't summon up how many ramps there are – the only figure that springs instantly to mind is too many, even for a fit lad in his twenties – but he does recall that they were constructed inside the tower to accommodate horses. Although why a horse would gallop up to the top of a minaret is a mystery to him, unless it was for some sort of equine suicide pact, which he can sort of understand.

William begins to climb. The psychological puffing starts in earnest way before any strain on the heart and lungs is plausible.

He is hardly onto the second ramp when he hears a noise up ahead, building rapidly in volume. William hopes this isn't a stampede of angry horses on its way down but it turns out to be a stampede of chattering Korean tourists, who prove almost as dangerous.

It is only when they and their lethal selfie-sticks have surged past him, forcing him to cower against a wall, that he wonders: what if the young couple really don't know who he is this time round? Even with all the guidebooks you can buy and every website you can google, no one has yet managed an advice line to the surreal, the occult and the downright perverse. There is no 999 or 111 to fate.

Where the spiral ramp ends there's yet another clamber for the now spent William. Up seventeen steps into the bell chamber, which in retrospect made the ramps seem like fun. On arrival he can see some incredible bells but unfortunately no familiar faces.

William can only pray that these massive instruments don't ring before he is well out of range. He has no idea of the time, because he gave an old Andalusian lady his inordinately expensive watch, for reasons that are becoming increasingly unclear to him.

He decides to work his way round the small bell tower, although he reckons that, even in all this bustle, he would have spotted the young couple by now. Especially as Will is a head taller than most other nationalities currently enjoying the sensational views. And, of course, he has that red hair, the bastard.

With immense sadness, William realises that it is finally time to throw in the towel. He gave it his best shot. A guy who dares to manipulate his own destiny has to finally accept meeting it head-on.

It takes a few intrepid climbers moving to one side, perhaps to catch a final procession way down in the old city, that he realises he should have set his own eyeline slightly lower. (So much for appreciating higher things.) There, on the ground, kneel a young, scraggly-bearded man and a pretty young woman. They are both scrabbling around for some coins that must have fallen out of a bag or a pocket.

William keeps his distance, making sure not to interrupt and quite possibly disquiet them. Until the massive bell right beside him strikes the late hour with inhuman glee and he hears himself screaming in shock.

The young couple, alongside everyone else from his own era, turn to stare at him, clearly impressed that a sound emanating from one slightly above-average sized man can match that of the famous bells in their clamour.

William's alarm, however, is swiftly overtaken by an intense despair at Will's and Lu's palpable lack of recognition. It takes a few agonising seconds before they squint their eyes, tilt their heads in unison and take a closer look.

"*Gordon*?" hazards Will.

Another spasm shoots through the older man. As he suddenly realises that it might not be the easiest task to explain to this smart young fellow why his very own name is proudly emblazoned on the rear of a vivid blouson that someone not apparently called William Sutherland is flaunting. For uneasy, read impossible.

Without turning, William casually removes the offending garment and sends it sailing over the parapet, as if this type of cavalier divestment is the most normal activity in the world.

"Oh, Will – hi!" he says, hardly missing a beat. Although he is already realising, in the cooler altitude, that he seriously misses his blouson. "And Lu! Well, fancy—"

"—seeing us here. I've a hole in my bloody pants and I dropped some pesetas. It's the end of our trip and my lovely winnings are practically gone. Jeez, pal, you've caught the old sun today."

"Oh, this," laughs William, self-deprecatingly. "It's just… Yes, it's sun. Sun. Yes."

He can't fail to notice the couple exchanging glances, but realises there is precious little he can do other than tread cautiously.

"Where is Fanta?" asks Lu.

"She's – not herself today, Lu." Moving on. "Great view from here."

"Right enough," says Will. "Hey, anyone'd think you were *following* us!"

William offers the most insincere laugh that probably ever came out his mouth, although of course he can't yet fully recall all of his game-show production years. "*As if!*" he says then wonders if anyone even said 'as if' thirty years ago. Perhaps it was he who started the trend. "So where *are* you going straight after this? Just – out of interest."

Lu disarms him with the most impish of smiles, her chestnut-brown eyes opening even wider with the pure excitement of it all. "Will has made the promise to me, Gordon. For this, our last night. We have the very special cocktail – *Aqua de Sevilla* – with a big cherry and a little umbrella!" This time her smile is just for William. It pierces him to the gut. "You British – you like the umbrellas – yes?"

Will has no idea what she is talking about and honestly doesn't care. "Lu, I didn't actually promise—"

Of course!

William finally recalls the missing pieces of that final Easter Sunday night and where they ended up so long ago. And just as instantly he sees his way in. Even if he can't as yet envisage a way out. "Hey, guys, my treat! I've no holes in my pockets these days. So no arguments." No arguments are forthcoming. "Actually, there's something I need to tell you both."

He can hear himself muttering under his breath, as he looks for hope in the relentlessly starry night, "Though *Jesucristo* alone knows how."

CHAPTER FIFTY-FIVE

WILLIAM SUTHERLAND REALLY HOPES that the famous old hotel, the special one his young couple appear so set on for their final Sunday night treat, hasn't been torn down for a motorway. Or had its historic roof terrace, overlooking the old city, converted into an infinity pool.

It would be just his luck.

Fortune, for once, is smiling. As they arrive in the plush lobby, an elegant blend of the timeless and the contemporary (with a lot of, in William's opinion, unnecessary clocks), he can see that its older incarnation is already impressing the hell out of Will and Lu. Even as it intimidates them.

"Can I meet you guys up there?" he pleads. "I just need to..."

Before they can acknowledge an old man's sudden incontinence, William has scurried off to somewhere behind the huge reception desk. He has no intention of stepping into a lift that hasn't yet arrived and freaking them out before the evening has even begun.

He also needs to work on what the hell he is going to say.

Perhaps, he muses, rather than any further notions of manipulation or deceit, I should just come clean. Reveal to them the whole extraordinary scenario, from start to finish. From careering phantom buses to brand-new versions of wife.

Or perhaps not.

*

The celebrated rooftop bar is, thankfully, not too crowded when William walks in.

At least not on the evening of Easter Sunday 2025.

At least not yet.

To his relief, it doesn't look like it has been excessively modernised in recent years. Almost as if history and a studied neglect is part of the charm. He is even more relieved to see that Will and Lù are already settled into their huge, shared cocktail. And that they aren't sitting on anyone else. He knows he is still totally unprepared, and terrified beyond reason, but at least his bladder is now empty, an unarguably sensible precaution.

The views are indeed spectacular.

Gazing into the panoramic night, William is treated to a magnificently evocative tableau of his own descent into madness and despair. Like the stations of the cross, he can pinpoint the exact locations of his torment, from the cathedral and La Giralda to Plaza de Espana and the old Triana Bridge. He thinks he can even spot the irrepressible yellow and black awning.

A sudden sadness envelops him, as he contemplates the excruciatingly fine mess he has gotten himself into and how impenetrable the psychic foliage through which he must now hack in order to emerge into sanity.

He doubts that he ever will.

William stares at the lovely young Spanish woman. She is deeply immersed in her drink and totally unaware of him. Her long hair gently brushes her husband's face as they suck the bright liquid through stripy straws, trying not to impale their noses on the little wooden umbrella they should have first removed.

William realises how dearly he misses Luisa.

This youthfully fragrant one, plus the lonely older version he just left, but most of all the person he has wished totally out of existence in an attempt to improve all their lots. The Luisa Sutherland of whom in this life there is no longer a trace, save for the younger model slurping before him, whose natural journey will very soon be remapped.

Thanks to him.

Unless…

What in hell's name was I doing? he asks himself, as he forces the smile back onto his face. Playing God in this city of all cities.

And what the hell am I playing at now?

"Hi, guys – oh, you started without me!" he berates them, with some relief. He would have had a great time paying for a thirty-year-old drink in a currency the country hadn't actually adopted until four years after the event.

"Aye, sorry, Gordon. Apparently I promised Señora Sutherland I'd do the honours on our last evening," Will announces, proudly, "and a Scotsman never reneges on his promises."

Not quite William's experience, but he is rather impressed with his younger self, truth be told.

"You can do the next round," continues Will. "Meantime, what are you having?"

"Er, nothing for now," says William swiftly. "Thank you, Will. It's the – diabetes, you know. Need to be a bit careful." The young couple nod sympathetically. "I'll just enjoy watching you."

Which he does, as he can't think what else to do. At least he hasn't sat down on somebody already there, he thinks, or on a chair no longer available. We have to be grateful for the smallest mercies.

Eventually, as the couple grow self-conscious about having an audience and the sound of mutual slurping begins to resonate, Lu feels a need to move the conversation on.

"Gordon? There is something that you wish to say?"

Ah.

"Well..." says the Panama-hatted imposter, because he feels he has to say something, yet absolutely nothing springs to mind that could lead to anything approximating an appropriate conclusion. Or indeed any sort of conclusion. I'm normally so hot on strategy, he thinks, ask anyone in marketing consultancy, ask my clients (no, don't; they're not my clients any more). But right at this minute, *nada*. He looks around the splendid old terrace for some sort of inspiration.

What he sees makes the situation at least ten times worse.

Make that a thousand.

Across the large room, at a well-placed oaken table, are the last people he needs right now.

The Barbadillos, with what William has to assume is their loving family.

Señor and Señora are waving at him excitedly, beyond thrilled to see him again after their earlier brush with fame. The Señora has a stunning and incredibly large red rose in her hair, which looks as if it has been lovingly tended and watered and is now attempting to win prizes. Señor Barbadillo, for reasons as yet unknown, still winks pointedly at William, like a man with an annoyingly persistent nervous tick.

William feels that he should at least be polite, so he waves back at the couple, whose clearly impressed children and their partners are also nodding *holas*.

He finally turns back to Will and Lu, to find their eyes peeping over their huge glass and staring at him. He has absolutely no idea what or who they think he has been greeting so effusively. By the looks on their faces, he has probably just been observed sending regards to a floral arrangement or an adventurous pigeon.

If he hadn't felt a sense of urgency before, this latest development has given him a jolt no cocktail ever invented could match, even if the tiny umbrella had pierced an artery. Unfortunately, his misguided preamble is less than encouraging.

"O-kay. Before they come over – *no*, no one's coming over. Ignore them. Me. Okay." He takes a deep breath, as he realises that the young couple are hanging precariously on his every utterance, the way eighteenth-century society would watch performances by the insane. "Will, Lu – I think – well, to be honest, I *know* – that I've made a pretty big mistake."

"The tan?" suggests Lu.

"Not the tan! Well, maybe the tan," says William, thankful that he hasn't as yet removed his worn but effective Panama hat. "See, I had the – what would you call it – the effrontery to interfere in the lives – aye, the lives – of two total strangers."

"Yeah?" says a suddenly interested Will, most probably sensing a juicy story. "Who were they, Gordy?"

William just sighs. He feels totally lost. There's just no way…

And then he hears the rumble.

It appears to be coming from just outside the main door. Almost as if a crowd out there have begun to stamp their feet. William tells himself it's most probably some type of cleaning machinery being wheeled past. Or inappropriate muzak played in error. He actually prays for earthquake but in the meantime chooses to ignore it.

"What I'm trying to say is, Lu – Will – what the hell *am* I trying to say?"

He is left with little time to find out.

The door to the roof terrace bar suddenly smashes open.

To the frenzied strum of finely tuned Spanish guitars, a troupe of high-class flamenco dancers bursts in, the men in tight black trousers with crimson sashes, the women a swirl of brilliant red.

Their accompanying musicians sway noisily around them as the flamboyant newcomers make immediately for the table full of beaming Barbadillos and proceed to perform solely for them, proud heads held high, arms raised and swivelling, as if no one else in the bar exists.

Although, of course, everyone in the room watches and cheers and whoops in delight.

Señor Barbadillo is grinning like an Andalusian Cheshire Cat at the "unexpected" visitors and at William (*see what I did!*), but mostly at his overwhelmed but adoring wife. Señora Barbadillo looks like she doesn't know whether to smile, cry or pick up a stray castanet. William has a pretty good idea that she will happily manage to do all three and more before the mad evening is out.

"*Oh, thanks a sodding bunch!*" he hears himself cry into the ether, as he senses his entire life being systematically crushed under a stampede of brilliantly polished, black patent leather shoes. While Will and Lu, not privy to the surprise but fairly surprised anyway, move swiftly from bemusement through bewilderment into the fast lane on the autoroute to terror.

It's all going really well.

CHAPTER FIFTY-SIX

"**CUMPLEAÑOS FELIZ, CUMPLEAÑOS FELIZ,** *Te Deseamos Todo, Cumpleaños Feliz.*"

The indomitable troupe bellow their version of *Happy Birthday* as the delighted instigator screams out "SORPRESA!", like the Señora didn't know.

William can only watch in panic.

The surprisers are clearly about to "work" the room and an all-too-brief moment later he sees Señor Barbadillo merrily pointing him out. Why not just crucify me now? thinks William, which he knows is sacrilegious but at least not untimely.

William turns back to the young couple and tries to block out the sounds of a dozen professionally disdainful and probably paid-by-the-hour Andalusians stamping their arrogant, Cuban-heeled feet, as if crushing a sudden outbreak of cockroaches, in rhythm to a repeated chanting of what he fears might be the *The More Soon You Than Me!* signature tune. It is hardly *Malagueña* but it appears to please the crowd.

Closing his weary eyes, William attempts with

commendable futility to block them all out, as they make a foot-stomping beeline for his apparently empty table. He prays, in a way he never has before, that having imprinted their presence on the shuddering floor of the roof terrace, they will feel sufficiently spent and creatively sated to return to their host's table for thoroughly justified refreshment.

No such luck.

They decide to dance, stomp, sing and play around him.

All around him.

As close to him as they can possibly get.

They are, of course, as he has to keep reminding himself, totally invisible to Will and Lu. Unfortunately, William's reaction couldn't be more in the young couple's faces if it were projected onto a state-of-the-art cinema screen lowered from the merciless heavens.

All that Will and Lu can see is a bizarre assortment of pissed-off twitches and despairing twists from a solitary and increasingly peculiar Scot. Whilst all William can think is that, if Spaniards are noisy when they're talking, you should hear them when they bloody dance.

It is when one over-exuberant *bailaor* tries to remove William's hat and he, not unnaturally, resists that he notices Will and Lu's eyes open wider than alcohol usually permits. Their jaws drop in unison, like characters in a cartoon. William soon computes that to them his hat appears to be wobbling right around his head entirely of its own volition.

"How the hell do you do that?" asks Will, not unreasonably.

"I used to be in a circus. Now, as I was trying to say—"

He moves his chair out of the orbit of the dancers, which proves totally fruitless, as they appear as determined as a swarm of locusts to go with him. So he has to make his impassioned address on the move, as the young couple's eyes follow his weird trajectory with undisguised wonder.

"The thing is, guys – the thing is—" *What* is *the sodding thing, William?* "Well, I'm afraid that sometimes—" *okay, go for it, pal,* "—sometimes older doesn't necessarily mean wiser. It just means – less young."

You think?

He knows that he is talking in platitudes – in fact, he knows that what he is saying would give platitudes a bad name – but he simply can't get a handle on it. The dancers aren't necessarily the cause, but they certainly don't help.

He gazes around the terrace, his current discomfort zone, which is rapidly filling up with excited patrons enjoying the free entertainment. Including the involvement of the poor stooge in the Panama hat. Some of them even applaud him.

As he squirms around, to avoid the plague of hat-snatching flamenco bastards, the room begins to spin. It can't be alcohol – he hasn't had any. And he isn't twirling nearly fast enough to induce the dizziness he feels. So perhaps he has finally succumbed to full-blown mental disintegration. A condition he recognises as having been in development long before he ever landed in Seville.

And suddenly the only thing William can think of doing is to laugh.

Not just a giggle or a vaguely disquieting titter.

He is talking full-throttled, big-bellied, frame-rattling laughter.

Laughter at the madness of it all. The sort of mirth-suffused, booming roar that comes from the gut and the heart and the soul and can float high over a balcony and resound way into the flame-filled, Iberian night. Laughter that he was born with and that is everyone's birthright. Laughter that sings with the innocence of youth, soars with the what-the-hellishness of age. No stiffness. No resistance. No worries, pal.

"AWAY YE GO!" he bellows, in his new-found glee.

"He likes to shout," explains Lu, who has some history here.

From her own perspective and that of Will, there are just a few guests on the roof with them, quietly drinking and enjoying the view. Along with one extremely loud, perma-tanned, Panama-hatted, jacketless, watchless, elderly, laughing lunatic, who came here on his honeymoon way back in 1965 and apparently hasn't matured much since.

So, when Señora Barbadillo herself rises gracefully from her family table and stamps towards him, making the classic movement of doves with her thickening but still nimble fingers, encouraging him to stop being British, if only for this milestone night, he can see just one way to proceed.

He rises from his chair and begins to dance.

William Sutherland, uptight and stuffy Scot, captive to a throbbing beat that could have been womb music had the womb in question not belonged to an illiterate factory worker from Greenock. Willo S himself, sashaying on a cool Spanish terrace, in the lush April evening, with a seductive local celebrity whose age is no longer a secret and whose special day this is.

Seeming to one fascinated, but justifiably wary, young couple as if he is dancing with absolutely no one, to absolutely no music at all.

And not terribly well.

William begins to shout even louder above the clamour, reminding Lu once more of yesterday morning's hitherto quiet jewellery store.

"What was it the late, lamented John Lennon sang, before he died forty-five years ago?" Why are they both staring at him like that? "*Fifteen*! Fifteen years ago!" He moves to the rhythm. Or at least he hears the rhythm and moves. "*'Life is what happens to you while you're busy – doing other stuff – making plans*'. Or something like—"

He stops, as if frozen into a dramatic pose.

Had he been a professional dancer, this might have been the stunning yet natural conclusion to a performance and the music would have reached a similarly exhilarating end. But, whilst he is clearly and surprising game, the man is no mover – in this or any incarnation – and to at least two members of his audience, there is no music at hand to be inspiring any sort of climax.

Yet no one watching this terpsichorean display, from either era, could fail to note the glorious sense of revelation that suddenly bathes the weary face of this middle-aged man, like those scintillating coloured lights that magically illuminate the old city facades as darkness begins to fall. And William knows that his young couple are totally attentive. If for no other reason than the sight of a hitherto respectable, weirdly-tanned, suspiciously unbalding man losing his grip on sanity – or at the very least on self-control – can't be anything other than horribly fascinating.

"For once in my life," he cries, "*I've run out of bloody plans!*"

As he laughs uproariously once again, he notices that Señora Barbadillo and her little troupe are laughing with him. Perhaps because they feel it is safest to do so or maybe they're just happy. And laughter – even that of a balmy, barmy Brit – is infectious.

"Not a spreadsheet or an agenda or a Window to my name!" he continues. Then adds, "Or a production schedule," in deference to his current calling.

He holds out a bronzed hand to Lu. "So I'll just have to go – *wherever the music takes me.*"

Lu doesn't rise immediately, so he beckons her upwards, gently and with a warmly avuncular smile. Nothing to fear here.

She looks at Will, who shrugs. Humour the old loon. So she nods and rises gracefully from her chair.

Like a young woman at her first formal event, Lu Sutherland moves with a shy smile to join William on what wasn't, until now, a dance floor. The only music in her ears the drumbeat echoes of a final procession way down below.

Yet, when his lovely young wife begins to dance unaccompanied, her lithe body swaying like a willowy sapling in the breeze, her delicate feet tapping in the flimsiest brown pumps, the grace and beauty of it almost breaks the older man's heart. He drinks in her glowing-eyed, innocent warmth, like the cocktail he doesn't dare order, and tries not to tell himself that all this will be lost to young Will in just two years, as it is lost to older William now. A loss he feels in every cell of his body, but especially those that still contain his most precious memories.

He attempts to match her movements, so effortless in their elegance, which of course is futile. Especially as the beat in Lu's head is most probably so very different from that of the musicians practically in his face.

And then he senses a different, more powerful movement directly behind him.

Señora Barbadillo has decided that she too will dance with William Sutherland. It would be impolite, she reasons, to allow this famous, successful, blouson-less and rather ridiculous man in the ill-fitting hat to writhe and contort all on his ownsome.

If William finds dancing with two formidable, accomplished women, of differing ages and from different eras – neither of whom is aware of the other's existence – unimaginably taxing, he tries bravely not to show it. Hopefully, he reasons, the perspiration he can feel running down his face, and everywhere else beneath his expensive summer clothing, will be put down by the casual observer to some highly unfamiliar exertions. Brought on by a spontaneous display of Caledonian flamenco.

"Legs are doing well, darling," he tells the older woman, because he feels they deserve some acknowledgement on their birthday. And this can't have been so misplaced, because he hears quite clearly two highly attractive Spanish women of differing ages murmur "*gracias*".

On an impulse, William grabs the red rose from Señora Barbadillo's hair, hoping its thorns don't rip her head open, and grips it between his now beautifully capped teeth. This is, of course, before he realises that to poor Lu it appears he has plucked the flower completely out of thin air.

"Conjuring school," he explains, to which Lu just nods, as if nothing about this man could possibly surprise her by now.

"What happened to your beautiful watch?" she asks.

He flashes his wrist, bereft of all the watches in his life, then adds what he considers a flamboyant touch by raising his arms and clicking imaginary castanets. "*Gave it to a tiny peasant! Ay ayy!!*"

Calming down, because he's exhausting himself let alone anyone else, he moves closer to Lu and tries to lower the level of near-hysteria in his voice. He ratchets it down to repressed panic, which he hopes she may not detect. "You have no idea what I'm trying to tell you, *cariño*. Could be because – after thirty years – I'm only just figuring it out myself."

Thankfully, Señora Barbadillo dances off. Perhaps because she wants to rejoin her family. Or maybe because the flying Scotsman is now talking in hushed tones to a large, potted plant.

"We can't *control* our whole world, Lu," continues William, with a gentle smile. "Believe me, no one can. Stuff – happens. Aye. It does. 'Fraid so. But you know what? *You know what?* It's not the bad stuff that does you in, Lu. Not really." He finds himself on the verge of tears, which he isn't certain will aid his cause, but neither can he help it. "*It's being someplace else when all the good stuff's going on!*"

There!

For reasons he can't totally fathom, he feels the urge to execute a move that will choreographically nail for all time the profound insights he has just received and felt impelled to share. He essays a bizarre manoeuvre that involve both feet leaving the ground and, inevitably, he stumbles mid-flight. Happily, a shocked Lu manages to catch him before he can do too much damage. For a second he savours the support and breathes in that particular scent he still recalls with such painful longing.

"Just keep going where the music takes you, Lu. *Wherever* it takes you. Spontaneity, that's the buzzword, kiddo. Go with your gut, go wi' the flow."

He glances across to Will, who is watching protectively. Patently hoping he hasn't surrendered his innocent young bride to some raddled Glaswegian lecher.

"And it wouldn't kill *you* to dance once in a while, pal!" says the raddled old lecher to his younger, stiffer self.

Yet he knows that respect and decorum dictate that he must reluctantly break away.

She isn't his and may never more be so. As yet William Sutherland fears that his raging epiphany may turn out to be nothing more than a one-man show.

Stepping back, he sweeps up their half-sipped cocktail from Will's hand, as if to propose a toast to his newer, wiser self. He notices, without huge surprise, that the glass and its contents at once appear to look their age. Yet, before the couple can spot this sudden desiccation, he swigs it down in one. Amidst the gagging and retching, he manages to complete his life-changing thought process.

"*You've just gotta go for the whole bloody cocktail!*" he proclaims, rather neatly in his opinion. He muses that he might have made a half-decent writer after all. Another life. "1995. Mm. Vintage!"

He hears applause from the Barbadillo family across the floor. He doubts that this is for his dancing, so he reckons it must be for his guts.

And then it starts to rain.

But it's 1995 rain. He watches as it lands on Lu and Will, but feels not a drop on himself.

"Come on, Lu," says Will, leaping up. "We'll get soaked!" He moves off to find shelter beneath an overhang at the central bar.

Lu watches him, then takes in the rain and finally lets her gaze rest on a smiling William.

Suddenly she cocks her head, clearly hearing something that William can't detect but knows is resonating deep within her. He suspects, from what his own ears have been telling him these wondrous days, that it is something primal. Something that strikes more than the ears, something that thrums with the soul. Perhaps the sound that has been so familiar this mystical week. That of distant drumming.

Whatever it is, it appears to be having some effect.

Lu shakes her head, at Will, at the elements, at the world. And stays where she is, lifting up her face to the skies and letting the glorious rain soak her. Because this is where she happens to be and here is where the rain is. She swings her head around, like a puppy emerging from a river, droplets singing into the night air.

William moves into her rain. Embracing it as it dances off her. "Go with the flow," he repeats, almost but not quite to himself. He smiles at her and raises his voice for one last plea. "Look, no umbrella."

She looks into his eyes, the same deep blue eyes, she notices now, as her husband, and just nods as gentle rain tips her fine dark lashes.

He knows that he can do no more, though he is far from certain that he has done anything. So he simply offers this joyous young woman the same brief, heartfelt *adios* he gave his last two "wives".

"Goodbye, Luisa."

She looks at him and smiles. A knowing smile, although perhaps she doesn't know quite yet what she knows.

As he passes the Barbadillo table, where they apparently can't keep still for a single moment, he turns back. To see Lu sexily enticing Will towards her, slender arms extended and weaving, drawing him sinuously closer, as if by an invisible cord. Will resists – until he can't resist any more. He picks up a minuscule wooden umbrella from the bar and, raising it jauntily above his head, joins her under the downpour.

Lu laughs. But then she neatly plucks the umbrella from out of his hand and lightly throws it away.

*

It is only when William reaches the lift that the realisation hits him.

He stands, frozen for a second. Glancing back, he can just glimpse the young couple standing even closer, if this were possible.

What has just stupidly and all too belatedly occurred to him is that this whole time, this whole Semana Santa, he has been devoting practically all of his attention to Lu. Whilst he can hardly blame himself, especially watching her now, her soft lips so close to – well – his, he is chastened to add one further damning insight to the evening's mix. And to all that he has learned this revelatory week.

Luisa was not – *and has never been* – the major "problem" to be solved.

He doesn't wish to disturb the couple, yet he has to go back. So he manages simply to tap Will on the shoulder and to whisper into the young man's ear.

"Look after her, pal," he warns, "or you'll have me to deal with."

By the time Will turns round, the older guy has gone. Out of the door through which he came only seconds before.

Wondering if he has just been talking to himself.

CHAPTER FIFTY-SEVEN

WILLIAM SUTHERLAND CAN'T RECALL entering the lift outside the rooftop bar, or exiting from it into the hotel lobby. Yet now he stands alone in the moonlight, shivering uncontrollably as he breathes in the scent of oleander and looks back up towards the terrace.

Wondering what the hell he has done.

Or, even more scarily, what the hell he hasn't done.

Was he too subtle, too oblique? Too downright weird?

William is also unusually aware of the hour in Seville, New York, London and Seoul, so he must have noticed the clocks on his way out. Despite the memory lapses, William knows only too well that time is painfully important, even though he realises that what happens from this moment on is totally outside of his control. (Not that he feels he has exactly been master of the universal control booth up until now.)

He stumbles out into the road, which is still full of happy humanity, most of whom have snacked on tapas and empanadas, lubricated themselves with their favourite *bebidas* and have probably only just concluded the 10pm dinners that are such a feature of Spanish life and tourism. William has never investigated the effect of full stomachs and late bedtimes on Spanish productivity. As he now apparently produces inexplicably successful game shows, there would appear even less necessity for him to do so, but it's still vaguely interesting.

Not entirely certain where he is heading, he moves off in the direction of the old quarter, where the landmarks are almost painfully familiar. As if to ram home this familiarity, he catches his voluminous corporate blouson drifting past him, just fifteen inches below his chin, as though propelled by its own little motor. Almost hidden inside it is the tiny rosemary woman, whose eyes are entirely focussed on the shiny Rolex watch weighing down her stick-like wrist.

William backs out of her way, just in case she covets the gold teeth he is certain must reside somewhere inside his expensive, tax-deductible mouth. A few more minutes of intensive, if somewhat aimless, walking delivers him through and beyond the raucous night-time crowds, to whom the message of Easter Sunday doesn't look as if it has been comprehensively delivered. At least he hasn't encountered any British stag or hen parties, which is always a blessing.

Finally, he discovers himself back at the entrance of the Hotel Herrera, which he guesses must have been his destination all along. Wasn't he just telling Lu she should go with the flow and take life as you find it? Surely this is what he is doing now, possibly for the first time ever, without even realising it. He almost smiles. "*Physician, heal thyself!*"

When he steps into the hotel lobby, less grand but just as bustling as the one he left some time ago, he has only to look at a solitary clock to realise that the day is nearly done. Easter Sunday and Semana Santa, in the worshipful city of Seville, are almost over. And most probably his former burdensome, less-than-exciting, never-less-than-stressful life along with them.

A life that suddenly means more to him than he could possibly have imagined.

*

"*If you like Piña Coladaaa…*"

Will and Lu tumble like crabs at a hoedown up the narrow, winding staircase of the Hostal Esmeralda, bodies locked so tightly that his song, sung loudly into her grinning face in broad Glaswegian, rattles the inside of her head. Normally she would giggle then tell him to shush, as there are people less besotted with each other who are probably sleeping nearby. But tonight she bellows "*Follow, follow, I will follow Rangers. And Patrick's Thistles..*" back into his own open mouth. A chant which inflames him, but she doesn't know the Partick Thistle song.

"You had less than half a cocktail!" he laughs.

"And a cherry! Do not forget the cherry."

"Talking of cherries—" He grins, which, of course, means nothing to her. It begins to explain itself when, with one firm hand, he presses her slim body against their locked door. Struggling wildly with the other to locate both key and keyhole, he finally unlocks it.

They topple into what Will has grandly called their

Bible-black bedroom, banging immediately into the small, solid-oak bed, a collision they find the funniest thing ever, even through the pain. Yet, instead of falling onto it, they manoeuvre themselves around the unyielding frame, stumbling over rucksacks and shoes and oranges as they try to unzip, unbutton and unencumber themselves and each other as swiftly and with as much of the requisite frenzy as possible.

Their yearning for each other's flesh, the perfumed softness of Lu, the wiry hardness of Will, has never felt so imperative. Perhaps because this is their last night and real life is about to begin, with all its strains and uncertainties. Or maybe because this has been the weirdest evening so far and something about the weirdness has infused their still-developing souls. Certainly Lu finds herself going back to that earlier, rain-sodden, curiously philosophical goodbye, from the strangest of strangers, even as she feels the chill of her newly defrocked, naked body.

Before a larger, warmer one lands directly on top of her.

*

For a moment, William stands outside the door to room 381.

He is trying to regain his breath and dial down his pounding heart – which is most probably now on that expensive medication – to some sort of normality. Although normal is not exactly how he would describe this night.

William wonders, for a moment, how come in his new persona he should have found himself in the very same hotel room, or even the same hotel, as before. But then decides that this is the least of his worries. Perhaps they hold it open for Brits in existential crisis or could be that some leading time-travel agency has the Hotel Herrera concession. He also wonders who the hell was Herrera, then puzzles why the human mind goes off in every direction at the same time, when it should be at its most focussed. Or is this just him?

He knows that he is putting off opening the door. But, finally, he does so and enters into a darkness that wears its vacancy like a musty gown.

"*Luisa?*" he hazards, without the slightest hope.

*

"I fucking want you so much," says Will, who knows there is a time for poetry and a time for action. He doesn't think he has ever felt so deeply in love and so unspeakably horny. And is still delighted to find that the two can function together, to the ultimate benefit of both.

"*Mi cariño*. My Willy."

He keeps kissing her, on her lips, her tiny chin, her silky, swan-like neck, where the scent of youth and whatever bouquet she prefers today is at its most captivating, travelling downwards, hotly yet delicately, as he reaches with a free hand for his bedside drawer. Giving the lie to those that say menfolk can't multitask.

She can hear him scrabbling around and briefly wishes his attention tonight was all on her and that she had fully captured his mind as well as his yearning.

"*SHIT!*"

"Will?!"

"I was sure I had one left. Bugger!"

He rummages with such renewed vigour that the flimsy bedside table keels over. Despite herself, Lu begins to giggle.

"It's not funny, Lu. I'm bloody bursting!"

"I can—"

"No!"

He springs up and starts to dress. "Sod it! Our last night! Can you hold on – stay there – I'll just go and find—"

"In a Catholic country? On the Sunday night of Easter? Near to midnight?"

She can hear him in the darkness, ripping open his rucksack with a frenzy, as if his drunken mother might have sewn an emergency supply into the lining, "especially for ma randy wee boy".

And she wonders, lying there so happy and so free, as yet unfulfilled yet so utterly fulfilled, what exactly it is that she, Luisa – Lu – Sutherland, with the secret knowledge she has and the private insights she perhaps has gained, is actually doing right now.

The words of a highly peculiar yet well-meaning gentleman, something about going where the music takes her, glide to her through the cool, round-midnight air, still speckled with incense and orange blossom and the myriad candles of Semana Santa, suffused with memories of gleaming, floral-strewn *pasos*, all of them now sleeping in respectful silence for another year.

And so too do her own words float back to her, the feelings she expressed to this same stranger, so honestly and frankly, about her deepest hopes for their future and her strongest fears. "*I think Will he will never have enough of the money. To be happy. Never enough to have the kids. Not even one kid. Even if he wins at the bloody casino every single day!*"

She gently strokes the chain on her neck and wonders again what in God's name she is doing.

*

William also wonders what he is doing, although perhaps not in His name.

He knocks again on the door of the room adjoining his own, which belonged briefly to the new Luisa and perhaps still does. For a moment he freezes, as a troubling thought takes hold. Could she be lying there in bed right now, drowsily reacquainted with their mutual old friend after a few *bebidas*? Seeking some comfort in this life as she did in the one before.

As the door slowly opens, William thinks his heart is going to burst.

A balding young man, drenched in sweat, stands there glaring at him.

"Oh. Er, *perdón*!" blurts out William, in patent relief, which only confuses the disturbed occupant even more. "You just – carry on. With whatever—"

The relief lasts only as long as it takes for the door to slam. He wonders now whether this same Luisa, the one content to settle for something less than happiness, has merely checked out and gone to stay in some other hostelry, with her most recent ex-husband.

Or did she simply prefer not to see William again?

He stands there in the corridor, lost in a weary suspicion that spans two existences, wishing he couldn't hear the less complicated sounds coming from behind the newly slammed door.

*

"There's a Canadian couple in the room down the hall."

"Is not like borrowing sugar!" She laughs in astonishment.

"We should've gone to—Y'know – *farmacia*?"

Lu gazes down at her handbag, roughly elbowed off the side of the bed as lust took over from tidiness. The worn zip is half-open and in the dim moonlight curling through the shutters, she thinks she can see the small *farmacia* packet peeping out. Even in these breathless moments, she finds herself catching what little breath she has.

She feels his eyes on her. His face, despite the urgency and the patent evidence of his desire, is the softest she thinks she has ever seen it. He gazes around the room at the debris, shaking his beautiful head, as if inviting her to share in the night's pure madness. And, somewhere, a voice he only half believes he heard this curious night, an older voice yet not unlike his own, seems to whisper inside his ear once again.

They begin to laugh at the same time, a laughter that turns into a helpless, snorting, undignified, marvellous blast that makes their eyes sparkle and their noses run. And she knows what she has to do, what she owes the truth and sheer honesty of this moment.

She rolls gently down to the side of the narrow bed and draws out the little packet from her discarded bag. Teasingly, her hands make the tiny flamenco movements of a pair of doves, just as they did on the roof terrace as she danced.

Their eyes meet.

He remains staring at her, following her delicate fingers, mesmerised. She holds her breath. Wondering what he will say – or do, but knowing at least that there will be no deceit. No games. The air grows still.

Until finally he smiles, laughs once more, throws caution to the wind and himself back onto the bed. Embracing the beautiful new wife he will look after forever, as instructed, whatever the world hurls at them. As he prays she will look after him.

As he knows she will.

The little packet floats out of her hand, dropping back onto the floor, as all the church clocks in the still-thrumming city outside their tiny room ring out their versions of midnight.

And announce the end of Semana Santa, this year of our Lord 1995.

CHAPTER FIFTY-EIGHT

WILLIAM IS CONVINCED THAT he can hear the bells tolling out his fate, even in the flaming lift.

He certainly can't check the time, as his watch is most probably on its way back to whatever wretched dwelling the poor rosemary woman inhabits. Unless she has already sold it on. But he can certainly check out his appearance.

The mirror inside the still-stationary chamber reveals an image that, in other circumstances, he might have been only too thrilled to flaunt – stylish, tanned and expensively thatched. Like a gent he now faintly recalls from a casino so long ago, a dapper man with a stunning and far younger woman on his arm.

He hears himself sigh like a Spaniard. Or, at least, like one Spaniard he used to know.

And then all the lights go off.

Before he can even gasp, the entire mechanism appears to shake and rattle in the suddenly terrifying darkness. There's an ugly grinding of machinery, far off yet deep inside his head, that sounds as ancient as the buildings all around him – making him think of some sort of medieval torture – just before the tiny, steel carriage begins to plummet at breathtaking speed. Curiously, he is aware of a total absence of muzak, which he normally hates but would currently kill for.

William feels as if he, and his increasingly airless mode of transportation, are totally out of control, heading on the express route down to hell. His body, which now appears mysteriously bereft of bones, flops helplessly against each solid wall in turn, at horrifying speed, as if he is in some sort of celestial blender. He wonders if this is what dying is like, but nobody tells you.

For a moment he thinks he spies Pablo reflected in the mirrored wall. Which shows him just how dramatically his tormented mind is addling, as – for once – there is no Pablo and barely even a mirror.

Beneath his own helpless screams and the ear-splitting mechanics, he hears another sound. More familiar perhaps but no less disconcerting. Two people yelling together on the brink of unfettered ecstasy.

What the—?

As suddenly as it began, the lift ceases to clatter and slows to a juddering stop. The lights blink on and William feels that the sweat from his body alone could cause an electrical accident. Alongside other accidents he doesn't care to imagine. He turns to look at the mirror. What he sees makes him almost retch in astonishment. And then smile in unabashed joy, as he finally greets an old friend.

"Yes! YES!! God, you're beautiful!"

The plush hair has gone, along with the wood-stain tan. He won't be missing either of them. Back are his trusty spectacles. Even more hearteningly, the elegant watch that Luisa bought for him so very long ago is once again strapped around his familiar, milky-white wrist.

And his back hurts.

The lift stops on a lower floor. The doors glide open. He holds his breath.

Marilyn and Shelby pour in.

"Hello, stranger," says Marilyn, juggling bag, phone and guide books with large, multi-ringed fingers.

William just nods politely; he has too much to think about right now. Although he does wonder where they could possibly be heading after midnight.

"Where've you *been* all this time?" asks Shelby, who, by the intense look on her face and her warm, wide-open eyes, has been thinking of little else.

"And this is a concern of yours why?" he says, not unreasonably.

Marilyn appears to take umbrage. He senses this when she presses a button and stops the lift mid-floor. "Because we've been comforting your poor Luisa, that's *why*, mister."

"Poor—? Oh God, you've bonded."

"Did you know that girl has Jewish blood from way back?" explains Shelby.

"I really don't think—"

"Sephardi. Trust me."

"That is a lovely lady, William," declares Marilyn.

William softens for a moment, as the hostilities subside. And nods in agreement.

"Despite the affair," says Shelby.

"She *told* you?" says William.

"A woman knows."

"You don't deserve a lady like that, William," says Marilyn. "Does he, Shelby?"

"He doesn't deserve shit. If you don't mind my saying so, William."

"What are friends for, Shelby? Would one of you mind restarting the lift, please? … The elevator?"

He can feel their eyes, kindly yet profoundly judgemental, locked onto his.

"I've lost her again, haven't I?" They shrug non-committedly and in perfect unison. "Where is she? Back in Richmond, packing up?" More shrugs. They aren't giving anything away. "No – *she's with him!* Bugger!" He thinks for a second. And nods. "It's what she wants – and, most probably, what I deserve. Who am I to—? *Bugger!*"

As soon as the doors open, the ladies shunt aside to allow him to rush out. It's like squeezing a pill out of a blister pack but he's hugely grateful as he bursts into the spacious lobby.

William has absolutely no idea where he is going or what he is doing. He knows simply that he has to keep moving. And, curiously, or perhaps not so much considering the events of this week, he is just beginning to trust in something beyond himself to tell him the answers.

It will come, whatever it is, good or bad. He is certain it will come.

Soon would be good.

Now?

He knows it surely won't come from the gnarled old guy in the smart denims ambling cheerily across the lobby towards him, even though William finds himself strangely pleased to see him.

"*Hola*, Pablo," he says amiably, as he rushes by.

"Watford Football Club – very nice strip. Yellow with a little black."

William stops.

There could even be screech-marks on the wooden flooring, from the old untrendy trainers now firmly back on his feet, as he judders to a halt inches before the revolving doors. He is not quite certain if what he has just heard is what he just heard.

"Who supports Watford?" he cries into the air conditioning. "*And when did you learn sodding English*?"

He doesn't have the time or the energy to delve deeper into the nodding retainer's education. Let alone his arrant duplicity.

Because he knows exactly what the driver/porter/lift attendant/wily old sod is trying to tell him.

CHAPTER FIFTY-NINE

THE CAFÉ AMARILLO, WITH its bumblebee-yellow awning and newly repainted black surround, appears much the same as in William's previous incarnations.

Luisa hasn't changed either.

She looks just as she did when he left her, another lifetime yet a matter of hours ago. Except that now her bulky suitcase squats beside her on the pavement and she is smoking, something that this particular Luisa hasn't done – or at least he hasn't caught her doing – since a time long gone, when their world collapsed in on itself and they each sought comfort in whatever way they could.

This same world that in the last few days William had single-mindedly reconfigured, with perhaps the best of intentions and an almost total absence of thought, and then only just restored to how it was and always should have been, with its unpredictable seasoning of sorrows and joys.

For better or for worse. The rough and the smooth. And every other cliché with more than a nugget of truth.

Yet, despite everything, is it all far too late?

William Sutherland doesn't approach his wife of thirty years straightaway. Perhaps, he reasons, it is pure fear that battens him down in this quaint plaza, now pleasantly cooler in the gone-midnight darkness. Or it could be that he simply wants to drink her in, like the white wine she quietly sips at the now deserted café, scarily certain that his days of being able to do this, days he so desperately wants, are not simply finite but quite probably non-existent.

He tells himself he knows so much about William Sutherland that he didn't latch onto before this night. He knows that he is overwhelmed with feelings he has never allowed himself to feel.

Which is all good stuff. Yet William is fast discovering that it still takes two.

Or, in this case, more than two.

The old lady and her surly helper, who run and possibly own the café, are looking wistfully in William's direction, as if willing him to drag the sad-looking woman with the suitcase away, so that they can please close up, for pity's sake, and have some well-earned rest after so intense a week. Use of force cannot be far away.

Taking the hint, William walks slowly towards the table.

Luisa appears so lost in her thoughts, watching the smoke from her cigarette drift upwards in the breezeless air, that it is some seconds before she senses his presence.

She raises her head to look up. There is little warmth in her eyes, only sadness. And resignation. He can hardly be surprised, yet the sheer relief of simply seeing her right here beside him, the original, authorised, less streamlined version, seems to overwhelm the reality of their situation and momentarily dampens his fear.

"You don't smoke," he says.

"Now you are telling me."

William knows that he is so full of things to say to her, after all that has happened. Meaningful things, words and sentences that could probably change everything. Yet they seem to be dissolving unvoiced into the air, like the smoke from her cigarette. Desperate to start afresh, he can manage nothing fresh nor even know how to start.

"Did you call the police to find me?" he hears himself asking and wonders why.

In the silence, he ponders that if "alternative" William, the bronzed one with the A-list hair (the presence of which he can still feel like some sort of follicular memory), has now never actually existed, where on earth has this current one been spending his time since he and Luisa last met? He must have been somewhere. Perhaps it will come to him in time, he thinks, as some of the more inane, game-show memories recede. He hopes so. He would be rather interested.

"I think I would have called the police," he concludes.

"Then you are much better husband than I am wife."

"No. No, I'm not, Luisa. I'd like to be. Not better – I'd settle for as good as." He looks determined. "And I *can be.* This week has taught me – how to change things."

He watches as alarm washes instantly over her face. "*Not the past!* Heaven forbid. Never the past. Yet just maybe the future?"

But he doesn't finish, because Luisa is leaning towards him and sniffing loudly.

"I know that fragrance!" she cries. "*You have been with me, haven't you?*"

"*Not the way you think!*"

William feels quite outraged, even though he couldn't swear to her that the notion has never, for a single moment, entered his deluded head. But not now. He has eyes for only one Luisa now, *this* Luisa, of all Luisas, yet in his heart he fears that it is already too late. That this beautiful, stately and sadly under-appreciated ship has sailed.

"Are you going to leave me, Luisa?" he asks. Adding quietly, "I can't honestly say I would blame you." He thinks for a moment. "Why *didn't* you leave me, in all these years – if it was so bad?"

When Luisa finally responds, it is as if she is talking to herself.

"I do not know, William. I do not know. Perhaps because it was never bad enough," Then she turns to him. "But now I tell myself that not bad enough to leave a marriage, is this good enough reason to stay?" She pauses. He doesn't dare interrupt. "And so I take the cab. I go to the airport." She laughs, but without much joy. "But I have not flown home alone in thirty years."

"I wish I could give you a better reason for staying."

She looks at him and shrugs. Which seems so very far from hopeful.

He senses the grumpy young waiter moving closer, desperate to clear the table and send the two old farts on their way. On our way to where? he wonders. Back to that barren place where we've been for so long?

William knows that he must do something.

It needs to be not a scintilla short of epoch-making

and must encapsulate all that he has learned along the way, the sum total of everything that he has discovered on this long and tortuous journey deep into the heart of Sutherlandness.

It has to be of the moment, which he now concedes, despite all the strategies and projections, is all that there is. It needs to come from somewhere at the essential root of his newly enlightened being. A truth so profound that it will resonate in an instant and strike a hopeful new chord within the souls and minds of the two of them. Uniting them once more, like two flares meeting in the night-time sky and surging upwards with impossible brightness.

Unfortunately, he still can't think of a sodding thing.

Not a sausage.

Zero. Less than.

His brain feels as dry as his tongue. There is far too much stuff from this crazy week roiling around inside his woolly head. And he is so awfully tired.

Away ye go!

The excruciating seconds pass. With them, his marriage. And his life.

Suddenly, from nowhere, he hears the sounds.

Not drums this time. Or trumpets. Simply words. New words. Words that seem to float out of his mouth – combinations of syllables he had no idea were even in there. Words he has, of course, known in harmless isolation most of his adult life but never imagined he would string together into such a simple yet volcanic sentence.

"Señor? Some *musica, por favor?* For the dancing!"

Despite being married to a Spaniard, William has never been fully cognisant with how exactly "oh, for fuck's sake!" translates. Until now, as he hears it emerge unambiguously from the mouth of a grumpy waiter. But he is gratified to see the old woman, who has clearly been listening, smack her sullen young colleague sharply on the neck and send him back cursing into the café.

He is not so gratified to watch the disdain grow on the face of his current wife. "You cannot fix a marriage by dancing," she mutters. "You especially."

"Can – if you believe in miracles."

She shrugs, not wishing to be party to any more lunacy, on this or any night. "William, please, it is very late."

"You're not the first person to tell me this," he says. "Not even the first Luisa," he adds to himself.

He holds out his hand to her.

She sees it trembling, just inches from her own, and looks up into his face. She can't pinpoint exactly how or why, yet somehow the man looks different. And perhaps – who knows – he *is* different. She will believe this when she sees this.

Luisa Sutherland, still of Richmond, Surrey for the time being, finds herself rising gracefully, if a tad wearily, from her chair, as if refusal might further unbalance her increasingly peculiar husband. The relief on that husband's face is matched only by the astonishment on her own, as to where her weary body might apparently be leading her.

He takes her arm gently. Perhaps it is this simple.

About four seconds later, the ear-shattering riffs of an obscure Spanish heavy metal track, with a particularly grating flamenco tinge, blast out from the café's speakers into the square, shocking any stragglers and traumatising every pigeon nesting in the eaves of the great cathedral.

William turns to see the young waiter staring defiantly back at him. Dance to that, you Brexiting British arsehole.

For a moment, William is fazed and can't move.

This isn't aided by a nagging itch inside his shirt, which impels him reluctantly to remove his hand from Luisa's. While she stands bemused beside her table, wondering whether this lunacy will ever end, William dips a hand down under the dull, brown cheesecloth to produce a squashed but still remarkably vibrant red rose, courtesy of Señora Barbadillo. He can't explain why this should still be on his person, whilst his hairweave is no more, but isn't he slowly learning that life is not here to be questioned? Therein lies madness and he reckons he's already used up his season ticket to that particular destination.

Better simply to go, as he recalls himself saying, with the flow.

Ignoring the painful decibels, he hands the flower to Luisa with a courtly flourish. Not overly charmed by where it has been, she takes it gingerly from his outstretched hand. He watches without breathing as, quite tentatively and despite her better judgment, she begins to soften. Slightly.

And so they dance.

Sort of.

Moving quietly, hands together but long-familiar bodies barely touching, they shuffle against the deafening music. Unsurprisingly (and not entirely due to 'D.J.' sabotage), the whole enterprise feels desperately, discordantly uncomfortable. And rather sad.

Hardly the stuff that dreams are made of. Or the kindling of hope.

Only one solution springs to mind. And it's certifiably bonkers. Yet, in a week of world-spinning dementia, it seems to William Sutherland, late of Govan, Glasgow, almost normal.

Summoning all his available strength, which isn't Herculean, he pulls a stunned Luisa more tightly towards him and spins her around, so that they're standing beside each other, hip to hip. Leaning his right hand over her shoulder to join hers, he abruptly pulls her left arm in front of him with his own to link hands. Once locked in place and knowing that she can't escape, he skips forward with her into the square.

"*What the hell?*"

"Just a touch of the Gay Gordons," he explains, as he segues into a jerkily recalled but still recognisable highlight of 'Scottish Country Dancing for Disadvantaged Eight-Year-Olds.' "Although I'm not Gordon any more. Nor, of course, am I—"

She attempts to end the derangement once and for all; to pull away as her spouse of thirty years prances at ever-increasing and distinctly erratic speed away from the café and the tables and the din. But, despite herself and her enchainment, she finds that her protests are less than half-hearted, as she suddenly can't seem to stop herself from finding it funny.

Luisa suddenly remembers a skinny young man, a man with red hair and a fuzzy beard, clutching his chest and collapsing outside a restaurant as he checks out the prices. A pale-skinned guy dropping his pants and spitting out water as he mimics a courtyard fountain. A grinning Scot using a wooden cocktail umbrella to 'protect' his new bride from the rain and pretending to be a bull in bed.

So, despite the pain and anger and sheer disbelief, and the grumbling desire to knee her infantile husband in the un-kilted crotch, she starts to laugh. Softly at first, but building gradually in both volume and lack of self-control.

He gazes at her in amazement, as they wheel around, Scottish-style, to heavy metal. He had forgotten what a glorious, full-throated, raspily Spanish laugh she has. And how very beautiful she can be when her wild eyes sparkle and her still-refulgent, dark hair shimmers. She lets the mirth that was always there and has never truly forsaken her fly carelessly out of her soul. A mirth made even richer by the sharp, distinctive tang of pure alarm.

When did I last make you laugh, Luisa? thinks William sadly. Perhaps the last time I asked you to dance.

The remaining café staff watch the display in stunned bemusement. Passers-by, on their way back home or to their lodgings, stop for a moment to catch this respectable-looking, not unattractive, middle-aged couple, who are most probably British and therefore drunk.

A huge, yellow street-cleaning truck moves in and starts its work around them. Like a fellow member of the dance.

CHAPTER SIXTY

BY THE TIME THEY re-enter room 381, with the heavy suitcase pulling once more at his dodgy spine (*hey, old pal!*) and the worst music they've ever heard in their lives still thumping in their ear-drums, William and Luisa Sutherland have left their singular dance routine far behind them.

Yet, somewhere, they are still dancing, even if the steps are a bit hesitant and the tune more than a touch ragged.

As he switches on the light, William finds himself wondering for a moment who might be here this time. Tazmin perhaps, returned with her cheap castanets and tapas tummy, to forgive him and see if their relationship/her career can take that second chance? Luisa, the famous but lonely writer of children's books, dreaming of the children she never had nor had ever lost? Perhaps even good old partner Sandy, come to whisk his erstwhile mistress away and afford her the attention she deserves but of which she has felt so cruelly deprived.

He wouldn't be altogether surprised to find Pablo himself between the sheets, ready to offer them bilingual words of wisdom as a highly exclusive turn-down service.

But, thankfully, it is just the two of them, closer perhaps than they have been in some while, yet still with that familiar distance lingering.

William is the first to speak. Even though there is probably no need and knowing, after the terrifying chaos of the past few days, that it might be infinitely better not to.

"I've fallen head over heels with three women since Wednesday, Luisa. And all of them have been you."

He sets down the suitcase, with some relief, and moves as if to hold her. But this time his hands don't caress her face or embrace her body. Instead they find themselves waving somewhat helplessly in the air, as if trying to encompass something that is too big ever to be contained.

"I am so *so* sorry." This is all he feels able to say. He hopes to God it is enough, but knows they have still so far to go.

"We could be saying the 'S'-word to each other all night," she sighs.

"You're right. *Perdón*, Luisa." She has the grace to smile, which gives him the courage to carry on. "I seem to have been trying to change everything this week, don't I? Wives. Lovers. Kids. Everything, that is, *except my bloody self!*"

Luisa nods wisely, although, not having been party to his wilder machinations, she isn't exactly certain as to what she is nodding.

"Perhaps I also am doing it this week, William," she concedes. "This really looking at who I am. My mama, she is always saying to me – Luisa, if you want to know the truth about yourself, *la verdad*, ask two New York Jewish lesbians."

"I loved that bitch for her wisdom. So what did you learn?"

Luisa mulls on this. "That while most things are your fault," she concludes, "not everything is."

"Seems fair," agrees William, resignedly. "I kept looking at that young couple, you know, and only ever thinking about what I'd lost. Seems about bloody time I started appreciating what I have."

He can't quite meet her gaze, as if he is suddenly sheepish about revealing too much. And, Lord help him, Glasgow hard man, coming over all sentimental. Yet neither can he find it within himself to stop, as the words finally start pouring out. "You've always taken care of me, you know, *cariño*. All these years. I just hope I've..." He shakes his head. "Mebbe in the only way I knew how."

To his relief, she nods, and he takes this as genuine. Perhaps, in its own way, he thinks, the advice he gave young Will last night didn't go totally unheeded over the decades. Then he decides he's not going to go there any more. He's exhausted. Semana Santa is over. And his head hurts.

"What about your 'Highland fling'?" he asks. Back on all too solid ground.

They stare at each other. She says nothing and ensures that her face and body are completely still, so that these say nothing either.

After a few seconds of this, he walks out onto the balcony.

He looks out at the sleeping city, wondering whether you can sense from the air and the sounds and the smells that something has ended. That the most important week of the year is over and normal, unmagical life, the life that plays no tricks with time or memory, that offers no mystery or miracles, will resume with the dawn. It's not even a bank holiday here, he reminds himself.

He hears a sound and instinctively looks to his left, onto the balcony adjoining his own. As if that other Luisa might have stepped out for a moment, in her bare feet and funky pedicure, to check a hundred emails and breathe in some orange-scented air. And with it perhaps some resilience, before embarking on her pre-arranged meeting, a reunion that could bring some semblance of companionship at this latter, lonely stage of her life. Something William now believes is a universal human need. He finds himself so glad the balcony is dark.

The sound, a clicking, has come from behind him.

He turns to find Luisa at the doorway, aiming her smart little camera in his direction.

Whilst this touches his heart, it also saddens him that it should feel so alien. Unsurprisingly, he recalls their first time in this city, when he was dressed in charity-shop clothing but had a mass of first-hand hair to be proud of. And Lu would forever hoist up that bulky machine she wore constantly, like a massive necklace, making him smile simply by smiling first.

The camera flashes and he blinks. He knows that this time he can ask to inspect the result straight away, but it isn't the first idea that springs to mind. "Maybe one together?" he suggests.

Luisa stares at him, as if he has proposed a sexual activity seldom performed without a safety-net. But she nods and very deftly sets the timer. Placing the camera gently on the wooden rail of the balcony, she looks to William, who is finding himself unsure where to stand. She yanks him briskly into the target area, yet it's still far from easy – finding a position of togetherness. It feels quite strained, but somehow they manage.

Until he suddenly strikes a pose.

"*I danced flamenco!*" he reveals, twisting his body and raising his arms.

"*Madre de Dios!*"

The camera flashes from its perch, capturing, for all time, William Sutherland in defiant flamenco pose and spouse Luisa with her mouth wide open. They stay still, even when the task is done, simply enjoying the early-hours daftness.

A small puff of wind breezes in from nowhere. They hardly notice it, until the camera begins to wobble. William instantly de-flamencos and rushes over, arms outstretched. Too late – Luisa's precious little camera disappears over the edge. They hear it make violent contact with the paving slabs below. He turns to Luisa, distraught over her loss and deeply apologetic, although he is pretty sure that it wasn't his fault. But, to his surprise, she simply shakes her head. Let it go.

Where did that come from?

He burrows into his pocket and pulls out his trusty old mobile. "Plan B!"

She looks at him in disbelief, as he fiddles clumsily with the camera function. She knows that he never takes photos. Mind you, until just now she would have told anyone that her husband never dances. Today, suddenly, he is Joaquín Cortés.

As she might have predicted, the technology is beyond him. Or else he is still too nervous to work out the basics. So, instead, with an exultant cry of "oh, sod it!", he chucks the offending yet once so very precious object over the side to join her shattered camera.

Luisa can only gasp, as if this is the most reckless thing she could ever see her husband – or indeed any fifty-three-year-old, workaholic marketing consultant – do. But William Sutherland is on a roll. And now, in this same mood of reckless abandon, he begins to reach for his laptop bag.

"NO!" she screams.

"Och, alright," he says.

CHAPTER SIXTY-ONE

IN A TINY UPSTAIRS room, at the pretty, "cheap 'n' cheerful" Hostal Esmeralda, a young honeymooning couple lie naked in each other's arms. Clothes are strewn all around the narrow and rigorously tested bed. The couple are not asleep. They have woken up from that surreal, post-coital dreaminess and are talking about the future. Their plans make no sense; minds are hardly at their sharpest right now, yet they love the sound of each other's voices and the fire of hope in their eyes.

As Will reveals to her the theme of his new story, a theme he has expounded several times before but never so nebulously, Lu grabs hold of his left arm, currently lying across her belly. He continues talking and to him at least the words make perfect sense, but she doesn't listen. She raises his hand and around it she wraps an elegant man's watch, an expertly crafted and designed piece of functional jewellery, with classy Roman numerals, such as he has never had before.

He senses the coldness on his still-warm wrist and tries to examine it by what little moonlight sneaks through the shutters.

"*Shit, is that the time!*" he exclaims.

She seems disappointed and ready to cry, until she sees the smile on his face and the look of pure wonder, as he admires the only precious thing he has ever been given, presented to him by the truly priceless, bright-eyed gift he may also never believe he truly deserves.

"*Muchas gracias*, Señora Sutherland," he says. "Now I'll always have time for you."

He places it next to his ear and immediately falls back asleep.

*

Seville hasn't slept for a week but she is sleeping now.

The Nazarenos sleep, proud hundreds of pious men who have been tramping and sweating in vivid anonymity, draped in the historic garb of their brotherhoods, alongside their cross-carrying brothers. The ancient *pasos* too, weary but still gleaming, sink back into their dusty chapels and churches, candles snuffed and flowers wilted.

The sturdy men-of-similar-stature snore as one, turbans unrolled and soaking, they themselves stretched out and equally scrubbed, thanking God in their dreams that they don't have to bear that heavenly load until another fifty-one far less holy semanas have passed. The righteous men, who have quit their balconies, slumber soundly, *saetas* of spontaneous devotion still ringing in their hearts and in the scented air. The pilgrims and the tourists, shopkeepers with their fans and castanets and marzipan penitents, the tapas makers, legions of azulejos sellers, footsore flamenco dancers, the surly and the over-friendly waiters. At least two surprised and satisfied Barbadillos, with bulging bellies and solid legs.

And the churros vendors.

All asleep, in the arms of their spouses, their lovers, Jesus Christ their Lord or someone they met watching a procession who is flying back home tomorrow but there's always WhatsApp.

In his toy-strewn room, a small Spanish boy dreams, blond hair damp and clinging to his contented face. Beside him, next to the dimmed Spider-Man bedside light, is a lumpy ball of wax that isn't quite as small as it was last year but nowhere near as huge as it will be the next.

No one knowing, as no one ever knows or should know, what tomorrow morning may bring.

CHAPTER SIXTY-TWO

THE HOTEL HERRERA BUZZES with the sounds of Monday morning goodbyes.

A discerning ear might pick up the nobly restrained sighs of relief from the staff, particularly those behind the reception desk, weary from a week of impossible demands ("Can the processions come nearer to the hotel?") and an unholy ignorance about the host country ("Where can I buy a sombrero?"). Tired too of the casual waves and cries of "hasta la vista, baby!" that so many visitors think is incredibly witty, its originality curiously building on repetition. As suitcases crammed with half of Seville rumble precariously away on unprepared wheels.

The casual observer might suspect that Marilyn and Shelby would be included in the Herrera staff's yearn-to-hit list, but the truth is that everyone adores them and is sad to see them go. Perhaps a generosity of spirit transcends boundaries or maybe people whose lives are possibly far from easy recognise kindred spirits beneath the bling and the bounce. So, whilst cries of *"Next year – Yom Kippur in the Vatican!"* and *"Purim in Mecca!"* aren't instantly accessible, the staff are happy to share in the joke, as the contented lovers from another faith and continent make their farewells.

Three floors higher, the man referred to by his more perceptive guests as "the ubiquitous Pablo" is proving he's not as ubiquitous as all that, by being in just the one place. He's strolling down the corridor, whistling a tune from his childhood and nodding to his various charges as they trundle contentedly away.

He drums out a brusque knuckle-roll on the door of number 381.

William hears it like a klaxon through the more calming sounds of his sleep and wakes up in a panic. He is immediately aware of smoothly soft legs, as they become even more tightly entangled around him.

The sleepy Sutherlands struggle to separate their conjoined bodies, like two people disengaging after a heady yet still exploratory one-night stand. They turn to face each other, breath catching breath, and somehow, quite suddenly, they feel at home,

Only, of course, they're not. They're well over a thousand miles away and their plane leaves in just a few short hours.

"Oh my God!" cries William, as if he has just discovered a corpse in his bed and has no memory of the night before. "*We've slept in!* I never ever—"

"Was it not worth it?" His sleeping partner smiles, in no hurry to leave.

He considers this. "Beats dancing." He kisses her lips softly, then taps her warm shoulder with businesslike efficiency. "Come on, old girl! Time and tide."

Although she has no idea what tide has to do with it, Luisa Sutherland lies back languorously, almost coquettishly, a mischievous smile on her face. "I thought we had another thirty years… Willy."

She sighs pleasantly and at some volume. He realises how appealing he still finds this. Why did he ever consider it irritating? William knows that there will be times in the future when he will find it intensely so, as indeed she will find his own trivial idiosyncrasies, but he's not going to mull on it right now. This moment is all that matters. For the moment.

He starts to get up, avoiding his naked reflection in the full-length mirror, one of those mirrors Luisa always demands or at least hopes for in a hotel room and which he would far prefer omitted from the inventory. But then he does sneak a look and is not altogether repelled. Not after last night. And not after the memories of that long-ago honeymoon, which are floating back with increased definition, like one of Luisa's old cameras pulling focus, and in which he could consider himself a contender. After all, he satisfied a beautiful woman, didn't he? And looking through his glasses at the contented face a few feet away from his own, now even more sharply defined, he reckons he might just have played a blinder once again.

The room phone rings. William stares at Luisa, as anxiety shoots back through his stomach and into his throat like bile. He stretches over to lift the receiver, although he is pretty sure that he doesn't want to.

They both know who it will be.

"He ask me last night if you are going to hit him again," says Luisa.

"Didn't work the first time," he responds, not wanting to contemplate this nor whatever else he has "rearranged" on this brief but epic visit. No doubt there will be more than broken noses awaiting him on his return home and not all of the alterations external.

He picks up the phone and shouts into it: "*And the Willy ye know's come back again!*"

Setting the phone down again, he smiles contentedly at Luisa. Who sighs.

*

When old Pablo grabs his heavy cases from him, just beyond the revolving doors, and hurls them into the boot of the hotel minivan, William Sutherland feels just as guilty as he did a few days earlier. Yet he can't say he is totally unrelieved, as his back is no better than it was on his arrival. If only that bit of his alternate reality could have remained with him, he thinks, wishing that he could have asked his other self for the name of his chiropractor.

Another employee is moving into the driver's seat. Clearly Pablo isn't accompanying them this time. William is fine with this, as he would quite like to talk to his wife on the journey home, rather than share her with a chatty compatriot. The two of them have a lot to catch up on.

Yet, even once the cases are loaded, Pablo lingers. Like an ageing dog, thinks William, waiting for a treat. He grabs a clutch of euros from his wallet and is about to stuff the lot into the old man's hand when reason intervenes and he restores half to his empty pocket. No point in being stupid about it; he's not a TV producer any more.

He swiftly persuades himself that an excess of generosity might almost be insulting.

"*Gracias*, Pablo," he says, before realising that he genuinely means it.

"No problem, Señor," beams Pablo, deftly pocketing the cash. "Have the safe journey home. Give my regards to United. 'We are the champ—'"

"Aye – okay. Enough now."

Luisa kisses Pablo with warmth and a real affection. As he watches her, an emotion William has begun to rediscover this fateful trip surges up from nowhere once again and catches him unaware. A genuine pride in his wife.

Well, that's it, he thinks, moving on. *Hasta la vista,* Pablo.

William helps Luisa into the rear of the minivan, then turns for a final moment to watch the old guy amble away, happily counting his tip.

William Sutherland won't ever quite believe this and it is most probably a trick of his reeling mind, which is naturally still in some turmoil after recent events. Yet he is almost convinced that, just for a moment, on this surprisingly ordinary Monday morning in the crown jewel of Andalusia, he sees the slightly bent, elderly man from the hotel suddenly stand straighter and taller, look up towards the cloudless sky and transform into someone different.

The handyman from Hostal Esmeralda.

Just for a second.

Almost as if that stocky, taciturn, burnished man of mischief has somehow been looking out for them all these

years, just waiting for them to return. But no, of course, this is fanciful. How can one man be two? Stay the same age, yet – wizen. It would take a miracle.

And the next time William blinks, it is just old Pablo there. Still counting.

CHAPTER SIXTY-THREE

THEY SIT CLOSER TOGETHER on the plane.

William is sticking to Diet Coke. Although, considering what has happened to him this week whilst remaining relatively sober, he can't imagine that alcohol could make him feel much weirder.

Yet he needs his mind to be clear, as he takes out from his laptop bag the brand-new notepad he has just bought in the airport. He smiles as he briefly wonders what else he might discover in there; books he has never read? Photographs that have magically altered? A small, waxen ball? The Holy Grail?

Luisa watches him as he begins to scribble. It doesn't appear to be work, or at least not the work he usually does, which is almost always on his laptop.

"Ladies of the Argentinian night?"

He has the grace to laugh. "Possibly!" A young child leans round from the seat in front of him. William smiles back.

Some time later, while the muse has a break, William looks across at his wife of thirty years. Her eyes are

closing, the large handbag lies open on her lap. Trying not to disturb her, he leans across and very gently pulls out the small photo album.

Luisa notices but simply smiles to herself. And softly, instinctively, she touches the shiny new cross at her throat.

*

They can see the dark clouds cluster, like a welcoming committee, as they begin to land. The anticipated rain won't be far behind.

By the time they emerge together onto the tarmac, the passengers in front have their phones out and their brollies open to protect them.

It takes forever to trudge through passport control and pick up their bags but Luisa notices how sanguine – well, comparatively sanguine – William is.

Finally they shuffle off, hand in hand, William dragging the heavier case and suddenly yearning for a Pablo. He sees the line of waiting minicab drivers. "We should have booked," he grumbles. "I just forgot. Still, there'll be plenty of cabs. No mad rush."

"*Mum! Dad! Over here!*"

They spin round to see Claire and Marcus, waiting nervously. Each holds up a white card, as cabbies do, one reading MAMA and the other PAPA.

"Did you know they were coming?" says a delighted William.

Luisa shakes her head. "They want to see which one of us has killed the other."

"Aye, fair enough. Going to have to be a wee bit

kinder to Marcus, aren't I? Maybe buy one of his godawful pictures… Or at least be kinder."

William stops and turns away, to shift the suitcase to his other hand. So he doesn't see what Luisa is staring at when he hears her say, *"Ay, Dios mio! William!"*

He spins around. And stops, open-mouthed.

Claire and Marcus have adapted their cards, using white cardboard flaps that they've clearly stuck on. The cards now read 'GRAND-MA' and 'GRAND-PA'. And they're beaming like loons.

William and Luisa Sutherland find themselves both tearing up.

"Oh, William," murmurs Luisa.

"*Away ye go!*" says William, with moist-eyed predictability.

He takes his wife's hand and they scoot, heavy cases and all, to embrace their children.

As they walk out of the airport together, William dumps his umbrella in a nearby bin.

EPILOGUE

THE BALL OF WAX *is hardly a ball at all. He has only just begun it.*

The grown-ups around him sense his nervousness. And his excitement. The man in the strange, pointed mask, with narrow slits for eyes, seems very kind. He is bending down as low as he can, ensuring that the wax from the huge candle drips only where it cannot hurt or burn a very small boy. There is a skill to this and the man appears very skilled.

The child looks up at his parents and grandparents. He seems to want them all to know how excited he is and what a time he is having, staying up so late in this distant yet somehow important country so far away. He feels a yawn coming on and tries hard to stifle it. In the process he almost blows out the flame of the candle.

The grown-ups smile. His grandmother takes his photograph then gives a tiny dance from her own long-ago childhood. His grandfather moves awkwardly yet contentedly to the beat of a drum.

And, even behind the mask, they can tell that the old man with the crinkly brown eyes, who seems somehow so familiar, is smiling too.

It is going to be a very special week.

POSTSCRIPT

BEFORE ITS PUBLICATION, ADVANCE copies of this book were sent out to people whose opinions we respect for (hopefully kind!) reviews.

One particular review stopped me short. It referred to the "aptly numbered room 381" (the Seville hotel room in which William and Luisa stayed). This completely bemused me. Was my choice, I don't know, unwittingly Orwellian or something?

So finally I Googled it.

Now, you may be well ahead of me here, but I admit to being totally gobsmacked when I read that "in text messaging and online communication, the number 381 is often used as a shorthand for 'I love you'. The number 3 represents the number of words, 8 the total number of letters and 1 signifies the single, unified meaning."

I had absolutely no idea.

So how come I picked this number out of hundreds for 'the room where it happened'?

Was it random? Fate? Serendipity?

Magic?

Perhaps I shall never know.

ACKNOWLEDGEMENTS

BEFORE *SEVILLE* WAS A novel, its first incarnation was as a thankfully well-received and much-repeated Afternoon Play on BBC Radio 4. This wouldn't have happened without my brilliant radio producer and dear friend, David Ian Neville.

Between drafts of the book, it re-emerged as a movie script, the only UK Finalist in the Screencraft Comedy Script Contest in LA. Since then, the input from my wonderful agent Seb Flatau and the esteemed film producers Niall Perrett and Stewart Till has been incredible. This author owes them all a great debt.

Yet even before all of this, it was a notion.

Some years ago, my late mother kindly gave my wife and me a special anniversary trip, back to the magical place where we had honeymooned. Seville. At the very same time as that first visit – Semana Santa. I said to my spouse, wouldn't it be curious if we happened to meet… (I'll keep her response to myself!)

So my final thank you goes, as ever, to her. My inspiration, my first reader. Whose sighs, whilst not Iberian, can match those of my leading female character in their richness and variety.

ABOUT THE AUTHOR

PAUL A. MENDELSON IS a BAFTA-nominated writer for TV, radio and film. He has created several classic BBC comedy series, including *May to December*, *So Haunt Me* and the long-running *My Hero*, starring Ardal O'Hanlon. He conceived *Neighbors From Hell* for DreamWorks Animation, starring Steve Coogan as Satan, and wrote the acclaimed ITV cancer drama *Losing It*, featuring Martin Clunes.

Paul has written five novels for adults, three story collections and four novels for children, including *Henry the Half-Time Hero* and its sequel. He scripts all his novels, and three have been optioned for movies. His comic novel *Must Have GSOH* was the only UK finalist in the prestigious Screencraft Cinematic Book Contest 2023.

His movie script for *Seville* is currently a Finalist in the 2025 Stage 32 Romantic Comedy Contest in LA, the largest contest of its kind.

Paul is married with two grown-up daughters and four grandchildren and lives quietly in hope.